By Brandon Webb & John David Mann

Nonfiction

The Red Circle

The Making of a Navy SEAL

Among Heroes

The Killing School

Total Focus

Mastering Fear

Fiction

Steel Fear

Cold Fear

COLD FEAR

Bantam Books | New York

COLD FEAR

A Thriller

Brandon Webb & John David Mann

Published in the United States by Bantam Books, an imprint of Random House, a division of Penguin Random House LLC, New York.

BANTAM BOOKS is a registered trademark and the B colophon is a trademark of Penguin Random House LLC.

LIBRARY OF CONGRESS CATALOGING-IN-PUBLICATION DATA
Names: Webb, Brandon, author. | Mann, John David, author.
Title: Cold fear : a thriller / Brandon Webb & John David Mann.
Description: First edition. | New York : Bantam Books, [2022]
Identifiers: LCCN 2022000433 (print) | LCCN 2022000434 (ebook) |
ISBN 9780593356319 (hardcover ; acid-free paper) | ISBN 9780593356326 (ebook)
Subjects: LCGFT: Novels.
Classification: LCC PS3623.E3913 C65 2022 (print) | LCC PS3623.E3913 (ebook) |
DDC 813/.6—dc23/eng/20220105
LC record available at https://lccn.loc.gov/2022000433
LC ebook record available at https://lccn.loc.gov/2022000434

Hardback ISBN 9780593356319
Ebook ISBN 9780593356326

Printed in Canada on acid-free paper

randomhousebooks.com

2 4 6 8 9 7 5 3 1

First Edition

Book design by Virginia Norey

Title-page and part-title-page art from
an original photograph from freeimages.com/ayla 87

Map design by John David Mann

To you, reading these words
A story is nothing but black marks on a white page,
until it sparks to life in the mind of a reader
And we have the most incredible readers in the world—
thank you from both of us!

Contents

Map: Reykjavik City Center   xi

Prologue   3

Sunday   7

Monday   37

Tuesday   85

Wednesday   137

Thursday   195

Friday   239

Saturday   295

Monday, January 2   385

Epilogue   401

Note from the Authors   405

A Guide to Pronunciation   409

Reykjavík City Center

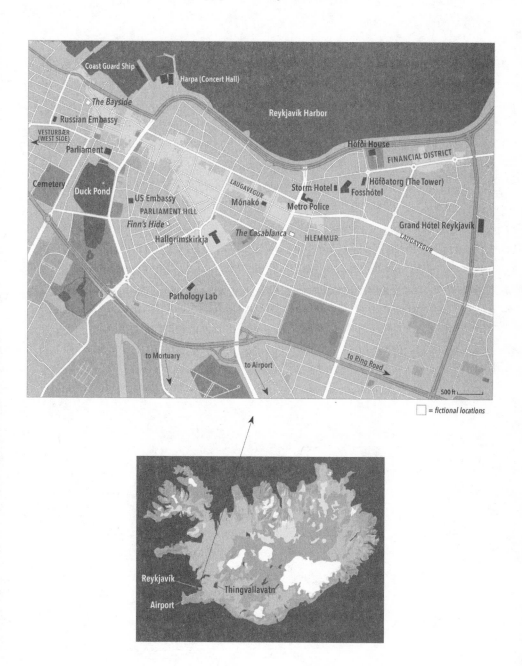

= *fictional locations*

COLD FEAR

Prologue

A deserted city street. The distant ruckus of drunken revelers, laughter, Christmas carol fragments. Under the faint glow of streetlights a flurry of snowflakes drifts to the frigid cobblestone surface, then swirls aside as a girl sprints past.

Bare feet. No coat. Mid-twenties.

She darts through an intersection. Then another. Street names she can't pronounce. On a wild guess she takes a left at the next corner and runs another block before stopping, bent over, hands on knees, breathing like a trapped animal.

There's nothing but the silence of the snow and her own rapid panting. She looks around, frantic.

Has she gone too far?

Takes off running again. Squinting at the street signs, pleading for them to make sense. Fighting back the urge to stop and scan the darkness behind her.

The sound of her feet slapping the slick street surface drums against her ears . . . images explode through her mind—

the mines . . . the Englishman . . . the lake house—

She pushes them away. Her feet are bleeding, but she has to keep going. She has to—

Wait.

Was that a glimpse of someone passing on the far side of the street?

She slows long enough to peer back through the murk. No one there.

She spat out the last pill, but the drugs are still too strong. She can't tell what is hallucination and what is real.

Keep going.

Her feet slapping the cobblestones . . . the mines . . . the Englishman . . .

She won't make it. It was a crazy idea. Should have known it was pointless to try. She reaches the next corner—

And there it is. Spread out before her like a banquet.

She stops again, hands on knees, gasping, the Arctic air searing her lungs. Squints into the dark and feels a rush of bitter relief. Not a hallucination. Really there.

A patch of open water.

The driver told her about this the day she arrived. In December the pond is covered in ice, he said, ice so thick they hold hockey matches on it. Except right here, at this spot. The city keeps this northeast corner heated year-round. "For the ducks!" he chortled.

And sure enough, through the gloom she can see their little bodies, tucked into themselves for warmth, still and silent. Living, breathing ducks, asleep on the water.

How do they survive the winters here?

How does anyone survive the winters here?

She whips her head around, suddenly alert, eyes and ears straining in the dark. There's no one behind her. The only sounds she hears are her own hard breath and the faint splish-splash as she steps into the shallow.

From her pocket she pulls a stick of lipstick, blood-red.

Stares at it, her heart pounding.

She isn't supposed to know.

Isn't supposed to know about any of it.

But she does.

Hands trembling from the cold, she twists the lipstick open, pulls up her shirt with one hand and with the other scrawls a single word upside-down across her abdomen.

Then lets the lipstick fall from her fingers.

She strips out of her clothes, tossing each item behind her. Stark naked, she takes a few more steps into the water. Another flurry of snowflakes falls around her, the air a blast freezer on her skin. Teeth chattering, she kneels. Places her palms down against the shallow pond floor. Slides down onto her stomach and pushes herself away from the edge with her feet, propelling with her arms, each stroke drawing her further toward the pond's center. After a moment her outstretched fingers find the lip of the ice sheet.

She slips underneath the ice, then twists around so that her back is to the pond floor, her face to the ice above. Stretches out her arms as wide as she can.

And pushes farther in.

Sunday

Temperatures in the low twenties (F°),

snow flurries; bitter winds.

1

Gunnar slipped out of his family's townhouse and closed the front door, soft as a spy. He wasn't supposed to be out there on his own, but his parents wouldn't notice. And anyway, he'd be back inside in just a few minutes. Quick as a flash.

It was past ten in the morning but still dark out. The sun wouldn't come up for another hour. He looked around at their street. It snowed in the night! Only a little dusting, but snow was snow. It looked just like the powdered sugar on the Christmas cookies his Danish au pair made the day before, on Christmas Eve.

Gunnar descended the steps and trudged around the corner, scooted across the street and out onto the ice. He knew it was safe. In fact, he'd be out there later that day with his parents to watch the college kids play hockey. Right now, though, there was no one on the pond, no cars on the streets. Christmas Day. Everyone was at home eating oatmeal and staying warm, or still in bed ("sleeping it off") like his parents.

He ventured farther out onto the ice, halfway to the middle of the pond, then lay down on his back, gazing up at the gray clouds against the violet morning sky, imagining bears and dragons and brave men with swords chasing them. He made snow angels. Laughed at the fresh tickle of snowflakes on his face.

After a few minutes of this glorious fun, Gunnar rolled himself over to get up on his feet. Gotta be home before they noticed him gone. He slipped on the ice and fell flat on his front side. *Good one,* klaufi! *That takes talent!* That's what his big brother would say if he saw that clumsy move.

Taking it slow and careful now, Gunnar got back up onto his hands and knees—and stopped.

This couldn't be real. Could it?

He was looking down at the ice, and someone underneath was looking back up at him.

He stared into the ice.

Into her eyes.

"The Little Mermaid" was Gunnar's favorite story. His au pair had read him all the Hans Christian Andersen stories, and that was the one he fell in love with. He'd seen the Disney movie, too, but that was different. It felt fake. He liked having the story read to him better. Closing his eyes and hearing the words, in her voice, it all came alive. He never admitted this to his big brother, or to anyone, not even his au pair, but in his heart of hearts Gunnar believed that mermaids were real.

And there was one staring up at him right now from under the ice!

His palms were starting to hurt from the cold, but he couldn't move a muscle. It was like he was as frozen as the ice.

He *wanted* this to be real.

He wanted so badly for this to be proof that he was right all along, that his brother and his parents and teachers were all wrong, that there really *were* mermaids, and that Gunnar—not his brother, not his parents, but Gunnar himself—had found one!

But there was this cold feeling in his tummy, a bad feeling, really bad, bubbling up like Geysir.

He was terrified.

Gunnar knew this was not a mermaid.

He knew this, because the lady in the duck pond wasn't moving.

Not at all.

Then Gunnar heard a horrible sound, like the shriek of a hockey referee's whistle, but he didn't stop to wonder what it was or where it was coming from, didn't even think to realize it was coming from himself.

Didn't think at all.

He was too busy running.

2

Krista Kristjánsdóttir stood over the vague form in
the ice and cursed a blue streak.

She pulled her phone from her vest and tapped the screen to life.
"Surface too opaque to see limbs and torso clearly." She held the phone
close and spoke low and quiet, enunciating each word. "Only the face
visible."

She paused, aware of how inadequate the word sounded. *Visible*. How
about *indelible*. *Haunting*.

The police had arrived within minutes of the boy's first screams, but
not before some citizen showed up with his phone and snapped photos,
then trotted off to sell them to the city's daily newspaper. Terrific. By the
time the cops had the scene locked down, the dead girl's face was staring
out through iPad screens in households across the country, over the
headline LITLA HAFMEYJAN Á ÍS!

The little mermaid on ice!

Krista's partner, Einar, plodded over, texting as he walked, and relayed
a brief from one of the officers on the scene.

No ID in the woman's clothing. A lipstick that might be hers, might
give up prints, might not. No other clues to her identity. A team of divers
was slipping in under the ice sheet right now to see if it was possible to
pull her free without damaging the body. Otherwise they'd need to cut
her out.

They waited in silence, puffing clouds of icy breath.

Moments later the lead diver emerged, looked over at Krista, and shook his head. They'd have to cut out a section of the ice, secure it with a tarp, and transport her to pathology that way. "Like a fly in amber," murmured Einar, his nimble fat thumbs tap-dancing over his phone again.

Krista glanced at the crowd along the duck pond's edge, pushing up against the barriers they'd hastily put in place, craning to catch a glimpse.

And cursed again.

Media.

She looked at Einar and nodded in the direction of the little throng of reporters. He stopped texting and grinned. *No problem*, he mouthed. He turned and trundled over toward the pack to give a statement that would say nothing at all, but say it in the most polite and interesting terms.

Krista hated this part, talking to the press. Always made her feel like a politician. Einar had no problem with it. Which Krista had never understood. It seemed to her that cops and reporters should be natural enemies. Or at least opposites. A detective's toughest job was getting people to talk. The hardest thing about reporters was getting them to stop talking.

She watched as an officer brought over a blue vinyl tarp and set it down next to her. Another officer with a portable saw kneeled at the foot of the young woman's frozen crypt and lowered the spinning blade to the ice.

Like a bone saw at an autopsy, its metal edge let out a scream that sliced through the brittle morning air.

Krista winced.

3

At the back of the crowd, a squarish face with over-size eyes watched from under its hooded parka as the little knot of police officers instinctively took a step backward from the scream of the saw. Their elongated shadows stretching out over the duck pond's frozen surface reminded the hooded man of the strange statues of Easter Island. Silent sentinels, watching over their people, keeping them from harm.

Too late, for the woman they were cutting out of the ice.

He looked around at the city's storybook architecture, everything illuminated by the liquid amber light. Eleven fifteen, and the sun was just now coming up, struggling to breach the horizon by a few degrees before falling again and plunging the city back into darkness barely four hours later.

Iceland, the "land of fire and ice," at the darkest time of year.

He'd been here before. Visited briefly, years earlier, just before they withdrew all American forces from the nearby air base. A lifetime ago. Before he made chief.

Back then he was plain Finn, a freshly minted Navy SEAL sniper, on his way to help train a Coalition team in Norway. It was summer then, balmy, sunny. Iceland's famous temperate summers. Herds of tourists—Americans, Canadians, Brits, Malaysians, French, Germans—there to experience the daylight that stretched clear around the clock, to see the glaciers and geysers, the lava fields and lunar landscapes, the milky Blue Lagoon, the ooh and the ahh.

Not now. Now the tourists were mostly gone. This was the island community in deep winter, when the sun showed its sallow face for no more than a few hours a day. The bitter Arctic climate that forged this people's national character for a thousand years. No midnight sun, no balmy lava-field tours, no ooh, no ahh. This was not the Iceland of the travel brochures and vacation websites. This was the Iceland outsiders seldom saw. Right now, the land of fire and ice was mostly ice and darkness.

And death.

The night before, after being dropped off a few blocks from his destination, Finn had walked the streets of the city. It was an eerie mix of old and new, a mash-up of Heidelberg or Prague or some other quaint European burg with a futuristic scene out of *Final Fantasy*. Rows of wood-and-corrugated-iron houses brightly painted in pastels and primary colors, a medieval village on an LSD trip. Even as he walked the paved streets of the city, images of the gouts of steam he'd seen geysering up out of the treeless landscape on his ride from the airport were a constant reminder that this was a land carved on the face of a volcanic crack in the earth.

When he'd gotten safely into his bolt-hole and turned on the tap, the water that poured out was near the boiling point and gave off the unmistakable smell of sulfur.

All the amenities of hell.

On the ride into the city his driver had asked what he was doing here in Reykjavík. "Research," Finn told him. "Crime writer." As good a lie as any.

The driver snorted. "Then you will have a boring time here, my friend. We've got no crime in Iceland worth writing about. We have husbands who beat up their wives and idiots who drink too much and beat up their friends. And this, my friend, is all she wrote."

Finn looked back at the pond, the milling crowd pointing at the saw-cut hole in the ice, conversing in whispers as one would in church.

All she wrote.

He slipped away and melted into the city, winding through the back streets of Parliament Hill until he arrived at an old townhouse on a quiet block. He mounted the steps and produced a makeshift house key, which he slid into the lock along with a slim torsion tool.

Finn felt the lock put up mild resistance for a moment, then gently give way. He turned the knob and the door clicked open a crack—

"*Halló!*"

He glanced over at the townhouse next door. An old woman's face poked out at him, its features twisted into a suspicious scowl.

Finn nodded. "*Halló.*" The torsion tool salted away in a pocket.

Her face darkened. "*Ert þú vinur* Ragnars?"

You a friend of Ragnar's?

Finn nodded again. "*Já.*"

The crone took a step out onto her stoop and eyed him up and down a few times, her scowl deepening.

"*He said nothing about any friend,*" she grunted in Icelandic.

Finn shrugged. "Ragnar," he said, rolling both R's hard, like machine-gun fire. He sighed and shook his head as if to say, *What a dick, am I right?*

The scowl relaxed by half a degree. The woman looked out across the street, gazing in the direction Finn had just come from.

"*Terrible, what happened,*" she murmured, still in her native tongue. The Icelandic words reminded Finn of someone gargling.

"*Já,*" he murmured.

Her scowl went harsh again, her voice low and guttural, like a dark priest casting a curse. "*Some drunk partier got a little too friendly. Like poor Birna in 2017.*"

"*Já,*" Finn agreed.

"*Too many foreigners,*" she added, spitting the words: "*Pólverjar. Finnar. Rússar.*"

Poles. Finns. Russians.

Finn looked back toward the pond, too.

"Fuckers," he said.

She looked at him in surprise and barked a laugh. "*Já,*" she said. "*Fokking fokk.*" She turned her gaze out toward the pond again.

"*Greyið,*" she said softly. To Finn it sounded almost like the word "crying," and the look in her eyes conveyed much the same thing.

Poor thing. What a terrible shame. Crying.

"*Greyið,*" Finn echoed.

The old woman raised one finger in a wave.

Finn waved a finger back.

They both retreated into their respective houses.

Finn closed the door behind him and strode silently through a nar-row hallway, coming out into a small dining room. The place was spot-less, meticulous, tiny. Polished hardwood floors, disappearing black acoustic-tile ceilings, soft recessed lighting. Old made modern, like an Upper West Side apartment. Walls hung in good art—except for one that lay bare, cleared of its artwork, the framed pieces neatly stacked against a far wall.

Prep, for the task ahead.

Finn slung his backpack off his shoulder, dropped it on the dining room table, which was empty save for three large sketch pads and a dozen charcoal pencils, purchased on an earlier swing through the neighborhood. He began unloading the results of his resupply run.

Two gaudy, traditional Icelandic wool sweaters, the kind only tourists wore. Two ratty pullovers. A second, scruffier parka and an oversize pair of cargo pants. Expensive suit jacket, dress shirt, and tie. Half a dozen cheap, preloaded phones. Two disposable cameras, ball of twine, small screwdriver, wire stripper, a foot of insulated wire, a few small screws. He didn't expect to need the hardware, but better to have it on hand.

As he unpacked his gear he thought about what the old woman had said.

Or at least, what he guessed she'd said.

Finn neither spoke nor understood a word of Icelandic. Other than "Já."

He knew the accent usually fell on the first syllable; knew how to put that assault-rifle roll in his R's with the tip of his tongue; knew that if he aped a Norwegian accent he wouldn't be far off. Although he didn't know any Norwegian, either.

Not that it mattered much.

Even in English, most people were a mystery to him.

Still, he was pretty sure he understood the old woman's final com-ment. More or less.

"*Greyið*," he murmured in her voice.

He took a breath, held it to the count of five, then let it out again.

This wasn't why Finn was here.

He had a quarry to hunt, and scarce time to do it in before the noose tightened.

No distractions.

Not his problem.

He opened one of the sketch pads, selected a charcoal pencil, and began sketching a layout of what he'd seen of the city so far.

4

Ten blocks to the east, Krista and Einar sat in their cramped office at the Reykjavík metro police station. The ice-encased, vinyl-wrapped body was making its short trip to the University pathology lab. The pathologist had been called at home and was on his way in, grumbling, to perform an immediate autopsy. Christmas or no Christmas, they needed to get in front of this.

Krista was especially keen on seeing the results of the tox screen. Drugs. Had to be. What else could explain a girl stripping naked in the middle of the night, in late December, and sliding herself under the ice? "Like a letter through a mail slot," she murmured.

"A dead letter," her partner added with a fat grin.

In her mind, Krista sighed. That vintage Einar humor: driving her nuts for the past twenty-six years.

An officer poked his head in the door and handed her the surveillance photos she'd asked for. Good. Take her mind off the scene she'd just left.

"I'll leave you to it, then," said Einar, as he hauled himself out of his chair and lumbered off to hunt down a pastry and hot coffee.

Einar thought she was wasting her time.

He was probably right.

Krista stared at the first grainy enlargement, a screen capture from CCTV footage taken at the airport the day before. The facial recog software at customs had flagged half a dozen travelers, Brits and Kiwis and one American, but it was just an A.I. hiccup, and after a cursory passport check by an actual human, they'd let each one pass. Now, at Krista's request, they were running another check on the ID the American had used to enter the country. It would come back clear, she'd bet money on it. But something still felt off about him to her.

It was the name on the passport.

Marlin Pike.

That seemed an obvious fake to her, but then what did she really know about American names? They all seemed fake to her; strange combinations with no logic or consistency to them. Marlin Pike. Two fish? She sighed. Real as any, she supposed.

Krista had no love for Americans. Some half a million of them flooded her country each year—half a million too many, in her view. "Their dollars help pay your salary," as Einar had pointed out a thousand times, to which she would reply: "I'd take a pay cut."

But why did this particular American bug her so? She couldn't say. Some foreigner with an odd name enters their city and trips a cyberwire, and on the same night an unidentified girl winds up dead in the heart of downtown . . . No, there was no logical connection. Nothing there but a random confluence of unrelated events. The very definition of coincidence.

And like any one of ten million other cops on the planet, Krista did not like coincidences.

Or maybe she just had too much time on her hands.

She tapped the screen on her phone and began voice-to-texting another memo.

"Marlin Pike . . ." She stopped.

Marlin Pike what? Looked odd? Bothered her?

"Fuck."

She set the thing down.

Krista hated her phone as much as Einar lived on his. It was only the relentless mocking from everyone else in the department that had made her finally give up her little notepad and pencil stub and follow the high-tech herd.

She studied the photo again.

Oversize eyes, set wide on a squarish face. Expressionless.

God, she missed that pencil stub. Made it so much easier not to smoke.

She switched to the second photo, shot at a distance from behind. A little blurred, but she could make out the figure. Short. Lithe. Thin wiry limbs, knobby joints.

Now she studied the two photos side by side, the face and the frame. Awkward-looking, like a cartoon. Almost geeky. But there was something wary there. An alertness in the eyes. A strange grace in the posture.

Who was this guy?

An officer burst into the room. "The mermaid!" he stammered.

Krista silently cursed and threw the man a weary look. Did her own officers have to refer to the deceased as a "mermaid"?

"What about her? Isn't the pathologist there yet?"

"*Já*, he's there. He just—he just went in to autopsy the girl."

"And?"

"She's gone!"

"Of course she's gone. She was dead when the boy found her. Probably been under the ice for hours."

"No, I mean . . ." He took a shaky breath. "Her body. It's *gone*."

5

Today the city was a ghost of itself, streets deserted, its buildings like bones of the long departed.

"Christmas is special here," Finn's driver had said. "In Reykjavík, nothing bad ever happens at Christmas."

Special. That was one way of putting it. Finn had never experienced a city so still, so silent. It was like walking through the aftermath of a nuclear blast. The only thing that told him he was awake, that this wasn't some post-apocalyptic nightmare, was the fresh sting of salt air and ice crystals in his nostrils.

That, and the faint, meaty, burnt-wood smell of smoked lamb shanks. *"Hangikjöt,"* they called it. "Hanging meat."

He walked due north, threading his way past closed cafés and restaurants, homes buttoned up against the cold. If it weren't for the scent trails of the hangikjöt, you wouldn't have known there were people inside.

After ten blocks he reached the lip of the harbor and stopped.

Listened to the wind's Arctic whispers and groans.

A gigantic double-cube of black glass rose up in front of him. The city's gleaming new concert hall. Next to that, a mammoth hotel, still under construction. When he last walked this path there'd been nothing but fishing piers and dusty boat sheds. Now a modern metropolis had sprung from the shores of lava and rocks. There was something geological about it, new mountain ranges bursting up from tectonic clashes, erupting volcanoes of steel and glass. Finn could practically feel the thrum of hot magma flowing underfoot.

He hadn't had time for a deep dive the day he learned his hunt was taking him to Iceland. But he'd absorbed what he could on the plane.

The plan, so he'd read, had been to put up a suite of high-rise constructions right on this spot—office towers, apartment complexes, a huge car park, all flanking a colossus that would house their central bank. "Iceland's World Trade Center," they were calling it.

The 2008 crash stopped all that. Iceland had soared higher than any other nation on the planet—and fallen harder. By the time the carnage was over, that bank and the country's entire economy had collapsed into nothing but dust and indictments. This hunk of black glass and a half-built hotel were the only survivors.

The wind sighed and whispered curses.

He turned and looked out at the harbor.

There it was.

The big flat gray Coast Guard ship, docked in exactly the same spot as it had been fifteen years earlier, now huddled behind the massive glass block like a sulking teenager. It was the only thing in sight that Finn recognized.

Last time he was here, they'd given him a VIP tour of that vessel.

Last time he was here, Finn himself was the tip of a mighty spear, the full weight of the US military machine behind him. That was before another decade of continuous war had blunted and corroded that spear. Exhausted it. Corrupted it.

Before Mukalla.

Before Finn was pulled from his team, hustled onto an aircraft carrier in the Persian Gulf, and sent home in disgrace to answer for an atrocity he didn't commit.

At least, he didn't think he'd committed it.

Though even now, four months later, he couldn't be sure of that.

The big gray Coast Guard ship stared back at him.

Last time, he thought. A lifetime ago.

This time, he was on his own.

He glanced to his left, up the coast, then to his right, taking in the measure of the territory.

Iceland was roughly the size of Ohio. You could drive clear around the country in twenty-four hours, if you wanted to. The Ring Road, they called it. Route 1.

Finn didn't need to drive around the country. He was pretty sure his business was all right here in the capital city. A quarter percent of the country's landmass, roughly ten miles by ten miles. About the size of Fort Wayne, Indiana, with less than half the population.

Which at that moment included three Americans he was there to hunt. And, once he found them, to engage in a friendly conversation.

Or not so friendly.

That part would depend on them.

He heard a faint disturbance, the slow scrape of feet through the moaning of the wind. He turned and clocked the source: a single human, wrapped in old blankets tied incongruously with a sash of electric blue silk, making his way along a sidewalk on the leeward side of a building.

A white Mercedes van rolled up the empty street and slowed to a stop a few yards past the homeless man. Red Cross emblem on its side. Finn had seen vans like this in a number of European countries, specially equipped to deal with addicts and homeless people, providing food and medical care, sometimes even clean needles.

Evidently they took care of their own here in Reykjavík.

Surviving, as far as Finn could see, was the country's principal industry. After plunging into that economic sinkhole, so he'd read, these descendants of Vikings threw their bankers in jail, let their currency collapse, took on crippling austerity measures, and had clambered up till they were back on top within a decade.

"The Iceland Miracle," the article's writers called it.

Finn had once heard a talk by a think-tank foreign policy analyst who described Iceland as "an unsinkable aircraft carrier in the middle of the North Atlantic." Unsinkable, perhaps, but not unshakable. Sitting astride a seismic fissure between the two tectonic plates that held North America and Eurasia, the entire country was split in half along the diagonal, like a cut lunchbox sandwich, its two halves pulling apart by another inch every year. They experienced something like seventy earthquakes a day.

No wonder they pulled together.

Nothing like scrabbling a living from an unstable volcanic jut of rock at the edge of the Arctic Circle for a thousand years to breed a little solidarity.

The white Mercedes van collected its charge, then rolled on, vanishing around a corner and leaving the street as spectral and desolate as before.

The wind groaned and wailed.

Finn turned northwest and walked along the coast for a few minutes, past the sea-angling sites and whale-watching sites, the harborside restaurants and farmer's markets. Everything closed. Everything silent.

In Reykjavík, nothing bad ever happens at Christmas.

Suddenly the air was shattered by a sonorous gong: the city's big church bells, a dozen blocks away, tolling the half hour.

Three thirty.

Only mid-afternoon, and the revenant sun was already dying again, the city's shadows returning to reclaim their territory.

He turned back and took his reconnaissance southeast, along the coast, past the big concert hall again, then veered due south a few blocks to the city's main strip, which ran parallel to the coastline.

Laugavegur: "Wash Road," so named by women of bygone ages as they lugged their dirty laundry to thermal springs a few miles off.

Now a mile-long shopping mall.

He followed Laugavegur east-southeast, threading his way in and out of the side streets, cataloging everything, observing the evidence of the city's epic struggle to pull itself out of the crash. Last time he was there it had been a street of cafés, galleries, mom-n-pop shops with local flavor that went back generations. Now it was all machine-stamped storefronts hawking gaudy tourist trash. Little models of the great church and concert hall. Shot glasses and pillow cases with puffins on them, hats and shirts with volcanoes and more puffins.

And hotels.

He came to a stop where the road angled at Hlemmur Square. What fifteen years earlier had been a seedy, run-down bus terminal was now reborn as an upscale food court, backed by yet another luxury hotel.

Hotels and more hotels. Everywhere Finn looked, new hotels had sprung up to fill every empty space. And he marked each one in his mind, noting especially the most upscale and expensive. Memorizing each one, its name and location.

Mapping his grid.

Three days, he figured. That's how long it would take.

Three days to locate, stalk, and strike.

Three days to get what he came for. And get out.

The giant church bells tolled the quarter hour, marking the sun's slide back into oblivion.

So many upscale hotels. Too many to cover on his own.

He would need help.

Normally in a situation like this he would have been through a detailed brief. Or, if left to improvise, he would liaise with local police, gain access to hotel records, airport customs logs, maybe engage local military intel resources. But right at that moment Finn had no access to any police or military intel resources.

Right at that moment the arrayed forces of his country's military intel were engaged in tracking him down.

In official terms, Finn was UA, Unauthorized Absence, the US Navy's version of the more commonly known term "AWOL."

In plainer terms, a wanted man.

A fugitive.

Hugging the shadows on the northern and western sides of the streets, he began threading his way back to his stolen bolt-hole.

6

"How is it possible, in a city the size of a handker-chief, to lose a human body?"

The admin woman looked confused. "A handkerchief?"

Krista sighed, then strapped on a smile as she wondered what it would feel like to strangle this woman to death right here and now. She had been on best senior-detective behavior—had not cursed once since arriving at the University Hospital. Still, her professional patience was wearing thin.

"It's no more than a five-minute drive from the drowning site," she began again. "How is it—?" She stopped herself and put up one hand to signal a change in question.

She had already grilled the few staff who were anywhere near the deserted pathology lab around the time the dead woman vanished. No one knew anything about a fresh Jóna Jónsdóttir.

No one even knew what she meant by "a fresh Jóna Jónsdóttir."

"You know," she'd said. "Like how they say 'Jane Doe' in America?"

She got blank looks.

The pathology lab's caseload had exploded over the past few years, as this useless admin had just explained yet again. They were overloaded and overworked. And today was a Sunday, which meant a skeleton staff. Worse yet, it was Christmas. Christmas was a dead zone.

Yes, the woman had really said all that. The head of a pathology lab. *Skeleton staff. Dead zone.* With a total lack of humor or self-awareness.

"Okay," Krista said. "So, could the body have been mistakenly sent out for cremation?"

The woman now pursed her lips and frowned, as if giving the question serious thought, which Krista knew was bullshit because she was shaking her head at the same time. "No," she finally concluded, "I don't think so. Don't think that's possible."

Krista went back to her car and headed over there anyway.

The city's only crematory—in fact, the entire country's only crematory—was located another five-minute drive away, at a cemetery on the south side of the city. Cremation was not big in Iceland. Krista found this ironic, given that her Viking ancestors were all sent off to Valhalla by way of flaming funeral pyres.

But then, these days she found everything about her homeland ironic.

No one at the crematory knew anything.

Correction: everyone knew something, but none of it added up to anything.

After another fruitless hour, Krista climbed back into her Volvo compact and assessed what she'd learned so far. Which was a shitload of nothing.

The driver reported delivering the body to the pathology lab, but the pathology lab had no record of receiving it. The mortuary's cremation records were conflicting; they'd either burned two bodies that day, or three.

Their system was overloaded, too.

And it was, after all, Christmas.

"Fucking fuck," she said to her windshield.

You didn't just lose a body. She'd never heard of such a thing happening. How could it? Lose a report, a piece of evidence, of course that *shouldn't* happen, but sure, it did, every now and then. Fine.

But a whole person?

Strictly speaking, the chain of jurisdiction from scene of death to pathology to mortuary was not entirely under Krista's watch. This wasn't her fault. But that's how it would land anyway.

On her desk, like a steaming pile of caribou crap.

She started her Volvo and addressed herself once more to the interior of the windshield.

"Merry fucking Christmas."

"So what have we got?" Even as she asked, she knew the answer.

While Krista was out collecting blank stares, Einar had interviewed the divers who recovered the body from the duck pond, then organized and dispatched a few officers to go canvassing possible witnesses in the surrounding neighborhoods.

So far, no one had seen anything. Everyone was inside.

Christmas.

No one from the public had come forward to identify the young woman from the photo in the paper. Nothing turned up in their files; facial recog software came up empty.

Iceland's entire national population was one-twenty-fifth the size of New York City's. It wasn't hard to keep track of their people. Her Jóna Jónsdóttir was not an Icelandic native, nor an Iceland resident, that much was clear.

Which only left the rest of the planet's twenty-something female population.

Because there was no body, there were no dental records or any other physical evidence. The woman's clothing, left behind at the scene, gave up no evident clues—no passport, no driver's license, no credit cards, no ID of any kind. They would run DNA on whatever they could collect from her clothing, but unless the girl happened to be a local felon, there was no reason to expect that her genetic fingerprint would be on file.

The lipstick found at the pond's edge had, in fact, yielded no viable prints.

Einar had gone through all open missing-persons files. Given its unpredictable and often brutal weather patterns, Iceland was legendary for its missing persons. No match.

"What we have," replied Einar, "is goose egg."

Krista closed her eyes.

God in heaven, but his summary pronouncements could creep under her skin. Especially his love of the idiotic American idiom. Spill the beans. Barking up the wrong tree. Piece of cake.

Goose egg.

She tossed her phone on her desk and searched her pockets for the pencil stub that wasn't there. "We should've . . . Fuck."

We should've done a more thorough forensic examination right there at the site.

"Hey," said Einar. "Under the circumstances?"

Excusable. Not our fault.

The frozen grave had been treated as a crime scene, since it was not 100 percent clear whether the death was an accident or a suicide, but in view of the difficulty of extracting the body intact, only one or two shots of the face were taken on site before they wrapped the ice-encrusted corpse in their police tarp. A more exhaustive photo and forensic documentation was to have taken place at the University's pathology lab.

Which, again, was only five minutes away.

Nobody expected the body to disappear.

So, yeah, excusable. But sloppy.

They should have taken more photos.

"She got drunk," her partner continued. "Or high. Both, probably. Some tourist who thought it would be a big kick in the pants to go skinny-dipping at midnight on Christmas. So wasted she got herself trapped under the ice sheet."

He shrugged, which Krista found supremely irritating.

She hoped he was right. Sorry though she was that the girl was dead, she hoped with all her heart and soul that the poor thing had been done in purely by her own recklessness. The duck pond was pretty damn shallow; it wasn't easy to drown in there. Still, though, if she were drunk and stoned? Then, sure.

Like drowning in your own bathtub. It happened.

That's what she hoped.

What she suspected, what she feared, was that the girl was assaulted by some drunk hard-partier.

Just like Birna.

"Anyway," Einar grunted as he hauled his girth out of his chair, "I'm off. Salvage what's left of Christmas, eh?"

He turned back as he reached the door.

"She got drunk, Krista. She was foolish. Stumbled in and drowned. Not your fault—and not your fault the cretins at the crematory burned the body."

Krista gave a vague wave, something between a *Thank you for the exculpatory gesture* and a *Get the fuck out of here.*

As Einar vacated the office Krista spotted a young officer passing in the hallway.

"Jón!" she called out.

He stepped in. *"Halló?"* Bright kid, motivated.

"Jón, why don't you start gathering whatever CCTV footage you can from a ten-block radius around the pond. All the shops, all the government buildings. Bring a partner."

"Halló?" He appeared confused. "But . . . it's Christmas. I don't think we'll find anyone there."

Okay, to be honest, not especially bright. But motivated, and that counted for something.

"Roust them. Ring them at home. Police business, Jón. Justice doesn't take holidays."

As Jón sped off to recruit a partner, she thought over what Einar had said.

She was foolish. Stumbled in and drowned.

Was he right?

Foolish? Possibly. Drowned? Clearly.

Stumbled?

Krista didn't think so.

So how in God's name did she end up under the ice?

Hopefully CCTV would turn something up. It would take hours to sort through whatever footage Jón brought back. That was fine with Krista. She wasn't going anywhere.

Christmas could go fuck itself.

7

Finn stopped sketching and stood back to look.

His work now covered several pages, which he'd stuck up on the blank wall with bits of adhesive. Edge to edge, they formed a partial map of the city.

His war room.

His quarry could be anywhere. In theory. But simple inductive logic focused the field significantly.

They weren't just three Americans, they were three fellow SEALs, deployed here on some sort of covert kill/capture mission. Finn knew nothing about who their target was, cared less than nothing.

He wasn't here for their target.

He was here for them.

Finn had executed k/c missions like this himself, dozens of times. If this op were being run by him, he would probably hole up in a hostel or a cheap room in a third-rate hotel. Lower profile, less chance of discovery. But this op wasn't being run by Finn. It was being run by three guys who saw themselves as BFDs. Big Fuckin' Deals.

Ergo, they'd have set up in some swanky hotel. Which was stupid. But that was the curse of smart, highly trained people: they saw themselves as incapable of doing dumb things, so they were blind to it when they did.

Besides, these three wouldn't have any reason to think they were being hunted themselves.

There were twenty-five 4-star hotels in Reykjavík. They'd be at one of them.

But which one?

He opened a sketchpad and wrote all twenty-five names on a blank sheet, then stepped into the back bedroom to retrieve the laptop he'd discovered there, then sat down at the dining room table with the laptop and list of names and began compiling intel on each one.

"Trendy boutique hotel offers simple, modern rooms . . ." Unlikely choice, not for these three.

"Features a famous fine-dining restaurant and extensive wine cellar . . ." That one was a possible yes.

"Whimsically styled . . . rooms on the small side but the design compensates . . ." A no.

He continued on, starring some, demoting others, based on what he knew of his targets' preferences and opinions of themselves, narrowing his list of possible locations down to a dozen candidates.

Still too many.

He powered up one of the half-dozen disposable phones he'd bought and punched in a number.

"Magnús." The voice rumbled through the phone like a bulldog being roused from a nap. Which was pretty much what the man had looked like when he drove Finn in from the airport the day before, jammed into the driver's seat of his Yaris.

"Magnús," said Finn, pronouncing it precisely as the other man had. *Mock-noose*. "It's Marlin Pike."

There was a brief silence, then the rumble again. "You mean, Marlin Pike the writer?"

Finn made no reply.

This was a loaded question.

The voice yawned, then continued. "Iceland has the highest literacy rate in the world, my friend. There is no published crime writer in America named Marlin Pike. Or anywhere else in the English-speaking world."

Finn almost smiled. There'd been a handful of drivers at the airport curb. He'd made a good pick.

"Ghost writer," he clarified. "I probably should have mentioned that."

"Ah. Well, then." Clearly not believing it. "You need a ride somewhere, Ghost Writer?"

"How much to hire you for the week?"

The big man promptly named an astronomical number. Didn't even have to think about it.

Finn was impressed. "Done." Though he didn't expect to be there anywhere near that long. But he liked a little slack in his rope. An old habit. Bake contingencies into the plan.

"When do you want me to pick you up?"

"No pickup. I don't need you to drive, just be on call. And provide information."

A pause. "What kind of information?"

"I've got some friends here in the city who may be in a jam. I need to find them."

Another pause. Mock-noose was thinking this over.

"Will this be illegal?"

"No. It's not illegal."

Another pause.

"Are you on the up and over, Ghost Writer?"

Finn had to think about that one. *Up and over.*

Oh.

On the up and up, the man meant. Icelandic English.

Icelish.

Interesting that he didn't ask why, if they were his "friends," Finn didn't have their phone numbers, let alone know where they were staying. The driver didn't waste time playing footsie. Just went right to the point. *Will this be legal? Are you on the up and over?* Finn liked that.

"Tell you what," he said. "When we're finished, if you think I wasn't, I'll tip you the full amount again. For the trouble to your conscience."

Another pause, but briefer.

"What information do we have to go on?" the voice rumbled.

Good. Mock-noose was in.

"Three American males, traveling together."

"Description?"

This was a challenge.

His intel had told him that three of the six SEALs who'd gone rogue that night in Mukalla were in Reykjavík on a k/c op—but he didn't know which three. His intel didn't go that far. It had taken three months just to get what he had.

Finn knew all six men, each more dangerous than a puma. But each was dangerous in a different way. Distinct strengths. Unique weaknesses. Exactly how he dealt with them would depend to some extent on exactly which three they were. Which meant he had to be prepared to adjust his tactics on the fly. SEAL training 101. *All situations are fluid. There is no normal.*

But first he had to find them.

"Late thirties," he said. "In excellent shape."

"That's it?"

"That's it."

"I'll see what I can do."

After arranging their terms of payment, Finn clicked off and sent Magnús the agreed-upon sum in bitcoin, using an untraceable mobile app. Then pulled his razor-sharp CPM steel ring knife and carved a single notch on the side of the phone.

Phone #1: the Magnús phone.

Was using Magnús a bad idea?

Of course.

It was a bad idea to take a taxi in the first place. Finn could have taken the airport bus. Less risk. A cabdriver was far more likely to remember him than a bus driver, should anyone come looking. As Finn had no doubt someone would.

Still, taxi drivers the world over were prime sources of local information.

Establishing a HUMINT network—human intelligence—always entailed the risk of exposure. But so did all intel, one way or another. Heisenberg: observe an event, and the act of observation itself becomes part of the event. You put out feelers, they could be felt by others. Basic physics. And whenever possible, Finn preferred low-tech to high-tech.

Walk barefoot and you could feel the lay of the cobblestones.

Talk to real people and you got context with your information.

So, yes, it was a bad idea.

But it was also a good idea.

Besides, Finn had a high tolerance for risk.

He spent the next few hours walking the lower circuit of the city, south and west. Ended up back at the center of town.

At the duck pond.

It was now full dark, the city's street lamps offering no more than scattered puddles of light. Starlight and a waning moon threw a ghostly cast over the snow-covered city.

For no reason he could name, he began walking the perimeter of the pond, starting at the top, modern city hall and ancient national parliament building on his right, and proceeding counterclockwise, down the western edge with its great, looming cemetery, then skirting the narrow southern edge along the bridge's footpath and continuing up the eastern shore, past the public park and national gallery to the head of the pond—

Where he stopped at an art installation.

A statue.

A statue of . . . well, of what, exactly?

It was a man in business attire, carrying a briefcase, his face invisible. His whole head was invisible. In fact, his entire upper body, from mid-thorax to above where his head ought to have been, was encased in a gigantic block of what appeared to be black granite.

A mid-level government official being eaten from above by a giant rock.

It was like they'd put Hieronymus Bosch in charge of the municipal statuary.

Finn remembered reading about this. They called it "Monument to the Unknown Bureaucrat." Other countries had monuments to the "unknown soldier." But Iceland had no army. So they made a monument to an office drone. A fallen hero in their battle to modernize, Finn supposed. Paper-pushers versus ancient gods.

Weirdest damn thing he'd ever seen.

He retraced his steps back to the pond's northeast corner, where the crowd had gathered that morning, gazing at the knot of police ice-fishing for the dead.

He looked out at the frozen pond, then turned around and gazed in the opposite direction, due east, toward Laugavegur—Wash Road—and the bus station that was only a ghost now. Wondering where the dead girl had come from.

He had the sense of being watched.

He stood motionless for a full minute, tuned to his peripheral vision, which his sniper training had taught him was more sensitive to movement.

Nothing. He was alone.

The streets were empty.

He left the site and headed back toward his tucked-away neighborhood, making no sound as he walked. As he slipped around the first corner he glanced back—and caught sight of a face in the shadows, illuminated briefly in a flicker of moonlight. Only for an instant, and then it was gone.

He could have sworn it was the dead girl.

Monday

Overcast; possibility of snow.

8

Finn awoke at dawn, only there was no dawn.

It was dark as a tomb when he gasped awake and thrashed up to a sitting position, panting like an ancient hound in its final hours. He waited while his breathing slowed and stilled, then rose silently and went to wash.

He filled the tub with cold water, stepped one foot in, then the other, then lay down, fully submerged.

Finn was lost in darkness, still in that Yemeni farmhouse in Mukalla, crouched in the suffocating heat of the little dirt-floor room, the dim space lit up at jarring intervals by brief bursts of heat lightning that revealed glimpses of the horrors that had happened there—

children's sightless eyes staring up at the ceiling, black blood pooling where their ears had been, courtyard outside littered with corpses . . .

Not combatants in war. Farmers and their families. Elders, infants. An orgy of mass execution that would end three days later with Lieutenant Kennedy murdered and Finn himself shuttled off into exile.

He lay still, buried deep under the water's surface.

The cold brought a hint of relief, but it didn't penetrate. He hadn't really slept for weeks, months even, not deeply enough to wash his mind clear. Fatigue had soaked into his bones; it moved through his veins like oil sludge.

Half memories of that night flickered through his mind, single-frame images stabbing at him like shards of glass.

There were moments when he wasn't sure whether he was there in

Iceland and dreaming about that night in Mukalla, or if he was still in Mukalla, dreaming about being in Iceland.

After an unknown number of minutes, he surfaced and stood, toweled off, climbed into his sweats, and went back out to the dining room.

The place had no living room, which struck him as unusual. More likely this *was* the living room, but the guy who lived there had skipped the usual couch-and-love-seat arrangement and set the place up as a classy little dining room instead—long polished table, upholstered hardback chairs, sideboard and hutch. Apparently his host liked to entertain.

Finn sat on the floor, by his bedroll and backpack. He reached in and pulled out a nondescript black canvas bag, pulled open the heavy-duty zipper, and extracted a cellphone. He powered up the phone, waited for it to boot, then checked for text messages.

Nothing.

Opened the browser, checked IN box and Drafts folder.

Nothing.

He powered down the phone and zippered it back into the bag.

Thought about his quarry.

There would be sex, which meant women to find and track. There would be drugs—X, K, coke, whatever—which meant someone to obtain the drugs from. The three SEALs would have left trails he could find and follow. Like slugs.

He felt in his backpack among the half-dozen throwaway phones and withdrew the one with the notch. Hit REDIAL.

Time for a SITREP.

The bulldog voice answered on the first ring.

"Good morning, Ghost Writer." A soft rumbled laugh. "Although to you it must feel like still night."

Among the fellow drivers he had talked with, Magnús reported, there were dozens who'd picked up American tourists at the airport over the past week fitting Finn's description, mostly traveling in twos and fours. Trios were less common, and most of those were composed of men in their twenties. Or in their fifties. Or they included a woman in the mix.

But three men, traveling as a unit, all in their late thirties, all in excellent shape? They'd reported exactly two such groups, each dropped off at a different hotel.

Neither driver had names for their passengers, but it wouldn't have mattered if they had. The SEALs wouldn't have used their real names anyway.

"Question," said Finn. "If I wanted to buy some drugs, who would I talk to?"

This was met with a long pause.

"Illegal drugs," the bulldog voice finally said.

"Yes." Drugs would be a simpler slug-trail to track then sex.

Another pause. Then: "This is research."

"Yes."

"To do with your friends, who may be in the jam."

"Yes."

Magnús sighed. "Okay." He gave Finn a phone number. "You send this guy a text, he answers if he trusts you."

Finn wondered what criteria the drug dealer used to decide whether or not he trusted you, with only a single text message as evidence. But didn't ask.

"Your friends," Magnús said thoughtfully. "Do they *know* they're in the jam?"

"Not yet," said Finn.

He clicked off and sat thinking about the last thing Magnús said.

Your friends. Do they know they're in the jam?

Your friends.

Finn didn't have what you would call "friends," per se. He'd never mastered the concept. It was like there was some sort of membrane separating him from everyone else. It had always been that way.

But if he'd had such a thing as friends, his best friend would have been Lieutenant Kennedy.

He reached into his backpack and took out a second throwaway phone, carved two notches onto its side, then used it to send a text message to the number Magnús had just given him. The message consisted only of his name.

Marlin Pike

He put away both phones and got to his feet. Sat up at the dining room table and studied his list of twenty-five 4-star hotels. Both hotels

Magnús's friends had named were among the dozen he had identified as prime candidates.

Of course, it wouldn't necessarily have been someone in Magnús's driver network who'd driven the three SEALs into the city. They could have taken the bus. Or picked up their own rental at the airport. But public transport in Reykjavík was sketchy around Christmastime. And these guys would hardly be pinching pennies.

Besides, he had to start somewhere.

He marked them both on his map.

One to the west, up on the waterfront, above the concert hall.

The other about three klicks to the east, a twenty-minute walk beyond Hlemmur Square.

He'd start with the one on the waterfront.

Locate. Stalk.

Then strike.

And get out.

Finn slipped on a pair of beige chinos and an obnoxious wool sweater. As he packed his gear he thought again about that oppressive dirt-floor slaughterhouse and the flash-bulb bursts of heat lightning that showed him everything but told him nothing.

Nothing about what had really gone down that night.

The three SEALs would know.

They would know, because they'd been in the middle of it all when it happened.

9

Einar stopped as he entered the cramped office and sniffed the air. "What is that?" He looked around, puzzled, then at Krista. "Mmm, that's nice. Is that perfume?"

"Fuck you, Einar."

All he was smelling was his own cologne, of course. Krista didn't wear perfume. As Einar knew perfectly well.

The first time he'd pulled this stunt was twenty-six years earlier. *Is that perfume?* At the time she had not replied "Fuck you, Einar." She'd been a younger, more gullible Krista then and she'd actually thought he was serious. "On this job," she'd said, all sparkly earnestness, "you don't want to be wearing any scents."

"Ah," the young Einar had nodded. "So the bad guys can't sniff you out. Verrry smart."

Asshole.

"Look," she said, nodding at the video monitor.

Krista had been there since early morning, scanning the CCTV footage Jón had collected, and the hours had paid off: she'd found a glimpse of someone who was almost certainly the girl from the duck pond. It was shot from a tiny corner storefront located nine or ten blocks to the east of the pond and a few blocks south of Laugavegur.

There was more CCTV coverage now along the main strip, ever since 2017. Ever since Birna. It still wasn't much, though, nothing like a big European or American city, and once you got a few blocks away, coverage dropped off considerably. Those shops and hotel lobbies that did have cameras mostly had them trained on their own interiors. Street footage was almost nonexistent.

This was a lucky shot.

It was only a moment, two or three seconds of a woman, shot from behind as she ran. For an instant she had turned her head back over her shoulder and toward the camera. It was only a single darted look, the resolution too poor to make out any facial features at all, but in that glimpse Krista had the distinct impression that the woman was frightened. As if she was running from someone or something.

She brought Einar up to speed.

Now that they had an idea of what direction the girl was coming from—and now that the Christmas "dead zone" was behind them—Krista had sent Jón off to track down more security cameras in that area.

There had also been a handful of complaints the night of the twenty-fourth about loud laughter and drunk-sounding revelry from tourists in a few hotel bars, and in the empty streets after even the hotel bars were closed. No arrests, nothing significant, but still, even that level of disturbance was unusual for Christmas Eve in Reykjavík.

Maybe it was the record cold, pushing holiday partiers to get even drunker than unusual.

Krista had dispatched a few teams of officers to canvas area hotels.

"What do you expect to find?" said Einar. "The girl got stoned, went for a dunk with the ducks, too high to realize how cold it was." He shrugged, then leaned in and peered at the image frozen on the monitor. Slowly shook his head.

"My opinion, I'm not seeing fright there. I'm seeing someone half off her gourd."

Off her gourd. Dear God.

Einar plodded over to his own desk and sat, his chair groaning its usual protest. Pulled a Danish out of its paper sack and set it down on top of the saucer that lived on his desk for that express purpose.

Krista sat back in her own chair, disgruntled and frustrated.

Too high to realize how cold it was.

She supposed that was possible. Because of the tempering influence of the Gulf Stream, the winters in Rekjavík were not normally as cold as outsiders expected. This winter was unusual, though, and they were in the grip of a fierce cold snap. Maybe the intensity of the freeze caught the girl by surprise.

"Bullshit," she murmured.

They'd already questioned dozens of pond area residents, and she had a gloomy sense that whatever interviews her officers conducted closer to Laugavegur, the results would be no different. No one saw anything, no one heard so much as a squeak.

How was it possible that this girl ran through the street for a dozen blocks or more and not a single soul saw her?

She looked again at the still image.

"Who were you running from, Jóna Jónsdóttir?"

10

This morning the city was no longer silent and empty.
The daily rhythms of Reykjavík had gone back to normal—but Iceland's
version of normal, which meant the street traffic and urban soundscape
amounted to barely a tenth of that in any midsize American or European
city.

And still blanketed in darkness.

Darker even than the morning before.

During the night a bank of clouds had moved in, blotting out even the
faint starlight and dwindling moon. Now a thick blackness spread out
around Finn. What sounds there were—the murmurs of occasional
buses, faint thudding of cars with their studded tires, clatter of vendors
rolling in trash cans and putting out displays, the faint crunch of snow
underfoot—seemed to be swallowed up by the darkness, as if it were
made of a thick, absorbent substance.

Even the streetlights struggled to penetrate more than a foot or two.

Reykjavík no longer had the overt feel of a ghost town. The city was
alive and awake now, no question. But just barely. It was as if the city
were lying very still, holding its breath.

Waiting.

Finn thought about that massive fault line, the ragged seam where
two continental plates crashed into each other. This morning he could
practically feel the tremors through the soles of his feet.

Retracing his northward trek from the day before, he turned left
a block past Laugavegur, then stopped at a sleek, glassy, modern hotel

set a few blocks in from the water, with breathtaking views in all directions.

The Bayside. Very classy.

Stepping inside, he judged it to be relaxed and convivial. Restaurant just off the lobby, open and brightly lit. Sky-blue chairs, polished blond hardwood tables. Guests lingering over their breakfasts. The restaurant abutted a well-stocked semicircular bar, a ruddy-faced Icelander behind the counter polishing glasses, already preparing for happy hour. The place had the feel of a social hub.

Good.

Finn stood at the maître d' station holding a menu, as if mulling over its contents while deciding whether to venture in for breakfast. Out of the corner of his eye he assessed their cadre of servers and singled out a portly, middle-aged man, a little red about the nose, who gave off a sense of being both experienced and affable. Requested a seat in his section and was ushered directly into a booth off to one side, not far from the entrance.

He sat with his menu, listening to the conversation from the booth behind him. Not tourists. Local businessmen, relaxing over a holiday breakfast. From what Finn could tell, three were Icelanders and one a Pole who hadn't yet mastered the language, so they'd settled on English.

". . . still don't know even who she was—"

"Okay listen, *nobody* falls into Tjörnin naked and drowning. There was someone else involved, I will place money on that—"

"Hush, now! You don't know that."

Talking about the girl in the duck pond. Of course.

Naked and drowning. I will place money on that.

Icelish.

Finn was fascinated with the sounds of Icelanders' speech. Their English was fluent, articulate, and 98 percent accurate—but still odd somehow, with peculiar little hesitations, each word spoken like a fresh mint being placed on a pillow. It conjured up the sense of a magical kingdom. How elves or naiads would speak if they had human voices.

He'd read that the majority of Icelanders believed elves were real. He didn't find that strange. Not at all. Icelanders believed in elves. Americans believed in Elvis.

Everyone had to believe in something, he supposed.

"And for you, sir?"

His waiter stood poised to nod and memorize.

The breakfast menu was a study in multiculturalism. There were the expected eggs with sausage and/or bacon; waffles, pancakes, assorted pastries. Cheerios and Cocoa Puffs were among the options.

Then there was skyr, Iceland's answer to Greek yogurt, with bowls of berries—bilberries, crowberries, brambleberries, and goji berries, along with the more familiar blueberries and wild strawberries. Assorted cold fish—smoked, fermented, pickled. Even a platter of hangikjöt.

At the end of the buffet bar he noted carafes of cod liver oil standing next to stacks of shot glasses and small plates of lemon slices. No Icelander started the day without their shot of fish oil.

Oatmeal, that universal Western breakfast staple, seemed to bridge the cultural gap.

Finn went with oatmeal, pickled herring, and water, then posed his question.

"I'm lookin' for three friends, stayin' here, sposeta meet them for breakfast," he said in a Texas twang that telegraphed "I am an American." He assumed a rueful look and added, "Ah overslept."

The waiter gave a sympathetic nod. "They just left. I believe they were headed over to watch for whales. Not the best season for it," he added confidentially.

Finn produced an expression of hurt irritation.

"Seriously?" he said. "Without me?"

The aggrieved buddy.

"You might still be able to catch them," his server volunteered. Then, in a quieter voice: "They weren't moving too fast. I think they overslept too." He said this last with a look of merry empathy. This was a man who'd tied one on himself, more than once in his life. Probably more than once in the past two days.

All three together? That right there all but ruled them out. The three SEALs wouldn't likely move as a pack. They'd be in a rotation, alternating surveillance shifts to provide each one a chance to sleep. And to avoid being conspicuous.

They weren't moving too fast.

Even more dubious.

Though he couldn't be sure, not without eyes on.

After downing his chow, Finn paid in cash, thanked his server, and left.

Exiting the restaurant, he moved silently to the lobby. There was an area carved out to one side, furnished with comfy chairs flanking an enormous bookshelf. Finn picked out a leather-bound volume on Iceland's "Cod Wars," picked out a chair with a clear view of the elevator, and sat, giving the appearance of being fully absorbed in his book.

Evidently the Icelanders were serious about their cod. They'd gone to war with Britain ten times in the past six centuries over fishing rights and maritime boundaries. Iceland had won every time.

Finn had just gotten up to 1973, reading about Iceland's first (and only) fatality in the entire conflict, when his peripheral vision flagged three American men emerging from one of the hotel elevators. Loud conversation. Loud wool sweaters. Mid-thirties; one hefty, bordering on obese, none in great shape.

He'd never seen any of them before.

Not his guys.

Okay.

There could be more than one group of three Americans staying there.

Time to take his recon a little deeper.

Finn slipped out of the reading nook and started in the direction of the hotel's interior—then stopped. A pair of women stood at the front desk, talking with the desk clerk. Black uniforms, black-and-white-checked hat bands.

Police officers.

This was unusual.

Reykjavík was not a heavily policed city. Officers didn't do street beats or regular patrols here the way they did in so many American cities. Which suggested that these two were out canvassing.

Reason? Unknown.

He left by a side entrance.

11

An hour later Marlin Pike was back at The Bayside,
only it was a different Marlin Pike. Not Pike the American tourist, but
Pike the European businessman.

Stopping back at his bolt-hole, he'd swapped out the tourist's chinos
and gaudy woolen sweater for his business suit and a nondescript pair of
glasses. An identity better suited for deeper penetration into the hotel's
inner labyrinth.

The change of clothes also served as added insurance, in the event
anyone had tracked him to Reykjavík and was there now, on the hunt for
him. Which was possible. Probable, even. Cause enough to deploy basic
precautions.

Field disguise 101: go simple.

The more elaborate the getup, the more it called attention to itself.
Adding or subtracting a pair of glasses, for example, was a more effective
disguise than donning some complicated latex-and-putty rig. This wasn't
Mission Impossible; this was reality. From a distance, most observers
tended to recognize you more by color and style of clothing than your
facial features. More times than not, just changing to a contrasting set of
clothes got the job done.

He strode on through the lobby, gave the desk clerk a brisk nod and a
barked *"Guten tag!"* and headed for the elevators. As he walked he withdrew what appeared to be a large phone from his suit jacket pocket and
began speaking into it in rapid-fire German.

He took an elevator up to the second floor, where housekeeping rounds were just wrapping up, and made a circuit through the hallways, still talking. On his return loop he bumped into a housekeeper backing out of her last room on that floor.

"*Verzeihung!*" he said. *Excuse me!*

She mumbled something in Polish and began pushing her cart of soiled linens toward the elevator. They both boarded. She got off at the next floor.

Finn took the car back down to the ground floor, got out, and strode back behind the check-in desk and down a back hallway, as if he knew exactly where he was going.

It took twenty minutes of searching through the warren of corridors and offices to find a door marked with both Icelandic and English terms:

ÖRYGGISMIÐSTÖÐ
SECURITY

The room where the hotel's CCTV monitoring station would be located.

He stood by the door for a moment, thinking.

The Bayside obviously catered to a top-end clientele, domestic and foreign. Security was a priority. But like all cutting-edge Icelandic establishments, they would place exceptionally high faith in technology, and would also be reluctant to spend money on human resources where it wasn't needed. In off hours, chances were good they wouldn't bother staffing a backroom spot like this. His best guess, they would have someone manning the monitors during high-traffic times: breakfast, dinner. Maybe evenings. But not right now.

Besides, Finn had a high tolerance for risk.

He slowed his breath, closed his eyes, and listened for five full seconds. No sounds of anyone coming in either direction.

He pulled out the "phone" he'd brushed up against the housekeeper's pocket and placed it against the door, just above the handle, so that it lay flat against the keycard slot.

The miniature RFID/NFC scanner gave out a barely audible *whirrrr*, followed by a soft *click*.

Then went silent.

The door's lock clicked open.

No one walked by.

Finn pocketed his keycard scanner, slipped in the unlocked door, and closed it behind him.

Once inside he set himself on a stool at the monitor that covered the hotel's snazzy fitness center. Took a moment to familiarize himself with the deck controls, then set playback to go at double speed and began reviewing footage starting back at six a.m. the morning before.

He watched as stressed-out Icelandic executives and visiting CEOs worked off their obscenely pricey dinners from the night before and worried about closing their next deal over breakfast. No conversation; no one looked to the right nor the left.

The exercisers left and were replaced by others.

He moved the controls to 8x speed, then 16x, slowing periodically to examine subjects of possible interest. He saw dozens of hotel guests come and go.

Nobody he recognized.

After the nearly ninety minutes it took to scan through a full day's worth of footage, he was satisfied. The Bayside was not the place. His three SEALs would not have gone a full twenty-four hours without using the hotel gym. Not possible. They couldn't help themselves. None of these guys could. It was like an addiction.

They weren't here.

Finn stepped to the door and opened it a few inches to check the corridor for foot traffic.

One of the phones in his backpack vibrated.

He quickly pulled the door shut again and felt inside the pack. Two notches.

The drug dealer phone.

He extracted the phone and saw he'd just received a text.

> We could meet for a drink at the Mónakó.
> Perhaps 14.00.

Interesting phrasing, that "perhaps." Especially in combination with the subjunctive "we could meet." It suggested a certain level of education. Not exactly street talk.

Evidently the man had decided Finn was someone he could trust. Based on what calculation, Finn had no idea. But the man must know his business.

Finn cracked open the door again and risked a quick peek.

Hallway empty.

He stepped out, quietly shut the door, and threaded his way back out of The Bayside.

The other hotel on the Magnús list would have to wait.

Time to go meet his very first Icelandic drug dealer.

12

"Look!"

Krista, Einar, and Jón had each been scanning their portion of the divvied-up footage for hours. Tempting as it was to zip through in fast-forward mode, none of them wanted to risk missing a crucial second or two. Which was unfortunate, because watching a second-by-second replay of downtown Reykjavík on Christmas Eve was about as exciting as watching moss grow.

A few hours of staring intently at a screen upon which absolutely nothing happened was making Krista want to scream.

It was Jón who had finally seen something.

"Look," he repeated, his face flushed with excitement as the other two gathered round the workstation they'd set up for him in their office. He pointed at the screen, unnecessarily, and said, "What do you think?"

He played what was clearly another brief clip of the girl running, this one a few blocks closer to the duck pond, by the big church, and this time shot from a front angle. Again, only a few seconds long—but just long enough to see a second figure in the background on the other side of the street, walking the other way.

The young officer backed it up ten seconds and replayed the shot of the second person, doing what he could to zoom in on that portion.

It was a rear view and too grainy to make out any detail—man? woman? anything distinctive about the clothing?—but to Krista, something about it sparked a faint flash of recognition.

"Again," she said. "Slow."

Jón played it once more, frame by frame.

"There!"

He froze the image.

Krista stared at it. She looked over at Einar. After a moment, he nodded. A slow, uncertain nod, but a nod nevertheless.

That screen capture from airport customs.

She nodded at Jón. "Get me yesterday's CCTV footage from the airport lounge."

It didn't take more than a phone call and a ten-minute broadband download to get what she was after: footage from every bar and lounge in the airport over a two-hour window, starting from when the odd American's plane touched down.

They spent another excruciating hour staring at Jón's screen, scanning through reams of useless footage, until Krista thought her back and neck were both going to break from her hunched-over position—when she suddenly shouted "Stop!"

Her backache forgotten, she jabbed her index finger at a young man in expensive threads, seated at the bar in the airport's main lounge.

The camera was positioned above and behind the bar so that it held a full wide-angle view of the lounge interior and entrance. The figure she pointed to was positioned in the lowest portion of the screen, facing toward them.

Just behind him, the frozen frame caught a slight figure walking past and briefly stopping. A slight figure with squarish face and oversize eyes.

Marlin Pike.

"Rewind, fifteen seconds," her voice now hushed in concentration.

As they watched, the American walked by and bumped into the young man. The two exchanged a few words—it looked like the American was making an apology and the young Icelander was waving it off—then the American took the empty seat next to the young man, placed an order, and the two exchanged a few more words.

His order arrived. Water, no ice. A small plate of Icelandic rye with butter and lava salt.

The three sets of eyes continued staring at the screen as the soundless image played on.

After four or five minutes, the American stood and left the screen.

And returned three minutes later. "Water closet," murmured Jón. Einar looked over privately at Krista and winked. *Proper young pup.*

The two subjects exchanged a few more words. The American finished his rye bread and water, stood, nodded at the young man, and exited the screen.

Krista looked up at Einar. "Did you see that?"

He frowned.

She tapped Jón twice on the shoulder. "May I?"

He stood, giving his seat up to her.

Krista backed the footage up fifteen minutes. "Watch."

She hit PLAY.

Once again, the American entered the lounge, casually ambling through.

"Look at his eyes," said Krista. "He's scoping out the patrons. Travelers about to leave the city, most of them, for the Christmas holiday. See . . ."

They watched the American scan the crowd, his eyes settling on the young, well-dressed guy.

"The approach," she said as the American strolled by his mark. "The bump."

The American sat.

"Small talk, small talk, small talk," Krista continued, narrating the silent action. "Yes, the guy is leaving for a week abroad—look! You see that?"

She backed up ten seconds and hit PLAY again.

"Look: when Marlin—that's the American's name," she added for Jón's benefit, "when Marlin leaves for the men's room, he brushes up against him. You can't see his hands, but he just lifted the man's wallet. Now watch . . . aaaand *there*! Lightly touches him again when he comes back. Wallet back in the pocket." She stopped the clip. "Now he's got the guy's name and address."

"So, what," said Einar. "You think he's going to go to the guy's place and break in?"

Krista shook her head. "Too risky. Even if you're good, it can take a few minutes. Neighbors could get suspicious. Here, keep watching."

She pressed PLAY. The three of them watched the footage carefully.

After another minute they saw Marlin's body sway close for a moment, and then once again a few seconds later. Krista stopped the play-back and looked over at Einar.

Einar said nothing, but she could tell by his frown that he'd seen it, too.

"He lifts the guy's house key," she explained, "then a few seconds later he slips it back."

Einar frowned again. "Because . . . ?"

"He clammed it."

"He *what*?"

"You press the key into something soft—maybe he's using a chunk of that rye bread, or a piece of soap from the men's. Anything that will hold an impression. Only takes him a few seconds. Now all he needs is a pair of scissors, a nail file, and an Appelsín can. All of which he can buy right there in the airport. Cut a piece of aluminum from the can, stencil out a piece to fit the clammed mold, and—" She snapped her fingers. "Instant house key."

Einar stared at the screen. "Are you serious?"

"Flimsy, and you'd probably still need a torsion tool to turn the cylin-der. But it'd work, and it cuts your break-in time down to seconds."

Einar reared back and gave her a look. "How the hell do you know this stuff?"

She gave him a look right back. How the hell did he think?

"I read."

Despite her general distaste for Americans, Krista had an abiding pas-sion for American crime fiction. Sometimes she was not sure herself whether a particular bit of knowledge came from her own police train-ing and years of experience on the job or a classic American crime novel. She always hoped it was the former.

Jón retook his seat, and within five minutes he had the young clothes-horse ID'ed. His name was Ragnar Björnsson and he worked—surprise, surprise—in finance.

"According to his itinerary, he was on his way out of the country for the holidays. In New Zealand." Jón beamed up at Krista. "I just sent his information to you. Both of you," he added in Einar's direction.

Krista looked at her phone, tapped the screen once. "Huh." She tapped the phone number and put the phone to her ear.

"Who are you calling?" said Einar.

"Ragnar Björnsson." Krista nodded at Einar's computer as she waited for the phone connection. "Check out where he lives."

Einar looked down at his own computer screen and opened the memo Jón had just sent them.

Ragnar Björnsson lived in Parliament Hill, on Baldurs Street.

Three blocks from where the girl drowned.

13

Now decked out in scruffy parka and oversize cargo pants, Finn picked his way through the neighborhood south of Hlemmer Square and the bus depot that no longer existed. The last time Finn was there, the place had been a location good citizens were careful to avoid after dark. Den of drunks, derelicts, and petty criminals, hub of a dark, sketchy neighborhood.

In fact, some of the old seediness had survived the tidal wave of gentrification. Finn noted a handful of vacant, run-down buildings, taken over by squatters, still dotted the pocked side streets.

The city's indigent underbelly, alive and well.

At Hlemmur Square he took a moment to step inside the sparkling new food court and saw that not *quite* everything had changed inside. The old bus station's red, rusted floor tiles were still there. As if the transformation had left bloodstains.

He turned back onto Laugavegur and walked west for a block. Halfway to his destination he noted a familiar figure on the other side of the street, trudging along with the vaguely dogged gait of a man who knew he had nowhere to go but was determined to get there anyway.

His street buddy with the electric blue silk sash, walking his beat.

Finn crossed the street and handed the man a 500-króna bill. Roughly enough for a cup of coffee. *"Heil og sæl,"* he said with a nod.

"Heil og sæl," Blue Sash mumbled back.

To your health and happiness.

The vagrant resumed his pilgrimage. Finn crossed back and entered the wreck of a building the drug dealer had selected for their rendezvous.

The Mónakó was a popular spot for addicts, gamblers, and other down-and-outs. The place was lit with low-watt bulbs designed to hide more than illuminate. As his eyes adjusted, he took in the décor: slot machines, gambling tables, pool tables, darts, none in great shape.

His contact sat alone at a far corner table that was set up for chess, with half the pieces missing. Finn had no trouble identifying him. Every other soul in the place was lost in their own existence. This one was watching the door.

The man was old way beyond his years: huge bushy beard, weathered face, barrel-chested, scrawny limbs. Grandpa on Skid Row. Still, his clothes were clean. Down and out, but hadn't forgotten how to take care of himself. And appearances notwithstanding, Finn could see he wasn't a user himself. The man was a living dissertation on the human capacity to deteriorate—but from booze, not crack or meth or heroin. There was a difference. Like rust versus a forest fire. In both cases you had corrosion through oxidation, but one was a good deal slower and allowed for the retention of more dignity in the process.

Finn introduced himself and shook the man's hand. When the other man withdrew his hand there were now three crisp American $100 bills tucked into it. Most retail business in Iceland was transacted through debit or credit cards—but restaurants and bars still took good old American cash.

"Ólafur," the man said. "Good to make your acquaintance, Marlin." His voice was distant but strong.

Finn took a seat and glanced around the place, taking in the clientele, memorizing faces. If Ólafur had met any of his three SEALs here, there might be other witnesses.

"Is this where you typically meet new clients?"

Ólafur shook his head. "Only reliable referrals, such as yourself."

"So, how does it work, normally?"

"You have seen our hotels."

"You have quite a few," said Finn.

"I frequent only the finest."

Finn nodded. In other words, he discreetly cruised the 4-stars, making himself available to wealthy tourists.

"Mostly I am seen as a local curiosity," the big man said. "Like a puffin, or a geyser."

Finn understood. Those clients who were in the market would spot him for who he was and deal with him quietly and privately. To the rest, he was a harmless eccentric.

"And the police don't bother you?"

Ólafur waved a hand grandly. "I have visited their establishment many times. They take care of me, feed me something warm, scold me, send me on my way. Look out for me. I keep an eye on things in my neighborhood, they do the same in theirs. The relationship is symbiotic. Like oxpecker and water buffalo."

Finn nodded agreeably.

"So, what can I do for you, young man?"

"I'm looking for a little information."

"That's all?"

"That's all."

Ólafur's eyes narrowed. "Information such as?"

Finn asked Ólafur if he'd had occasion to do business with any American men over the past five days. Mid-to-late thirties, in good shape. Three traveling together, though chances were good it would have been just one who interacted with him.

Ólafur seemed reluctant to reply.

"I'm not with any kind of law enforcement," Finn added. "I'm not here to get these men in trouble. I'm here to help get them out of trouble. Trouble they don't even know they're in."

Good a lie as any.

Or maybe a half-truth. Finn himself could be trouble enough.

Ólafur considered, then relented. "As a matter of fact, I have lately encountered two such men, either of whom might fit that broad description. The first was staying at, I believe, the Grand Hótel Reykjavík . . ."

The second hotel on the Magnús list.

"And the other . . . I don't have a hotel for that one. We met at the Casablanca, a few blocks from here, but I don't believe he was staying there."

The Casablanca. Finn had seen the place on one of his circuits, a few blocks off Laugavegur. A run-down operation, bottom of the heap. One-star, or more likely no-star.

Dubious. Meeting up at a cheap hotel was not their style.

But the Grand sounded perfect.

He thanked Ólafur and left the dark-lit café. It was now mid-afternoon. Still time to change and go scope out the Grand Hótel Reykjavík before night fell, at least give it a preliminary recon.

Arriving back at his appropriated base of operations, Finn found an envelope taped to the door.

For "Marlin Pike"

Addressed to him: not a good sign.

And quote marks around the name: not a good sign at all.

He didn't bother looking around. He knew he'd been alone when he approached; whoever left the note was long gone.

He brought the envelope inside and set it on the dining room table, where he carefully slit it open and extracted a single sheet of notepaper.

Lögreglan
Hverfisgata 115

We'd like to have a conversation, if you have a moment.
You can reach me at

And it provided a local phone number. It was signed, "Krista Kristjáns-dóttir."

Lögreglan.

Icelandic for "law and order." Also the Icelandic word for "police."

The Reykjavík police wanted to have a conversation.

Unexpected.

Finn hadn't wanted to rent anything, not even under an assumed name. Didn't want to leave a trail, not with a full-court press military manhunt for him in progress. So he'd gone dirt basic and fallen back on skills he'd picked up as a teenager on the SoCal docks. Found someone leaving town, lifted a copy of his housekey, and gone to ground.

No one had followed him from the airport.

No one knew he was here.

And this Icelandic cop had found him inside thirty-six hours.

Impressive. And disturbing. Either she was very good, or he was off his game.

Probably both.

And that worried him.

14

Krista was staring at the still shots from the airport when her cellphone buzzed.

Number unknown.

"This is Krista," she said in English.

"I'm sitting in a coffee shop down the street from your office." A quiet, measured voice. "It's got a sign out front with a picture of a French press coffeepot on it."

He didn't identify himself.

"Two minutes," she said.

Upon entering the French Press she recognized him immediately, in a booth off to the right, seated facing out, a bottle of water in front of him.

"Mister Pike," she said, sliding into the seat across from him.

"Detective Kristjánsdóttir."

She gave a pro forma smile. "Thank you for coming so promptly."

He said nothing. No "Happy to help," or "What's this about?" Which she found interesting. In her experience, people facing a police inquiry invariably reacted, growing either defensive or overly helpful. Sometimes both at once.

This American showed no reaction at all.

He'd also set the parameters of the meeting himself, rather than coming in to the police station, say, or simply returning her call when he got the note. And had chosen his seat strategically: back to the wall, clear view of both front and back exits as well as the street. Seizing the high ground: basic battle tactics.

Military?

"So," she said. "What exactly are you doing here in Iceland?"

"Research," he said.

"Oh? What sort?"

"Human behavior. Crime, mostly."

"You came to Reykjavík to study crime?"

"It's research for a crime writer. A novelist, back in the States. He's working on a novel set in Iceland."

"Uh-huh," she said. "You have a background in that sort of thing? Let me guess. Intelligence community? Special operations?" He didn't look or behave like anyone she'd known from the armed forces, but she knew how to see past exteriors.

"I . . . was a rescue swimmer for the navy. At one point."

Huh. He'd hesitated briefly, which surprised her. And he'd said a little more than he'd needed to. *At one point.* Implying that something else came after.

She sensed a deep fatigue about him.

A server came to her side. She took advantage of the moment to think about her next tack as she placed her coffee order, then turned back to the American.

"I see you flew in from . . ." She pretended to check some notes in the file folder she'd brought with her. It tended to wear down witnesses' defenses if they thought you had some hard facts on a piece of paper, and not just in your head. "London?"

She looked up at him.

"There was no direct flight from the US, not on Christmas Eve. So I came in through Heathrow."

"Your itinerary shows only the one flight from London."

"I bought two tickets. Two separate itineraries."

"Uh-huh," she said. "And it was important to come on that particular day?"

He shrugged. "I had work to do. I wanted to get to it."

"May I ask, what brought you to Ragnar Björnsson's house?"

"I'm a friend. He loaned it to me for the week."

He hadn't asked her how she'd found him, how she knew he was staying at that particular address. Which was also interesting. Wouldn't most people be surprised? Burning with curiosity, even?

"How do you know him?"

"Is that important?"

She looked straight into the American's eyes. "I just put a call in to him, half an hour ago."

Marlin Pike gave up no visible reaction, just returned her gaze. "And what did Ragnar have to say for himself?"

For five full seconds she looked at him, studying his face for a reaction.

Five seconds is a long time.

"Nothing," she said, finally. "I left a message."

He nodded. Tilted his head two degrees to the left. "You don't like Americans, do you?"

That threw her for an instant, and she had to struggle not to show a reaction—but she knew that she had, and that he'd seen it.

"If you don't mind," she said, reaching her fingers into the folder and withdrawing a still of the two figures on the street. She laid it on the table, rotated it 180 degrees so that it was facing his direction, then pointed to the man in the photo. "Is this you?"

"Hard to say. Looks like me. But . . ." He spread his hands out in a *Who knows?* gesture.

She pointed to the girl in the foreground.

"Did you see her, Rescue Swimmer?"

He leaned back slightly in his chair. "I was out walking. That's all."

"You've heard about the girl who drowned in the duck pond."

A question, framed as a statement.

"Yes," the man said.

"We have reason to believe the girl was running from someone, possibly someone in the general neighborhood where you're staying. Was that someone you?"

"Detective Kristjánsdóttir—"

"Krista."

He said nothing, just looked at her.

"'Kristjánsdóttir' isn't a last name," she explained. "Like 'Pike,' for example. It's a patronym. We don't use them like last names. We just use what you'd call first names. And we don't use titles, like 'Detective' or 'Officer' or 'Ma'am.'" She cocked her head slightly, reflecting back his gesture from a few minutes earlier. "Ragnar never told you this?"

"It never came up," he said. Matter-of-factly. No defensiveness. He clearly knew she was playing with him, yet it didn't seem to unnerve him in the slightest.

She waited a beat. "You were saying," she prompted. "About the woman in the photo."

"I really can't help you, Krista. I don't know who she is. I don't know anything about this."

She returned the printout to its folder, placed the folder off to the side, and folded her hands on the table in front of her.

"Marlin Pike. Good professional name. You should publish under that name."

He shrugged. "It's my name."

"Of course."

She made no effort to hide the fact that she didn't believe him. But she had no cause to hold him.

She handed him a card with her name, cellphone, and email. "You know what we customarily say in a situation like this."

Pike took the card. "Don't leave town?"

She reached for her folder, then stood and walked out of the French Press. The best parting line, in her experience, was no line at all.

Leave them guessing.

She crossed the street and walked the short block back to the station, still thinking about the man's maddening lack of reactions—and that single moment he'd hesitated.

I was a rescue swimmer. At one point.

She took the stairs to the second floor and down the corridor to the back of the building.

When she walked into her office she found the dead girl sitting at her desk, smoking a cigarette.

15

After the detective left the coffee shop Finn sat for a moment, sipping his water, thinking about her. The ice-blue eyes that didn't miss much. The coolly aggressive interview style. The skillful placement of questions.

Her little parry-and-thrust with Ragnar's name was smooth, practiced. Obviously she hadn't actually spoken with the guy. He was off the grid for at least a few days, a detail Finn knew and the detective clearly did not. It was a feint, designed to smoke him out, or at least throw him off balance. The fact that it didn't work had pissed her off, though she hid it well.

He wondered if that hostility was about Americans or foreigners in general. Or just a part of the uniform.

His thoughts turned back to his mission.

He knew they had arrived at least a day or two before Finn himself did. They would have located their target, holed up nearby, as close as possible, and set up their own surveillance rotation the moment they arrived.

By now they'd be well into the process of watching their subject's comings and goings. Monitoring pattern of life. Studying his or her every move, cataloging, learning the routine. Getting copies of keys, entry codes, and so on. Looking for windows and cracks. Opportunities to exploit.

Which meant they themselves would be following a routine.

Which made them easier for Finn to find.

When you hunted prey, you tended to adopt the patterns of your subject. In many respects, you became your target. Which made you as vulnerable as your target.

Made *yourself* prey, in other words.

"Scuse me—American, yeah?"

Finn glanced around, already placing the accent. Half-Americanized
British? New Zealand? No, Canadian. But not Toronto or Montreal.

"You were at the duck pond," the man stated triumphantly, like he
deserved a bonus for working it out. "Yesterday morning."

Central Canada. The prairies: Manitoba or Saskatchewan. A flatter,
plainer accent. Like the US's Midwest.

The man's face, ruddy from the cold, wore an eager grin, and he had
one hand stuck out in front of him.

Finn gave the hand a single shake.

"Ben Stewart," the man said, in reply to a question Finn hadn't asked.
"CBC Winnipeg."

Finn remembered the face all right. From the throng of media at the
duck pond's edge, the morning before. Hanging back, not pushing in to
snap photos or fire questions at the police.

He was a photojournalist, the man explained, there in Iceland to do a
nature piece on the Arctic fox. "Only mammal native to Iceland. Arrived
here at the end of the last Ice Age, long before humans, though no one
knows exactly how it got here. Elusive, highly intelligent little creature.
Fascinating subject, really . . ."

Ben the photojournalist from Winnipeg was clearly aching for Finn
to invite him to join, yet just polite enough not to sit without being asked
first.

Finn didn't ask.

A server came by to see if Finn's friend would like anything. It didn't
seem to bother her that the man was standing by the table and not seated.

"Yes, thank you, miss—tea, if you would. Hot. No milk, just plain."

Once the server left, Ben No-Milk-Just-Plain broke down and slid
into the bench across from Finn. "May I?"

Finn gave a tilt of his head that could have meant anything.

Sipped at his water.

"They told me Reykjavík wouldn't be as cold as I expected," the man said cheerily, rubbing his hands together and blowing on them. As if his topic needed an audiovisual aid to be clear. "Ha! Joke's on me!"

Finn nodded. In terms of small talk, that was as far as he was willing to go.

After a few moments of silence, the man spoke up again. "I couldn't help noticing you talking with the detective. Just now, I mean. Was that about the drowned girl? Do they know who she was yet?"

Which was what Finn had figured the man was after from the start. A story.

He told the journalist the same thing he told the detective.

"I really can't help you. I know nothing about any of this."

Ben's plain hot tea arrived and he made a bit more small talk over a few surprisingly noisy slurps of tea—how sad it was, hoped they'd be able to identify the poor girl and notify her family, and so on—then eventually left a few Canadian bills on the table for his tea and excused himself.

Alone again, Finn drank more water and thought about his situation.

He was too exposed.

Way too exposed.

He should get out of Iceland now while his exfil path was still somewhat clear. Though he'd need a new passport. And it would mean cutting loose a lead it had taken him months to track. He might not see another chance like this for a long time.

He considered the pros and cons.

High tolerance for risk, yes . . . but still. He'd been on the run for more than three months now, ever since vanishing from the USS *Abraham Lincoln* into the cold Pacific ten miles off the San Diego coast. At this point any number of intelligence agencies could be closing in. And evidently he wasn't that hard to find.

So: Abort?

Serious question. Elements of the most powerful military machine on the planet were arrayed against him, wielding accusations of major war crimes. And they wouldn't do the accusing unless they'd planned to make it stick. Not much of a future there.

He should abort.

The café staff began making a circuit through the place, switching on their lights. Daylight was fast draining away and the clientele had dwindled to almost nothing.

Finn didn't move.

What would Lieutenant Kennedy do?

He would stay, that's what he would do. Not even a question.

More of an answer.

Finn reached into his backpack and pulled out his third throwaway phone, the one he'd used to place his call to the detective. He scrolled through a few photos he'd taken earlier, around the pond. Selected one, keyed in a phone number, and sent it as a text message attachment.

He stood, took the last sip of water, and walked to the front entrance.

Just inside the door he stopped, removed the phone's SIM card and crushed it under his boot heel, then broke the phone in half, placed its pieces in the trash can, and exited the French Press.

16

It wasn't the dead girl, of course. But she looked a hell of a lot like the dead girl. Which made sense, once she told Krista who she was.

They were sisters.

The deceased's name was Kateryna Shevchenko, and she had traveled from their native Kyiv to Iceland to work as an au pair—against her big sister Oksana's advice.

"Our parents are gone," the smoking woman told Krista. "I am Kateryna's guardian, since we were teenagers."

Krista gave a brief outline of what they knew about her sister's death, which was painfully little. CCTV had glimpsed her on the street, running in the direction of the duck pond; she appeared to be alone. A witness had passed her in the same area, an American, but was unable to add any details. Upon reaching the duck pond, she had apparently stripped and entered the pond at its northwest corner, alone, gone under the ice, and expired.

They were truly sorry for her loss.

Krista resisted the impulse to preface her next question with an apology. In her experience, preemptive apologies only made the hard questions harder.

"Was there any chance your sister had been using drugs?"

"No." Oksana's reply came cold and fast as the drop of an axe. "No drugs."

Krista waited. After a beat she saw the woman's shoulders sag, and she registered the sense of defeat it conveyed. A tiny gesture with the weight of too many lost battles behind it.

"Kateryna, at one time . . ." She seemed to search for the right English idiom. "For a while, she ran with the wrong crowd. Drugs, then. No sleeping, too many boys."

She sucked in a drag from her cigarette. Reykjavík was as non-smoking as a city could get, but Krista wasn't about to stop her.

"But this is all past. Kateryna is clean now, not touching drugs, not once in three years. *Three years.* Making a good life for herself."

The shoulders came up again. Troops back in position.

"So, no. No drugs."

Oksana said she'd known the move to Iceland was a bad idea, she had felt it in her gut, but she couldn't stop Kateryna, and besides, at some point her little sister had to stand on her own two feet.

Now she knew her gut had been right.

She learned of her sister's death, she said, when she saw that photo online. The one with the tacky headline.

"Two hours later, I was on a plane."

Einar poked his head in the office and spotted the woman smoking. "Hey, you can't—"

Krista cut him off with a frown.

He silently crossed the cramped office space and took a seat at his desk, where he bent his head over some paperwork, leaving the two of them to continue talking.

Oksana threw a brief glance in Einar's direction. Dropped her cigarette into her cup of take-out coffee and blew out a stream of white smoke.

"So. I'm here to bring little sister home."

Krista sighed inwardly.

"There's an issue with the body—"

"Yes, yes." The woman made no effort to hide her impatience. "I understand this. Procedures. How soon you are able to release?"

Krista's heart sank. The sister assumed that by "there's an issue" she had simply meant they couldn't release the body *yet*.

Fuck.

How did you tell someone her only sister's corpse was misplaced and accidentally popped into an oven for an hour at a thousand degrees Celsius?

"We're still looking into it," she said. "Please be patient."

"So now we have a name." After the woman left, Einar had scooted his long-suffering chair over to Krista's desk. "Did she say who the employer was?"

Krista lifted her phone and activated the memo software, looking at Einar by way of reply as she dictated the name into the phone: "Tryggvi Pétursson."

Einar whistled. "That'll be some interview. I'll go have my uniform pressed." He hauled his bulk up again and chuckled as he headed out into the corridor. Not, in fact, to have his uniform pressed, but to engage in the eternal Einar pastry hunt.

She wrapped the silence of the office around her like a cloak and sat thinking about the girl in the duck pond, no longer Jóna Jónsdóttir but now with a name of her own. Here in Krista's city, under the patronage of one of Iceland's wealthiest citizens.

Tryggvi Pétursson.

Krista puzzled over the name. It was now well over twenty-four hours since the dead girl's photo had been blasted out over the news. Everyone in Reykjavík knew about it. Probably everyone in Iceland knew about it.

Why hadn't the man contacted them?

"Halló?" Jón at the door.

Krista raised her eyebrows. *Yes?*

"We just got a call from Tryggvi Pétursson's office? He'd like to have an audience with you at the Tower tomorrow morning?"

Ah. Speak of the devil.

Looking up, she realized Jón was still at the door. Like he was waiting for permission to enter the inner sanctum. "Yes, Jón?"

He came over and placed a stack of printouts on the corner of her desk. "Report on the canvassing."

"Good," she said.

She dismissed her diligent protégé and began reading through the report, the results of their efforts to follow up on the Christmas Eve disturbances. Everyone else filed and read their reports online, on the department's intranet. Krista liked her reports on paper.

It wasn't only vacationing tourists who'd disturbed the Yuletide peace. Her officers had also counted among the rowdy a few British bankers there on business, an Australian med student enrolled at the University, and a visiting Swedish hockey team.

No one had anything significant to add.

Her phone buzzed. She glanced over at it.

A text from Marlin Pike. No message, just an attachment.

She pulled the phone closer and tapped on the attachment.

It was a photo of a man walking casually with a briefcase, one hand in his pocket. The entire upper half of his body, including his head, was encased in a large block of granite.

She recognized it, of course. Anyone in Reykjavík would recognize it. The Monument to the Unknown Bureaucrat, a statue on display at the head of the duck pond, an easy stone's throw from City Hall.

She frowned. Was that supposed to mean something? An unidentified man at the pond, not far from where the girl drowned. Or was it supposed to be some sort of joke?

What exactly was Pike's role here?

Did he even have a role? It wasn't at all clear from the CCTV footage that the girl had been running *from* him. Just that they had been on the same street at the same time. Not even the same side of the street. Could be, he just happened to be there.

Another random confluence of unrelated events.

Uh-huh.

She turned her attention back to her printouts, reading every detail of every conversation, word for word.

The Swedes had been having drinks with a gaggle of flight attendants, though that was well before midnight. (The time stamp on her running girl footage was closer to one a.m.) The Aussie said he'd maybe seen a car on the street on his way back to his room (staggering, no doubt), but he couldn't be positive. The bankers were worthless.

Terrific.

In the name of thoroughness, she'd run a check on all flight attendants in the city over Christmas, but expected nothing there.

She went back to her report, starting from the top and poring through it all once more, trying to establish in her mind a clear timeline of the events of that night.

Which was difficult, considering that those events were still largely unknown.

Still, to Krista it wasn't simply a random series of meaningless interviews. It was the jumbled-up pages of a story.

She just couldn't see the plot yet.

17

Finn sat on the floor of Ragnar Björnsson's dining
room, looking up at his spreading map of the city. Off to the left, taped
onto the wall, was a photo he'd printed out on a little inkjet printer that
lived in the bedroom, next to Ragnar's laptop.

It was the photo from the newspaper's website of the drowned girl,
her face staring up at him through the ice, eyes wide, mouth half-open,
as if about to speak.

What did she see?

What did she know?

The truth was, *he saw her*. Of course he did. The retreating figure by
the great stone church in the detective's CCTV still, that was him.

Of course it was.

He'd been walking the other direction, coming from the west in his
initial circuits of his neighborhood, when she ran past him on the far
side of the street. He'd caught only the briefest glimpse of her face as he
walked.

He looked back at the news photo, the staring eyes and half-open
mouth.

What was it about that picture that held him in its grip?

She reminded him of someone, but he couldn't put his finger on who.
Which was unsettling in itself. Finn remembered everything he'd ever
seen. Or at least normally he did. Among the Teams, his powers of recall
were legendary. It was one reason, possibly the prime reason, the US
government had poured a small fortune into training and retaining him,

since military snipers were deployed far more as intelligence assets than as marksmen.

Except that over the summer he'd found gaping holes in that flawless memory, mental canyons he had yet to bridge. "Lacunae," a navy psychologist had called them.

Like the hours surrounding that bloodbath in the farmhouse.

He reached into his backpack, pulled out the black canvas bag, and extracted his personal cellphone, the one he'd brought with him to Iceland.

Cellphones were a digital security nightmare. Putting one in "airplane mode" didn't make it secure; he'd still be visible to short-range snooping technology via signals like Wi-Fi or Bluetooth. Even turning it off was no guarantee of invisibility.

Hence the rotation of anonymous disposable phones.

His own instrument he kept completely powered down and enclosed in a bag laced throughout with a tight wire mesh, which acted like a portable Faraday cage, cutting all electrical signals traveling in and out of the bag to near zero.

Still, the instant he removed it from the bag and powered it on, he became as visible as if he were standing silhouetted on a ridgeline. So he was reluctant to use it, and did so as briefly as possible, and only when it was important.

This was important.

He powered up the phone, waited for it to boot.

No messages.

He wasn't sure if that was good news, or bad news.

He shut off the phone and placed it back into the canvas bag. And looked again at the photo.

What did she see?

What did she know?

He began taking down all the paper sheets from the wall, stacking them carefully in sequence, then spent the next few hours going back and forth between research on the borrowed laptop and refining his pencil sketches and lists, updating his map and information.

He could have simply printed out sections of the city from Google Maps, rather than taking all that time to survey it on foot and then sketch it all from memory. But for a sniper, sketching an AO—area of operation—was a tactical essential. It was how you learned the lay of the land, not just to memorize it but to *know* it down to your bones.

Finally, he put everything back up on the wall. Looked at the map.

Looked over at the photo again.

He turned off the lights and headed back outside into the night, zig-zagged east a few blocks until he arrived at the location documented in the detective's freeze-frame, the precise spot near the big church where he'd caught that glimpse of the running girl.

He looked back west toward the duck pond. Then east again, the way he'd just been walking. She would have been coming from that direction.

What did she see?

What did she know?

He retraced his steps all the way back to the edge of the pond, where he stood for a moment looking out at the spot where she drowned.

I was a rescue swimmer, he'd told the detective.

Another lifetime.

He felt someone's presence behind him and turned.

The dead girl stepped out of the shadows and walked over to him.

18

The resemblance was striking, though up close it was clear that she was a few years older than the young woman in the photo.

Sisters.

Lit cigarette in hand, the woman gestured to the west, across the pond, in the direction of the big cemetery. "You know this place? Oldest graveyard in city. Famous poets and politicians they bury there."

She took a long drag on her smoke and gazed into the distance, her eyes focused on nothing.

"There is a cemetery like this in Kyiv, where we have our family plot. This is why I came. To bring my sister home."

Finn nodded. Waited to see what else she would say.

After a quiet minute she dropped her cigarette to the ground and crushed it under the toe of her boot. "Come."

They walked a few blocks north in silence, the woman leading, Finn following. She stopped at the steps of the parliament building and sat. He sat down next to her.

She lit another cigarette.

"Longest-running parliament on earth," she said, gesturing behind her with her cigarette hand. "Modern world's oldest representative democracy." Now she turned and pointed out the national symbols that decorated the building's exterior, naming them as she did.

"Dragon, eagle, bull. Giant with big club."

He said nothing, just let her talk on as she explained the significance of the country's patrons.

Finally she stopped herself mid-sentence. "Sorry," she said. "Historian, national university in Kyiv. I talk history, it takes my mind off of here and now."

Finn nodded.

"Oksana Shevchenko," she said.

"Marlin Pike," said Finn.

She looked at him and took a long, appraising drag. "You are also a researcher," she said.

"Not an academic," said Finn. "I do groundwork for a crime writer."

"Hah." She nodded. "The detective I spoke with, she mentioned there was a witness." Now she nodded vaguely in the direction of the duck pond. "I saw you, there, last night. Am thinking, witness must be you."

Finn glanced over in the pond's direction, then back at her, but said nothing. In his experience, silence was a more useful communication tool than most words.

"She said you saw my sister."

"I told her I didn't."

The sister gave up the hint of a smile. "I don't think she believed you."

Finn was not surprised to hear this. The detective hadn't believed anything he'd said. Except perhaps the part about being a rescue swimmer.

Still, it was interesting that she had mentioned him to the dead girl's sister. Finn didn't know much about police procedure in general, let alone how they did things there in Iceland, but that seemed like an unconventional move.

Maybe she thought the sister would get more results with him than she did herself.

Oksana Shevchenko's eyes bored into him. "What did you see? How did she seem?"

"I can't help you," he said. "I'm not part of this."

She took another drag and blew the smoke out in a long thin stream. "Why?" she said. She looked at him sharply, then looked away again. "Why you tell detective you didn't see her?"

Finn didn't reply.

He noticed how, when her emotions swelled to the surface, her English disintegrated into a sort of Slavic-English, losing its articles and leaning into the present tense.

"She came here to Reykjavík," she said, tonelessly, "to work as au pair. For Tryggvi Pétursson."

Finn recognized the name but didn't show it.

"One of the most powerful men in Iceland."

"Okay," he said.

"But not so powerful," she added softly. "Not powerful enough to keep her from being killed."

She dropped this cigarette on the pavement, too, and fiercely ground it out.

A passing couple gave her a dirty look. *Littering foreigner.*

"Killed," he repeated.

Not *from dying. Keep her from being killed*, she'd said.

She looked at him. "I think my little sister fell in with some bad people."

Finn considered this. "What did the detective say when you told her this?"

"I didn't."

"Why not?"

"Why I should trust police? Police don't trust me."

Finn cocked his head two degrees.

"They never ask me to ID the body." She looked at him. "Photo is enough, they say. I am no policeman, but I'm thinking, this is strange."

Finn had no comment on that. It did sound unusual.

"Why tell me?" he said.

She stood and looked down into his face. "You saw her."

He stood, too.

"I can't help you," he said again.

What was she expecting from him?

She regarded him for another moment, then leaned in, her face just inches from his.

"You *saw* her," she repeated.

She turned and walked away.

He sat for the next hour on the Parliament building steps, in the cold, reflecting on the sister's suspicions. Though it was hard to say exactly what it was she suspected. She played her cards close to her vest.

Cautious.

And patient. How long had she stood in the freezing cold, waiting for Finn to show up?

And sure enough, show up he had.

He shook his head.

A *little* off his game? Here he was, just forty-eight hours since setting foot in this city, and so far he'd been found by, let's see, a local detective, a Canadian bird-watcher, and a university professor.

"Scrotal disaster," he murmured.

One of Kennedy's many sayings.

Scrotal disaster.

Moses blows us.

Christ on stilts.

He pushed the thought back. Don't think about Kennedy.

Don't think about the girl in the ice.

Don't think about Ray.

Focus on the mission.

Let the dead be dead.

Tuesday

Clear and cold.

19

It was hot and dark, the air shot through with elec-tricity. Heat lightning trembled, illuminating the scene in brief slashes. He stood before a great wooden door set into a mud-brick wall. The timbers of the door were smashed in.

He pushed aside the shattered fragments, stepped through the opening— and all at once, like a jump cut in a horror flick, he was inside the house, entering a room.

Jump cut.

Now he was on the other side of the room, sitting on the earthen floor, back to the wall, legs splayed out. A flash lit up the room—

And now he was eight years old, on the floor of an enormous closet, screaming—

Finn awoke panting, covered in blood.

Gradually, he became aware that it wasn't blood.

Of course it wasn't.

It was nothing but a thin film of his own sweat.

He lay still on his back, slowing his breath until it settled into a quiet, normal rhythm.

Then opened his eyes.

Finn had been working on a technique Carol told him about. He would let himself walk through the dream, and when he got to the point of sitting in that childhood closet in eastern Oregon, he was supposed to picture something peaceful, so that when the scene lit up he would be somewhere else.

Like a field of butterflies, or an Alpine mountaintop.

"Those are just my examples," she'd said. "Your ending has to be something you come up with yourself. Something that bubbles up from your own subconscious, so it has a chance of showing up naturally when you're in REM."

It was like finding an organ donor with compatible blood types, she'd explained.

A compatible fantasy.

Finn had settled on Vieques, a little island paradise off the eastern tip of Puerto Rico. Every day, he spent a few minutes sitting still and conjuring up an image of himself diving into the clear turquoise water under an azure sky. The clearer and deeper he could cut that particular neural groove into his brain, as Carol explained it, the more likely it became that it would start firing in the middle of the night, when he needed it.

That image was his anti-nightmare.

So far it hadn't worked.

He felt in his backpack and pulled out the black canvas bag again. Undid the heavy zipper, withdrew the phone. Powered it up.

There were two people on the planet Finn knew he could trust; staying in touch with both was the only reason he had brought his own phone.

He keyed in a text message to squidink28@gmail.com.

> here

After a moment a reply message appeared.

> have you slept?

He shut off the phone.

The absence of reply would be his reply. Carol would understand that. Carol understood Finn. Maybe better than he understood himself.

Admittedly, not that high a bar.

The two rarely exchanged more than a few words on email.

They rarely exchanged more than a few words in person, for that matter. Mostly their overlapping existence lived in shared silences. Like radio signals beamed through space between two distant planets, both far from any known sun, held in mutual orbit in the outer rings of some unnamed solar system.

have you slept?

No, he had not. Not longer than a half hour, anyway, which was about how long it took him to hit REM.

Until that summer, the childhood event in the Snake River cabin gun closet had been sealed in a time capsule somewhere deep in his neurology, shut in and cauterized to keep it from infecting the rest of the organism. It had been explained to him by the same navy psychologist who taught him the term "lacunar amnesia."

"The mind knows how to wall off a traumatic event," he'd said, "encapsulating it to protect the rest of the system. Much like the body cordons off an abscess."

Up till that summer Finn had been completely unaware of the entire event, and yet—again, like an abscess—its toxicity had been leaking out for years, bleeding into his everyday existence. Unexplained symptoms. Reactions that made no sense. He just soldiered on.

It was Carol who pointed that out.

"You adapted. Toughed it out. Never gave it a thought."

Until that summer, and Mukalla.

Finn had seen a good deal of death in the course of his military career. Like all special operators—like all people thrust into the face of war, for that matter—he had learned to inure himself to its horrors. But what he saw when he walked into that Yemeni farmhouse opened a crack in the time capsule. When that crack finally split wide open a month later, those childhood memories came pouring out.

And now he was cursed.

However hard he tried, he still couldn't fully remember what happened that night in Mukalla.

Yet try as he might, he couldn't forget what happened that day in the Snake River cabin gun closet.

Before putting the phone away he risked switching it on once more and saw there was now a new message waiting for him.

Not from Carol.

From stanl3099@gmail.com.

> Spoke with Diane about the boys' jungle gym, should
> be delivered no later than Friday. Claudia confirmed.

He parsed through the message as he powered down the phone and zipped it back into its Faraday pouch, which he secured in his backpack. He stood and swung the backpack over his shoulder.

Time to move.

He didn't know anyone named Diane.

He didn't know anyone named Claudia.

But his timetable had just accelerated.

20

Thirty miles away, another American ambled in through airport customs.

Soft sandy blond hair, tied in a ponytail. Tinted wire-rimmed glasses.

As the man stood smiling at the customs podium, the official holding his passport looked up at him. "Jack Lansdale?"

"That's me."

"May we speak with you for a moment?" A polite *This way, please* gesture, directing him to one side.

"Sure. I mean, what's this about?"

"It'll just take a moment."

They led him to a small room. Asked him about his business in Iceland.

"I'm a security consultant," the American explained. "I run what's called a 'red team operation.' It's highly specialized work."

A red team op, he told the official, was basically a mock invasion of a company's headquarters, just like a real attack, whether from criminals or from the competition, except in this case without malicious intent. Quite the opposite, in fact. A red team op was designed to probe the system for any security weaknesses so the leaks could be plugged.

"Every system has its flaws. Folks like me, they bring us in to test the system's limits. Find its weaknesses. 'Fore someone else does, someone with bad intentions. See?"

The immigration official regarded him with a whiff of skepticism he couldn't quite disguise. The man did not look like a security expert. He looked like an accountant and a hippie got together and had a love child.

Reykjavík was home to hundreds of high-tech security firms. It was a big-bucks business. They couldn't do better than this guy?

"And they bring you all the way from America to do this? To break into their offices?"

Lansdale shrugged and grinned. "It's pretty specialized work."

The official blanched, then immediately tried to hide it. There was something about the man's grin that made him feel queasy. "May I ask, which firm brought you here?"

Lansdale shrugged apologetically. "See, that's the thing. I'm not supposed to say. Part of the contract." When the official looked puzzled, he added, "Part of the deal is, they can't know when I'm coming. 'Cause that would kinda wreck the surprise." Suddenly a look of concern came over his face. "Is that a problem?"

"No, no, you're fine." The man closed up his passport and handed it back.

"Are you guys looking for someone?"

"Just a routine check."

Exiting the customs area, Lansdale strolled directly through the airport and out to the bus stop by the curb. He had no luggage, only a carry-on.

He never had luggage.

As he went through customs he'd done some pocket-switching with his glasses case and a second, identical glasses case, squirreling case number two into a concealed pocket sewn into the inside of his shirtsleeve.

Simple sleight of hand.

Now, standing outside at the curb as he waited in line to board the bus, he went to surreptitiously switch the two back. Easing the second case out of its hiding spot, he couldn't help smiling again, thinking of the young official's naivete—

And fumbled the case.

He made a lightning-fast grab for it, but the thing tumbled out of his grasp.

He saw what happened next in slow motion, like the choreography of a nightmare, the little case somersaulting in a graceful little arc through the air and down to the asphalt, the front wheel of the arriving bus rolling over it, crushing it before he could reach down and snatch it back. The bus lurched to a stop and the door swung open directly in front of him with an imperious screech.

There were people behind him.

He was first in line.

He stared down at the street, in disbelief at his own carelessness.

Nothing he could do about it.

He gave the man behind him a sheepish grin and kept it glued to the front of his face as he boarded the bus and found a seat. Kept it glued to his face as the bus driver jolted into gear and pulled away from the curb.

Kept it glued to his face as they merged onto the highway.

He was really annoyed with himself.

Really, really annoyed.

The ride to the Airport Express stop at Ingólfur Square took fifty-two minutes.

He grinned all the way.

21

Finn walked the dark streets, heading east for the second hotel on the Magnús list as he tried to sort and catalog the hyperreal input of his senses.

The *thump, thump, thump* of studded tires. Murmured greetings between passing pedestrians. Buzzing flies. The faint smell of snow and pine, crisp and clear. Salt air. Smoked lamb. Wet straw, chicken manure, the astringent sweetness of burning khat—

He stopped walking.

Buzzing flies?

Chicken manure?

Memories and nightmares bleeding into his waking hours.

His senses were starting to short out.

Finn had dealt with torture, both in training and in the field. He understood how it worked, and how it didn't.

Causing excruciating pain—peeling away pieces of skin, snipping off digits, high-voltage shocks to the genitals—that played well in the movies, but in reality such techniques weren't used all that often, at least not by people who knew what they were doing, because they weren't all that effective.

Threatening family members was more likely to deliver results. Especially when the victim knew you meant it.

But the most effective torture scenarios by far, in Finn's experience, involved sleep deprivation. Take away a prisoner's sleep and you take away his capacity to make sound judgments. Sleep deprivation was to the military prisoner what propaganda was to a population: an erosion of the fabric of reality.

You can't vote intelligently if you no longer recognize fact and fiction.

You can't resist interrogation if you've lost touch with reality.

In BUD/S and SEAL workups Finn had been trained to survive extreme levels of sleep deprivation. But this had been going on now for four months.

And if he couldn't trust his own senses, what was there left to trust?

He looked around, taking stock of his surroundings. Drank some water from a bottle in his backpack. *Hydrate,* said a familiar voice in his head.

Sleep deprivation. Dehydrates the crap outta ya.

He started walking again.

And thought about Kennedy.

"How ya doin? Ya look like shit."

Finn did look like shit. He felt like shit.

"Hold still a sec. This is gonna hurt like you're getting laid by a pair of pissed-off porcupines."

Finn was more than happy to hold still. After what he'd just been through he was thankful to be in the hands of another SEAL and not a few hundred pissed-off Taliban locals. And while the guy disinfecting and stitching the worst of his wounds was not a corpsman, he looked like he knew what he was doing.

Helmand Province, southern Afghanistan, summer of 2009. The "surge" had just started and would do a whole lot more surging before it was done, taking a whole lot more American lives with it. Finn had just seen two men shot to pieces and would have lost a third, too, if he hadn't picked the guy up and run the last mile with him in a fireman's carry.

He'd been on loan to a tiny Army special forces element to help take out an HVT—high-value target—deep in Taliban-held territory, which meant crossing on foot, single-file, through miles of landscape as hostile as hostile gets.

Four days, no sleep.

They arrived at midnight, staked out positions flanking the main route exiting the village, waited for dawn. Except that when dawn came they were ambushed by a battalion's worth of arsenal coming at them from all directions at once. Finn and his five companions were forced into a full-bore retreat, running nearly two full miles between opposing walls of gunfire to meet a Marine element coming in to rescue them.

Of the six, four made it.

Half a SEAL platoon had hitched a ride with the Marines to come re-trieve Finn. It was a young SEAL officer who stitched him up. And hooked him up to an IV bag of saline. "Sleep deprivation," he said. "Dehydrates the crap outta ya."

"We lost two," Finn said after the officer put enough water into him that he could talk.

"Yeah, ya dumb shit," the officer said. "But you saved three. Your mama must have done something right."

And just like that, Kennedy was in his life.

Finn didn't understand how that worked. He didn't understand how Kennedy worked. Finn could "make friends" with anyone on the planet, any age, any background, for purposes of gathering intel. But he'd always been incapable of forging actual friendships.

Which Kennedy did without even trying.

In most ways they were opposites. Kennedy was a natural-born leader. Finn was no kind of leader. Too self-sufficient. Kennedy had an innate empathy that made it easy for him to connect with anyone and everyone. Finn didn't do empathy. He did insight. Keen observation.

Kennedy was the kind of person no one could dislike. Everybody's best friend. Finn was the guy nobody quite liked. It wasn't that he made enemies. Quite the opposite. He helped the other guys out, guys who didn't have his gift for stalking, his ease with the water. Whenever another Team member needed any kind of leg up, Finn was there. Everyone appreciated him. Just, nobody especially liked him.

You didn't get close to Finn. No one ever had. Carol, in her own way, but Carol was a special case.

There was no one like Kennedy.

And now he was gone.

Just like that.

Which was why Finn was there, in this land of fire and ice and darkness.

He had a question.

And he wasn't leaving without an answer.

22

Krista stood at the foot of Höfðatorg Tower 1 and looked up, craning her neck in an effort to see the very top. Thirty-six years she'd lived in the city, and she still stared at the skyscrapers like the rube she was.

After the iconic Lutheran church, the Tower was the tallest building in Reykjavík, black and forbidding, a soaring monstrosity that exemplified the eruption of Iceland's sudden financial clout. Crown jewel of Tryggvi Pétursson's harbor world of steel and glass. It reminded Krista of the monolith in Kubrick's *2001: A Space Odyssey*.

The fact that she couldn't see the top bothered her.

No one else knew it—not the chief of police, no one else in the department, not even Einar—but she planned to put in for a transfer the following Monday, the day after New Year's.

Krista didn't recognize this city anymore. She'd been on the force for thirty-one years, and she wanted out.

There was an opening coming, she'd heard, for a new chief of police in Eskifjörður, the tiny town by the eastern fjords where she grew up. She thought she would enjoy working there, in a place where she could see the tops of buildings and understand the people.

Eskifjörður's police force totaled five officers.

She entered the monolith's front lobby, flashed her badge at reception, and was taken up the secure elevator to the eighteenth floor, where she was promptly ushered into his inner office.

The first thing she noticed was the man's face, puffy and red-eyed. Despite his formal bearing, he had obviously been weeping.

He did not wait for introductions. "I must apologize," he said with a nod, directing her to sit. "I should have contacted you earlier. Would have done so, in fact, had I known." He spoke in the manner of a man accustomed to not wasting a second of his own or anyone else's precious time.

Krista obediently took a seat, yet Tryggvi remained standing.

"Yes?" said Krista, unsure what else to say.

"I learned about—" He paused and pressed his lips together, then began again. "I learned about what happened only late yesterday. Just before I spoke with your officer. I was in Europe for a few days, departed from Keflavík on the evening of the twenty-fourth. My private jet," he added in reply to her brief look of puzzlement, as the last commercial flight out on Christmas Eve would have left by early afternoon. "I was in meetings continuously. When I touched down again yesterday, they told me."

He paused again. Appeared unable to continue.

"I'm so sorry," she said.

"We knew her only a brief time, but already we had all grown fond of her. Lovely girl. This is . . ."

He paused once more, evidently searching for the right word to convey the depth of grief but unable to find it. Finally he abandoned the sentence altogether.

"Tell me, please," he said instead, "what is the status of this case. Who is responsible. What leads you have. The situation."

Krista was not especially surprised at how, even in the grip of such emotional turmoil, he could slip into command-and-control mode. She had never put much stock in the "stages of grief" concept. While Iceland had comparatively little violent crime, it had plenty of death and loss, and she dealt with grief routinely. In her experience grief didn't fit a neat pattern. Grieving was a mess, mostly an unpredictable combination of denial, helpless fury, and collapse, sometimes in sequence but just as often all at once.

Which was what she saw happening here.

She spoke carefully.

"While we cannot be sure at this point, the death appears to have been purely accidental. Though we cannot rule out suicide." She saw him wince at the word. "There is at this time no indication of foul play, but we are pursuing a number of leads. Our information is still, unfortunately, quite incomplete."

Coward, she told herself. Get on with it.

She might be able to withhold the most damning information from the young woman's sister, but she knew she couldn't hide it from one of the most powerful men in Iceland.

"The body, I'm afraid, has gone missing. Before we were able to complete a forensic analysis, it seems it was sent to the crematory in error."

Tryggvi Pétursson's face went stony. He hid his fury well, but Krista saw it, all right. He was livid.

Krista felt enormous respect for the man, for the way he stood for Iceland. Yes, he was obscenely rich—but even within the onslaught of rampant commercialism, Tryggvi Pétursson had always led the charge for programs and institutions that preserved their native culture and traditional values.

She felt like she was letting down the soul of Iceland.

Krista was the one to break the silence.

"May I ask, how long was she working for you?"

For a moment Tryggvi said nothing, then gave a slow exhale. Now he pulled out his own chair, a gesture that seemed to convey a fatigue of infinite depth, and finally took a seat as well.

"She did not work 'for' me, strictly speaking. I was more sponsor, you would say, than employer. I have a placement service for select clients in various parts of the world, helping them find reliable au pairs of high character. My staff does the screening and flies in qualified candidates.

"Kateryna was here, in residence at my lake house on Thingvallavatn, for an eight-week orientation and training period, after which she would have been placed in another household overseas. It's not really a business, per se," he added. "Just something I do now and then for friends."

Now that he was talking it seemed difficult for him to stop. Krista had seen this before, too. The reluctance to face the silence that followed words. Because silence allowed the grief to seep back in.

With a little prodding, she hoped he would keep talking.

"How did she come to be out on the streets of the city, do you think, alone, in the middle of the night?"

"I frankly have no idea. My staff—chauffeur, housekeeper, cook—were all at their own homes for Christmas. I have a live-in groundskeeper who spent the day quietly with his wife in their own adjacent quarters."

"So she was on her own?"

He gave a vague wave of one hand, as if to say, *There are some things in this world even I do not control.*

"She had free rein of the kitchen. Everything she needed was there. My groundskeeper invited her to go to mass with himself and his wife, in the afternoon, and then join them for Christmas dinner. She declined, said she would be fine on her own. No one even realized she was missing until yesterday."

"And they didn't think to call the police at that point?"

"They should have, of course. But my flight was due in soon, and they . . ." He paused again. Let the next wave of grief crash over the rocks and subside. "They waited to tell me first."

"You mentioned her pending placement. May I ask who the client was?"

"You may ask, of course, but I am afraid this I cannot answer. There is diplomatic confidentiality involved. However, my staff can send you a copy of her background review, medical history, whatever else we have in her personnel file. And of course you'll want to speak with my groundskeeper."

"Thank you," Krista murmured, grateful that he understood the process. "That's most helpful." She hesitated before posing her next question.

"Was there any way she could have been using drugs?"

Tryggvi's reply was swift and sure.

"Impossible."

"How so—" she began, but he cut her off.

"We screen our young women quite thoroughly before arrival, and they are in our care from the moment they arrive at Keflavík. Before that, in fact—from the moment they board my plane in the country of their origin."

"Yes," said Krista. "But—"

"Then," he continued over her, "I have my own expert medical staff assess their health, both when they arrive and before they depart for their ultimate destination. There was no way that she or any of our au pairs would have access to any illicit drugs, street or otherwise."

And with that Tryggvi stood, signaling that the interview had come to an end.

She reached out to shake goodbye.

He held her hand in his grip, looking her in the eyes for a moment before releasing her.

As she turned to leave he spoke up once more.

"Inspector."

She turned back, struck by the oddly formal style of address.

"I must know what happened," he said. "I *will* know who is responsible."

23

"Jack Lansdale" arrived at the Express terminal by
the harbor and disembarked, still seething with frustration, still grin-
ning.

His name was not Jack Lansdale, of course.

It was Boone.

And while Boone truly was a security consultant who provided red
team operations (for ginormous fees, and worth every damn cent), that
wasn't strictly speaking why he was there in Iceland.

Although, probing a system for its security weaknesses? Yeah, you
could say that was exactly what he was doing there.

'Cause, hey: What was Chief Finn, the vexatious little pissant, but a
security leak?

A leak that most definitely needed to be plugged.

Boone walked west seven or eight blocks until he found himself in
what seemed like a sedate, affluent neighborhood on the west side of
town. The kind of place where people would have lived quietly for years.

He looked around. Began threading his way through the neighborhood in a random zigzag pattern till he found a small grocery store that
looked perfect.

Among the handful of patrons inside the little store he spotted an elderly woman loading a small shopping cart. The cart was of good construction, and she looked reasonably well off. The kind of old lady who
could afford to hire help but insisted on doing things for herself.

Boone admired this.

He ambled closer to her, focusing his attention on the shelves so that it was clear he wasn't watching where he was going.

Bumped into her, knocked her cart right over.

"Oh no!" he exclaimed, horrified. *"Fyrirgefðu, fyrirgefðu!"* he exclaimed. *Sorry, sorry!* He smacked himself in the forehead, then dropped to his knees and began hastily collecting the scattered items. *"Fyrirge-fðu!"* he said again. *"Ég er klaufi!"* *I am a klutz!*

He righted her prone cart and looked up at her, mortified.

She was smiling at him. "Please," she said, in English. "Don't be worry. It's be fine. Thanks you."

"Ég er klaufi!" he said again.

She smiled. "Your Icelandic is very good."

He shrugged, embarrassed. "I don't have much. Just a few phrases."

"American?" she said.

He blushed. "Does it show?"

The woman paid for her groceries—Boone insisted she go first. After thanking him and assuring him once again that she was fine, she set off walking, her sturdy little cart loaded with bags.

Once Boone had made his own modest purchases, he ambled off in a different direction. After a block or two, he hooked a left, then another left.

And what do you know: there was the same elderly woman he'd seen just minutes earlier!

He grinned at her. *"We meet again,"* he said in clumsy Icelandic, and he tipped an imaginary hat.

She smiled back and gave a graceful nod, then began mounting the steps to her little residence, pulling her cart up after her.

His grin turned to alarm. "Oh, please, that's heavy!" he said, reverting to his native English. "You must let me help you with that."

"It's not the bother," she said.

"I insist." He took hold of the little cart, paused while she mounted the steps to her door, then lifted the load of groceries up, step by step by step.

Held the door open for her, with a little bow.

She smiled, stepped inside, then turned to take the cart's handle. "Thank you," she said. "Well, that is very kind."

"Pish-posh," he said, which made her giggle.

He smiled at her, making no motion to leave.

She seemed to hesitate. "Can I . . . can I offering you something hot?"

"Oh, no," he said. "No, no, no." Then tilted his head and frowned slightly, perhaps feeling an obligation to give the offer fresh consideration.

Not wanting to be rude and reject such a neighborly gesture.

"Well, that is very kind," he said finally.

He followed her inside and softly closed the door.

24

The Grand Hótel Reykjavík loomed over the city's east side like a Vegas casino.

The hotel Ólafur had mentioned was also the second of two properties on the Magnús list. Two independent vectors touching the same point didn't mean certainty, but it did imply strong likelihood.

Which suggested he adopt a more direct approach this time. No quizzing waiters or skulking around monitor stations today.

Finn walked around a corner of the building, came in a side entrance. Hunted down a housekeeper on her rounds and executed another clumsy collision. Then located the nearest bank of elevators. The Grand had sixteen floors. He stepped into the first available car and hit the button for 14.

They would be on an upper floor. Force of habit. In the event of hostile incursion, an invading force would typically work its way up from the ground floor, so upper floors offered a tactical advantage. Besides, you'd want an unobstructed line of sight on your surveillance target. An upper floor maximized your field of view while minimizing your own visibility.

Also, the executive suites were up there.

But not the topmost floor, not in a property like this, where putting a small helo down on the roof was also a possibility. No, his guys would automatically select a floor *near* the top, but not *at* the top. Probably floor 15.

Which Finn would approach on foot.

He exited the elevator at 14 and walked to the end of the corridor, stepped out into the stairwell, and walked silently up one flight.

Opened the fire door and poked his head out.

Stepped out and looked around.

Made a single circuit around the entire floor to get the map in his head.

His guys would look for a room more or less equidistant from stairwells and elevators; too far, and you'd be at a disadvantage in the event of immediate exfil. But also at a remove from utility rooms, linen closets, and so on, locations that could expose you to higher risk of ambush.

Force of habit.

All of which narrowed his hunt down to four suites.

Three had privacy signs hung on their doorknobs. Of those, two had trays of used room-service dishes sitting on the floor outside the door. One tray was a mess of half-finished food and spilled condiments. The other held a pile of dishes, neatly stacked from largest to smallest.

That would be them.

Into the lion's den.

He pressed his keycard scanner to the door lock, covering the action with his body. Heard the *whirr* and soft *click*.

One SEAL, he could handle, especially with the element of surprise. Maybe even two. Three could be sketchy, even for Finn.

These were, after all, SEALs.

But he didn't think he'd find three SEALs on the other side of that door.

Chances were, this time of day, there'd be just one of them there on a daytime sleep rotation, with the other two out on location.

He entered silently.

Stood inside the door for five seconds.

Heard nothing.

Proceeding room by room, he cleared the suite.

The closets and bathrooms confirmed that there were currently three occupants in the suite. A cursory search turned up nothing that would suggest they were anything but normal tourists.

No surprise there. No surprise at all. They wouldn't be that obvious about it.

This wasn't Pakistan or Nigeria. This was a friendly, extremely peaceful nation, about as unlikely a site for a covert American op as one could imagine. Insane, actually. They had to be there under some seriously deep cover.

He continued his search.

No small arms: again, hardly a surprise. If they'd been foolhardy enough to smuggle anything in, it would be on their person. Likewise any fancy electronics.

There was a hotel safe, but Finn didn't bother breaking into it. No SEAL would use a "secure" containment that was readily accessible to hotel staff. Even trusted, name-brand properties could be susceptible to graft and corruption. Finn knew of 5-star hotels that had placed certain guests in specific rooms that were wired for surveillance. Even in the US.

No, "hotel safe" was an oxymoron.

Nor would they use fancy concealment spots, like stashing things behind radiator grills and so on. Made for great television, but no realistic operator wanted to be tied down in a fast-moving situation with having to unscrew the front plates of power sockets, back panels of TV sets, or grills off heating ducts.

Although . . .

He went through the closets a second time, examining the heels on each boot. A guy he'd known in Team 6 used to keep his stash in a slider in the heel of a combat boot.

The last boot he checked, the heel slid open.

Little white bag tucked inside. A little sniffy sniff.

Clients of Ólafur's.

Nothing to do now but wait for one of his teammates to show up.

Former teammates.

He lay back on the little living room couch, hands folded behind his head, stared at the ceiling, and wondered if Paulie was dead.

25

There were a lot of things he still didn't know about that night in Mukalla. And a few things he did.

For example, he knew he and Paulie had been set up from the start.

When Finn's group blew the door and rushed in, Finn himself at the head of the stack, they found nothing but an empty compound. They stood there, hoods and zip ties at the ready, sounds of the breaching charge and flash bangs still echoing through their earplugs, and had nothing to look at but each other.

Meanwhile, five klicks to the east, an entire farm community was being massacred.

By a crew of his own guys.

They'd planted false intel to set up the bogus raid in order to get Finn, Paulie, and Kennedy out of the way so they could go execute their mission of death.

Finn knew the crew who'd done it.

He even knew why.

Some unfortunate Yemeni farmer had witnessed the SEALs killing an American journalist who'd stumbled onto their little criminal enterprise. Maybe a whole group of farmers had seen it. Or maybe just one. Either way, the entire extended family paid for it with their lives. Every last one, from toddlers to great-grandparents. Tortured, defiled, slaughtered.

Trophies were taken.

Some of this, Finn had known, or guessed, at the time. Some he'd learned in the intervening months, with the help of Stan L. and a few other deep contacts. None of it was public knowledge. In fact the number of other humans alive who knew about any of it could probably be counted in the single digits.

Command kept the whole thing bottled up, quietly blamed the deaths on a fictional al Qaeda terrorist cell. The press never knew about it. The locals weren't about to say anything. All of Finn's local intel network went dark on him.

And when the story started to show cracks, Finn, Paulie, and Kennedy were already set up to take the heat.

Kennedy was their OIC—officer in charge—and Finn was platoon chief, the highest-ranking enlisted, which meant he was Kennedy's right-hand man. In fact, when it came to operational planning, Kennedy often deferred to him.

And then there was Paulie, their AOIC—assistant officer in charge. The AOIC typically played a relatively minor support role, but Kennedy and Paulie had known each other forever, grew up together in South Boston.

Paulie's name wasn't actually Paul at all, it was Beck. But Beck had two loves in life, aside from being a SEAL: German beer and busty blondes. "Like the St. Pauli Girl," he'd explained one day in BUD/S, whereupon Kennedy pointed out that St. Pauli Girl beer was in fact brewed at the Beck's brewery in Bremen—and bingo. A name was born.

Kennedy and Paulie were inseparable; Paulie was the Affleck to Kennedy's Damon.

Also the class comedian.

Legend had it that during BUD/S, an especially sadistic instructor had kept Paulie out in the freezing surf for hours one morning, doing eight-count bodybuilders while the guy screamed at him and kicked sand in his face. When the instructor finally let him up and onto his feet, Paulie looked up at him and said, "Sir?"

"What is it, you worthless pile of pig shit?"

Paulie reached both hands out toward the man and said, "Sir, you . . . complete me."

Finn had no idea if it was true or not, but either way, nobody could repeat the story without both teller and audience laughing so hard they cried, imagining Paulie's earnest Jerry Maguire hand gestures and the instructor's apoplectic expression.

And that was Paulie: he could keep the other guys in the platoon laughing even under the most wearing circumstances—which was as useful in the field of war as any combat or reconnaissance skills. Paulie was a master at it.

And a hell of a solid second O.

They were all solid, all three of them: Kennedy, Paulie, and Finn. Best leadership troika in the Teams.

Which made the whole scenario even more of a gut punch.

That night, the platoon was divvied up into three squads. Paulie was with Finn, leading first squad, breaching and clearing the compound, Kennedy ran second squad, covering their six. Third squad was under Dixon's command.

It was a classic tactical move.

Finn should have seen it ten klicks off.

Isolate the leadership with the bulk of the platoon, tied up on a wild-goose chase, while Dixon led his gang of renegades off to the farm to do their dirty work. And blame it all on some nonexistent terrorist cell they'd cooked up as their boogeyman.

Except that Finn had somehow shown up at the farm compound later that night.

Which must have thrown a hell of a wrench in their plans.

They'd had to get messy to cover their tracks.

They threw suspicion on Finn as the massacre mastermind, got him shipped home to take the fall.

Then killed Kennedy.

And probably killed Paulie, too, or else he was on the run like Finn himself, holed up in some other far-flung location on the planet.

All that, Finn knew.

But how exactly had Finn known where to go that night? How did he know what they'd done?

How did he end up at that farm family compound, sitting in the midst of the slaughter?

26

Boone sat erect at the tiny kitchen table, still as a cat, looking at the small collection he'd assembled on the polished wooden surface.

Twenty rows of ten, one row of three.

Two hundred and three little orange pills.

Exactly as it should be.

Adderall was illegal in Iceland. This was not a problem. Boone was scrupulous in his research and had foreknown this, had known to smuggle in a full supply, which he had done, sealed tight in a secure pouch and inserted, slick as spit, right up the old wazoo. Cavity searches were not part of commercial airport protocol. At least not so far.

The orange pills situation was hunky-dory.

But, as Jesus told Satan in the desert, man did not live by bread alone. And as Boone could have told Satan, if he'd been hunkered down out there in that Palestinian desert with those two batshit-crazy dudes, Boone did not do his best work on Attaboys alone.

And right about now he'd do fine with a little hit of that sweet kettle corn.

Gimme a break
Gimme a break
Break me off a piece of that
Kit Kat bar

But his supply of Special K was lying in a gutter outside Keflavík airport. Crushed into powder inside a shattered glasses case. Which annoyed him greatly.

Really, really, really annoyed him.

Bread alone was not good.

Bread required butter.

Bread and butter.

Bread and butter.

Bread and butter.

Butter-butter-butter-butter sah-*wiiinnnng* butter-butter—

Boone's face twitched.

He heaved a big old country sigh.

"Well, shit," he said to the empty room.

This was a problem.

Boone needed to fix this.

27

Krista paused in the corridor, her hand on the door to the office she and her partner shared. Trying to come up with a way of saying it without exploding.

It had been a long morning and a longer afternoon. Meeting with Tryggvi had told her nothing useful. Her investigation into the girl's death had ground to a halt. There were firings at both the pathology lab and mortuary, but these had not mollified her boss, the chief of police. The media were not going especially easy on her, either.

And now this.

She took a slow inhale/exhale. Then pushed open the door and stepped inside.

And there was Einar, at his desk, eating a fucking Danish.

She erupted.

"So when exactly were you planning to tell *me* about this?"

He looked up, face frozen mid-chew, then worked his jaw twice and swallowed his bite. "What."

She stood at his desk, glowering down at him. "So I'm on my way back from a chat with the chief and run into Árni, who's on his way out."

"Árni," Einar repeated. "Right, I—"

"Who happened to mention a detail from Sunday morning that caught me, let's say, by surprise."

Árni Jónsson, one of the divers.

"When they were cutting her out of the ice, Árni tells me, he noticed the girl had a *lower abdominal scar*. A lower abdominal scar *that looked recent.*"

Einar quietly put his Danish down.

"So naturally I ask Árni why the *fuck* he didn't report this—and you know what he said? He said, 'I did.'"

Einar stared at his Danish. Finally he looked up.

"I know, I know. I was just—"

"*He also said,*" she talked over him, shutting him down. "He *also* said he'd noted something had been scrawled on her belly, in red. Red ink, blood, he didn't know what—I'm sorry, is any of this sounding familiar?"

They glared at each other. She could hear his breathing, thick and angry.

"I was working on it," he said.

"*Working on it.* Oh, well in that case." She took a step back and looked at him. Grimaced. "And you look like hell."

He did, too. Haggard. Face all pasty and splotchy. Detective Danish, they called him behind his back. The man could afford to lose twenty kilos. Maybe thirty.

Without another word, Einar got to his feet and walked out of the office.

Krista sat at her desk and fumed for a few minutes. Then finally forced herself to focus instead on what the diver had just told her.

A scar. Lower abdomen, right side. Recent.

And a red scrawl, in some foreign language he didn't recognize. He'd caught only a glimpse before they levered her out and the attending officers wrapped the body into its tarp. There was an O in the word, Árni thought, maybe an "OM"?

She tapped the memo app and spoke quietly into her phone.

"Part of a word—OM. Something religious? Red ink, maybe blood. The lipstick?"

True to his word, Tryggvi had sent over the girl's medical file, which Krista had read as soon as it pinged her IN box. Now she spent ten minutes poring through it again.

There were the usual childhood illnesses, nothing significant. Kateryna's drug history was there and, just as Oksana had said, it wasn't a pretty picture. Evidently, though, she had indeed been clean and sober for more than three years.

"Good for you, Kateryna," she murmured.

There was no record of any surgery or injury that could possibly account for an abdominal scar.

She woke up her laptop and began reading up on the most common types of abdominal surgery, then tapped her phone's screen and read her results into a short memo:

"Appendectomy. C-section. Gall bladder. Incisional hernia. Inguinal hernia . . ."

If Árni weren't so goddam vague on the details of the thing, she could have narrowed it down. "If I'd known nobody else was going to get the chance to examine her," he'd said when she brought this up, "I'd have looked more carefully."

Krista had tried her best to ignore the caustic tone, but it stung.

They should have taken more pictures.

She spent the next half hour on the phone. Surgeons, OB/GYNs, walk-in clinics. While on hold and in the gaps between calls she dictated further notes on her findings—or rather, her lack of findings.

She couldn't locate a single surgeon or facility who had any knowledge of the girl.

She thumbed the intercom on her desk. "Jón?"

A moment later he appeared at the door.

"Halló?"

She held up her canvassing report. "The noisemakers on Christmas Eve. There was a med student who thought he saw a car."

"Yes. But no description or license plate."

"Find him. I'd like to talk with him."

She clicked off and considered the pages scattered over her desk. Still couldn't read the plot.

Lake Thingvallavatn was nearly an hour's drive from the center of Reykjavík. It was fairly isolated out there; at Christmastime that isolation would have been magnified. Even if one had wanted to hitch a ride in weather like that, the chances of being picked up would be slim to none.

Tryggvi was out of the country at the time, his staff all at their own homes, excepting the groundskeeper, and he, according to Tryggvi, was at the lake house the entire weekend with his wife. She would want to talk with the groundskeeper to confirm, but expected no surprises there.

Kateryna herself didn't have a car.

So how did she end up in town?

After returning from their interview earlier that day, Krista had called every cab company and limo service that would have been available to make the drive out to Tryggvi's lake house and back.

Nothing.

There were no formal ride-share companies operating in Iceland. There was a local Facebook group called Shuttlers with over 20,000 members, and she'd spoken with a representative of the group. It took a little wrangling, but she secured their cooperation in searching their trip data for that address on the twenty-fourth.

Goose egg.

She looked at her phone. Pulled up the private cellphone number Tryggvi had given her, in the event she had further questions or there were any new developments on the case.

She pressed CALL.

One ring. Two.

"Tryggvi Pétursson."

She felt her spine straighten at the sound of his voice, and it occurred to her that he probably had that effect on most people. Hard to believe she'd witnessed any vulnerable underbelly there. But then, everyone had one.

"You mentioned putting us in touch with your groundskeeper?"

"Of course," he said. "I'll have him arrange to come in and speak with you tomorrow."

She was silent.

"Anything else?" he said.

"One of the divers from that morning mentioned a small scar on Kateryna's abdomen, said it appeared to be recent. Would you know any-thing about that?"

"A scar," he said. "No. I do not have the slightest idea. Is your diver quite sure of this? She was free to come and go," he added without wait-ing for a reply to his question, "so in theory I suppose anything is pos-sible. But if anything traumatic enough to cause a scar had occurred, I would think someone here would have known."

"I'll recheck my source," she said. "Thank you for your—"

But he was already gone.

She put her phone down and sat back in her chair, his parting words from their meeting that morning replaying in her head.

Inspector. I will know who is responsible.

Responsible for the girl's death. Surely that was what he meant.

But she had the sense he was also talking about whoever bore respon-sibility for losing the body.

Stop it, Krista. She sighed and turned her thoughts back to the matter at hand.

She needed to talk with Árni again. Maybe he *had* got it wrong. Shal-low pond, full of debris. He'd been underwater when he caught that glimpse.

Maybe the scar was a good deal older than Árni had guessed. From childhood, perhaps, and for whatever reason not in her records. A play-ground mishap. Krista had a few of those herself. Or maybe it was even fresher than he'd thought, and it wasn't surgery at all. Perhaps she'd scraped herself that night getting herself under the ice.

Or maybe something else happened that night. Something that had to do with whatever—or whomever—she was running from.

She tapped her phone again and spoke to the screen:

"Knife wound?"

28

The light, what little of it there was, was already fading. Finn got up and switched on a few lamps, then lay back down on the couch, hands once more folded behind his head.

He had a lot of questions about that night. Questions he'd been asking for months. The biggest of which might also be the hardest to get answered:

Who was at the top of this shit show, calling the shots?

Think chain of command. There had to be someone above Kennedy, someone up the line who had his fingers in it. Someone in a position to pull some mighty long strings.

But not *too* far up the line.

The decision to whitewash the whole thing, to bury it all and Finn along with it, that could have come from some shadowy figure back in the States. Someone thousands of miles removed from the reality of it, someone for whom covering it all up with a nod and an unspoken understanding was like correcting an administrative rounding error. Someone who would sleep just fine at night, knowing he or she had taken responsible steps to keep the US military's reputation squeaky clean in these increasingly unclean times.

But masterminding their whole corrupt enterprise—the graft, the dope-running, the intimidation and assassinations, the murder of a journalist? And then giving the order to eliminate one of their own? An *officer*? That had to come from someone closer to the whole thing.

Someone with authority over their platoon.

Which narrowed it down to three people.

The platoon's CO, directly above Kennedy, was Tommy Keyes, their task force commander on base in Yemen. Then came Commander Dugan, the O-5 above Keyes. And finally Admiral Meyerhoff, the O-6 in charge of the whole operation, who was stationed in Bahrain.

For the past three months not a day had gone by without reexamining his reasoning. It had to be one of those three. Couldn't be anyone else.

Keyes.

Dugan.

Meyerhoff.

Three officers. Two solid, one rotten. Which one?

Who gave the order to kill Lieutenant Kennedy?

One of his disposable phones buzzed. Phone #4, so far unused. He pulled it out and looked at the screen.

> Hnífsár?

The detective was writing a new memo.

The instant she'd opened the Unknown Bureaucrat photo he sent her, it had planted a piece of spyware on her phone that mirrored her keystrokes. Now he could scroll back and forth through her texts and notes and follow the thread of her investigation. At least whatever portion she conducted through text messages or recorded as typed memos.

Except that it was all in Icelandic.

So Finn had to select each entry, then copy and paste it into Google Translate to learn what she was thinking.

Which he did now.

Hnífsár? . . .

> Knife wound?

He scrolled back to look through her entries from the past hour, copying and pasting each one into the translator as he went.

> Appendectomy. C-section. Gall bladder. Incisional hernia. Inguinal hernia . . .

Some notes on what must be phone interviews with medical facilities.

It seemed she was making inquiries relating to the girl in the duck pond, looking at possible explanations for an abdominal scar.

And then, an entry that struck him as odd, once he got the translation:

> Part of a word—OM. Something religious? Red ink,
> maybe blood . . . the lipstick?

Part of a word. Meaning there were, or might be, more letters than those two, for some reason obscured. WOMAN? WOMB? Was that a scar from a Cesarean?

Or was it even English?

For that matter, what if it wasn't "part of a word" but the word itself, just the two letters and no more? OM. Some sort of mantra she'd had tattooed, or someone else had carved into her? Obviously the detective was thinking along similar lines: *Something religious?*

But that wasn't the odd part.

> Red ink, maybe blood . . . the lipstick?

That was the odd part.

They had the body, which meant they should know the answers to those questions. But they didn't know the answers. Which meant they didn't have the body.

They lost the body?

He wished he could scroll farther back in the detective's notes, all the way to Sunday morning, when he'd first seen her, standing at the pond over the body, surrounded by her colleagues. But his spyware had only started capturing her keystrokes from the moment she opened the photo he'd sent her on Monday afternoon.

Still, he could see no other conclusion.

They lost the body?

No wonder they hadn't asked the sister to make a positive ID. She'd flown from Ukraine to Iceland to recover her little sister's body and bring it home for burial. And they didn't have it.

Which they weren't about to tell her. Or at least not yet.

And now it seemed Oksana wasn't the only person who thought there might have been foul play. The detective was thinking in that direction, too.

Knife wound?

Even Ragnar's ancient neighbor seemed to think there was something dark about the whole affair. He didn't understand a word of her Icelandic, but he remembered the sounds of it, syllable by syllable, and he got the gist.

Eins og Birna greyið, árið 2017.

Something about "Birna," whoever or whatever that was.

Something *greyið.*

His reverie was broken by a buzz from phone #1, the Magnús phone. A text message, just a single word, in English.

Call

He was about to comply when he heard footsteps approaching.

One of his three, finally returning to their suite.

He took a breath and readied himself.

Moment of truth.

The door's locked whirred and clicked.

The door swung open.

A man Finn had never seen before took two steps into the room and froze mid-stride, staring at him.

And said, "Who the fuck are you?"

29

Boone walked toward the harbor to an upscale vegan restaurant he'd been wanting to try. Boone had been to Reykjavík quite a few times. Boone had been everywhere quite a few times.

He selected the vegan bibimbap.

When it came, he sat with both hands in his lap and looked down at the dish. After a minute, he raised his head, and with a nod called the server back to his table.

"Sir?"

"What's your name, son?"

"Björn, sir."

"Björn. Good."

"Sir?" Boone had spoken so softly that the boy had to lean in to hear. "Do you see anything . . . *off* about this plate? Björn?"

"Off, sir?"

"Off. Like it doesn't belong." He lifted his left hand from his lap and pointed down to something toward the center of the plate.

Björn peered closer. "Ah. Maitake, sir. It's . . . it's a kind of mushroom."

"Yes."

"Sir?"

"What's your name, son?"

The server was clearly thrown. He had already given the man his name several times.

"It's Björn, sir."

"Björn. Good. Tell me, Björn, what you know about mushrooms."

"They're, ah, fungi, sir. A kind of plant."

"Really."

The boy nodded.

Boone's voice dialed back one degree softer still. "Do you know what fungi exhale? Björn? They exhale carbon dioxide. Cee oh two. And they inhale oxygen. You know what else does that?" His eyes twinkled. "You do, Björn."

He looked at the boy.

The server looked like a rabbit staring at a cobra.

"In fact," Boone continued quietly, "fungi are more closely related to animals than to plants. I'm surprised more people don't know this. Surprised and disappointed. So, you tell me: Can we really say this bibimbap is . . . vegan? Björn?"

"I'm so sorry, sir." The server reached for the plate, completely flustered. "Let me take this back and bring you something else."

Boone held the dish firm with both hands and continued speaking.

"Do you know what mushrooms eat?"

"What they . . . eat, sir?"

"Dead things. Dead trees. Dead plants. Dead flesh. They eat dead things."

Björn moved his lips but nothing came out.

In fact, Boone loved mushrooms.

He was just fucking with the kid.

Now he leaned forward and murmured, "Son—what was your name again?"

"Björn, sir." The boy's face was white as the underside of a gull.

"Björn. Good. Good name. Strong. Björn, you got any idear where a visitor might score him some K?"

A long silence.

"Sir?"

"Some K. Special K. Super C. Kit Kat."

Another silence.

"Are you—are you trying to get me in trouble, sir?"

Boone released his plate and sat back in his chair. His lips broke a faint smile, but his eyes did not. The twinkle was gone.

"No, son, I'm not trying to get you in trouble. Just a visitor to your fair city, in the market for a little stress relief. Looking to resupply a little stash I seem to have misplaced in transit."

He held the boy's gaze for a long beat. Then slowly withdrew a sleek silver pen, clicked out the point, and handed it to the boy.

30

Finn left the Grand Hótel Reykjavík by the delivery
dock, accessed through the main kitchen.

He'd given the man in the fifteenth-floor executive suite some fish
story about cleaning their rooms (the Privacy sign notwithstanding).
Incredibly, the guy bought it. Good for him. Not that it would have mattered to Finn. Either way, he would have left the place undetected.

Better this way for the guy, though.

That exhausted the Magnús list and left him with nothing but Ólafur's dubious Casablanca lead. Unless Magnús had something new for
him.

He waited until he was locked away into the seclusion of Ragnar's
townhouse to call the big cabdriver.

Who did indeed have something new for him.

Magnús had found one more driver, just back from a Christmas
break. On the twenty-second, two days before Finn's arrival, he drove
three men who fit Finn's parameters. Magnús relayed the driver's brief
description.

Finn thought one of them sounded a little like Peyton.

Could definitely be Peyton.

Where did he take them?

To the Fosshótel.

Which was no more than a few blocks from the Casablanca, the no-
star place Ólafur had mentioned and Finn had dismissed.

Was it possible that Ólafur's dubious Casablanca lead and this driver's more solid Fosshótel lead were one and the same? More than possible.

Fosshótel had been high on Finn's priority list among the twenty-five 4-stars. Tall, modern, as flashy as anything in Reykjavík. And positioned at the gateway of the city's financial district. Which could well be the heart of whatever action it was their target was involved in.

He would move on it the next morning at first light. Or first semi-darkness.

"This is good, Magnús. This is excellent."

He moved his finger to the END CALL button but stopped before pressing it. Put the phone back to his ear.

"Magnús?"

"Still here, Ghost Writer."

"Who, or what, was Birna?"

He heard a slow, heavy sigh on the other end, followed by a moment of silence.

Then Magnús told him what happened.

One night in January of 2017, a young woman named Birna Brjáns-dóttir spent the evening clubbing along Laugavegur with friends. The friends went home. Birna stayed. Left the last club at closing, five in the morning. Still dark out, of course, but the street was brightly lit. Strolled the avenue, eating a falafel pita, according to CCTV. Ambled by the famous Lebowski Bar ("twenty-four variations of white Russians!"), then a coffee-and-waffle shop.

And vanished.

Up to that point the Laugavegur nightlife was considered relatively safe, even for young women walking the streets at night. Iceland had barely any violent crime, and certainly not the kind that involved the snatching of random victims off the streets.

That all changed on January 13, 2017.

The entire city became involved in the search for Birna. Then the entire nation, nearly a thousand volunteers and a hundred vehicles. The biggest search operation in Iceland's history.

Eventually, of course, they found the body. And the fishing boat employee who killed her. A Greenlander, not a local. (Which came as a relief to many, though few would say so out loud.) Two thousand people attended her funeral, including the president and prime minister. Smaller services were held throughout the country.

"It changed Iceland," the cabdriver's voice growled. "Even more than when the economy went crash. Before Birna, there was a kind of innocence. A purity. And after Birna?"

He huffed.

"Maybe that's the crime you should write about, Ghost Writer."

"The Birna murder?"

"The death of innocence."

Finn extracted his personal phone and checked for messages.

Nothing from squidink28@gmail.com.

Nothing from stanl3099@gmail.com.

He thought about that morning's warning from stanl3099 as he powered down the phone and zipped it back into electronic oblivion.

> Spoke with Diane about the boys' jungle gym, should
> be delivered no later than Friday. Claudia confirmed.

"Stan L." was a Teams guy Finn knew from way back in the days of BUD/S and SQT. Now he worked in the catacombs of some private-sector defense colossus—but Stan L. was a believer in old loyalties. He had no problem moonlighting as Finn's pipeline to tidbits of intel no one on the planet should have had access to.

And he always communicated like this, like they were in some seventies paranoid thriller. Ad hoc code, made up on the fly. That was Stan L.'s genius: there was no system to it. No key. It was different every time.

Finn had understood the message the moment he read it.

The boys' jungle gym. Swings . . . slide . . . rope ladder . . . monkey bars.

Bars.

I.e., confinement.

I.e., arrest.

Diane. Claudia. Both fictional—except for the three letters they shared: d-i-a.

DIA. Defense Intelligence Agency.

Definitely not fictional.

US military intel had homed in on his coordinates and the DIA had mobilized. The jungle gym was on its way. Bars for Finn.

But *only* DIA. "Diane" began with those three letters, "Claudia" ended with them. Ergo, it started and ended with DIA. No other agency involved.

Not at this point.

Which meant they were still trying to keep the whole thing corked up tight.

If someone from CIA were involved, say, then Stan L.'s message would have included a *Marcia*. Or a *Felicia*. If there were any NSA spooks on it, then a *Hansa*, or *Esperansa*. And so on.

They wouldn't want to be public, either, so no cops would be involved, no liaising with other countries' intel agencies. No Interpol. Nothing fancy or complicated. Nothing that would risk leaks to the public.

Not yet, anyway.

Which was why the detective with the ice-blue eyes didn't know who he was. They wouldn't have notified even local authorities, not the police, not the coast guard. No one.

Just a team from DIA.

Diane, Claudia.

A team of two.

Whether they were in-country already or on their way, what they would look like, what their cover would be, Finn hadn't picked up any of that from the message. Stan L. probably didn't know. He just knew there were two of them, and they were on their way.

No later than Friday.

No later—but could be earlier.

For all Finn knew, they were there now.

He turned off all the lights and lay down on his bedroll on the floor.

Have you slept?

He thought about Birna, and about Kateryna.

About Kennedy.

About Ray, and the death of innocence.

Greyið.

He closed his eyes.

Hoping that sleep would come, and that dreams of blood and death would not.

31

Pharmacies in Iceland had limited hours, closed by suppertime. There was a big chain pharmacy by the Hilton off Laugavegur that stayed open till one in the morning. Not ideal. A smaller, out-of-the-way clinic would be preferable. And unlike pharmacies, some clinics in Reykjavík were located in odd places. Top floor of a bookstore. Jammed in the back of a library. Or set off in the back corner of a small mall.

Like this one.

Boone stood on the far side of the street, obscured by the pervading darkness, watching. Foot traffic was zero.

He crossed, slipped around to the back corner of the building. Switched on a penlight, held it in his teeth. Felt among the wires and located the one he wanted. He produced a single-edge razor blade and slid it gently into the wire's rubber jacket, wiggling it through the braided rubber-and-metal shield until it made contact with the wire's copper core.

He took a step back and surveyed his work.

Switched off the penlight.

Left in place, the blade would short out the security camera's signal, temporarily disrupting the video feed and leaving the monitor to record nothing but static. Later, when he removed the razor again, the signal would return to normal.

Like he was never there.

He walked back around to the front and entered the clinic.

It was empty, except for a staff of one, a young woman sitting on a tall stool behind the reception desk, reading on her phone.

Graveyard shift.

Boone heard the faint sounds of a second person out back, talking quietly on the phone. Attending physician. From the voice, a male. Young. Possibly talking with a girlfriend.

He told the girl at the counter he had just arrived in Iceland and needed to fill a prescription, but the pharmacy had said he needed to talk with a doctor first.

"Please, I'm in kinda a hurry." He smiled an apology. "Wife back at the hotel, got the allergies somethin' awful." Handed her a piece of paper.

She smiled as she took it, but her look turned doubtful as she glanced over the neatly hand-lettered specifications. "Just a moment," she said. "Let me talk with our nurse practitioner."

Ah. Not a physician, then.

While the young woman consulted with the male nurse through her desk phone intercom, Boone strolled around idly among the sparse shelves of braces, supports, heat/cold packs, and crutches. He noticed a display of canes and walking sticks and picked up one carved hardwood number that looked like it had character. Brazilian walnut, his best guess. One of the hardest woods on this fine planet. He found the handiwork impressive.

Send a text to this number, Björn the waiter had said. *He'll text you back and meet you.* Boone had followed his instructions, but the drug dealer had so far not returned his text.

Boone might have to take some initiative there.

Trouble himself to locate the man and stop by for a visit.

Meanwhile, he could do right now right now *right now* with a skosh of sweet, sweet balance. Diphenhydramine hydrochloride: the antihistamine that put the "PM" in Tylenol PM. Trade name Benadryl—or as they called it in Iceland, Benalyn.

Another option might have been Doxylamine, the sleep aid (Icelandic brand name: Unisom), but this was a weak choice. Boone had also seen guys in the Teams try to modulate the effects of Adderall with alcohol.

This was a complete shit idea in Boone's view: too difficult to calibrate. Besides, Boone didn't care for alcohol. Too fucking sloppy.

No, until he could replenish his supply of ketamine, Benadryl would have to do. Available here over the counter, but only in liquid form, which was another shit idea. For tabs or caps, a fella needed a prescription.

Hence this visit.

"Mister Lansdale?"

The male nurse was at the counter now, wanting a word with Boone.

The nurse apologized all over himself. Explained that he would need to have a doctor sign off on an order of this size. He spread his hands out in the universal sign of apologetic impotence. "I'm so sorry," he said again.

Boone smiled. "It's all good," he said.

More'n one way to skin a possum.

He withdrew a pair of cloth booties from his pocket, like the ones worn by crime scene technicians.

Never left home without them.

Bent down and donned the booties, left first, then right.

His boots properly protected, he straightened again and thanked the two for serving him, then said, "And now it's *me* who gotta apologize."

They both looked puzzled. Apologize for what?

He held up one index finger.

Whether this meant Shush or Wait was impossible to tell, but to be on the safe side the young woman and young man did both.

Boone cleared his throat. Closed his eyes.

Began to hum, hearing the music in his head.

Ravel's *Boléro*.

The softly tat-tat-tatting snare drum, barely audible. The cellos and violas, pizzicato pianissimo, three-quarter time, like a waltz. And then, the single flute, its sinuous, hypnotic solo.

Boone drew in a slow inhale, then pushed out a slow exhale, one with the flute's serpentine melody.

A slow inhale. And slow exha—

On the final third of the out-breath he erupted into motion.

Spinning counterclockwise in a full circular arc, he came around and bashed the young nurse on the left side of his head with the walnut walking stick, crushing his skull.

Blood and brain matter flew with tremendous velocity.

Spattering the young woman's face.

She froze—but only for a split second.

During that split second Boone absorbed the energy of the heavy hardwood object bouncing off the man's skull and followed it, backward and around, now executing a full spin in the opposite, clockwise direction, coming back to front and bashing the young woman on the right side of her skull, driving her into the collapsing nurse so that the two crashed together before sliding down into a mangled, ruined heap on the floor.

The flute continued.

The snare drum rat-tat-tatted its delicate triplets.

Boone closed his eyes, rolled his shoulders, cracked his neck.

Took a deep breath. Let out a sigh.

First time since boarding the damn bus that morning that he'd felt like himself.

He came behind the counter, making a wide berth around the inert pile of bone and tissue, and began rummaging through shelves for the product he wanted.

Correction. Not the product he *wanted*.

The one that would have to do for the moment.

A 50-milligram dose would slow most people down. Boone thought he would go with 75.

Ah. There.

He popped open the box and carefully tore open one packet. The hell with 75, make it 150. Two for the road. He would take a slow walk back.

Give the Ravel time to finish.

He slipped his supply into a coat pocket, then turned and looked at the inert figures on the floor.

Stared at them for a long beat.

Ah, what the hell.

He crouched down between the two bodies, balancing on the balls of his feet so that nothing else touched the ground. Withdrew a clean plastic sandwich baggie from another pocket and set it balancing on one knee while he pulled a tool from yet a third pocket, the same one that held his penlight. Finally, he donned a pair of latex gloves.

Just one task to finish before he left.

Wouldn't take but two minutes.

He bent down and pried open the young woman's mouth.

Wednesday

Colder.

32

"Fuck."

Krista stood over the two mangled bodies, the pools of blood garish in the ugly fluorescent lighting.

This had always been a point of pride for her about her homeland: the near-total absence of predatory danger. There were no wolves in Iceland, no coyotes, no snakes, no poisonous spiders. Not so much as a mosquito.

Yet there was always blunt human cruelty.

That, apparently, was universal.

So now they had a homicide to deal with. A double homicide, yet. And where was Einar? At home "taking a sick day." At home sulking, in other words, still nursing his hurt feelings after being yelled at.

She sighed. "Fucking fuck."

Jón, eager as ever, poked his head out of the office in back. "Krista?" he said. She followed him into the cramped room and stood by the video monitor as he put his hands back on the keyboard. "Watch," he said.

He pushed PLAY and the two dead staff people sprang to life on the little screen, viewed from above and behind so the customers' faces could be caught on camera. The young man disappeared from the screen, leaving the young woman alone, sitting on a tall stool behind the reception desk, reading on her phone. Jón put up one finger and said again, "Watch."

A few seconds later the image cut out and turned to snow.

The young officer hit STOP. "It's like this for another twenty minutes.

Then," he moved the cursor forward to a spot he'd marked and hit PLAY again. More snow—and then it vanished as quickly as it had come, returning them to the normal view of the clinic's interior.

Except there were now two corpses piled on the floor.

Jón turned to face Krista. "There was some kind of glitch with the video feed," he explained unnecessarily. "We checked the equipment and the lines. Everything's working fine, nothing broken, no sign of sabotage. It just . . . glitched."

She walked back out and stood over the two bodies again. Took out her phone, tapped open her memo app, and described what she saw.

Another detective, a lean, dour colleague named Daníel who was standing in for the absent Einar, came over to fill her in on the results of a hasty inventory. Nothing appeared missing. No cash—not that there was any cash on hand to speak of in a place that ran on government-sponsored health insurance. "Plenty of prescription pain meds and narcotic agents here," he said. "None of it disturbed. But look here."

She looked at the shelf where he pointed. A gap suggested several missing boxes.

"Who kills for Benylan?" said Danni.

The two detectives walked back to stand over the bodies.

"Guð minn góður," muttered Jón as he came up beside them. *Oh my God.* "How awful. Such a random, senseless . . ." His voice trailed away. Which Krista understood perfectly well. She knew the boy had never seen anything more violent than a bar fight.

Was it really "senseless," though? Wasn't there something almost deliberate in how the two bodies were positioned?

And how did a perfectly timed twenty-minute gap in the video feed suggest "random"?

"Guð minn góður," he murmured again. He pointed with one knuckle at the woman's mangled mouth. "The blow knocked out a few teeth."

She leaned in and used a pen to lift the upper lip as Jón stepped back, his face whiter than usual. Sure enough. Two teeth missing. But not contiguous.

Danni was already quietly dictating into his phone.

"Number six, number eleven," she reported to him quietly. "No other oral cavity damage."

"The brute," muttered Jón.

Krista shook her head. "Don't think the blow did this, Jón."

She turned to the second body and bent over the young man's ruined face to examine his dentition as well. "Male subject," she said over her shoulder to Danni, who turned to join her. "Same." She straightened, cleaning the pen with a wipe and returning it to her pocket.

Jón watched her, horror-stricken.

"I think the killer removed them postmortem," she said as Danni snapped a few pictures with his phone. "Not that hard. Just takes a methodical back and forth movement. Once you snap the periodontal ligament, it doesn't take much force to extract. And the PDL isn't difficult to break."

"Jesus," Jón said softly. "How do you know this shi— this stuff?"

"I read."

Jón stared at the carnage. "Jesus," he murmured again. "Talk about overkill."

Krista stood frowning down at the bodies.

Overkill.

A term coined in the 1950s in the wake of the first atomic blasts. In the reading of crime scenes, overkill was typically a sign of rage. Normally suggesting that the killer knew the victim. Though was there anything here that said "normal"?

"An affair?" offered Danni. "Vengeful spouse?"

Krista shook her head, still frowning. "Don't think so. Too methodical. Look at how they're positioned. Here, step back."

They took three steps back together, looking at the bodies as they did. From that perspective, the symmetry became more obvious. Danni pursed his lips. "What would drive that kind of rage, yet still have that kind of precision?"

Jón's phone buzzed, startling him. He tapped the screen and put it to his ear, then looked up at Krista.

"That's the station," he said. "You have a possible witness."

"Already? That was fast."

"Not for this. For the Little Mermaid."

33

This didn't sound like your everyday street violence.
Not remotely.

Sitting in the lobby of the Fosshótel, Finn finished Google-translating Krista's brief summary of their fresh crime scene and watched the clinic killing as the sequence played out in his head. The notes were broad strokes only; maybe she left the detailed observations to a colleague. But it was enough for Finn to do a basic reconstruction.

One staff member, the young man, head bashed in on the left, falls to his right toward the young woman, who is still reacting when the right side of her head is crushed, driving her in the opposite direction, all of it happening so quickly that she collides with the first falling body as she, too, crumples to the floor.

Two coordinated attacks, one from each flank. Two assailants? Or just one, working with practiced efficiency?

No, not your everyday killing.

Didn't look random, either. It looked like a page out of the organized crime handbook. That was not Finn's area, but not hard to surmise.

There was a reason mob hits favored the good old-fashioned lead pipe. Bullets were efficient, but they left forensic traces. Bashing some-one's skull in got the job done just as well and had the added advantage of giving the appearance of a random street kill. And there were at least a dozen organized crime groups with their tentacles in this city. Though it was mostly white-collar stuff. The cost of prosperity.

But why would a pro walk into an out-of-the-way street clinic and execute the staff?

Maybe one of the two victims had something going on, some line into a drug supply chain, something bigger and darker than they could handle. Seemed like a stretch to Finn. Though again, this wasn't his area.

Or maybe they were just in the wrong place at the wrong time.

We have no crime in Iceland worth writing about.

They did now.

Something in the detective's brief description had set off a distant alarm bell, but he couldn't quite identify it. He was about to rewind the scene in his head and watch the murders a second time when one of the hotel's elevator doors opened and a tall American stepped out into the lobby.

Finn recognized him instantly.

Tom.

This was the place.

Tom wasn't with them the night of the raid, not in Finn and Paulie's squad and not in Kennedy's. He was part of the third squad, the one supposedly watching their six.

The squad that silently split away to execute the massacre.

The next day, the entire platoon was recalled to Bahrain.

The day after that, Finn and Kennedy spoke about it, albeit in code. "Give me twenty-four," Kennedy had said. In other words: *Within twenty-four hours I'll know exactly who was responsible—and we'll hold the fuckers to account.*

But Kennedy didn't get back to him within twenty-four hours. They never spoke again. That night, they hustled Finn out of Bahrain and onto a nearby aircraft carrier. By the next day, the third day after the massacre, Kennedy was dead.

There'd been a bullshit story about a classified op in some unnamed hostile territory, heroic actions, tragic consequences, blah blah, yada yada. There was nothing heroic about that day. There was no classified op. The hundreds who turned out for Kennedy's memorial service in

Boston had no idea they were mourning a lie. The posthumous medal of honor they awarded him did nothing but stain the fingers of the men who presented it to his family.

And while the world grieved the loss of the best man Finn had ever known, the snake who actually killed him slipped away scot-free.

Was Tom that snake?

It had to be someone who was right there in Mukalla, someone on the ground. Someone, in other words, in third squad. Could Tom have been capable of something that cold-blooded? Of murdering their own OIC?

But Finn knew the answer to that one, knew it from personal experience.

Anyone was capable of anything.

Now Tom was crossing the lobby and heading for the exit.

Finn examined a wall rack of tour brochures and timetables, his back to the lobby, his peripheral vision trained on the faint reflection off the museum-grade glass fronting a piece of the hotel's expensive artwork display.

Tom's reflection disappeared out the revolving door.

Finn waited a full twenty seconds before following.

He stepped silently out into the cold and glanced in all directions. Tom's form was disappearing around a corner off to the left.

Finn trailed him down that street and followed as Tom hooked another left, past a restaurant, then veered onto a walkway on the left that took him into the front entrance of an enormous office building.

Höfðatorg.

The locals called it the Tower.

Which backed up catty-corner to the Fosshótel. The two buildings no more than a hundred yards apart. Maybe that was why they were staying at the Foss.

Maybe their target was located there in the Tower.

Finn set his internal stopwatch to twenty seconds.

And waited.

—

Finn knew Tom back in the early days. College kid, top athlete, went into BUD/S two classes before Finn but washed out, then came back through in Class 251, Finn's class. Straight arrow. Clean-cut kid. God and country, fiancée. Didn't fuck around with other women, not even on port call in the aptly named city of Bangkok, which was an impressive display of abstinence in the face of considerable temptation.

Fast forward ten years.

Finn could see how it would have happened. Tom and Jean had a kid back home with a life-threatening condition, a condition that called for an insanely expensive surgical procedure that insurance wouldn't cover. Tom needed the money.

That was how it started.

That was how it always started.

With the money.

At first, chances were, he didn't participate in what the others were doing, the drugs, the theft, the extortion. Tom would have been paid just to keep his mouth shut. But from there it was a slippery slope. Soon he was in up to his neck—and their crimes turned ugly. Assassinations. Atrocities. Full-out war crimes.

Now the others owned him.

Now he was one of them.

Tom had started out as a good guy, a solid operator. He didn't stay that way.

And anyone was capable of anything.

When his internal counter reached twenty seconds, Finn moved. Halfway through the doorway to the Tower he spotted Tom, standing in line at the coffee bar.

This couldn't have been set up more perfectly if he'd planned it.

Of the six men on that rogue squad, Tom would be the easiest to crack. And right now, with his full attention on surveilling his target, he would be less vigilant about an approach from his own flank. All Finn needed to do was engineer an opportunity to confront the man. Lock him into an elevator. Isolate him in a men's room. Something.

Improvise.

If Tom hadn't pulled the trigger himself, chances were good he would know who did. Chances were at least 50 percent it was one of the two SEALs he was rooming with right now.

Finn was about to move into surveillance position when he spotted a woman walking across the lobby space, directly toward Tom.

The dead girl's sister.

Christ on stilts.

What did *she* want with Tom?

It was clear to Finn that she was making an effort to be casual, to not be noticed. Amateurs always did this. Failing to realize that by putting your focus on not being noticed, you practically guaranteed that you would be. Might as well shout your intentions through a bullhorn. The key was to ignore the whole question of whether or not you are being noticed and concentrate on your subject. Take the focus off yourself. She was trying too hard.

She walked past Tom without even a glance. Took up her own recon position at the far side of the lobby.

Okay. She wasn't there for Tom.

She was there for some other reason.

Now Tom was being served his coffee order.

Finn needed to be ready to follow. He needed to corner Tom, get what he came for, and get out. He was on a clock.

Diane and Claudia.

The boys' jungle gym.

One of the building's bank of elevator doors pinged open.

Someone stepped out. Older man in a suit.

Finn saw the sister stiffen imperceptibly, carefully not looking toward the elevator.

Whatever she was about, it concerned the old Icelander.

Finn recognized the face. Tryggvi Pétursson. The dead girl's employer. He'd looked the man up on Ragnar's laptop Monday night, after the sister mentioned him. Financial bigwig. They'd referred to him as "the father of modern Iceland."

Was Tryggvi Tom's target?

Why would a SEAL team be dispatched to kill or kidnap a respected civilian financier in an entirely friendly nation? Made no sense.

But no.

Finn had Tom in his peripheral vision, and he had not shown a glimmer of interest in the man, not even a practiced stalker's well-concealed interest.

Tom was not here for the old Icelander.

But the sister was.

The Icelander strode across the lobby and out the revolving door at the building's front entrance.

After barely a heartbeat, the sister followed.

Moses blows us.

Strangely, Finn felt yanked in two directions.

Which he didn't understand.

Tom was right there, barely twenty yards away.

Why would he want to follow the sister?

This was the moment he'd spent the last three months laying the groundwork for. The chance to learn who gave the order for that royal fuckup in Mukalla. The chance to find out who murdered Kennedy.

If he followed the dead girl's sister he could lose all that. He would certainly lose the critical window in front of him at that moment, which could push his stay in Reykjavík another twenty-four hours, maybe more, which he could ill afford. For all he knew, Tom and his two teammates would move on their target today and be on a plane out before Finn had another shot at it.

And besides, there was no conceivable reason to follow the sister.

Not his problem.

There was no question here.

None at all.

Choice was clear.

Ignore the sister. Stay with Tom.

Tom had now picked up his coffee drink and was walking with it back toward the interior of the building.

The sister disappeared out the revolving door onto the street.

Follow him in.

Ignore the sister.

Stay with Tom.

Finn crossed to the front of the lobby and slipped outside into the cold.

34

His name was Logan—and Krista loathed him on sight.

According to her officers' interview notes, Logan came from a wealthy family and had an excellent academic record. According to the face sitting across the table from her in their cozy interrogation room, he also had excellent teeth and a smug outlook on life that said, *I can do and have whatever I want.*

They'd brought Logan in for questioning concerning a complaint from one of his fellow medical students, who claimed Logan had been dealing stolen pills. Once they had him in the station, they realized he was the self-same Australian med student Jón had said Krista wanted to talk to. The rowdy Christmas Eve partier.

So they'd stuck him in an interview room and called Jón.

Krista studied the report in front of her, taking her time. Logan waited with an air of bemused tolerance. Danni just sat, his face in neutral. The silence was broken only by the periodic turning of pages as Krista read, leafing back a few pages, then forward again as she went through it a second time.

"So, Christmas Eve," she said in English, not looking up.

"Christmas Eve?" A little thrown off guard. Good.

"Yes, Logan. The night before Christmas Day. Why were you and your friend out in our streets, making noise?"

"I— What?"

God, it was good to hear that composure shaken, even if only slightly.

But it lasted only a second or two before the grin slipped right back into place.

"Hey, we were partying. No law against that, right? Not even here in Iceland?"

She ignored the question, still studying her report.

"Our officer says you told her you saw a car. What kind of car would that have been?"

"I said I *thought* I did," he corrected. "I wasn't sure."

She looked up at him, finally. "You *thought* you did. Well, then, let's *think* some more. What kind of car?"

Logan shrugged.

She could hardly believe it. No Icelander would be that rude. And to a cop?

Danni sat forward. "Give us something, Logan," he put in gently. "Work with us here. This could be important."

"I'm really not sure. An SUV, I think . . . maybe black. Just kind of cruising the street. No big bickies."

"Okay." Danni nodded. "A black SUV. Why do you say, 'cruising'?"

"Maybe . . . it was going slow. Like the driver was looking around as he drove."

Krista stared at him. "A black SUV."

Logan nodded, looking around at the walls, avoiding those ice blue eyes. "Again, though, I'm really not positive about that."

"Really not positive," Krista echoed. "Been watching a lot of American movies, Logan?"

"Movies?" He smirked, still glancing around the room like it was all one big fucking joke. "No, why?"

"*Logan.*" Krista's spoke softly but the syllables cut sharp as steel.

He looked at her.

"We've gone through every frame of every piece of CCTV footage in midtown from that night," she said. "There is no footage of any black SUV. At any time that night. Anywhere."

Silence. He looked away.

"Why do you suppose that is, Logan?"

"Honestly, I can't say." Now he looked back and met her gaze head-on. "I was a little drunk." Like he was proud of it.

"Were you."

"Yeah."

A little pissed. Uh-huh. According to Logan's companion that night, he was stumbling drunk. "Bombed to smithereens" was how the other boy put it.

"Your mate doesn't remember seeing a black SUV on the street that night. Or any other vehicle. He also doesn't remember you, Logan, not after he went back inside the hotel to throw up in the loo. Doesn't remember where you went or what you did."

"Yeah, well." A dismissive shrug. "That's Bryan."

"Logan? I think you're lying to me."

"I'm not—"

"I think you're giving us a bullshit story about some bloke who doesn't exist driving some scary car you saw in a spy movie. Now, why would a good boy like you do something like that?"

"It's not a bullshit—!"

"Maybe, say, to distract us from taking a closer look at what our good boy Logan himself was up to that night?"

Silence.

"Logan," Danni spoke up again, softly as before. "We want to believe you. But you need to help us. Is there something you're not telling us?"

Logan glared at Krista, then took a breath and looked over at Danni.

"Yeah, maybe. Okay?"

"Maybe what, Logan?" said Danni.

He gestured vaguely with one hand, as if to say, *What the fuck does it matter anyway?*

"I may have seen her."

Krista and Danni glanced at each other, then back at Logan.

"Seen who, Logan?" Danni prodded.

"That sheila, you know. The one you lot have been asking about. Running on the street."

Krista sat alone in the interrogation room, thinking about the conversation. After ten fruitless minutes of further questioning, Danni had escorted Logan to a holding cell, pending action on the pills allegation.

He'd said he couldn't be sure it was the same girl as the one in the newspaper photo, and he insisted he'd caught only a brief glimpse, and that was all there was to it.

Maybe. Maybe not.

Why hadn't he said anything about this before, when the cops interviewed him on Monday?

It wasn't his business, he said. He didn't want to get mixed up in it.

Oh, you're mixed up in it now, Logan. You're mixed up in it big bickies.

Pills, Logan's mate Bryan had said. (Unbeknownst to Logan it was Bryan who'd blown the whistle on him.)

Krista thought about that.

Rich medical student. Access. Hubris.

Pills could be the tip of the iceberg.

Illegal drugs were far more rampant in Iceland than most outsiders knew. Oxy, Fentanyl, cocaine, Ecstasy . . . who knew the extent of young Logan's trade?

And she was still thinking about her conversation the day before with Tryggvi.

Decades of interviews had given Krista a finely tuned bullshit meter. She could pick up all the tells, read all the clues. Tryggvi hadn't hesitated or equivocated, not for a moment. He was being truthful, she would bet her badge on it.

Still, there were one or two things about that conversation that bothered her.

For example: when she asked him if the girl could have been using drugs, that *"impossible"* had come back a little too swiftly, a little too emphatically. She had the sense Tryggvi might be fudging the truth there, perhaps in an effort to protect the girl's reputation, even in death.

Which Krista could understand.

Perhaps he felt guilty that his own staff had not been more attentive that night, allowing her to slip away on her own like that. Perhaps that swift "impossible" came blurting out because Tryggvi was having doubts himself.

Kateryna's sister said she'd been clean for over three years, and her medical record concurred.

Maybe. Maybe not.

Could Kateryna have been using drugs without her sister knowing it? Without her employer and his entire lake house staff knowing it?

Sure she could.

Could she have snuck into town to hook up with someone—an enterprising young med student, for instance—for a quick dope buy?

Sure she could.

Krista sighed.

She knew they couldn't hold her witness for one second longer than the legislated twenty-four hours. The pills allegation wouldn't stick. She couldn't help wondering if he were somehow connected to the murders at the clinic, with its tantalizing element of stolen pills. But there was not a whisper of evidence to suggest that a young medical student with a promising career ahead of him had gone and bashed the brains out of two medical staff in order to heist a little Benalyn. If his family had a smart lawyer on speed dial, which they almost surely did, he'd be out by dinner.

But he was guilty, she was sure of it—guilty of something, anyway, even if she didn't yet know exactly what or how. She felt it as sure as if he'd walked into their interview wearing a T-shirt that said "HI, I'M LOGAN! I'VE DONE SOMETHING BAD."

So let him stew in a holding cell for the day, see how smug he was after another six hours.

And she wanted to know more about that scar before they talked with Logan again. Just how old was it? Could it have been a fresh wound from that same night, sealed over by the hours spent in the freezing water?

But Árni, their diver, was out on Faxaflói Bay, assisting a rescue operation. Some tourists got stuck on an ice floe. Could be hours.

Had to be Americans. No Europeans would be that stupid.

As she exited the observation room she bumped into Danni, who'd come back looking for her.

"Chief wants to see you in her office." He leaned in and murmured, "Careful, Krissý. She's not happy."

35

Stalking without being detected was a skill that had always come naturally to Finn. It was only in SEAL training that he began to understand its component parts.

Part of it had to do with situational awareness. Staying alert to 360 degrees of light, shadow, and movement. Another part of it was being completely awake to the sense of one's own body in space. "Like you're moving through water," one instructor had told them. Feeling the air currents slipping over your shoulders, through your fingers, around your legs.

It also required an understanding of the concept of "dead space." Positioning yourself so that an obstructing piece of scenery came between you and your subject: a car, the corner of a building, even a slight rise in elevation, that last being especially relevant in a hilly environment like Reykjavík.

But the major part of it—the X factor—was simply being able to disappear.

Some people couldn't do this. It just wasn't in their nature. They took up too much volume. When they entered the room, all heads turned in their direction. Gregarious. Charismatic. Life of the party. The kind of person who couldn't be unseen if they tried.

To Finn, being unseen was as natural as breathing.

The dead girl's sister was not a natural, but she was better than he'd expected. Most civilians, unless they were hunters, had no clue how to stalk; they'd try to slip through streets unnoticed and might as well have been banging on trash can lids. The sister wasn't like that. Despite his impression in the Tower lobby, now that they were out on the street it was clear she had a decent feel for it.

Still, she was in over her head.

The man she was following: now, he was skilled.

Finn turned the sonar of his mind onto the old Icelander.

Not a serious pro—Finn didn't see any Spec Ops training there. He was old enough to have lived through the Cold War, but it was clear to Finn that he'd spent those years in business, not in the military or intelligence. Yet he was practiced. Canny. The kind of businessman who had successfully built connections with power brokers all around the world, made friends with the enemies of his friends, survived global conflicts and government upheavals and economic meltdowns and always come out ahead.

You didn't do that without being aware of your surroundings.

The three made their way west, crossing over Laugavegur and threading through the back streets of Reykjavík 101, Finn tailing the woman as she tailed the old man, then continued on, skirting the city center with its parliament building, city hall, and duck pond.

A few blocks farther west, the man abruptly turned and entered an impressive white Gothic Revival–style house surrounded by an iron fence. Just outside the entrance a flagpole stood sentry, flying a tricolor flag of three horizontal stripes: white on top, then blue, red along the base. Mother Russia.

The sister took up position across the street half a block down and waited in the bitter cold.

Finn waited, too.

The cold tightened around him like a noose.

The temperature was dropping.

"You know The Divine Comedy? *Dante Alighieri?"*

It was his third day of sniper school, held up in the mountains of northern California in the dead of winter, where it could get as cold as a meat locker. These were the first words anyone had spoken to him, or at least any of his classmates.

Finn nodded. "'The Inferno.'"

The guy laughed. "Exactly. My theory is, military Spec Ops training is structured along the same lines as Dante's nine concentric circles of hell."

They were sitting at breakfast, the classmate putting away eggs and pancakes, Finn taking down a bowl of oatmeal and a can of smelts. Finn cataloged the guy's features as he talked: broad forehead, delicate jaw, short-cropped dark brown hair, hazel eyes. Mouth set in a permanent smirk.

"First few circles," Hazel Eyes went on, "you're beaten by violent storms, dragged through toxic sludge, tortured by monstrous three-headed dogs."

Not a bad description of BUD/S instructors, Finn thought. Monstrous three-headed dogs. Copy that.

"Graduate to the inner circles, and now you're fed on by harpies and thrown in a lake of fire. From boot camp to BUD/S and all the rest of Spec Ops training—deeper and deeper circles of hell."

Half a pancake, chomp of bacon, slurp of coffee.

"But then you get to the ninth circle. No fire, no monsters—no no, not here. Here in the ninth circle you're frozen in a lake of ice. Surrounded by silence. Congratulations. You've reached the epicenter of hell.

"And that, my friend, is sniper school."

Finn had no trouble agreeing with that one, either. Hazel Eyes had nailed it.

Sniper school wasn't physically as demanding as BUD/S, but in a way the torture was worse. In BUD/S you carried heavy logs and beat the crap out of your body. In sniper school you beat the crap out of your brain. You pushed your capacity to focus, to observe and think and act with precision, as far as was humanly possible. And then pushed it further.

Sniper school was BUD/S for the central nervous system.

First day there the instructors loaded them all into a truck and toured them around the property, all fifteen acres. Second day, after six solid hours of intensive studies in the physics of internal and external ballistics, they took them on a five-mile run, then ran them through a series of calisthenics, then just as muscle fatigue was setting in they pulled the students back into the classroom, sat them down, gave them each a pen and a blank piece of paper, and addressed the class:

"Along the route we drove yesterday there were fourteen random man-

made objects placed around the property that didn't belong there. You have one minute to write them all down, location and approximate distance from the road. In sequence."

By the time Finn was sitting down to breakfast his third day there, a quarter of the class had washed out.

"I did a Land Nav evolution up here when I went through SQT," his classmate was saying. "One night, out in the hills, my toes froze so bad I was afraid they'd get frostbitten. Before heading out I wrapped them in plastic bags under my socks to insulate. Smart, right?"

He laughed. The way his features relaxed into it told Finn the guy laughed often and easily.

"Oops. All they did was hold in the moisture. Come morning all my goddam toenails had sloughed off. Never grew back. My girlfriend says it made me a better lover."

Hazel Eyes leaned in close and lowered his voice to a conspiratorial whisper.

"Learn from my travails, young man. You can let 'em take your toes, but don't let 'em take your balls."

He stuck out his hand and introduced himself.

And that was the first time Finn met Paulie.

A few years later Paulie enrolled in OCS, came back up as an officer, and ended up as Second O in his old childhood pal Kennedy's platoon, where the two took up like they'd never left Southie.

Kennedy was from a big Irish Catholic family, seven kids in a house that functioned as the social center of the neighborhood. Paulie was a kid from two blocks over whose parents were never around. "For all practical purposes," Kennedy had once told Finn, "Paulie may as well've been an orphan."

Finn could relate.

Kennedy's mom felt sorry for him and took him in—adopted him, more or less—and the two boys had been inseparable ever since.

Finn wondered what it would be like to have the kind of friendship Kennedy and Paulie had.

He wondered if he'd ever know.

He shifted his position slightly to boost his circulation and ward off the intensifying cold.

For the past three months he had tried to make contact with Paulie, but he'd vanished. Even Stan L. didn't know where he was, and Stan L. could snorkel up just about anything. Finn had no idea if he was even still breathing. He hoped so.

He hated to think the only one left of the troika was him.

36

"Where are we on the double homicide?"

Never a handshake or a "Good morning." The Reykjavík chief of police conducted all her meetings standing, and she invariably got right down to business the moment you showed up on her doorstep. Ylfa, her name was, an old Icelandic word for "she-wolf."

Ylfa: a she-wolf with a blond bob so perfect it would have given Hitchcock heart failure.

"We're just getting started," Krista replied.

Conversations with Ylfa also worked in code. "We're just getting started" meant *We are absolutely nowhere.*

"It's an ugly scene," Krista added. Translation: *So far there's nothing to go on.*

"Well, you don't have long," said Ylfa. "Before it gets uglier, I mean."

Oh, Krista knew what she meant.

Mercifully—miraculously—the press had not yet caught wind of the clinic murders. Krista had given strict instructions to keep the story buttoned up as long as possible, instructions everyone in the department was only too happy to follow. They wouldn't be able to contain it for long, though. Probably no longer than they could hold on to young Logan.

And the moment it leaked out, the thing would erupt faster than you could say "Eyjafjallajökull."

Also, not that this especially concerned the she-wolf, but the moment it leaked out, the Little Mermaid would be instantly forgotten. The prime minister wouldn't be attending that funeral. But then, there wasn't even going to be a funeral, was there? No body. And whose fault was that?

"Why are we holding an Australian medical student? Pills, I'm hearing. Do we have anything connecting him to the clinic?"

"No, actually, we're questioning him in connection with the drowning on Christmas Eve. I believe the girl may have been running from someone."

"Christmas Eve?" Ylfa looked up with a frown that Krista knew from experience said something on the order of, *That's the most idiotic thing I've heard today.* "Are there any witnesses who actually saw him *with* the girl? CCTV footage of them together? or even in the same location?"

The chief would already know the answers to all these questions, and know that Krista knew that.

The rhetorical bludgeon was one of Ylfa's go-to instruments of torture.

Krista plowed on. "He's admitted to seeing her that night. He was drunk. The girl had a history with drugs; there may have been a drug connection. And we believe the assailant was most likely a foreigner, given that there were virtually no Icelanders out and about on Christmas Eve."

"The assailant," repeated the chief.

Another one of Ylfa's rhetorical favorites: repeating your words back to you as a form of ridicule.

Had she picked that up from Ylfa, or was it the other way around?

"A young girl drowns on Christmas Eve," the chief continued, having bullied her senior detective into silence. "Alone with the ducks and the geese. It's a tragedy. Like a fairy tale from some depressive's version of Hans Christian Andersen. I get it. But it is what it is."

"Of course. But . . ." Taking the bait, despite herself. "From the CCTV footage it does seem clear she thought someone was following her—"

"Yes, a reasonable thought, when you have no concept of how safe our city is because you're a stranger to Iceland. Which she was. Also possibly so high she was suffering from paranoid hallucinations. But since we don't have a body, there's no way of knowing, is there. Correct me if I'm wrong, but I'm not really seeing anything to investigate here."

As Krista knew better than anyone else in the building, when the chief began a statement with the words, "Correct me if I'm wrong," it always meant the precise opposite.

To Krista, the Christmas Eve drowning was an unexplained death crying out for resolution. To the department, it was a national embarrassment, begging to be filed and forgotten.

Message received.

"So. The clinic. Do we have any leads?"

Absolutely. The killer was fastidious and had anger issues. Which narrows it down to 95 percent of Iceland's male population.

"No, no leads. Not so far."

"Well, get one."

Back at her desk, Krista found an email waiting from her friend at Airport Police, the one who'd sent over the CCTV stills of Marlin Pike. She'd asked him to look into the A.I. glitch that flagged the American in the first place. It seemed her friend had something to report.

She called his office at the airport and was immediately put on hold.

While she waited, she thought about her meeting with the chief.

Like some depressive's version of Hans Christian Andersen. Ylfa's literary horizons were none too broad; she'd obviously never read the original "Little Mermaid." One of the darkest fairy tales there was, crammed full of sexual creepiness, suicide, and conspiracy to murder.

If Krista was smart, she would comply with her boss's unspoken order and close the file on Kateryna. If she wanted to secure that transfer to a quiet post on the other side of the island, she would need the full backing of her chain of command.

She needed the she-wolf, in other words, on her side.

Not, unfortunately, their normal everyday relationship.

Krista knew cops who drank, or collected porn, or spent hours gazing at Instagram. Every cop had their own private vice. Krista read American crime novels. As much as she revered Inspector Erlendur and Lisbeth Salander, there was something about a good Philip Marlowe or Travis McGee that quickened her pulse. It was Krista's guilty pleasure. And it occurred to her now, as she sat on hold, what it was about those cynical Yankee samurai that she resonated with.

Their perennial distrust of the broken system they were a part of.

"It wasn't a glitch." Her Airport Police friend was back on the phone and sounded out of breath. "It was an alert."

Apparently Immigration had gotten a brief about some foreign-national bad actor referred to in the chatter as "The Englishman," either entering the country or already there, associated with an operation un-helpfully referred to as "Pandora." Tentative links to known terror net-works. No photos, no description, no bio. Not a clue as to purpose or scope of activity.

Nothing more than that "Englishman" handle, for what it was worth, which could be nothing at all.

So the facial recog A.I. engine had gotten a little twitchy, especially right around Christmas, and pinged on any Anglo inbound travelers looking remotely out of the ordinary.

Krista thanked her friend and opened a new memo on her cellphone.

"Pandora," she said into the phone.

Like the Greek myth? or the music streaming service? or the Danish jewelry company?

"The Englishman," she added. "Sleeper cell? Black money courier?"

Could Logan from Australia possibly be mistaken for an Englishman? That seemed like a stretch. And she had a hard time picturing him as part of any international terrorist plot.

The software had flagged Marlin Pike, but he was American, not English.

She frowned. Where had Pike flown in from? Not New York or Boston. Not Atlanta. He'd come over in two flights, hadn't he? Stopped over somewhere. She flipped back through her phone, checking her notes.

Heathrow.

She brought up a picture of Pike in her mind's eye and tried to match it with her concept of "terrorist." It didn't fit. But it didn't exactly *not* fit, either.

There certainly was a lot going on with that odd-looking American that he wasn't saying.

She looked down at her phone again. Went to her photos and scrolled back through to Monday afternoon.

Monument to the Unknown Bureaucrat.

Why did he send her that? Was he saying he was just an unknown worker-bee himself, a researcher on someone else's project? Or that he saw *her* as a bureaucratic nonentity? Or did Marlin Pike know something, something he was only hinting at?

It was driving her nuts.

She called Jón on her intercom. "Can you bring up records for this cellphone number?" She read out the number Pike called from Monday, which was the same number he'd used to send her that weird photo.

Jón was at her office door in less than five minutes.

"Whose phone was this?" he said.

"Jón," said Krista, snapping her fingers impatiently. *Spill.*

"Right. So, it was a brand-new line. Just one outbound call, Monday afternoon. One text message, also Monday. Both of those to—"

"I know, both went to my cellphone. What else? Do we know whose phone it is?"

"Nothing else. It's one of those cheap prepaid phones. After those two entries, the line shows as inactive."

A prepaid disposable, used only once, and only to contact Krista. Then tossed.

Why would Marlin Pike be using a burner phone?

37

A vicious wind sliced through the streets, bringing
with it a scatter of smells. Seaweed, salt air. Ice crystals. *Hangikjöt.*
Chicken manure, wet straw, burning khat—

Finn took a slow breath, in and out, and adjusted his position an inch
to bring fresh blood flow to his chilled extremities. Tried to get the smells
of Mukalla out of his nose, to tell his brain they weren't real.

His experience of that night was like a twenty-second trailer for a horror movie he'd never seen. A series of stark images stitched together with
jump cuts, jarring but incomprehensible.

He remembered giving the call to breach, the percussive *Thump!* as
they blew in the compound door. He remembered Paulie leading the
stack in, then finding the place empty—and then?

Blank. A skip in the playback track.

Next thing he remembered was standing before that shattered wooden
door in the farmhouse wall, hours later, under a sky riven with heat
lightning.

Blank.

Skip.

Sitting on the dirt floor of the room, death all around him, two children staring up at him through blank eyes.

Blank.

Skip.

Waking up on the ground the next morning, wrapped in his Gore-Tex
blanket, back at base camp.

Lacunae.

He half closed his eyes and began going through it again. The smell of chicken manure, wet straw . . .

The room lights up with a flash, like an instant of daylight, and then it's gone. Finn sits against the wall, legs splayed out, blinded by the afterimage seared into his brain: the dead children, their sightless eyes, blood oozing down the sides of their heads.

Flash—then darkness.

And something else in the darkness.

Something moving, just for an instant, but he can't see what.

Finn took a deep, slow breath, peering down the long corridors of neural pathways, letting himself sink into the fragmented fabric of memory.

Standing at the gate, pushing through the shattered door—skip—walking through the darkened farmhouse—skip—sitting on the earthen floor against the far wall, facing the room's open doorway—flash of heat lightning—the bodies of the two children in the darkness—Ray's startled dead eyes staring at hi—

Finn jerked, his eyes snapping open, and forced himself to start breathing again.

It was no good.

Every time he tried to remember, every time he tried to peer into the darkness that followed that moment of heat lightning, he ended up back on the closet floor in the Snake River cabin in the moments after the blinding flash of the handgun, eight years old, staring into the semi-dark at his big brother, Ray, thudding to his knees, the light gone from his eyes.

The childhood memory stood like a cursed hound guarding the gates of hell.

He couldn't penetrate the darkness in that farmhouse room, couldn't see behind the flash's grisly afterimage.

There was a soft buzz in one of his pockets. Burner phone #4, the one he was using to track the spyware he'd placed on the detective's phone.

"Pandora" . . . "The Englishman." Sleeper cell?
Black money courier?

The detective was dictating a memo.

He followed along in real time as she made a few more notes, copying and pasting and translating as fast as he could. The words "Pandora" and "The Englishman" were in English, everything else in Icelandic.

Apparently their intelligence was tracking some character known only as the Englishman who'd entered their little island nation, likely with malign intent. Possibly related to an op, code name Pandora.

Or maybe Pandora was a person. Or a place. It wasn't clear.

He considered this.

Sleeper cell . . . in Iceland? Seemed unlikely to Finn. Black money courier? Much easier to picture.

Hang on. She was still typing.

A phone number.

His phone number—burner phone #3, the one he'd used Monday to call her and send that photo and then destroyed.

Interesting.

Did she think *he* was this "Englishman"?

In his peripheral vision Finn saw Oksana stir.

The Icelander was on the move again.

On the walk back Tryggvi took a slightly different route, once again keeping to the side streets to the south of Laugavegur. Once again on foot. In the bitter cold. In the dead of winter.

Which Finn found curious.

Finn noticed Oksana zipping her parka up an extra two inches on the front of her neck. Everyone in Reykjavík wore parkas. Everyone but the old Icelander, who marched grimly up the street in nothing but his wool business suit.

The walk was well over a mile.

Why would he not take a car?

Finn had recognized the name when the sister first mentioned it. A little research on Ragnar's laptop had filled in some details of the general picture he was already vaguely aware of.

Tryggvi held a wide range of business interests in and around Reykjavík, including three securities firms, a financial brokerage, a high-tech data center, an aluminum smelting business, and a shit-ton of real estate. To tourists, the Reykjavík skyline was famous for the soaring church tower, the sparkling new concert hall, the glass dome of Perlan. To those in the know, Tryggvi towered over all of it. Rumor was, when Russia offered to bail Iceland out after the 2008 crash, it was Tryggvi who back-channel-brokered the deal.

So no surprise that he was paying a visit to his friends at the Russian embassy.

But why was the sister following him?

When they arrived back at the Tower, the old Icelander strode directly through the lobby and into a waiting elevator.

The sister stood at the edge of the lobby, looking uncertain, as if wavering over the question of what to do next.

Finn walked up to her and spoke.

"If you're trying to stalk that old Icelander without him knowing it, you're doing a pretty terrible job."

She looked at him for five seconds, unblinking.

Then said: "You like cup of coffee?"

38

Oksana took Finn around back and up a service elevator to the top of the Tower, through several sets of heavy doors, and out onto the roof, which offered up a magnificent view of the city.

How she knew her way around, how she had access to these restricted spaces, Finn had no idea. She was one resourceful history professor.

They stood, side by side, looking out at the frozen city. Finn waited for her to speak.

"Is beautiful," she finally said.

"You grew up in Kyiv?" he replied. She obviously had a story to tell. That seemed a logical place to start.

"Kyiv is most beautiful city in Europe," she said. Finn caught the fierce note of defiance in her identifying her country specifically as part of Europe. "You know Bernard Henri-Levy, French philosopher?" she said, as if reading his thoughts. "He called my country 'the beating heart of Europe.'"

She paused for a moment, then continued.

"Our parents were intellectuals. Outspoken. They criticize Soviet Union. This is a very risky thing, back then." She looked to the right and to the left, taking in a sweep of the cityscape. "Now, too. Always risky."

She produced a cigarette from a parka pocket, lit it, took a drag, and blew out a thin stream of smoke. "You know Novichok?"

"Soviet-era nerve agent," he said.

"This is what they use to assassinate Sergei Skripal. Same way they try to kill Alexey Navalny."

Finn said nothing.

"This is what they use on parents," she said softly.

Finn looked at her. "On *your* parents?"

She nodded. "I was teenager." Her voice low and coarse with emotion. "Old enough to read autopsies. Old enough to not buy official bullshit story. I know all about Novichok. Is ugly death."

He waited a moment, then said, "You were there when it happened?"

She shook her head. "Small mercy. But I know."

Finn knew, too. Muscular pain, often severe. Vomiting. Slow suffocation. *Is ugly death.*

"According to Ukraine police, case is 'unsolved.'" She shrugged and looked out at the skyline. Took a long drag.

"Saddam, Assad, they are amateur. No one knows chemical and bioweapon like the Russians."

She was silent for a moment. Then she beckoned him over to the roof's north-facing edge, looking out over the harbor.

"Look."

She pointed directly across the street to a little white gabled house, fronted by a pair of gambrels, sitting by itself on a patch of incongruous lawn amid the glass-and-steel financial district.

"Höfði House," she said.

"Reagan-Gorbachev summit," replied Finn. "Eighty-six. Beginning of the end of the Cold War."

Oksana gave a derisive snort. "End of nothing. You know what local people call this place? Ghost House. British ambassador living there, many years ago, moved out, took his consulate with him. Never went back. Why? Because place is haunted."

Finn was silent.

"Reagan, Gorbachev." She spat the words, turning away again toward the city's old town. "Summit was a mirage. A ghost. Cold War never ended. Just went into hibernation. Like bear."

Now she pointed out over the city. "You see church?"

Finn saw it, about fifteen blocks to the west: Hallgrímskirkja, the great Lutheran church that towered over the city like a gigantic inverted icicle.

Where he'd passed Oksana's sister, running to keep her appointment with Death.

"You cannot quite see it from here, but just beyond that, below Parliament Hill? Duck lake."

Finn nodded.

"Just this side of duck lake, there is American embassy. Just above, Iceland parliament. Opposite side, Russia embassy."

The building to which they'd tailed Tryggvi earlier that day.

Finn could clearly see it all in his mind's eye—and it struck him that the landmarks she'd just described were laid out like a perfect map of large-scale geopolitical tensions: America and Russia sitting on opposite sides of a body of water, little Iceland perched to the north between the two.

Oksana took another drag on her cigarette.

"Your police detective went to see Tryggvi Pétursson yesterday. Immediately after this, he goes out, alone, on foot." She gestured with her chin.

"To the Russian embassy," said Finn.

"To Russian embassy."

"And your theory is?"

"Tryggvi has a Russian client. Very important man in Russian government. Very high up. He cannot simply pick up the phone and call this client. He has to visit on foot, alone. Name is Petrov."

Finn looked at her. She knew the man's name?

She shrugged. "I have a good friend in Kyiv, military intelligence directorate."

"And you believe this is connected to your sister."

Another long drag. She didn't look at him, continued keeping her gaze fixed to the west as she spoke, as if not wanting to see in his face whether he believed her or thought she was crazy.

"I think this au pair business is . . ." She waved her cigarette, like a magic wand to summon up just the right word. "Bogus." She took another fierce drag. "I think they run sex traffic operation. I think they did not recruit Kateryna to be some au pair in New York. I think they recruit her to be some rich person's property in New York. Maybe friend of Petrov."

Finn did not find this especially far-fetched. Contrary to Iceland's mostly deserved image as a crime-free, high-social-justice society, the island nation had also become something of a destination spot for human trafficking, and sex trafficking in particular.

Still, he had no compelling reason to think that that was what was happening in Kateryna's case. And he could understand how Oksana might be looking for an explanation more grandly conspiratorial than a simple, random street assault or a drug-related accident. Or suicide.

This was, after all, someone whose parents had been victims of a state assassination.

And who was pissed off at Iceland for not protecting her little sister.

She spoke up again, her voice now soft and low.

"You're thinking, okay, so, if she is running from someone, how does she end up naked in duck lake? Or if this someone catch her, why put her there?"

Finn nodded slowly. He wouldn't have posed the question out loud. But, yeah. Regardless of who may have been after her, why drown her in the pond and leave her body there on public display?

"Makes no sense," he said.

She finally turned and looked into his face.

"All makes no sense."

"What do the police say?"

"They say, must be accident. I know what they think. They think Kateryna is drunk, stoned, goes swimming, and drown. They don't say this, but they think it."

She turned away again, face downcast.

"I don't care what happened." She spoke so quietly Finn could barely hear her. "I don't care about revenge. I don't care about justice. I just want to bring my sister home."

She paused, then added: "That legend? Dead spirit haunting Höfði House? Local people say, is young girl. Young girl who drown."

She dropped her spent cigarette to the rooftop and crushed it out with the toe of her boot.

"Now coffee."

——

They went back down to the ground floor and took side-by-side seats at the lobby's coffee bar. She ordered a double espresso. Finn had water. They waited for their drinks in silence.

After her first sip of espresso, the sister looked at Finn.

"So. I tell you about me. Why I follow him. What about you? Why do you follow me? Why do you care about any of this?"

She sucked in a breath, then blew it out again. A dedicated smoker in a non-smoking country. "Because you are crime writer?" she added with a smirk. Like both Magnús and the detective, she obviously hadn't bought that cover story for a second.

Finn didn't answer her question. Instead he said, "Why haven't you told the police about your suspicions?"

She huffed out a single laugh. "When you grow up in Ukraine, police are last people you trust."

Finn could see that. Still. "These are Icelandic police," he said.

Another sucked-in breath. This time she held it for a moment, thoughtful, then let it out through pursed lips. "In Iceland," she replied, "people assume no one is corrupt. In Ukraine, assume everyone is corrupt."

She sipped at her espresso.

"Something else I didn't tell detective. Kateryna, she stayed in touch with me by text. She made a friend here, Zofia, Polish girl, also training to be 'au pair' in New York. Maybe they will be friends there together, she said."

She took a sip of her espresso, then took another sip, and another, until she had drained the little cup.

Then sat back in her seat and continued.

"Kateryna is not much for writing. Short text, one line, maybe three, four words."

Finn thought Kateryna sounded a little like Carol.

Oksana reminded him a *lot* of Carol. Resourceful. Direct. No bullshit.

"One week before Christmas, she send text. 'Last night I dream I visit mines.' I write back, mines? What mines? No answer. Next day, 'Not feel well, resting.' Next day, 'Feeling little better.' Then nothing."

Finn was not aware of any mines in Iceland.

"After a few days more, I write again. No answer.

"I tell detective, I am on a plane two hours after I hear news about girl who drowns in Reykjavík, see her picture in papers. This is a lie. I am on plane the day *before*. Before news. Before she drown. I know, in my heart, is something wrong.

"So: long flight, slow change in Warsaw. Twenty-four hours my trip takes. I am in the air when she dies. I am—"

Oksana fell silent, her face turned away, quietly weeping.

Finn didn't know what to do but sit still and wait while she wiped her eyes with the tiny napkin that came with her espresso.

After a moment she looked up and said, "You have brothers, sisters?"

"An older brother. Ray. He was killed when I was eight."

She was silent for a moment, then said softly, "I am so sorry." Another silence, then: "Sibling is closest person in all of life. Closer even than parents."

Finn said nothing.

"Do you weep for him? For Ray?"

Finn shook his head. "I don't. No."

This was the truth. Finn had never wept for Ray. He hadn't wept for Kennedy, either, though the news of his death, when Finn learned of it, felt like a two-thousand-pound stone crushing down on him.

But no, he'd never wept for anyone. He didn't mourn. It wasn't how he was wired.

Let the dead be dead.

"But you miss him," she said.

Finn didn't know how to reply to that.

There were two things he knew about Ray.

He had been the center of Finn's universe.

And Finn had killed him.

39

Two officers led a shaken Logan from the interview room, taking him back to his holding cell for a late supper. Whether he'd be able to eat right now was anyone's guess.

"Jesus, Krista," murmured Danni. "Why not just beat him with a rubber hose?"

Krista looked at him thoughtfully. "Wish you'd brought that up before."

It was daybreak in Sydney, early evening in Reykjavík, when they finally got Logan's full record. It was worth the wait.

Turned out, a year earlier he'd been questioned in connection with an assault charge. Seemed he had been playing rough with his girlfriend, according to the girl's father, who filed the charges. The girlfriend declined to confirm the allegations. The matter was dropped.

The file included color photos. Mostly the colors black and blue, with patches of bilious yellow.

With this information in hand, Krista had Logan brought in for a second, somewhat less polite interview.

She pushed him hard. He denied everything, stuck to his story, shit-eating grin firmly in place.

She pushed harder.

Once it dawned on him that they weren't after the business about the pills, that they were serious about linking him with that girl who wound up dead in the duck pond in the center of town, his composure started to crack.

He got loud. Swore up and down that he knew nothing whatsoever about the stupid girl, his mate Bryan was an ass, his parents were going to sue the entire Reykjavík police department. Yada yada. By the time he was sent back to his cell, he looked like he was on the verge of tears.

Good.

"Hopefully we can pick up tomorrow morning where we left off," Krista said as the two got to their feet. *If we can find a way to hold him that long*, she thought glumly.

Danni swore under his breath. "Careful, Krissý. You're on thin ice here."

She turned and looked at him. "Piss-poor choice of words, Danni."

They walked out into the hallway in silence and continued on through the building, stopping at the front entrance.

"I'm off," said Danni. "Long day." When she made no move to walk out with him he looked back at her.

She shook her head. "Some stuff to look at."

He nodded.

Halfway out the door he paused and turned.

"He's just a kid," he said softly.

Krista took the stairs up to her floor, feeling in a blouse pocket for her pencil stub, wishing she had a cigarette.

He's just a kid.

Meaning what? Boys will be boys?

The crime photos from the clinic were still spread out on her desk. She tucked into her chair and sat staring at them.

Thinking about Logan's black-and-blue Australian girlfriend.

Thinking about the dead girl in the ice.

Thinking about Birna.

Tragedy didn't get to Krista; in fact, it barely affected her. To her, tragedy was familiar, almost comfortable. She was three when her parents were killed, drowned in a storm when their fishing boat went down off the eastern coast. She'd been with her grandpa at the time, sitting at a window. They sat together and watched the ship sink.

So, no, tragedy came as no shock.

What she couldn't handle, what had bludgeoned at her sensibilities for every one of her thirty-one years on the force, was the brutality.

The human being's capacity to brutalize another was something she simply could not grasp.

When the sea snuffed out those twin brilliant lights that were her parents, Krista Kristjánsdóttir was branded by a grief that had never left her. But she *understood* it. The violence of nature, majestic and impersonal, was native to the Icelandic soul; it echoed millions of years of continents ripping apart and spewing up the tons upon tons of molten rock that had formed their volcanic homeland.

But human beings turning on each other for no reason at all, clubbing each other senseless?

It made no more sense to her now than it did the day she walked in on her first domestic violence call as a twenty-two-year-old rookie. The thin woman sitting at the kitchen table weeping silently, bloodied and bruised, ice pack to her fractured jaw. Husband on the floor, on his back. Contentedly snoring.

Iceland had the broadest social net in the world, the most generous health-care system. It boasted the strongest "gender parity" and was routinely held up by other nations as a paragon of equal rights and social justice. It was rated the safest country on earth.

So why did so many Icelandic men still beat their women?

Why were those two innocent lives at the clinic abruptly terminated in an explosion of blood and brain matter?

Why did the Little Mermaid have to die?

She reached into a desk drawer, pulled the surveillance photo of the running girl on Christmas Eve, and set it on top of the others.

That frightened face.

Einar believed she was high as a kite, and that was that, no assault, no assailant. So did the rest of the department. So, clearly, did Ylfa, her boss.

They were all wrong. That was no drug high she was looking at in that photo.

That was fear.

"Who were you running from, Kateryna?" she whispered. "Was it young Logan?"

Just before going in to give the medical wunderkind a good sear before his overnight braising, she'd finally gotten to talk with Árni the diver. He was insistent: it was a scar, no older than a week or two, but definitely not fresh. At least a few days old.

So, no, assuming Árni was right, she hadn't scraped herself on the ice. And it wasn't from an assault that had just taken place that same night.

Maybe the scar was irrelevant. Some dumb accident a week earlier.

"Like what," she muttered. "She dropped a wineglass in the bathtub?"

What kind of ordinary household accident put a scar on your lower abdomen?

Or had she been with Logan the girlfriend-beater not for minutes but for days?

Was Tryggvi concealing the fact that she'd gone missing, not just on Christmas Eve, but days earlier?

And speaking of Tryggvi.

As fiercely as she resisted the thought, there were a few more points in his testimony that didn't quite add up.

When she'd visited his office, he gave the clear impression that Kateryna was under his staff's constant supervision. "In our care from the moment they arrive at Keflavík" were his exact words. Which was why it was "*impossible*" that the girl could have had any access to illegal drugs.

Yet when she spoke with him later by phone to ask about the scar, he stressed that the girl had been free to come and go.

So which was it, "constant supervision" or "free to come and go"?

Go ahead, Krista. Ask the question.

Was it possible that the girl was being abused right there at the lake house?

And the other one. Go ahead, let the shoe drop.

Could she have been pregnant?

She'd dismissed the thought when she first learned about the scar. The timing was off for a C-section; the girl would've had to have been pretty far along when she arrived in Iceland, and surely Tryggvi's people would have known. Nobody hires a pregnant au pair.

But what about an ectopic pregnancy? That could have been recent. And ectopic pregnancies could lead to a burst Fallopian tube and emergency surgery, typically within the first eight weeks of pregnancy.

Exactly how long she'd been in the country.

According to Árni's observation, whatever caused the scar would have happened within the past week or so. The time frame fit.

Was Tryggvi hiding something far darker than a case of staff carelessness?

Was Kateryna raped?

40

Boone sat like a stone Buddha, nothing moving but the slow pulling back of his right arm, followed by the lightning snap of the wrist. He stood, walked, retrieved the knife. Returned to sitting Buddha.

Clothed in nothing but his necklace and a sheen of sweat, he felt the power surge through him. Stripping off his clothes had also stripped him of his mild, genial manner. Underneath, Boone was all steel limbs and mercury movement.

He held the knife between thumb and forefinger. Sighted through imaginary crosshairs on the spine of a book in the bookshelf in the far corner.

Slow pulling back. Lightning snap.

The long black obsidian blade flickered like an adder's tongue.

Bull's-eye.

Stood and walked. Returned.

He'd been doing this for hours, throwing his dagger into different surfaces, at different distances, different angles, cataloging each with a sense of urgency that had no mooring in anything but the act itself and what it represented.

The black blade's accuracy wasn't the point.

The point was the accuracy of Boone's mind. Weighing and balancing aerodynamic information.

The point was for Boone's mind to merge fully with all the elements involved in the projectile's flight. To become pure ballistics, only without the gunpowder and its attendant mess.

For the blade itself to disappear.

It was Boone's thoughts, not the sharpened obsidian, that penetrated the room's furnishings.

It was a meditation. A pathway to placid perfection.

Boone drew the knife back—and stopped.

Lowered the blade to the floor. Turned and picked up his phone.

It suddenly occurred to him: he had not contacted Papa Bear.

Really?

He thought back. No. He definitely had not contacted Papa Bear.

Twenty-four hours in-country and he hadn't phoned in.

Unbefuckinglievable.

He reached down, picked up the phone. Stared at it.

Ten hours had gone by. And Boone had been completely unaware of it. Had spent the entire fucking day in the zone, a state of hyperfocus his little orange pals helped him achieve and which was excellent for accomplishing those sorts of tasks Boone was regularly called upon to accomplish.

But it was ratshit for keeping track of time.

The Benalyn wasn't cutting it.

He needed to replace that lost stash.

The first time Boone took ketamine was under a doctor's supervision. It was pushed on him; the unit commander said Boone "needed therapy." Boone's view was that he needed therapy about as much as a cottonmouth needed Nikes.

Still, it was an illuminating experience.

They posted some woman in his room to serve as his, what, chaperone? Babysitter? As things got rolling Boone came to understand that this woman was Satan himself, come to test Boone, to wrestle with him. Which colored the experience. He didn't tell the doctor.

To this day, he was not entirely convinced he'd been wrong.

Boone didn't get any other insights from the therapy, but he did get ketamine.

Other guys said it made them disoriented, gave them hallucinations. Not Boone. No, sir. For Boone, it gave him just one thing: clarity.

Sheee-yit.

He touched the phone's screen.

Brought up a number.

Tapped out a message.

In country.

Hit SEND.

He should have done this twenty-four hours ago, when he first landed.

Papa Bear. What a fuckin' stupid handle. Like a bad spy movie. As if Boone didn't know the man's actual name.

Boone was not 100 percent impressed with Papa Bear's logistical performance. He'd already fucked up once. Back in mid-September he'd sent Boone to the dock in San Diego, where he'd waited three days for the opportunity to plunk a high-speed round into the little fucker's beano—and the little worm never even showed up.

Boone hated that.

Hated it when you put in the time, when you told the whole joke but never got to deliver the punch line. It was like switching off *Boléro* just before the big key change and explosion at the end. You walked away with one miserable case of blue balls.

Boone'd had to spend the next three months sniffing him out.

Boone was a professional. He never let his personal feelings on the matter, if he had any, color the situation. But goddam, his balls hurt.

bzzz!

He looked down at the phone.

A reply.

Fosshótel

"All-right-all-right-all-*riiight*," he murmured. Now he knew where the three were hanging their hats. Which meant that, sooner or later, Finn the Freak would show up.

When he did, Boone would be there, too.

At the Fosshótel. Fossss. Fosssssss

Fosssssssssss

Boone saw himself leap to his feet and stride to the front door . . . burst out of the little house into the cold and set off naked through the streets . . . saw himself running over the frozen cobblestones and lift off the ground, soaring through the air like a turkey vulture, grunting and hissing as it homed in on the Fossssssssss—

Dust motes hung in the air around him, mocking him as he sat motionless.

He glanced at the phone in his hand.

Another forty-five minutes had passed.

Shit.

Boone touched his necklace.

Took a breath.

Looked down at the obsidian blade by his feet.

"Whatcha waitin' fer, pilgrim?" he drawled.

He knew damn well what he was *waitin' fer*. Same damn thing he'd been *waitin' fer* since he started his damn routine hours earlier.

That sense of perfect balance.

It hadn't come.

He couldn't function like this.

Björn the waiter's drug dealer still had not replied to his texts.

The Fosshótel could wait.

Boone reached down and picked up the knife. The obsidian blade caught glints of light as he turned it in his hand.

He could have sworn it winked at him.

He smiled.

"Whaddya say, pilgrim? Think we got us a social call to pay."

41

Finn returned to the Fosshótel, but he knew he was too late. His chance to grab Tom alone was gone for the day.

He'd have to come back the next morning.

Now that he knew Tom was here, he had a pretty good idea as to who the other two would be. Peyton fit the vague description from Magnús's driver friend. And if Peyton was here, Dixon probably would be, too.

"The SEAL teams' own George and Lennie," as Kennedy put it once when no one else was around. Finn never forgot the image.

Peyton put up a swaggering, superior front, but he was nowhere near as smart as he thought he was and he orbited Dixon like an orphan moon. No atmosphere of his own.

Dixon was mean as a malarial mosquito. And smart, which made him dangerous.

Which meant a modification of plans. Now that he knew he was dealing with Dixon, he wasn't going busting into their suite. Not without the right equipment.

He spent the next two hours roaming hallways, riding elevators, walking the stairwells, learning the hotel's layout inside and out. Bumped into another housekeeper, intending to load his keycard scanner for future use—but at the last minute he changed his mind and instead lifted the passkey itself, which he pocketed after loading its code into the scanner. Not that he'd need it. But he didn't know where his encounter with his old teammates might lead, and his training had taught him that redundancy was the mother of good outcomes.

In plain English: *always have a backup*.

Groundwork fully laid, Finn was slipping out of the hotel when he heard someone call his name.

"Mister Pike."

Christ on stilts.

What was he, a goldfish in a bowl?

He turned.

It was the old Icelander, standing by a small couch in the lobby. Clearly intending for Finn to come over and join him.

In his peripheral vision he noted a man standing by the elevator, watching him. Dressed like a chauffeur but with the unmistakable bearing of a bodyguard.

He walked back through the lobby and over to where Tryggvi stood.

The old Icelander made no move to sit, so neither did Finn. Evidently they were going to conduct this conversation standing up.

"My people told me you were here."

His people.

His city.

Finn knew the type, had seen them, or evidence of them, in every city he walked. Men who believed that their amassed wealth and years of successful maneuvering gave them a kind of ownership of the realm. And they were not entirely wrong.

"I am aware that Miss Shevchenko has been following me," the man said. "I know of her suspicions. I do not blame her, nor does this surprise or offend me. I am a rich, old man, Mister Pike. The rich are always targets. Someone with all that money, all that power, cannot have accrued his wealth and station without having done bad things. So goes people's thinking."

Tryggvi shrugged. The gesture seemed slightly incongruous with his stiff bearing, as if he'd had to rehearse it in a mirror.

"I have no intention of approaching her, not now. She must be given time, given space, to grieve in her own way. She'll come to what peace she can in her own time. I have no wish to interfere. You might do well to follow my example."

He paused, giving Finn the space to reply.

Finn said nothing.

"The police seem to think you are, as you so delicately say in America, a person of interest. That is, there is at least one detective who seems to think so. Though I doubt the police will pursue this matter much further, which to me is a crime unto itself. They are distracted by a more"— he seemed to search for the right word—"a more *sensational* tragedy. Any moment, the media will catch hold of the scent, and it will then consume everyone's attention. I would suggest they've already all but forgotten about the Little Mermaid in the Ice."

He paused again, this time purely for emphasis.

"I have not."

He leaned in so close Finn could smell his breath. Old lamb and wood smoke.

"I don't know who you are, Marlin Pike. But if I were to snap my fingers, I would possess that knowledge by the time I sat down to breakfast tomorrow. You Americans, you think we're polite. We are not polite. Just tolerant. We have been here a very long time. But that tolerance has its limits."

It was pitch-black outside.

Finn took a left out the front entrance and thought about Tryggvi as he made for the cross street.

If Tryggvi believed he was involved in Kateryna's death, he would make a run at Finn with everything he had. And Finn suspected that the old Icelander had resources that went well beyond those of the police, beyond even those of Iceland's intel community, a private network with tendrils that reached everywhere. Maybe even into places like Yasenevo and Fairfax County.

Tryggvi had known that the detective had an interest in Finn, yet she would hardly have offered up that information herself.

And that comment, "They are distracted by a more sensational tragedy." Meaning the double homicide at the clinic. But that was still bottled up; no one outside the police (other than Finn himself, of course) had heard about that yet.

Yet Tryggvi knew.

Oksana was convinced that Tryggvi was behind her sister's death, and whether or not she admitted it, she wanted revenge. Or at least the justice she'd been denied in her parents' murder.

Tryggvi seemed to suspect Finn was somehow involved in the girl's death. And he, too, wanted retribution.

The detective was tracking Finn and suspected him of . . . well, whatever it was she suspected him of. Assault? Stalking? International terrorism?

And he'd blown off a chance to interrogate Tom in order to dig himself further into this mess.

Why, exactly, had he done that?

As he reached the cross street and took a right to walk back toward Parliament Hill, something drew his eye in the opposite direction.

He glanced up the street toward the harbor, through the gap between the Tower and the buildings on the opposite side of the street to the little gabled house by the coast. The house where Reagan and Gorbachev shook hands, the house a British ambassador had vacated a generation before because of bumps in the night.

The night was cold and clear as glass, the sky above laced with a spectral explosion of green and orange, a Christmas tree angel of electric ribbons and phosphorescent glitter.

The Northern Lights—hovering directly over the Höfði House.

Like a ghost.

42

I tell you about me. Why I follow him. What about you? Why do you follow me? Why do you care about any of this?

Alone in his stolen bolt-hole, surrounded by his surveillance sketches and the news photo of Kateryna's face staring up out of the ice, Finn asked himself this same question.

Why?

Why did he follow Oksana and blow his shot at getting Tom alone?

What was his deal with the dead girl? It had nothing to do with him.

He reached into his backpack and pulled out the Faraday bag. Checked for messages. Nothing from Stan. Nothing from Carol.

Have you slept?

He tapped out a quick text to stanl3099@gmail.com.

> Getting a little chilly in my room.

He switched off the phone and stashed it away again in its secure pouch, then sat at the tiny dining room table and opened Ragnar's laptop. Navigated to Gmail and started a draft, leaving both recipient and subject line blank.

> Have you seen this show on cable everyone's talking about? The Englishman. Seems to be a big thing here.

Saved it in the Drafts folder. Next time he checked, it would be deleted.

Getting a little chilly.

Meaning: *There's a draft.*

It was an old trick Finn had learned from civilian assets embedded in authoritarian regimes. Compose your email, but don't send it. Leave it in Drafts. Your contact had access to the same account. If you left something in the folder, your contact could see it without you ever having actually sent it. Less visible.

Though still not foolproof. So he and Stan still couched even their draft folder messages in some level of code.

He closed the laptop and thought about Carol.

Have you slept?

He couldn't remember what it felt like to really sleep.

He stood and walked back to the wall of sketches.

Why do you care about any of this?

Why did he need to know what happened in Mukalla? What was he looking for?

Justice?

Revenge?

No, Finn wasn't interested in revenge. To Finn, revenge was a fool's game, a pointless waste of energy. After all, if he believed in revenge, then by that logic he would be compelled to avenge his own brother's killer.

Which was Finn himself.

Their parents were gone, off on one of their save-the-world missions. Or maybe destroy-the-world missions. Finn was never clear on that. Left alone in that remote cabin in eastern Oregon, the two boys broke into their dad's gun closet to look at the guns.

A handgun went off.

It was in Finn's hand when it fired.

The first time Finn saved a life, he was fifteen.

The first time he took one, he was eight.

So, no, he didn't believe in revenge. And he wasn't big on "justice," either. From what he'd seen of the world, justice was generally in short supply.

What did he believe in?

He didn't have a clear answer to that question.

Finn had never been strong on understanding his own feelings, or even identifying them. Much of the time he was convinced he had no feelings at all. So what drove him? Why was he there in Iceland?

Carol, who knew him better than anyone else on earth, once said his driving force was *loyalty*.

Was that true?

Loyalty?

Maybe so. Maybe that was what brought him there to Reykjavík.

He really didn't know.

Did you see her, Rescue Swimmer?

It occurred to him that he believed in *rescue*. And that was something that predated his joining the service. He remembered as a teenager, rescuing that drowning kid off the Southern California beach. First time Finn ever saved a life.

And it happened again after that. He had taken lives. He had saved lives. Quite a few. That time on the beach, and on the battlefield dozens of times more. Even once in training.

There were also those he tried and failed to save, and every one left scars. Or maybe open wounds. He couldn't tell which.

Carol said his deep-rooted impulse for rescue had something to do with the fact that as a kid, no one ever rescued Finn.

His parents weren't there the day his brother died, and they weren't there when Finn was pulled out of that closet slaughterhouse in the Oregon woods and locked up in a hospital ward. And of the parade of agency reps and foster homes that blundered in and out of his life for years after that, not one had truly looked out for him. They'd each had their own angle.

Carol could have a point.

Though there had been a few exceptions.

There was the detective who pulled him out of that bloody hellhole. Finn didn't know his name, couldn't bring up the face, but he still remembered the smell of the man's wool hunting jacket and cigarettes, the soothing rusty-hinge sound of his voice.

And there was Kennedy.

At age eight, when he sealed off that horrific event in the gun closet, he'd sealed himself off, too. That was how Carol explained it anyway. They'd had him in that hospital for weeks. When he finally woke up, he screamed until they strapped him down and drugged him. He had no idea how long. Weeks.

"When you finally came out the other end, the part of you that went through that nightmare was sealed up like a bug under glass." So said Carol. Who knew him better than anyone on earth.

By the time he reached the SEAL teams, it felt to Finn that he had lost all connection to the human race. A balloon floating away into the sky.

Kennedy tethered him.

So, yeah. He owed Kennedy.

And he believed in rescue.

He looked up at the news photo of the girl's face, frozen in the ice, staring at him.

Like a bug under glass.

And wasn't that, right there, the answer to her sister's question.

Why?

Because he wanted to rescue her.

It sounded crazy, too crazy to say out loud. Still, there it was.

But rescue her how, exactly?

She was already dead.

43

He hummed as he stared nose-to-nose into the shaving mirror, watching years of facial hair fall away.

Iceland's national anthem—not the easiest tune to hum, but Ólafur had been a decent singer in his day. Back when his shop was popular and his business was flourishing. Or at least, when it did well enough to get by, to raise a family. To be happy. Before the boom and bust, before Iceland's banks all defaulted, before the worst economic collapse of any nation in recorded history.

And somehow, when the country rose from its ashes and astonished the world by rebuilding its economy, the Iceland Miracle had passed him by.

Shaving off his beard might give the appearance of turning back the clock, but Ólafur knew this was an illusion. A clean-shaven face couldn't bring back his wife. Couldn't reverse the collapse of his life, his descent into whatever this world was he was living in now.

Perhaps, though, it could give him a little boost in his pending encounter. A little credibility. Or at least a chance. A crack in the door.

Ólafur's wife was gone and buried more than a decade now, but he had a grown daughter who lived only a few miles away, in a nice little house on the western coast. Ólafur hadn't seen her in years, not since the crash.

And whose fault was that? His own, of course. Ólafur's life may have spiraled down the piss hole, but he had never stooped to blaming others. He still had some self-respect.

And finally, finally, he'd decided to take the risk. To make contact again, even to arrange a date to go see his daughter—and to meet his granddaughter!

The granddaughter he'd never seen.

"So far," he murmured. "Haven't seen *so far*."

It was never too late to turn the page and start a new story.

Tomorrow morning. Just hours away.

His shave complete, he took up a pair of scissors and trimmed his hair, doing his best to clean up his appearance in every way he could. Far from polished, but at least he didn't look quite so pathetic. He wanted his granddaughter's first glimpse of her *afi* to be as perfect as possible.

When he was satisfied with what he saw in the mirror, he turned and walked out of the bathroom and into the little hallway.

And stopped.

A man stood in his living room.

Ponytail, wire-rim glasses, round affable face. The kind of face that would put you instantly at ease.

Not that it put Ólafur at ease. Far from it. The opposite, in fact.

Because Ólafur knew at once who he was.

This was the man who'd sent that text, the one Ólafur had chosen not to respond to.

For all his weaknesses, and they were manifold, Ólafur was a shrewd judge of character. A terrible judge of the market, perhaps, but an instinctively good assayer of human beings.

One had to be, to stay safe in his current line of work.

The moment that text had popped up on the screen of his little phone, Ólafur had sensed this was someone from whom one would do well to keep one's distance.

And now that someone was right there, standing in Ólafur's living room.

"*Fyrirgefðu!*" the man said hastily, apologizing in Icelandic. He laughed merrily, then apologized a second time. He didn't mean to startle Ólafur, he explained. But he was in a hurry. "*Although I imagine you hear that a lot in your line of work,*" he added, still in Icelandic, and he laughed again.

There was something wrong with that laugh.

"What is it you seek?" Ólafur spoke in English. He didn't like the feeling of this man using his language.

"Well," the man began, in a drawl that made the word sound like *whale*. Or maybe *wail*. "Two things, matter fact, now that you ask."

Ólafur said nothing, wagering that the less he said, the sooner the man would leave.

"I understand you deal in a product I'd like to purchase, name of ketamine. I've got American dollars, Icelandic króna, PayPal, whatever floats your boat."

Ólafur strove to keep his face as neutral as possible, but he could not quite keep his eyes from darting in the direction of his hidden supply closet. Which the man of course noticed.

Ólafur cleared his throat. "And the second thing?"

"I expect a man of your trade comes into contact with all manner of travelers in the course of his day. I'm wondering if you may have made the acquaintance of a certain American, last couple days. Late thirties. Kinda squarish face, big eyes. Odd-looking fella, like a meerkat, or maybe a possum. Not that I guess you folks have any such creatures here in your little island habitat."

Ólafur did not want to give this man any information. He knew that if he did, it would bring Marlin misfortune. Marlin had seemed like a decent sort.

He frowned for a moment, as if thinking it over, then gave a slow shake of the head. "No," he said. "I don't believe I've seen anyone fitting that description."

The man looked at Ólafur, his expression a complete blank.

Ólafur could tell the man knew he was lying.

"Now, if someone were to come by asking about me, Ólafur, what would you say?"

"I will say nothing. I—I never met you."

The man took a step closer, still looking right at Ólafur.

"Y'all have an honest face," he said.

The way he said it made it sound like the most degrading insult imaginable.

Then the man's face changed.

It broke open in a wide grin, but the grin was all wrong. There were strange gaps in the teeth. The pupils were tiny and dancing, like jittering little insects. The overall effect was nauseating.

Ólafur closed his eyes.

He'd known the face would do that the minute he first saw it.

Somehow he'd known it when he first read the man's text.

When he felt the bony hand grab his throat with the strength of a steel vise-grip, Ólafur wasn't ready.

He did his best to hold his focus on the image in his mind's eye of the little girl with the long blond hair.

"Ólafur." The man's voice was soft and steady. "Open your eyes."

This Ólafur would not do. He kept his focus on the little girl, her long blond hair, her laughing eyes.

"Ólafur," the man repeated. "I'll be needing your left arm, pard."

Eyes closed tight, mind's eye on the laughing girl, maybe playing jump rope, he held out his arm. He knew it would only be worse if he didn't. No need for the ghoul to tell him that.

The grip on his throat released, but Ólafur didn't cry out or call for help. It would be futile. They both knew it.

Now he felt the vise grip clamp onto his arm at the wrist, turning it so that the inside of the arm was facing up.

When the tip of the blade punctured his skin at the elbow, he let out a gasp, then held his breath, and he kept holding it as the knife point slit its way slowly up the length of his arm.

As the river of blood swelled, spilled over its banks, and flowed into the floor, Ólafur did his best not to scream.

He wished he'd gone to meet his granddaughter just one day earlier.

Thursday

Colder; wind with gusts up to 30 knots.

44

The crown jewel of Iceland's most prestigious hotel chain, the Fosshótel Reykjavík was built out of two tiered structures, like a huge two-step ziggurat. The lower, main portion housed a world-class restaurant, an upscale pub featuring premium beers from around the world, a two-story gym, the obligatory conference rooms, and seven stories of 4-star guest rooms. At the hotel's back side, the second tier climbed an additional ten stories, providing the seven luxury suites on the topmost floor with one of the best views in the city.

The Tower's roof stood 192 feet from ground level. The distance from that point down to the flat roof of the lower structure was approximately ninety-eight feet. Which meant the body would have traveled for about two and a half seconds, reaching a velocity of roughly eighty feet per second by the time of impact.

Eighty feet per second was a lot of impact.

At eight o'clock on Thursday morning, the location where that impact occurred was now lit up by Klieg lights as uniformed Lögreglan officers moved quietly around the crumpled form lying bloodied in the snow, half-buried in drifts piled up by fierce overnight winds.

The senior detective on the scene stood over the body, morose and irritated.

"Fuck," she pronounced.

Down at street level, a crowd of reporters, camera operators, bath-robed and sleepy-eyed hotel guests, and random passing pedestrians stood massing outside the lobby, craning their necks and staring seven floors up, trying to catch a glimpse of whatever was going on up there.

It was freakishly reminiscent of the scene at the duck pond Christmas morning—only this was a grotesque parody of that other tableau, this death displayed on a rooftop, like the stage at the Harpa concert hall, its audience spread out below, beyond the footlights.

They should charge admission.

Krista heard the soft crunch of footsteps on the crisp snow.

"Fall, or jump?" murmured Danni as he came up beside her.

She looked up ten stories to the floor where the man had been staying. Not the top floor but the next one down. Those windows opened only enough to let in fresh air, but a grown man could conceivably force one open a bit farther and slip through. Or could he have been up on the building's roof?

She shrugged.

Fall, or jump?

Krista didn't know which would be worse. If he fell, the hotel was in big trouble. If he jumped, the Iceland Tourism Commission was in big trouble. Either way the media was in full-blown outrage heaven—and she was fucked.

"Tell me he wasn't trying to get a selfie," she muttered.

Danni chuckled quietly.

His ID said he was American. Of course he was. Another one thinking they were invulnerable. Had the man actually ventured out onto the roof? In these high winds? Idiot.

Unless, of course, he was pushed. She sighed. *Krista, Krista,* her grandfather would have said if he were here. *Only you would think such dark thoughts.*

She nodded to the pathologist kneeling by the body. "Let me know if all his teeth are there."

The pathologist looked up at her, frowning. "Teeth?" He noted her scowl, murmured, "Yes, Krista," and bent back to his work.

Krista walked with Danni to the edge of the roof and looked down at the milling crowd. The media were clamoring for a statement. And Einar wasn't there.

Damn him.

Fuck, she hated this.

Danni nodded at the reporters. "I'll talk with them. You take the two friends." They both watched as a young officer steered the two Americans carefully away from the crowd and around to the side of the building, no doubt expecting one of them to come down and take it from there.

"Oh, for God's sake," said Danni. "Why does he have them down there, and not up in their rooms?"

Krista recognized the officer. Jón, of course.

"To avoid having them contaminate the crime scene, I imagine," she said drily. She glanced at Danni and added, "He's just a kid."

Danni looked at her, as if about to say something, then turned away.

The two detectives withdrew from the roof's edge and headed for the safety door, which had been propped open with a cinder block. As they walked she pulled out her phone and punched in a number; her fingers knew the sequence by feel. A ring, followed by another, and another, and a fourth, then:

"This is Einar. I'm occupied right now, solving the crime of the century . . ."

Voicemail.

Of course.

"Einar," she said after the requisite beep, "don't be an asshole. Let me amend that. You *are* an asshole. But you don't have to sulk like an asshole."

She clicked off.

It wasn't the first time he'd taken a "sick day" out of pure pique. But this was Grand Sulk, Day Two. And in the worst possible week of either of their careers.

Dead girl in the duck pond on Christmas day, body missing (just the thought of it hurt her brain), her own boss pushing back on her investigation. Double murder at the clinic, so far unsolved. Now a dead American tourist at the Foss—and after this she and Danni would be heading over to poor Ólafur's miserable squat to see what little sense they could make out of yet another wretched death.

And this was the week her partner picked to stay home from work?

When he did eventually slink back in, she might just push him off a building herself.

45

Finn stood watching, his anonymity secured by the
crowd around him, thinking through his next steps.

If he'd acted on the opportunity to confront Tom when it presented
itself the day before, he might well be already on a plane over the Atlantic. As it was, that particular window was now closed for good. There'd
be no asking Tom.

Not today, not ever.

Now the interrogation would not be quite so easy.

In the thick of the media gaggle he spotted Ben the photojournalist,
Mister No-Milk-Just-Plain, craning his neck along with the rest. So
much for the clean life, out in the wilds shooting zoom-lens video clips
of the Arctic fox in its natural habitat. Ben from Winnipeg was on the
hunt for a sensational byline, just like every other journalist there.

He sidestepped to the far side of the crowd, farther away from the
man.

As he moved, a delivery truck rumbled slowly through the crowd,
people parting like a school of fish and regrouping around it again as it
passed. Finn flowed with them.

He caught a glimpse of a young officer leading two men, presumably
hotel guests, out of the lobby and around to the far side of the building.

Two men he recognized.

It was Peyton and Dixon, all right.

The SEAL teams' own George and Lennie.

He watched them walk. Though Peyton was the weaker-minded of the two, he covered it well with practiced poise and a glib vocabulary. Wealthy family, Ivy League, athletic. Impressed with his own good looks. But basically a follower. No real convictions of his own. The kind of guy who drew his identity from being near the center of power. In the Teams they called him "GQ."

Dixon was the veteran ringleader. Southern boy, violent and greedy. They called him "Rat."

Tomboy, GQ, and Rat. All three of them part of third squad that night. The one supposedly hanging back to cover their flanks.

Glancing up, Finn spotted Krista the detective, peering over the roof's edge and down at the crowd.

One of his cellphones buzzed. He felt with his thumb. A single notch: the Magnús phone. He picked up but said nothing.

"Hope I didn't wake you." The voice made a brief indistinct rumbling sound. It took Finn a moment to recognize it as laughter.

Now Krista was talking with the thin man next to her. Another detective, judging by the collegial body language.

"Hello?" said Magnús.

"I'm here."

Collegial, but Finn saw some kind of tension there. Not as tight a team as they ought to be.

"I have sad news about our friend in the distribution business," Magnús reported. Meaning Ólafur the old drug dealer. The taxi driver had taken to his new role and developed a penchant for talking like a character in a crime novel. "He has breathed his last. Slit up his wrists in the night."

"Okay."

The two detectives had now disappeared from the edge.

"Also," Magnús rumbled on, "before he crashed and did himself in, the man had a little cocaine party and went a little crazy. Place was torn to piecemeal. Chairs, table, bed. He did not own much, but what little he had was all smashed to toothsticks."

"Okay," Finn said again.

He clicked off, watching the action as he did.

The two detectives emerged from the lobby now, the man striding toward the media huddle, no doubt to make a statement, which interested Finn not at all. If it was for the press, it would be devoid of useful content.

The other one, Krista, was now by the side of the building, talking to Peyton and Dixon.

Now she was ushering the three of them to go inside, no doubt to question them.

Finn would have to wait his turn.

The crowd surged forward to hear the thin detective's statement. Finn surged with them.

He thought about Ólafur, the Hlemmur Square sage whose ship had sailed its final lonely passage out to sea. Who drank, but didn't use. Whose inclination to rage and violent outburst, it seemed to Finn, hovered at close to zero.

Torn to piecemeal. Smashed to toothsticks.

Magnús would win no awards for his mastery of English, but Finn got the general idea.

Slit up his wrists in the night. Had a little cocaine party.

Finn knew better.

And now the murder at the clinic Tuesday night made sense.

Lead pipe to the head, suicide in a junkie's den, fall from a high place: the assassin's holy trinity. All designed *not* to look like the work of a professional.

Only thing missing was a car crash.

Except that whoever did it had gone a little overboard in the drug dealer's place. Carefully choreographed execution in conjunction with over-the-top violence.

A signature of sorts.

Boone was here.

The crowd fell back, aimless and impatient, Finn moving with them.

So it was Boone they'd had waiting at the dock in San Diego the past September to meet the USS *Abraham Lincoln*, the carrier Finn was supposed to be on. His welcoming committee.

He had known they would send someone after him. Someone outside the normal channels. And he knew who sent him. The same people responsible for the Mukalla cover-up.

The same people who, with a quiet nod and a few murmured words, signed Kennedy's death warrant.

Now Finn had two parties on his trail. A DIA team. And a former SEAL turned contract killer.

If they wanted Finn gone, whoever "they" was, they couldn't have tapped a better man for the job.

The two had known each other vaguely during training, served together for a few tours in Iraq. Boone was a corpsman who was endlessly fascinated by injuries, especially those of the mortal kind. Healing them, inflicting them, he didn't seem to care which, so long as he could be there to observe what happened.

In Finn's experience there were two kinds of corpsmen in the service. One was the guy who gravitated to the role because he actually wanted to take care of people. The other kind treated you like a farm animal—looked you over, punched a needle in your arm, and said, "I gave you a local, now shut the fuck up and hold still while I stitch you up."

The first kind took to medicine as a calling; the second took it as a job.

Boone was the second kind.

Still, he'd saved Finn's life once. One of Finn's teammates had stepped on the wrong patch of dirt and been blown to bone fragments. Finn was positioned far enough from the blast not to suffer fatal injuries, but close enough for it to punch a chunk of shrapnel through his right shoulder and concuss the shit out of him. Severed his left subclavian artery, would have bled to death on his own. Still had a massive scar to show for it. Boone clamped the artery, dragged him two miles to safety.

Though Finn could never tell if Boone was relieved that he pulled through, or disappointed.

Probably neither one. Probably just watching to see what happened, like a middle-school boy studying a bug.

Saved his life.

Now here to take it back.

Finn shifted with the crowd as it made way for a meat wagon, there to give Tom an escort to his chilly new digs at Pathology. As he moved, he thought about the sequence.

The clinic Tuesday.

Ólafur Wednesday.

No question. Boone was waist-deep in some haywire drug cycle. Not heroin or oxy, not cocaine. Not practical, not here. Probably Adderall and some industrial-strength downer. Ketamine maybe. Hell of a spin cycle.

A gust of frigid wind swept through the crowd.

Finn felt a faint stirring at the back of his neck.

Like a static charge in the air.

He scanned the perimeter.

Boone was probably right there, right now, scanning the crowd for signs of Finn.

Moses blows us.

All at once he felt more exposed than ever.

Evading a DIA team was one thing. All they wanted to do with Finn was quietly arrest him, lock him up, maybe throw away the key. The people who sent Boone were different.

They weren't looking to lock him up.

From up the street a bus approached, passing the Storm Hotel a few doors away and slowing to a halt at the curbside bus stop by the antique store directly across from the Fosshótel to discharge a few passengers, then rumbled on past.

The crowd parted, then merged again.

Finn had vanished.

46

The three rode up the elevator in total silence. The only words exchanged between them so far had been a single sentence, spoken by Krista upon being introduced to them out by the side of the hotel:

"We should talk inside."

Now she stood between the two, all three mutely facing the elevator doors as they rose. That she had placed herself between them was not an accident; she preferred to keep them as isolated as possible.

A trained observer could of course pick up reams of information from the way a person spoke, the words they chose, the topics they plunged into and those they avoided, the pacing and tone of their speech, the cant of their head, the look in their eyes, all this and more.

But there were things to be learned from people's silence, too. In some ways, more revealing. Particularly with foreigners. Icelanders were by nature experts in silence. Americans, and to a lesser extent Europeans, found silence uncomfortable and would invariably rush to fill it.

Not these two.

On the outside, the dead man's two friends were horrified, in shock, just beginning their long slide into what would become a deep lagoon of grief. At least that was what their exterior conveyed.

Yet they betrayed none of the typical signals of extreme stress—the uneasy shifting of position, the dry-swallowing, the ragged, uneven breathing. None of it. They were, as Einar might put it, *cool as cucumbers.*

An officer stood sentry outside the door, standing straighter as they approached from down the hallway. Placed there by the ever-eager Jón, no doubt. (*Bright-eyed and bushy-tailed.*) Krista dismissed him with a nod and ushered the two Americans into their own suite.

With another nod, she indicated that they should proceed through to the living room area for their interview. She put the two side by side in the two-seater couch, their backs to the windows, and placed herself facing them in one of the room's café chairs, putting her seat a good three inches higher than theirs.

Now she took a moment to look at them. The handsome smug one and the wily-looking one with the pinched features.

She strapped on a smile.

"So," she said. "Let's start from the top. What exactly are you doing here in Iceland?"

The elevator ride down was as silent as the ride up, only this time because Krista had the car to herself. The descent went quickly. She wished it would take longer. The interview had been brief, but there was a lot to think about.

The two had no idea what happened. Of course not.

They were in shock, stunned, horrified. Of course they were.

They were there in Iceland for a week's fun vacation. Take in the sights. Ring in the New Year with Reykjavík's famous fireworks. Had no idea how this could have happened. Or even exactly what *had* happened. They'd all gone to sleep the night before, and when they woke up this morning, their friend Tom was just . . . gone.

Yes, he'd seemed fine, totally normal.

No, he hadn't been depressed, nor anxious. No, there was no trouble at home, nothing like that.

No, they didn't hear a thing.

Of course not.

When she'd pulled out the surveillance photo of the girl running through the street and showed it to them—this was, after all, the direction the girl had been running from, and the three Americans were staying right there on Christmas Eve—they seemed genuinely puzzled. What did this girl have to do with anything?

No, they hadn't seen her.

When she asked them to take a second look, to see if there was any chance, any chance at all, that they might have seen someone answering this description, she sensed pushback, a faint defensiveness. Hostility, almost. Yet with no specificity to the bristling, no distinct denial underneath it. Like maybe they'd done a lot of things to a lot of girls, but none of them to this girl in particular.

They didn't ask who she was. They didn't ask anything. Which was unusual, in her experience.

And they were in good shape. Better than good. Certainly more than your typical weekend warrior or ski-bum tourist. More like trained warriors.

Like Marlin.

Her descent bumped to a stop. The elevator doors slid open. She stepped out into the lobby and veered off to the side, sequestering herself for a moment in the hotel's cozy reading nook, where she murmured a brief summary of the interview into her phone.

Still thinking about Marlin, she then placed a call to Ragnar Björnsson.

Two rings . . . a voice.

"It's Ragnar here, it's you there—you know what to do."

Voicemail.

Krista hated voicemail.

"Ragnar, this is Krista Kristjánsdóttir again, with Lögreglan, Thursday morning. I know you're on holiday, but I'd really like to speak with you at your earliest."

She shook her head as she pocketed the phone. Four days without answering his voicemail. She felt a twinge of annoyance and was surprised to recognize it as envy. She'd always thought these young buck finance guys lived tethered to their phones (like Einar!), and if she were honest with herself, she looked down on them for it. But wasn't it really she who'd become tethered to the damn thing?

She emerged from the hotel's revolving-door front entrance, took two steps, and stopped, stung by the eerie sensation of being watched. Not just by the thinning crowd out front, but by someone specific.

As if through a telescope.

Her phone buzzed.

Number not recognized

She picked up.

"*I can give you a description,*" the voice said.

47

"I can give you a description," Finn said softly into the phone as he watched her out the window. It was burner phone #2, the Ólafur phone. He'd just finished deleting the man's number and their brief text thread. He wouldn't be using it to communicate with Ólafur anymore.

The detective stood stock-still, standing just outside the hotel lobby, her breath a white nimbus billowing up around her head.

"Of the dead guy?" her voice said in his ear. "Don't need it. I've just seen him."

"Of the guy who pushed him."

Still riveted to her spot, the woman began slowly scanning the area in front of her, searching each face in the crowd. Searching for him.

"What makes you think he was pushed?" she said.

"Six one," said Finn. "Sandy blond hair, usually wears it in a ponytail."

"Where are you, Pike?"

"Hippie glasses," he continued. "Round face. A face you'd trust your children with. And it would be the worst mistake you ever made."

A brief silence. She peered to her right up the street, past the Storm Hotel, then back in the opposite direction. "And you've seen him here?"

"He's here."

An officer approached the detective and she shushed him with her open palm, then held up one finger. *Give me a moment here.* "And what makes you think—"

"It was him."

The detective was silent, thinking. Phone still glued to her ear, she started walking out into the street.

"Same man who killed your favorite drug dealer," Finn added. "And the two at the clinic."

She stopped walking.

From his vantage point across the street and three floors up, Finn could see what she was thinking. *How the hell does he know about the murders at the clinic? And Ólafur?*

He heard her take a slow breath. Watched as she put her head down, free hand to the back of her head. Thinking fast and hard.

"You know how many murders we have per year, Marlin Pike? On average? One or two. In the entire country. Some years, none at all. You know when was the last time we had a serial killer in Iceland?"

He watched her slowly turn and look back up at the big hotel. Scanning the windows. Looking for signs of him.

"I'm guessing not recently," said Finn.

"Sixteenth century."

"Your victims at the clinic yesterday. Were they missing their canine teeth?"

He heard a sharp intake of breath.

How did you know that?

Krista's mind was racing at 100 miles per hour. For a minute she said nothing, just turned slowly, rotating a full 360 degrees as if to take in the entire city.

Where was he?

"Marlin Pike," she finally said. "Can you see the harbor from where you are?"

"His name, his real name, is Boone," said the voice on the phone. "No idea what name he's using right now."

"You're not hearing me," she said.

"Don't bother looking at hotels. He won't be there. He'll take over a resident's home, stay as close as possible to zero footprint."

"Like you?"

Silence on the other end.

She nodded to Danni and the others who were waiting, indicating that they should go on ahead without her. They started off down the street. It was only a three-block walk back to Hlemmur Square, another few blocks to poor Ólafur's squat.

"How do you know this Boone?" she said.

More silence.

"If you can see the harbor, look at the mountain across the bay, due northwest. More than a hundred kilometers away, but it's visible. You see it?"

No answer.

From where she stood, down at street level, her own view was blocked by the other buildings—but she had no trouble seeing it in her mind's eye. Clear as crystal.

"Snæfellsjökull," she said. "It means *snowfall glacier*. A volcano, covered in ice."

"Jules Verne," the voice said. "*Journey to the Center of the Earth.*"

Ah. So Americans did read. Or at least this one did.

Her mind kept spinning hard.

If he could see the volcano, he would be behind her, up in the hotel's tower structure. But then he wouldn't have seen her as she first emerged from the lobby's revolving door.

Her best guess, he would have taken up a frontal position, where he could surveil the whole scene. For what reason she had no clue, but that seemed to her the logical positioning.

"I just came from talking to your friends," she said.

"Not my friends."

"Who is 'the Englishman,' Pike?"

No reply.

"I don't know why your friends are here. I don't know why one of them is now a smear of jelly on our hotel roof. I don't know what you're doing here in my country, Rescue Swimmer. But I'll tell you a few things I do know."

She turned back to face the hotel again and to resume slowly scanning the upper-floor windows.

Or at least to give the appearance of doing so.

Directly behind her, three floors of small office spaces sat above the antique shop across the street. She knew these spaces. Only one was empty. On the far right, closest to the stairwell. The windows were impossible to see in against the daytime reflection.

That's where Marlin Pike was. Had to be.

But if she crossed the street in that direction and entered the building, he'd be gone before she reached the stairwell.

She had to go about this strategically.

"Reason I ask about the teeth," the voice in her ear was saying, "Boone has a thing about canines. He has this belief that they're an atrocity, an evolutionary holdover from caveman days. So he takes them. Don't ask me to explain the logic of it. And you don't ever want to see the man smile, but if you do, you'll notice there's something strange about it."

She couldn't not ask. "Strange, how?"

No answer.

"You're telling me . . . he had his own canines extracted?"

"Took them out himself. With his knife and a pair of dental forceps."

She shuddered.

"If you go looking for him," the voice continued, "you want to find him before he finds you. And don't go alone."

"This may come as a shock, but I'm actually competent at my job."

No answer.

"Listen to me, Pike. I know you and your—"

"Be careful, Detective," the voice said, and the line disconnected.

Krista took the phone from her ear and stared down at it in her hand.

The son of a bitch hung up on her!

"Oh, no you don't, you fucker," she muttered, stabbing her forefinger at the goddam phone screen.

She succeeded in bringing up the "Number not recognized" and hit DIAL.

Finn saw the incoming number and almost smiled. Persistent. Good.

He hit the TALK button to connect the call, but said nothing.

"You asked why I don't like Americans," the detective continued as if there'd been no interruption at all. "I'll tell you. To you, Snæfellsjökull is a famous volcano, a curiosity. To us, it's our guardian. Our protector.

When I was a girl, America was like that, standing guard over our little island nation. When I was a girl, I worshipped America."

He could hear the intensity in her voice. She wasn't bullshitting, at least not about this part.

"I grew up in the middle of the Cold War. We always turned a neutral face to the world, but we understood who were our enemies, and who were our friends."

He saw her turn and walk away, following the direction her colleagues had taken. Leaving the scene. But still talking to him on her phone.

Playing him.

Finn put her on speakerphone, then sat down, his back to the room's front wall, and opened his backpack. As she continued talking, he withdrew the two disposable cameras he'd purchased on his first day there, followed by the small screwdriver, wire stripper, length of insulated wire, and four small screws.

"*Most Americans today don't even know where Iceland is,*" Krista continued, the intensity coming through despite the tinny sound of the instrument's cheap speakerphone. "*You know Björk and volcanoes. We are a dot on the map. But we are the key to the north. Tom Clancy understood this. He wrote about a World War Three between the Soviets and NATO forces. And you know what the turning point was—the geopolitical hinge upon which victory turned?*"

Finn knew. He'd read *Red Storm Rising*. He had a sense where she was going with this. *An unsinkable aircraft carrier in the middle of the North Atlantic.*

But he kept silent. Let her talk.

He needed to focus.

He stripped off the cheap cardboard housing from the first camera, then carefully removed the circuit board, flash, film, and battery.

This was a delicate procedure. As a teenager, he watched another kid electrocute himself trying it.

"*It came down to which superpower controlled Iceland. Which worked out fine in the novel, because you did. America did. Except that fifteen years ago, you pulled out all your forces. You lost sight of the big picture, Rescue Swimmer. You, America, you took your eye off the ball. You broke my heart.*"

He clipped the length of electrical wire into two shorter lengths, clipped one of those in half again, then stripped each of the shorter pieces at both ends.

Next, he wrapped the ends of those two wires around the heads of two of the screws, then began twisting the screws into the camera housing, right at the spot where the film roll had sat.

"For the past two decades, while you focused on your 'war on terror,' exhausting your military resources and the political will to wield them, the real threat sat quietly watching. You thought Russian aggression was dead after the Soviet state collapsed—but it wasn't dead, it was regrouping. And you went right on squandering your finest. You bled out. As Russia gathered strength, you did the opposite. And then?

"And then the North Pole melted."

Now came the delicate part. One at a time, he needed to wrap the opposite ends of the two tiny wires to the two capacitor posts, avoiding any contact with the capacitor itself, which would reroute the charge from the camera's battery into the two protruding screws.

This was the step where his teenage acquaintance had gotten fried.

"Remember Snæfellsjökull, Pike? Our volcano covered in ice? Ten years ago, for the first time in history, the ice on the summit was gone. All volcano. No ice.

"And suddenly, you needed us again.

"We didn't matter as long as everything was about the Middle East. But now Arctic shipping lanes are opening up. You know how many icebreakers Russia has? A fleet of fifty. You know how many America has? Three— and two of those are nearing their expiration date."

The wire ends now snugged tight on the capacitor posts, Finn began securing them with bits of tape he'd scrounged from Ragnar's kitchen.

He didn't disagree with anything the detective was saying. And she was sounding a hell of a lot like Oksana, the history professor. *Those two should work together,* he thought. But they were both too independent, too untrusting.

He could relate.

He remounted the circuit board back in the camera, then snipped off a short piece of the discarded film and slipped it in between battery and battery terminal post, to keep the thing from accidentally discharging before he was ready. He hoped.

"Clancy was right. If conventional war should break out, it won't happen in the Middle East, or in Asia. It will happen right here, up in the north. And you know who sits in the northern gap between Russia and North America? Iceland. That's who."

Finn went to work on the second camera.

Snip!

There it was again. What the hell was that?

Less than a minute after she'd started walking away, Krista had heard a faint *snip!* then another. And now, a third. Like small wire cutters.

What was he doing up there, building a bomb?

For half a moment she regretted not bringing Danni with her as backup.

"So now here comes America again," she continued into the phone as she walked, "hat in hand, wanting to rebuild your air base here—but you have to tread on eggshells, because it's not so easy, trying to put that particular toothpaste back into the tube."

She was behind the building now, circling around to the back entrance that would bring her to the enclosed stairwell.

"And now here *you* are, you and your two buddies and their dead friend. Special forces, paramilitary, black ops, whatever you are. You know what will happen if anyone realizes you're here? Uncovers whatever it is you're really doing here?"

Silence.

What was he doing?

"When the Icelandic people protest, they protest hard," Krista continued. "They don't just hold up signs and give speeches. They toss out the entire government and put in a new one. And the new one they put in won't be so accommodating to American troops and your NATO friends. The people get wind of who you and your friends are, they will rise up and say 'Fuck No' to America. No alliance. No air base. No American presence.

"And then Russia will have North America by the balls. Look at Crimea. We are the Crimea of the north."

There was still silence on the other end, but she could sense Marlin Pike there, listening. She was now halfway up the staircase. She lowered her voice, growing progressively quieter as she ascended.

"You know this one, Pike?

"For want of a nail, the shoe was lost.

"For want of a shoe, the horse was lost.

"For want of a horse, the battle was lost.

"For want of a win, the kingdom was lost—

"And all for the want of a nail."

She stood at the door, feeling his presence on the other side.

"We are that nail, Marlin Pike," she whispered. "Whatever it is you're doing here, don't fuck it up."

If this were one of Einar's American TV shows she would now kick open the door and burst into the room, her sidearm held out in front of her with both hands, and yell "Freeze!" But this wasn't TV, she wasn't an American cop, and Lögreglan officers carried no firearms.

Though neither did Pike. At least she hoped not.

She took a breath, then pushed open the door and shouted, "Pike!"

And heard her own voice, tinny and small, echoing—

"PIKE!"

"Pike?" she repeated, scanning the darkened room.

"PIKE?" the echo mocked.

She stepped to the front window, overlooking the street. On the ledge there sat a phone, its screen emitting a pale green light. She picked it up. On the screen, a note in bold.

It's not easy, flying solo.
Watch your six.

She looked back at her own phone.

The call was still connected.

But the caller was in the wind.

48

When Boone was a kid, he used to take little scraps of stripped-off tire treads, light 'em on fire, and drop 'em on ants' nests, watch the little fuckers skitter in all directions as the thing burned. He could watch them for hours, if they'd keep it up that long, which of course they wouldn't, but there were always more ants' nests and more tire treads.

Once he got into the service, he did it there, too. Stir things up, and watch. And no one ever complained, because Boone got results. It was one of his favorite moves. Dial up the heat a little, tighten the screws, squash a few people, and see what happened. You learned things, usually useful things.

Like right now, for instance.

The lady detective had spent the last twenty minutes slowly skittering. Circling the AO, searching her perimeter. Looking for Finn. Sure as Shinola. She'd made the connection between Finn and the three in the hotel.

"Good for you, little lady," he whispered.

Lying prone in the snow on the roof of the Storm Hotel, Boone peered through his spotting scope and smiled a secret smile.

This would make his job just that much easier.

The three SEALs didn't have Clue One where Finn was. Didn't even know he was in town. Tom had made that clear as the Kentucky sky. A man tends to come clean with what he does and don't know when he's dangling off a sixteen-story building and can tell you ain't bluffing.

Boone never bluffed.

"Truth'll set you free, man. John eight thirty-two. Just tell us where our good buddy Chief Finn is hanging his hat."

"I don't know!" Tom had shrieked into the wind. "Honest to God, I don't know!"

"C'mon, pilgrim, you can do it. C'mon now. Spill, or you drop."

"I DON'T FUCKING KNOW!"

Turned out old Tom couldn't answer Boone's question, because he truly hadn't fucking known. But that was old Tom's problem, not Boone's.

He didn't spill.

So he dropped.

Stir up the ants' nest a little, see which way they skitter.

See what he could learn.

The damnable thing about it was, he was sure Finn was there somewhere, right now, watching all this. Boone could feel it. But could he see him?

No, sir. He could not.

For a moment there he'd caught a glimpse of someone in the crowd who *might* have been Finn. But then a bus had passed through and—poof!—little fucker was gone.

If he'd really been there at all.

The three SEALs in the hotel were the kind of smart that showed up as dumb sometimes. Oh sure, they'd taken care not to be seen by the target they were hunting. Surveillance one oh one. But that wasn't their greatest vulnerability. No, sir. Being burned by your target, that wasn't how missions got blown. Of those surveillance teams that fucked up, nine out of ten were burned not by the targets they were tracking but by some unseen third party. Someone they didn't even know was there.

Someone stalking the stalkers.

The three SEALs had either forgotten that basic rule or just been plain sloppy. So they hadn't been hard to find. Schoolboy stuff.

Not Finn, though. Little weevil knew every goddam thing there was to know about evading detection. Even if the little freak were standing right there, forty feet away, Boone probably wouldn't see him. That little stream of piss could melt into the scenery like water on sand.

Boone knew his limitations. If it came down to physical combat, he could crush Finn like a bug. But he was no match for the little weevil when it came to stalking and evasion. He had no idear where the little tick had dug himself in.

And Papa Bear's intel channels were silent on that question.

Which was why he needed to stir up the ants' nest.

And he'd found himself just the right ant to watch.

It looked like she was leaving the AO altogether, heading out to meet up with her team. Probably on their way to the drug dealer's place. More skittering ants.

Boone'd been pretty sure that exfil was a feint, though, so he'd scuttled over to the back of the Storm building, repositioned himself at the rear lip of the roof, raised his spotting scope again, and watched.

One minute. Two minutes. Two and a half.

And sure as dog shit on your shoe, there she came, sneaking around the back of the antique store building.

Skitter skitter skitter.

Boone didn't bother following her in. Finn'd be well and gone by that point. And sure enough, out she came again five minutes later, empty-handed.

The lady cop was good, though. You could see that from a hot-air balloon a mile away. And here was the thing: she had local resources that Boone didn't have. CCTV footage, a network of cops, probably the country's entire intel and security forces. Yeah, good as Finn was, she'd figure out where he was staying, Boone'd lay odds on it.

And Boone would be right there with her when she did.

Right at that moment, as if she'd heard his thoughts, the lady cop looked up at the rooftop of the Storm fuckin' Hotel, as if she were looking straight at him. Fuckin' spooky. But no. Now her eyes were moving on, scanning everywhere.

She was looking up at the back of every building in the area, doing a 360-degree horizon scan.

And now she was walking away, headed back toward the Square, for real this time, Boone's guess was.

All righty, then. Time to go to work.

He fished another orange pill from his breast pocket and popped it, swallowed it with snow scooped from the roof, thought about it for two seconds, then fished out and swallowed another. Then down the back wall of the Storm Hotel to follow after her.

Damn, but he did love his work.

49

Finn waited in a third-floor supply closet of the Fosshótel for another fifteen minutes, just long enough to make sure any remaining police presence had fully cleared out, then took the elevator up
to the sixteenth floor and stepped out into the hallway.

Looked up and down the hall. No Lögreglan. No foot traffic. It was
too early for linen service up in the Tower. He was alone.

He walked softly down the hallway toward the end, stopping at the
suite number he'd pulled from Krista's brief interview summary. Listened at the door. Two voices, not enough to make out the words, but
enough to know they were there.

He let himself in with his keycard scanner, leaving the PRIVACY sign
hung out on the doorknob, and silently shut the door behind him, then
strode into the living room where the two SEALs sat talking through
their next move. "Gents," he said without breaking his stride.

He took advantage of their split second of surprise and confusion to
whip out the two doctored cameras, one in each hand. Peyton had just
managed to get out a "The fuck *you* doing here?" when Finn jammed the
two protruding pairs of screws against their necks and pressed both
flash buttons at once.

A loud *Zap!* shot through the room, accompanied by the acrid stench
of burning flesh as the cameras' stored charge hit both men with 200
volts.

The bolt radiated through their tissue and nerves, generating a static
charge that shut down their internal communication systems and left

them collapsed on the floor, convulsed with involuntary muscle contractions.

Finn tossed the cameras aside, knelt down and hog-tied both men with zip ties, then positioned them so that they were lying on their sides, facing away from each other.

Then came around and hunkered down in front of Peyton.

"Hello, Peyton," he said.

"Mrrr. Mrrrr," gritted Peyton. "Mrrr frrr."

Motherfucker.

"Good to see you, too. You're looking well."

"Ffffhh. Ffffhh."

Fuck you.

"How's Tom? Not here with you, I notice. Guess you guys are taking turns?"

Peyton managed a staggering breath, then another.

"Muhhr. Ffffhukkr," he croaked.

Now Dixon spoke up.

"Shhuhh, Puhh."

Shut up, Peyton.

"I'll give you boys a minute, collect your thoughts."

He stepped away and rummaged around the kitchen for a moment, came back with two hand towels, a corkscrew, and an empty ice bucket. Placed the objects on the floor next to him.

Then leaned down to face Peyton.

"Got a few questions for you, GQ."

"The fuck you doing here?" Peyton said again, his voice little more than a hoarse shiver. The tase was already wearing off.

Finn reached down and applied backward pressure on Peyton's arm until he felt the joint give way with a soft crunch. Peyton jerked and let out a loud *"Fuck!"*

"Point being," said Finn. "I ask the questions. You supply the answers. Ground rules."

"Like hell," Peyton said through gritted teeth.

"No, like church. Call and response."

He reached back behind the arm, bracing Peyton's body with his knee, and pulled forward on it until he felt it snap back into place.

"*Fuck! You!*" said Peyton, though not as loud as the first yelp.

"Separation," said Finn. "Not as painful as dislocation. Which comes next. Hey, we've got a whole menu here."

Peyton just glared at him and worked at his ragged breathing.

As Peyton watched, Finn picked up the corkscrew, turned it over in his hand, considering it. Looked Peyton over. His lower back. His groin. His eyes. Considered the object in his hand again. Then placed it back on the floor and frowned.

The corkscrew was just for effect.

Finn knew the threats were futile. A dislocated shoulder would hurt, sure, but these guys had been through all the same training he had. SERE, BUD/S, SQT, and a shitload of worse. They didn't respond to pain the way normal people did.

That was okay. All part of the play.

"They think we've, what, lost our edge?" Dixon's voice was a barely audible scratch. "Seriously?"

Finn glanced over at Dixon's back but didn't move. "Your edge?"

"Why do you think we're still here? Some limp dick bigwig in his Georgetown penthouse suddenly gets a case of cold feet."

"Fucking ROE bullshit," muttered Peyton.

"So we're sitting here jerking off," Dixon growled, ignoring Peyton, "and getting nothing but radio silence. Meanwhile, our fucking HVT catches Tom watching him and tosses him off a roof. And they send *you* to finish *our* job?"

"Fucking Tom, man," Peyton echoed.

"Shut *up*, Peyton!"

Finn looked at them each in turn. Then shook his head. "Boys, boys. I don't care about your target. I don't even know who it is. This isn't about your target. It's about Mukalla."

"Fuck you," spat out Peyton again. "We had no—"

"*Shut the fuck up, Peyton!*" Dixon growled. Then, to Finn: "Mukalla is *bullshit*. There was no Mukalla."

Finn glanced in Dixon's direction again. "You'd like that, Rat, wouldn't you. Just let the whole thing disappear. But here's the problem. Making the whole thing disappear means making you two morons disappear, too."

Dixon went silent.

"Your dipshit HVT didn't kill Tom, and whoever's sponsoring your dipshit HVT didn't kill Tom. Let me give you a clue, gents. The guy they sent out to the docks at Thirty-Second Street last fall to be my welcoming committee—you think he's only after me?"

"Fuck you, freak," muttered Peyton.

"Peyton, you really might be as stupid as you look." Then to Dixon: "They sent him out to clean up *all* the mess. Someone up the food chain does, in fact, want the whole thing gone. So this guy, the guy they send, has simple orders: *Make it go away.* All of it, everyone involved. Silently, invisibly. Completely."

He waited while that sank in. Then he added:

"Boone, gents. Boone is in-country."

"Mother *fuck!*" Peyton murmured under his breath.

"Coming for me, coming for you. Came for Tom. You gents know Boone as well as I do. The man does not have an OFF switch."

They were both silent.

"So, walk me through it, GQ. While Paulie and I were breaching the safe house, were you boys already over at the farm compound? Or was that later?"

"You fucking serious? You followed us to fucking Iceland for this sh—?"

Finn smacked him hard across the face with the flat of his hand.

"What the FUCK!"

Peyton stared at him, outrage and disbelief smeared over his Ivy League features.

On the scale of pain, being slapped in the face ranked somewhere behind stubbing your toe. As an interrogation technique on a seasoned warrior, about as useful as gnats' wings in a windstorm. But that wasn't the point. It wasn't the pain or threat of pain. It was the humiliation. Slapping one of your own was possibly the most effete, most girly-man thing you could conceive of, on a par with a curtsey and a "Pretty please?" And especially humiliating when you were hog-tied and couldn't do anything about it.

It was like . . . well, there was a reason for the expression "a slap in the face."

Would it make Peyton talk? Of course not.

Which was fine.

All part of the play.

Finn continued in the same calm tone. "What happened that night, GQ?"

"You know goddam well what happened!"

Smack!

"Fuck!"

Smack!

"FUCK! You want me to say it?"

"I want you to say it."

"You know as well as—"

"Peyton!" Dixon cut him off with a feral growl. "Don't say a goddam thing!"

The room was silent again, except for Peyton's furious rough breathing.

"This is what," Dixon snarled. "Some kind of bust? NCIS have you now, like a monkey on a string?"

"No string, Rat," Finn said evenly. "No agencies. Just you guys and me. So tell me, Peyton. That night, in Mukalla. Was I there?"

"The *FUCK* are you talking about?"

"Peyton," Finn said, his voice level and cool. "Man to man. SEAL to SEAL. Was I part of it?"

Peyton stared up at him.

"Jee-zuss," he said. "You really don't know."

Finn had thought this through a thousand times since that summer.

He didn't think he'd been part of it, didn't want to think he was. Saw no earthly reason why he would have been.

But the honest fact was, he couldn't remember.

And if he wasn't part of it, then how did he end up there, sitting in that darkened room?

"Peyton," shouted Dixon, "if you give that psycho motherfucker one squirt of information I will personally hack off your balls and feed 'em to you with hot sauce!"

Finn put his hands on his knees and stood upright.

"You know what, that kind of gives me an idea."

Finn picked up the ice bucket, walked it back out to the suite's kitchen area, filled it with ice, then brought it back and plunked it down on the floor next to Peyton.

The shoulder manipulation and face smacking were pure theater. He'd just wanted to establish a clear before and after.

It was time for the "after."

People misunderstood torture.

In the popular view, the inflicting of pain, and the threat of inflicting greater pain, would eventually induce a subject to talk. But that was exactly the problem. To avoid pain, people *would* talk. And say anything. Truth, lies, fantasy, whatever they thought you wanted to hear.

The BS you saw in movies was just that.

Real torture was not about pain. It was about threatening to take away whatever you cared about most. If you really wanted to pry out some deep information it was far more effective, say, to threaten family members.

Which would have worked, for example, on Tom.

It wouldn't work on these two. Dixon didn't have any family, and Peyton didn't have one he gave a shit about.

Finn needed to threaten to take away something Peyton cared about.

And he had to demonstrate that he was serious.

He picked up one of the hand towels, walked around to face Dixon, and worked the towel into his mouth, far enough and tight enough that he couldn't spit it out. Then came back around to Peyton's side and did the same with the second hand towel, although this one he left slightly looser. He then undid Peyton's belt, pulled down his fly, and yanked his trousers and boxers down around his knees.

"Here's the deal."

He held out his razor-sharp ring knife in one hand, ice bucket in the other.

"I slice off one testicle. That's happening, regardless. Price of admission. Nothing either of you can do changes that.

"You talk, I drop it in the ice bucket. They've got talented doctors here, probably right here in the hotel. Dixon will find someone to sew it back on.

"You don't talk, I slice off the other bad boy. You lose some of that toxic masculinity and learn to love singing soprano. The second slice is optional."

Dead silence in the room.

"So, choose. Which nut do the girls favor, GQ? I'll start with the other one."

Now Peyton let loose with a string of screamed obscenities, mostly swallowed up by the hand towel. Dixon yelled into his own hand towel, no doubt telling Peyton to shut the fuck up.

Finn touched the edge of the knife to Peyton's scrotum, just above his left testicle.

"Who killed him, Peyton? Who killed Kennedy?"

Peyton stared at him, his face a perfect mix of fury, disbelief, and unbridled panic.

"Whuuhh uh fuuhh?"

Finn knew he'd only get one shot at this. One question, one answer.

He needed to push on the one that mattered most.

Who gave the order—Keyes, Dugan, or Meyerhoff? That was a stone he'd turn over eventually. It could wait.

The question of his own involvement in the massacre? Burning as it might be, that was secondary, too.

Kennedy was all that really mattered.

Call it loyalty. Call it justice, or revenge. Call it whatever you want.

Kennedy was the reason he'd tracked these men to Iceland. Getting that answer was why he was here. It was the roll of the dice on every dollar you owned, the stakes you gambled your life on. For a whole range of reasons, some of which he understood and some he didn't, he needed to know the answer.

"Who, Peyton?"

He applied pressure to the knife, just a little. And jiggled the point slightly, to make its presence undeniably clear.

"Which one of you two fine men killed him, GQ? Or was it some other upstanding warrior? I just need a name."

He began to slice.

Peyton screamed into his hand towel.

It was only a tiny incision, drawing no more than one or two drops of blood. But in terms of pain and especially in terms of terror, it packed a hell of a wallop. And Peyton was just vain enough, just weak enough, and just dumb enough to believe that Finn really would follow through and actually take off the man's balls.

At least Finn hoped so.

"Who pulled the trigger, Peyton, and you keep your goolies. I just need a name."

Peyton thrashed against his restraints, his muffled screams now forming a single desperate syllable, over and over.

A name?

Finn put down the knife and took hold of the hand towel.

"I'm going to pull out the towel, dipshit, and the only word I want to hear is a name. Who killed Kennedy?"

He yanked out the towel.

Peyton swore at him.

Finn smacked him across the face again, this time purely to focus him.

Peyton looked up and spat a gob of blood in his face.

"Who killed him, Peyton?"

"YOU DID, YOU WHACK JOB!"

Finn fell back a step, as if he'd been struck.

Stared at Peyton.

Peyton glared back, panting with fury and adrenaline.

The words ringing in Finn's ears.

YOUUU DIDDD YOUUU WHACKKK JOBBBBB . . .

Finn blinked twice. Three times. Staring at Peyton.

"I wasn't. Even. There." All at once Finn could hardly hear himself speak. It was as if his ears were stuffed with cotton. "They shipped me out. The night before. I was on a helo bound for the *Lincoln*. Kennedy was killed the next day. August first."

Peyton rolled over on his back and let out a weak laugh. "Yeah. If you believe the fucking press release."

His head lolled back to look at Finn again.

"His body was cold before that bird ever fired up its turbine."

50

Krista stood in the spot where they found poor Óla-fur's body, turning slowly in a full circle, taking it all in. His decrepit bookshelves, overflowing with dusty volumes, every one of them cherished and dog-eared. The hand-carved and hand-painted birds—Arctic terns, ravens, white-tailed eagles—now mostly in pieces.

The place had been destroyed, smashed to pieces, as if in a blind rage. Yet there was something almost systematic about the mayhem.

She thought about the two meticulously mangled corpses at the clinic.

Those two certainly hadn't killed themselves.

She didn't for a moment believe Ólafur did, either.

Although that was, at least for now, the official position.

Krista would be the one to go tell his daughter. Sweet girl, lived out on the west side, near the coast. Had a little girl herself.

She should drive out there and do it now, before anything leaked to the press and the daughter read about it herself on her damn phone.

Krista heaved a sigh and thought about the week's relentless march of dismal news.

They'd had to let Logan go that morning. Much as Krista wanted him to be guilty—guilty of something, anything—there was not a shred of evidence tying him to the dead girl in the duck pond. While Krista was playing her futile game of hide-and-seek with Marlin Pike, the arrogant little Aussie prick was walking out of the metro station a few blocks away, free as a preening oystercatcher.

Within hours after his release, he'd boarded a flight to Australia. "On holiday." Uh-huh.

She couldn't decide what she thought about Tryggvi. Was there something reprehensible going on there at the lake house? Or was he simply grief-stricken over the loss and feeling embarrassed and guilty about his own staff's negligence?

She was aching to confront him and ask about the inconsistencies in his statements. In their interview at his office, he'd made no reference to Kateryna's history with drugs. Yet he had to be aware of it; it was right there in her file. If his business was grooming "reliable au pairs of high character," as he'd claimed, why import someone with a past like Kateryna's? She wanted to go see him, ask him to his face if Logan had been out there to the lake house.

But she knew she was powerless to pursue that line of thought, even breathe a whisper of it, without something rock-solid to back it.

And maybe not even then.

Tryggvi was a powerful man who no doubt had the commissioner— her boss's boss—on speed dial. If Tryggvi didn't want her investigation to go any further, it wasn't hard to imagine the sequence of quiet phone calls that would start in the office suite at Höfðatorg and end at the she-wolf's desk.

Maybe that had already happened.

In any event, Kateryna's case was stone-cold dead.

Meanwhile, they still had their double murder with no suspects but a blank spot on a videotape. A ghost.

A ghost who may or may not have stood in this very spot and done this terrible thing to poor Ólafur.

And all she had to go on was a description of a ghoul, provided by another ghoul.

Were there really two ghouls? Or were they both the same person?

Was Marlin also Boone?

The phone in her pocket buzzed. She glanced at the number. Someone calling from the station.

"Yes?"

"Krista?"

She sighed. Who else would be answering her phone? "Yes, Jón. It's Krista."

"Where are you?"

She felt her spine stiffen. She'd never heard his voice like this, subdued, serious, none of its usual eagerness.

"I'm at Ólafur's place," she said. When she heard him hesitate, she added, "What."

"Chief wants you to come in. Right away."

Ylfa was still furious with her for the grilling she'd given young Logan and for holding him as long as she did.

"Tell her to fuck herself," she said. She heard Jón's gasp and realized he just might take that seriously. "No, don't," she added hastily. "Figure of speech. I suppose she's got her panties in a bunch over today's menu of mayhem?"

When he didn't reply right away, she felt a chill go up her spine.

"Jón. What happened."

He hesitated again, then told her.

They found him in his bathtub. When he hadn't called in to the station after two full days, they sent someone around to his house. He didn't answer the door. They forced their way in.

Heart attack, they figured the moment they saw his gray face, upturned and half-submerged.

Coroner said it was hard to fix exact time of death, but it'd been probably thirty-six hours, maybe a little more, maybe a little less.

Which meant that when the two of them had their little spat on Tuesday morning, he'd had less than twelve hours of life left to him.

Which also meant that the whole time she was furious with him for sitting at home sulking, leaving voicemail messages for him telling him not to behave like an ass, he wasn't sitting at home sulking at all.

He was lying dead in his bathtub.

The tub was empty now, and Einar's long-stilled body was absent, but otherwise the scene remained intact, a perfectly preserved museum exhibit.

Three items perched on the lip of the tub, untouched since the body's discovery. Rocks glass, the ice long melted, vestiges of vodka still clinging to the sides of the glass. A candle, burned down to the nub. And a paperback, placed upside down, presumably to hold the page where he was reading when he paused to take his final sip of spirits.

It was a book she'd given him as a birthday gift a few years back. The first Travis McGee novel, one of Krista's favorites. *The Deep Blue Good-by.* How many times had she needled him for not reading it yet? Einar, who loved his telly, lived on his phone, and never seemed to go near a book. He kept saying it was "on the list." Like he had a list.

It seemed he'd finally started.

Turned out, the heart attack wasn't what killed him. Soapy water was found in his lungs. According to the coroner, the heart attack simply immobilized him.

He drowned.

"Pig," said Krista quietly, her vision blurred. She blew her nose and stuffed the Kleenex back into a pocket.

He did love his Danishes and coffee. "And booze," she said to the empty bathroom. "Let's not forget the booze."

The chief's request notwithstanding, she had gone straight from Ólafur's sad living room to Einar's house in Vesturbær, where she spent the next two hours walking through room after room. She couldn't compute it. It was like a column of numbers that added up to a sum that made no sense.

Einar?

Dead in his own bathtub?

Einar drove her crazy. Annoyed the shit out of her. He was an oaf—but a dedicated oaf. And a brave one. She had seen him face off with men twice his size, men in blind rages slobbering about "tearing his Gucci head off and feeding it to him," and he never flinched.

And not stupid, either. Her partner-in-crime had not risen through the ranks to senior detective by accident. He was shrewd.

And despite everything, one seriously devoted cop.

This is Einar. I'm occupied right now, solving the crime of the century.

It was like the entire left side of her body had gone missing.

She began again in the kitchen, mentally logging every item, picturing him building his drink, following his movements through the house, to the bathroom, watching him shirk off the old robe and climb into the tub, light the candle, place the paperback next to him, upside-down to hold his page, watching him take a long pull on his drink and set the glass down again.

A column of numbers that added up to nothing but emptiness.

51

"Help me!"

It's cold out today. Unseasonably cold. It's after Labor Day. Why haven't they closed the beach?

But of course, they have. Which he immediately realizes as he glances around. No families, no beach towels, no lifeguards. No people, period. The place is deserted.

So what are those three little dipshits doing here in their trunks?

Two of them back on the beach now, scattering like sandpipers when they see his approach, laughing their heads off in the distance. Not even occurring to them that they're leaving their buddy out there in the wind-blown water, alone.

"Help m—"

The sound is swallowed by coughing, the coughing swallowed by the surf.

He's already running.

There's riptides out there, he thinks, but before the thought fully lands he is already out of his shoes and plunging into the surf.

"Hel—"

One last sputtering cough and he knows it's the last sound he'll hear, the kid is under and staying under.

Now in his fifteenth year on earth, Finn has already seen his first OD, another kid his age, and he's seen a number of other kids with gunshot wounds, some of them bad, some fatal. Seen one kid, name of Llewellyn, when they cut him down after he hung himself.

And now it occurs to him as he churns freestyle through the surf: he's about to see his first drowning.

Fuck that.

Not on his watch.

Halfway there.

Finn is a skinny kid, but hardbody-swimmer thin, not scrawny thin, and he shoots through the water like a bullet, craning his ears as he goes, listening for the kid's voice, a cough, sputter, anything.

Silence.

Three-quarters there . . . and . . . there!

He grabs the kid's opposite arm and spins him into a perfect cross hold, grabbing him from behind the way he learned. But the kid moves like a desperate eel, wriggling around until he's positioned behind Finn. The kid shimmies up him like an acrobat up a pole, wraps his legs around Finn's neck in a vise grip, his arms like iron bands around Finn's face, pushing Finn's head a good two feet underwater.

Finn distantly hears the kid cough out a gout of seawater and suck in a long wheezing breath, then sputter and cough again, then wheeze in another breath of pure air—and he's holding Finn's head underwater, his vision now going black around the edges, his lungs struggling to pull whatever O_2 they can from that last gulp of air he took, now gone stale, the instant before he was pushed under.

His eyes roll skyward, searching for air.

The water's surface is a phantom of ghostly light a mile away, a flicker at the far end of a long, dark, blue-green tunnel.

For some insane reason, at that moment his brain sparks and fizzes and brings up the kid's name.

Sebastian.

The other two dipshits are lost to his fading brain, but he remembers Sebastian. The one the other kids pick on.

Sebastian is two years younger than Finn, but Christ, he's strong. Or maybe it's just that kind of death-struggle strength that people find somehow.

Either way, Sebastian isn't letting go.

He tries to backward-head-butt the boy in the balls. Can't get enough mobility.

He tries to get his teeth free to bite down on Sebastian's leg, but he can't break the boy's iron grip.

He's weakening.

Finn is about to see his first drowning, all right.

From the inside.

The freezing cold water lapped up against his bare feet, then spilled over his ankles.

Where were his boots?

Where was *he*?

Finn took a long cold breath and looked around. He was sitting on the snow-dusted bank of a small semi-frozen lake. His boots on the ground next to him. Shoreline a few hundred yards off, ocean stretching to the horizon. To his right, maybe a half mile away, a lighthouse.

To his left, a thin ribbon of highway, then more ocean.

He looked straight up.

A thread of blue-green phosphorescence laced the night sky.

An engine, the grinding of gears.

Looking around behind him, he saw a white van in the distance, trundling up the highway on his left. A logo, a big red plus sign, on its side.

He recognized that van. He'd seen it before.

His first day of recon.

He was in . . . Norway? Sweden? Russia? Some place up by the Arctic Circle.

He watched the van's slow approach.

Reykjavík.

He was in Reykjavík.

And now he recognized the location, though from photographs only, not from ever having been in this particular spot before. It was Reykjavík's western coastline, a bird-watching pond they called "Bakkatjörn," meaning the pond out back.

Western coastline.

He must have walked the entire city. Why, no idea.

What was he doing here?

What was he doing in Reykjavík?

He felt dislocated in time as well as space.

Dislocated in every sense.

Separation—not as painful as dislocation. Hey, we've got a whole menu here.

Who had said that?

The van pulled off the road and came to a stop, a football field away. For the first time Finn noticed another figure sitting over there by that side of the pond, huddled into an old blanket. The van door slid open. Someone stepped out and helped the blanket man into the van. The door slid closed.

Now he remembered. The van was to help homeless people.

He couldn't recall where he was staying. Or if he was staying anywhere.

Maybe he should get in the van, too.

The big vehicle did a careful K-turn, then shifted into DRIVE and pulled away in the direction from which it had come.

Finn thought about Sebastian, the kid who almost got him drowned off the California coast when he was fifteen. He remembered sitting by the beach, afterward, when it was all over, just like this, feeling the water lap over his feet and ankles.

The first time he saved a life, he was fifteen.

Was that true?

The van dwindled to a dot in the distance.

How had he survived that drowning? He couldn't remember. Had he somehow managed to turn the tables? To pull the kid under and climb up on top himself?

Did he survive by drowning Sebastian?

Friday

Warming, into the mid-forties by noon;

dense fog.

52

He became aware of lying on his back, gazing up through a semi-opaque surface at a dim diffuse light, confused at what he saw. What medium he was looking through—ice? Water? Death?

Death.

He was lying in a coffin of ice.

Out of the gloom an image resolved: two eyes peering through the darkness. Then a face, pale and terrified. A young boy, staring at him through the glassy membrane, or dimensional veil, or whatever it was.

A hole opened in the boy's face: a mouth, gaping, about to scream—

Finn grabbed hold of both sides of the coffin and wrenched himself up out of the water with a gasp. Threw up a gout of cold water, then another, his stomach convulsing, the contractions coming in waves.

The waves slowed, then stopped.

The sound of his panting filled the tiny room.

He was sitting upright in a bathtub filled to the brim, cold water slopping over the sides in time with the heaving of his respirations.

He sat like that for a few minutes, eyes closed, slowing his breath, periodically coughing up dregs of bathwater. Trying to remember the night before, how he got back to this place. He searched for images of himself filling the tub, stripping down to the skin, climbing into the water.

None of it came to him.

Dislocation . . . more painful than separation.

Hey, we've got a whole menu here.

He remembered hearing the words, but not who said them.

He opened his eyes and held his fingers in front of his face. Deeply puckered fingertips. He had to have been in the water for a good length of time.

Had he drowned?

No, he was breathing. He'd come close. But he hadn't drowned. He was still here. Still alive.

He was better than 50 percent sure of it.

He climbed out and toweled off, pulled on a pair of sweats he found laid out for him (by him?), and went out into the little dining room.

And there she was.

On the wall—that face. Looking up at him through the ice.

He knew her.

No.

He'd *seen* her.

Did he know her?

His gaze moved along the wall to the right. He stood looking at the tapestry of sketches, placed there in an array that described a partial map of a city bordered to the north by a harbor.

Reykjavík.

He knew this city. He had walked these streets, every one of them.

When?

Why?

He was gripped by a gust of shivers. In an effort to bring back circulation, he absently rubbed his arms and hands and fingers.

They were going numb.

Now it was seeping back into his brain, disconnected fragments of it, the trickle swelling to a surge. Hotels . . . looking for the three SEALs . . . Dixon and Peyton—

YOU DID, YOU WHACK JOB!

Finn staggered back and collapsed into a sitting position on the floor, the sound of Peyton's voice echoing in his ears like peals of black thunder.

YOUDIDyoudidyoudidyoudidyoudid . . .

He couldn't feel his arms and legs. Couldn't feel his face.

With a start, he realized he wasn't breathing.

He forced himself to inhale, then exhale.

For the next few minutes, breathing was all he could do.

In through the nostrils, hold for four, five, six, seven seconds, then slowly let it out through the mouth.

And in: four, five, six, seven, and out through the mouth.

And in . . .

Finally he clawed his way back onto his feet.

Turned away from the wall.

Reached down into the backpack on the floor and hauled out the ring knife with its worn leather sheath.

Walked with it into the little kitchen.

Every movement took a singular effort, as if he were learning to operate a large and unfamiliar machine.

Pulled open the fridge doors.

Icelandic rye, pieces hacked off with the knife, spread thick with butter and lava salt. Slices of smoked Icelandic char.

He sat on a stool at the kitchen counter with his breakfast. While he ate, he did nothing else. No thoughts, no plans. Just trying to feel himself in his body.

When the plate was empty, he washed, hand-dried, and put it all away in the cupboard. Cleaned the knife, slipped it back into its sheath and into a pocket.

A vague memory came to him: standing over the two SEALs, fishing in one of their pockets and extracting a pocket knife, leaving it on the floor within crawling distance so they could cut their zip ties once he was gone . . . and then being out on the streets, walking, walking, a dull buzzing in his ears that came and went like a distant air raid siren in a nightmare, *YOUDIDyoudidyoudidyoudid* . . .

He sat staring at the kitchen wall but not seeing it, seeing only what he could pull up of memories from the past summer.

And went through it once again.

The last time he saw Kennedy was at the base in Bahrain, two days after Mukalla. Walking through the hallway of the admin building that afternoon. Kennedy leading him outside into the blistering heat to talk, away from prying ears. *Give me twenty-four*, he'd said. They'd parted, Kennedy back to the admin building, Finn headed in the direction of the hotel where he was billeted, then—

Skip

—walking onto the tarmac of the airstrip in Bahrain that night to meet the Knighthawk that would take him out to the *Lincoln*. Where he would spend the next month sailing back to the States. And not learn till the end of their passage that Kennedy was dead.

Killed the day after Finn left.

If you believe the fucking press release.

The images came to him again: standing at that big wooden door, pushing aside the shattered fragments to enter—

Skip

—sitting on the dirt floor of a dark inside room lit only by sporadic heat lightning, his back to the wall. Surrounded by carnage.

Was it him who smashed in that door?

Was he the author of that carnage?

He'd shot his own brother at the age of eight, then buried the memory for three decades. Who was to say there weren't other people he'd killed and forgotten?

Anyone was capable of anything.

He thought back to that final encounter with Kennedy.

His lieutenant clearly knew, or at least suspected, that the massacre at the farmhouse was an inside job. Had Finn thought he might get too close to learning the truth—that Finn himself was involved?

When they parted ways that afternoon, did Finn follow Kennedy back to the admin building and wait till he was alone?

He didn't believe it, didn't want to think it was even possible.

But he couldn't remember.

53

He walked back into the tiny dining room, where he
sat on the floor in front of the tapestry of pencil-drawn maps.

He still could not quite feel his body as he moved.

He took a deep breath, reached into his backpack for the leather bag,
withdrew the phone, and fired it up.

There were two messages.

The first was from squidink28@gmail.com. Carol.

> Remember who you are.

He shut off the phone and set it on the floor next to him.

Remember who you are.

YOUDIDyoudidyoudid . . .

He looked up to the left at the newspaper photo taped to the wall, the
dead girl in the ice looking at him.

Like she was telling him something.

His fingers still numb, he fumbled with the phone until he got it
turned on again.

The second message was from Stan.

> I checked out *Hitchhiker's Guide to the Galaxy,*
> got nothing from it. Guess I just don't get
> British humor. By the way, I brought your
> Steinbeck back to the library.

He read the message a second time. It was like reading tea leaves. Or staring at pebbles in a storm drain and looking for some kind of embedded meaning.

He took a few slow, deep breaths, then read it once more, slowly.

As his mind became engaged, he had a sense of settling into his body, like the contents of a shaken snow globe slowly starting to clarify.

>   . . . got nothing . . .
>   . . . British humor . . .

British humor.

He took a deep breath.

The shaken snow settling, another memory sifting through: the detective with the ice-blue eyes and her memos.

The Englishman.

Okay.

Stan had looked into the Englishman and come up empty.

>   I brought your Steinbeck back to the library.

What could he be getting at there? Finn started sorting through titles in his mind. *East of Eden. Grapes of Wrath. Tortilla Flat. Of Mice and Men. Travels with Charley. The Winter of—*

Wait.

Of Mice and Men.

George and Lenny.

Dixon and Peyton.

Back to the library.

Ah. So the two SEALs had been recalled. Brought back to the library. No big surprise there. Hadn't Dixon predicted as much? *Some limp dick bigwig in his Georgetown penthouse suddenly gets a case of cold feet.* Whatever beltway commando held a choke collar on their kill-or-capture op had finally choked it all the way. Or maybe their own chain of command had decided that with Tom's death being so public, it was too risky to keep a team there at all, and they'd felt forced to scuttle the operation.

Finn was more surprised at the code Stan chose for his message than at the message itself.

Kennedy was always meticulous about not dissing people, any people, but especially other Team guys. You had to be mighty tight in his inner circle to know that George and Lenny reference.

Evidently Stan knew Kennedy a lot better than Finn had realized.

Which meant the code itself was a message, too. It was Stan's way of letting Finn know how well he knew Kennedy. And whatever inside scuttlebutt there might be about what went down in Mukalla and after, whatever role they were saying Finn had played—or whatever role he *did* play, for that matter, a question on which he himself was still pretty well in the dark—Stan was still talking to Finn.

Stan, at least, did not believe Finn was Kennedy's killer. Which was encouraging.

Finn hoped Stan was right.

He took several long, slow breaths.

Thought it through.

There were only three possibilities.

Peyton was lying.

Peyton was telling the truth.

Peyton was repeating what he'd been told and had no fucking idea whether it was a lie or the truth. Which sounded a lot more like Peyton than either of the other two possibilities.

And if Peyton didn't know, that was because Dixon didn't know.

But there was someone who did know.

Whoever sent Boone to kill him.

Because that person would also be the person who had orchestrated the whole thing.

Keyes.

Dugan.

Or Meyerhoff.

Three officers; two solid, one rotten.

And Boone would know which one it was. Which meant that Boone would know the one man who could positively name Kennedy's murderer, whether Finn or someone else, and if someone else, then who.

Which meant Finn needed Boone.

He powered down the phone, cracked it open, levered out the SIM card, took that to Ragnar's impeccable little kitchen and placed it in the microwave. Nuked it for a solid minute, then extracted the remains and dumped them in the trash, followed by the Faraday pouch and now brain-dead phone.

Too dangerous to keep it any longer.

According to Stan L., DIA was closing in. Krista's police force might be looking for him. Boone certainly was. Too many ways his phone could end up in someone else's hands. Which could lead back to Stan. Or Carol.

And they both had to be protected, had to be safe, even if Finn wasn't.

He went back to his dining-room HQ and retrieved the burner phone with the single notch—the Magnús phone—pulled the SIM and gave it the same treatment. No point leaving the big driver exposed, either.

Time to cut what few ties he had.

It's not easy, flying solo.

He pulled an empty, lightweight bolt bag out of his backpack and loaded it with his compact first aid kit, Marlin Pike passport, most of his remaining cash, one extra change of clothes, and his two remaining unused burner phones. Burner #4, the one he'd been using to track the detective's memos, he pocketed. That one didn't link him to anyone but the detective.

The bolt bag he stuffed into his backpack, along with his keycard scanner, a glasses case containing a pair of horn-rimmed flat-lens glasses, and two full changes of clothes in contrasting colors.

He walked down the narrow hallway and poked his head out the front door.

The weather was turning unseasonably warm.

Unexpected.

Back inside, he hit Ragnar's closet and borrowed a lightweight wool sweater, dark gray. It was all he'd need for now, and come twilight it would make decent camo.

His parka went into the backpack with the bolt bag and the rest.

Good to go.

He looked around the place. Maybe he'd be back.

Maybe he wouldn't.

If he were smart, he would stay as far away from Boone as possible and focus on getting off this island. But it wasn't about being smart.

It was about getting answers.

Finn exited the townhouse, making no sound at all, and started walking.

54

It was Friday morning when the volcano finally blew.

Krista was sitting in a little corner café out by the University, gazing through the front window at pedestrians navigating the streets, which were starting to melt into a slushy mess.

The sudden reversal in temperature made her feel queasy. Everyone around her seemed to believe this meant the cold snap was finally at an end. Krista was not so confident. The pendulum, it seemed to her, was out of whack; all it had done was swing wildly the other way. It felt untrustworthy, like the city had suffered a knock on the head, resulting in temporary amnesia.

And it only served to aggravate the weirdness of what was already an unnerving day. One more time, she silently thanked God, or Snæfellsjökull, or whatever force had prompted her not to go in to the office early, as she normally did. Right at that moment her office was the last place on earth she wanted to be.

Ground zero of the eruption.

Heart of the volcano.

Some idiot in the department had leaked to the press, and the hot magma that was their double homicide at the clinic had finally burst open. A drowning in their duck pond, a dead American, a dead drug dealer—and on top of it all the brutal, random murder of two young innocents? For Chicago or Tijuana, that might be a normal week.

But Iceland? It was too much—far too much.

A DEADLY WEEK FOR ICELAND! screamed the headlines. The European papers were more colorful, especially the British tabloids. GEY-SER OF BLOOD!! ICELAND GONE BONKERS!! FIRE AND ICE, MURDER AND MAYHEM!!

They'd even made American headlines. ICED IN ICELAND!

Reporters from other countries were already pouring in through the airport.

Worst of all by far, from Krista's point of view, was the headline in their own city newspaper. It was the least sensationalized of them all, yet it was the one that would cause the most damage.

"POLICE IN THE SPOTLIGHT."

The media was screaming about poor security (a dead American!), the royal fuckup at the mortuary on Christmas (criminal incompetence!), murders at the clinic (with no suspects three days later!)—it all spelled rampant, systemic police ineptitude. There were loud calls for resignations and radical reform of the entire department.

Krista's phone was blowing up with alerts.

It was an Icelandic shitstorm.

Thankfully no one was drawing any actual, functional connection between the clinic killings and poor Ólafur's passing. The death at the Foss-hótel had been deemed a tragic accident. No one was uttering the words "serial killer," thank God, nor even thinking them, as far as Krista knew.

Other than Krista herself, of course.

And the elusive Mister Pike.

Still, the eruption was loud enough, the lava hot enough to scorch to a cinder everything it touched. And it wasn't only the press. It was the people. Now a crowd was gathering outside the police station in what looked like the first sparks of a major protest. Some were saying there were plans to stage a march outside the Parliament building. Krista knew where that could lead.

Her phone buzzed.

She picked up.

"Where the hell are you?" hissed Danni in a strained whisper. "The chief is ballistic. Demanding to know where we are with the clinic homicides. Wanting to know where the hell *you* are."

Krista rubbed her forehead with her free hand. "Tell her I'll be in shortly," she lied.

"*Krista.* You can't stay away. This is serious."

"I have a lead."

Silence on the other end.

"Tell Ylfa I can't come in right now because I'm out tracking a lead."

"Is it true?"

"Yes."

There was a long pause, Danni waiting for her to say more, her saying nothing at all. Danni wondering whether or not she was telling the truth.

She heard Danni give a sigh. "All right," he said. "I'll tell her."

"Thanks, Danni."

She clicked off, placed her phone facedown on the little café table, and rubbed her forehead again. Danni knew she wasn't going to tell him anything about her "lead," if it really existed, and he was not happy about it. Not at all.

And she didn't blame him.

So why wasn't she?

She hadn't said a word to Danni about Marlin Pike, let alone what Pike had told her about the terrifying Mister Boone and the possibility of a serial murderer.

Why not?

Maybe because the thing was so flimsy, so tissue-thin, that there was no point saying anything about it to anyone until she had something at least slightly more substantial.

Yeah, it could be that.

Or it could be that she really meant what she said to Marlin Pike, the day before. That if he and the three Fosshótel Americans really were some sort of Spec Ops team, here in Reykjavík on an active mission, operating without the knowledge or permission of Icelandic authorities, then doing anything to blow their cover could result in a social upheaval that would make this morning's protest seem tame. It could be that when she said it could lead to an overturn of the government and a chill in Iceland-American relations—a chill with potentially cataclysmic consequences—that she wasn't exaggerating.

Or it could be that she just wanted to give Marlin Pike a little more time to . . . to what?

To do whatever it was he was doing, she supposed.

Which was what?

"Fuck."

She had no idea.

Her phone buzzed again, the screen lighting up with a name that thankfully was neither Danni's nor Ylfa's.

Jón

She clicked TALK and said, "Tell me."

"I might have something," the young officer said in a voice so hushed she could barely hear it, yet not hushed enough to disguise his excitement. "Hang on. Sending now."

She watched her phone as it received the incoming text. Still being voice-connected was crowding her bandwidth, and the thing crawled so slowly she wanted to whack the instrument against the table.

As she waited, she contemplated the fact that it was the young officer she'd called that morning to run down this possible lead for her, and not Danni, her fellow detective and nominal partner.

If Einar were there, he would've been the one she called.

When the text finally finished loading, she tapped on it, tapped the attachment, and watched the eight-second CCTV clip, then watched it a second time.

Sandy blond hair, usually wears it in a ponytail. Hippie glasses. Round face. A face you'd trust your children with.

"And it would be the worst mistake you ever made," she murmured.

She put the phone back to her ear. "When?" she said.

"Tuesday morning, about eight forty-five."

"What else can you tell me?"

"That's it. I don't have a name yet, or itinerary, or anything. Just the clip. Hang on." She heard him cover the mouthpiece, then come back on. "Have to go."

"Thanks, Jón. I owe you one."

She practically heard his grin. Poor kid.

She was putting him in a terrible position. Danni, too. Concealing information, sneaking around behind even her own colleagues' backs, recruiting a well-intentioned young officer into her unreported inquiries? She was fucking with everyone here.

"All for a good cause," she murmured, hoping it was true.

She drained the espresso cup, got to her feet, and headed for her car to make the 45-minute drive to the airport.

55

She was on the move now, heading southwest, out of the city. Looked like she was on her way to the airport.

Good.

"This way, everyone . . ."

After an hour of skulking around the city's back streets, staying alert for the static charge in the air that announced the presence of Boone, Finn had ducked into a café restroom to change into his tourist outfit (gaudy wool sweater), then joined up with a downtown Reykjavík walking tour. Right now the group was being herded into an elevator to ascend to the top of Hallgrímskirkja, the church that rose over the city just a stone's throw from Ragnar's townhouse.

Sometimes the best place to stay hidden was out in the open.

As Finn walked, he kept one eye trained on the tiny screen of burner phone #4, watching the detective's movements via his bugging spyware's geolocation feature.

Boone was a preternatural killing machine, but he'd never been especially skilled in tracking or stalking. To find Tom, he hadn't needed to be. Whoever sent him would have just given him an address and said, "Go." But whoever sent Boone wouldn't have a clue where Finn was, and Tom wouldn't have been able to tell him, either. Boone would be on his own on that one. So where would he start? How would he proceed?

Finn had no idea.

Which was why he'd given the detective Boone's description. She had access to resources he didn't. She'd found Finn, most likely through

CCTV surveillance at the airport. No reason she couldn't do the same with Boone.

Follow the detective. She would lead him to Boone.

Going off Finn's description, she must have turned up some footage or eyewitness description of Boone coming in through the airport, whenever it was he arrived. Probably Monday, Tuesday afternoon at the latest, since by that night he was already busy bashing in skulls.

The tour guide was saying something about how much the church's pipe organ weighed and how many thousands of pipes it had.

Now she was at the airport. Probably hunting down someone Boone came into contact with there.

A string of letters appeared on the phone's tiny screen. She was starting a new memo.

"Jack Lansdale" . . .

Could be the name of the customs official who'd cleared him. Or more likely the alias Boone was using.

More words followed, now in Icelandic.

Finn copied and pasted and translated.

> Security consultant. Red team operation. Wouldn't say what firm . . .

Definitely Boone's aka.

The string of Icelandic words stopped.

Now she would be on the phone to someone back at the station who could track records, looking for signs of a "Jack Lansdale" making any transactions anywhere in the city.

If it were Finn there'd be no trace at all, other than the unavoidable passport scan at Keflavík on entry. Once he was out of the airport, the only thing that came out of his pocket was cash.

But Boone was just arrogant enough to feel invulnerable in his freshly minted alias. Since he would figure there was not a soul in Iceland who knew who "Jack Lansdale" was or that he was there in town, he wouldn't hesitate to use Jack Lansdale plastic.

His strength was his weakness.

The tour group shuffled out the church's front doors to gawk at the massive Leif Eriksson statue out front. A gift from America back in 1930, the tour guide explained, the work of the American sculptor Alexander Calder.

The dot on Finn's screen remained fixed in place.

The tour guide droned on.

"There was actually quite a controversy about this. The US insisted the statue be placed right here, in this prominent spot, but many Icelanders objected, as it meant tearing down an existing tower, which at the time was one of the most beloved landmarks in Reykjavík. Some wanted Iceland to reject the statue altogether . . ."

Finn knew how that story ended. The US had its way, the revered old tower was razed, and the fifty-ton American statue was planted in its place.

You, America, you broke my heart.

The dot was moving. East on Route 41 . . . she was headed back into the city. Which would take her at least forty-five minutes, possibly an hour.

Finn kept watching the phone.

As the dot edged slowly northeast, Finn's tour group straggled like a herd of ducks through the little city blocks, making their way through landmarks and food stops: City Hall, Parliament, fermented shark, sheep's head, a zillion local craft beers . . . Finn skipped the beers but enjoyed the shark, which everyone else said made them want to throw up.

The dot moved slowly up through streets west of the duck pond and wound into a quiet neighborhood on the old west side.

The tour guide was saying something about how famous these particular Icelandic hot dogs were, how Bill Clinton had stood right in this spot and eaten one with mustard, how some said they were the best in the world.

The dot stopped moving.

Finn zoomed in for a closer look. It was hovering over a spot the map labeled as a business. Finn copied the name and looked it up. A restaurant. Trendy, vegan.

Boone.

They probably served their most upscale clients an amuse-bouche of cocaine out behind the valet parking station.

"Hey," said one of the tour group patrons. "Hey, we gonna see the clinic where, you know, where the murders happened?"

There were a few nervous chuckles in the back of the group. The tour guide's smile faltered. "Terrible thing . . ." he murmured. Temporarily silenced, he led the group a few more blocks to view Harpa, the concert hall, while the tourists traded tidbits of gossip about the murders.

The dot settled next on another location. A grocery store.

Another memo. More copying and pasting.

> Shopkeeper remembers seeing him, could be Tuesday, no more details. Nothing useful.

The screen went blank again. No memos, no movement.

The tour guide talked on about the concert hall's 714 individually controlled LED windows and how they could go through a kaleidoscope of colors, how they could be used to paint massive moving electronic murals, even to play building-sized videogames. One or two listened; the rest dished quietly among themselves about the latest grisly news.

The phone's radio silence stretched on for another thirty minutes. Forty-five.

Finn considered his strategy.

Boone was bigger, stronger, and hopped up on speed. And his objective was simpler: to kill.

Finn didn't want Boone dead. He needed to immobilize him, not kill him, which put him at a critical disadvantage. A more complicated goal, one more prone to going off the rails. Boone wouldn't fall for a field-rigged taser. Finn didn't have access to tranquilizer darts or a hypo full of fast-acting sedatives. He had his arms, legs, and wits.

It would have to be a full-contact takedown.

While Boone might be the more ferocious fighter, Finn was preternaturally fast. Normally, at least. But he hadn't slept in months and his nervous system was shorting out. The numbness had backed off, but he still felt less like himself and more like a marionette trying to work its own strings.

His best bet would be to maneuver Boone as quickly as possible into a sleeper hold and choke him out long enough to get zip ties on him.

And then?

Improvise.

At fifty minutes the phone buzzed. Letters started marching across the screen. Memo. A list of area hotels.

Moses blows us.

He'd told her that was pointless. Boone would stay away from hotels, even cheap hostels and Airbnbs, for all the same reasons Finn did: anonymity, flexibility, autonomy. He would take over a hide, just as Finn did.

The detective was neither stupid nor careless. If she had resorted to running down local hotels despite Finn's advice, either she didn't trust that he was right, or she'd run out of leads and was grasping at straws. Hoping to get lucky.

Finn had never put much stock in "lucky."

The "Jack Lansdale" trail must have gone cold after his purchases at the grocery store. The grocery store was the end point.

So that was where he'd start.

He slipped away from the disintegrating tour group and walked west.

56

"Marlin Pike, *Reykjavík Grapevine.* We're doing a story on the police effort to track down the clinic killer."

That was all it took for the shopkeeper to drop everything he was doing and usher Finn to a pair of stools by the window, eager to be part of the excitement.

"How can I help?"

"The police asked you about an American, six-one, sandy blond—"

"They did," the man said at once. "And I told them they had the wrong man."

"Because?"

"I don't believe he'd be capable of doing such a terrible thing. A nice man, I mean not just polite. Genuinely nice. You can tell these things, you know?"

Finn did not know, and didn't think the shopkeeper did, either.

"Was there anyone else here when the man shopped? Anyone local?"

"Hard to say. People are in and out all the time. You know how it is." He thought for a moment. "Oh."

Finn looked up at him, eyebrows raised, pen poised over his reporter's notepad. He didn't think journalists actually used pens and notepads anymore, but figured the shopkeeper wouldn't know that.

"He knocked over Helga's grocery cart. It was actually kind of funny. He practically fell all over himself apologizing, picked everything up. I'd forgot about that."

"Helga?"

"Helga Guðmundsdóttir. Shops in here all the time."

Finn jotted this down. "Do you have an address for Helga?"

He frowned. "No, that I do not. She's in her eighties, you know, but still walks everywhere, so I'm sure she can't live far from here."

"And how often does she come in, would you say?"

"Oh, most every day. Helga, she likes her fresh groceries."

"Did she come in yesterday?"

He thought again for a moment. Grunted.

"What," prompted Finn.

"Now that you ask . . ." He frowned. "Guess I haven't seen her since, maybe, Wednesday?" Another frown. "No, Tuesday? The day he knocked over her cart."

So that was that.

"Say," Finn said, "do you have a phone I could borrow for a moment? My phone's out of charge."

The shopkeeper's face clouded over.

"It's been a crazy day," Finn added ruefully. He watched suspicion and hardwired civility battle it out on the man's face. Civility won. "Sure," the man said reluctantly, handing over his cellphone.

Finn called Magnús.

"Hey, boss," he said when the driver picked up.

"Ghost Writer!" the voice rumbled. "I was starting to wonder. You know your phone is out of the service?"

"I need to tap your network." Finn stepped away from the shopkeeper and lowered his voice. He described the woman, giving her name and approximate neighborhood, then disconnected so Magnús could get to work.

He gave the shopkeeper an apologetic shrug and held the phone up. "My boss. He should be calling back in just a minute or two."

Even if he had seized Helga Guðmundsdóttir's home for his base of operations, it was highly unlikely that Boone himself would actually be there. He'd be out in the city, hunting for Finn. But if you wanted to track a wild animal you started with its spoor. If you could locate its den, that was always a bonus.

When the shopkeeper went to ring up another customer, Finn surreptitiously checked the tracking software on phone #4. The detective was headed east again. Where was she going now?

A second peek a minute later gave him his answer.

She was headed back to the metro police station.

Either she was getting ready to tell her boss about himself and Boone, in which case the entire Reykjavík police force would now be on the lookout for Finn, or she was being called onto the carpet.

The shopkeeper's phone buzzed.

"I have an address," the voice growled.

57

Damn her. Piss on her.

Airport. Restaurant. Grocery store. She was supposed to be tracking the weevil. The fucking weevil. But she wasn't following the script. Instead, she was tracking *him*.

Evilbitch.

If he were pitching the movie version of this whole fuckaroo, that's what her character name would be.

Evilbitch Ladycop.

Boone scratched again at the left side of his rib cage, then opened his mouth wide, stretching his jaws. His skin kept tightening up on him, like he'd left it in the dryer too long at too high a temperature.

Though that wasn't what was bothering him, and Evilbitch Ladycop wasn't really what was bothering him, either.

It was the situation.

The whole setup.

If he'd been sent to track the weevil, what if Papa Bear and his toadies hadn't also sent someone to track *him*?

He knew goddam well how crazy that would sound if he said it out loud. But it wasn't crazy. Not at all. It's what he would do if he were them. And they were fucking devious.

But they were not all that smart, not to Boone's way of thinking.

They'd gotten greedy. Greed begat sloppiness, and sloppiness begat clusterfucks. Like that train wreck in Mukalla. And now they'd had to send him in to clean up their mess, vacuum up every last soul involved.

And Boone knew what that meant.

It meant that eventually, when the chairs were all empty and the music stopped playing, they'd have to vacuum up Boone, too.

He knew how it worked.

He scratched at his side again.

Had they sent someone already?

He felt the thought moving in his head like a bug crawling along a kitchen counter, walking itself from point A to point B, proceeding from ludicrous, to possible, to probable.

It was a short bug-hop from there to certainty.

He would have to be on the alert for a fuckin' tail. Not that he thought—

His head jerked up.

He'd sensed movement.

He stretched his jaw again and got silently to his feet.

Evilbitch Ladycop was on the move.

Boone followed.

58

"Let me ask you, Krista, what does it say on your badge? The little words in the circle."

Krista did not take out her badge to look. She assumed the question was rhetorical.

"Humor me," he added.

She stifled a sigh. Without looking away from his gaze, she recited, "MEÐ LÖGUM SKAL LAND BYGGJA."

By laws our land is built.

"Lögum," he repeated, smiling and nodding, as if she were a fifth grader who'd just done very well on her exam question. "As in, Lögreglan. This is what we do. This is who we are."

Krista had been talking with her fourth hotel clerk when Danni called her again. "You've got to come in now. No shit, Krista. This is serious." And she knew he was right. She could avoid Ylfa. She could not avoid the commissioner.

So here she was.

The problem with laws, she wanted to say, *is that they're enacted and executed by people. And people can be so fucking cruel.*

Instead, she said simply, "Yes. I know."

"This morning," the commissioner continued, the meaningless smile now gone, "I experienced the three things I dislike the most. A flurry of cheap headlines aimed in my direction. A breakfast gone stale while I sat on the phone. And the phone call itself, which was from the Minister of Justice."

The Minister of Justice stood at the very top of Iceland's law enforcement food chain. For the commissioner, it didn't get any more serious. If the minister wasn't happy, that meant the commissioner was even less happy, which meant Krista was in line to be fucking miserable.

As Einar would have put it: *Shit rolls downhill.*

"The commissioner wanted to know if I thought we needed to bring in NBI." Iceland's National Bureau of Investigation. Not a happy development. "He also made some rather unsubtle hints that, barring that action, the detectives on the case might need to be evaluated."

Evaluated. Meaning *reassigned.* Meaning *banished.* Which pissed her off. Reassignment to some backwater post was exactly what she'd planned for herself—but not like this. Not in disgrace. Not as a punishment.

Her phone buzzed.

"I told him . . ." The commissioner's lecture rolled on.

Krista glanced at the number—then abruptly held up her right index finger, cutting him off mid-sentence.

"I'm sorry, I have to take this."

Turning her back on the astonished man, she tapped her phone and held it to her ear. "Hello? Yes, thank you for calling back! Can you hold one moment?"

She turned to the commissioner. "I'm sorry, this will just take a moment." She swiveled back to the door and exited the room, phone to her ear, so she could hold the conversation out in the hallway. The commissioner was probably in the first stages of a stroke, but he was a big boy and could take care of himself.

"Hey, I'm sorry I haven't called till now," said the voice on the phone. "I just got your messages."

It was Ragnar Björnsson, the absent owner of Marlin Pike's appropriated townhouse.

Who, it turned out, had been whitewater rafting in New Zealand and cut off from his phone since Christmas Day. And who was a little freaked out that he had gotten a string of voicemails from the police.

"Do you have anyone watching the place while you're gone?" she asked.

"No," he said. "Why?" She heard the growing alarm in his voice. "Why, what's happened?"

Krista hesitated.

"There was, a break-in . . . in the neighborhood. I just wanted to let you know. No, no burglary, no problem. We're just contacting everyone on the block. Listen . . . do I have permission to enter your home? Just to look around, make sure everything is all right?"

"Yes, of course. Please! I left an extra key with the lady next door. Hey, I just read about the murders there, it sounds like the whole city is going crazy! Is this related—"

"No, no, there's no connection, probably just some kids getting into mischief. It's fine. We're simply taking precautions."

She clicked off.

And wondered what the hell she'd just done.

She looked up the hall to the office where the commissioner sat, or more likely still stood, fuming and waiting for her to return and finish having her ass handed to her.

She turned and walked the other way, out of the building, and began striding toward Parliament Hill.

59

Finn stood on the front stoop of the elegant little detached house, considering the front door. No time for subtlety. He jimmied the lock open with his ring knife, pushed the door open, and stepped through the entrance.

The air was dead inside. Place felt like it had been empty for at least a day, maybe a little longer than that.

Finn remembered a scene in Iraq, taking over a home in a residential neighborhood to set up a surveillance operation that would last a few days. Boone was there, too. It was not a hostile op; they weren't seizing the property, only borrowing it. The family had done nothing wrong. They were ordinary citizens. The group just needed to infiltrate the neighborhood, to get eyes on. They needed a secure spot.

The first thing they did, after surprising the hell out of the residents by showing up in their living room, shushing them all, and explaining their reason for being there and assuring the stunned family that they would come to no harm, was to herd them all into one corner of the room and collect their phones.

They kept the family buttoned up for three full days. Took good care of them, kept them calm and reassured. Then let them all go and vanished into the night.

This was the same sort of operation—only a photonegative of that experience. Like the version you'd encounter in a nightmare.

Which Finn supposed was exactly what it was.

For their urban recon ops in Iraq, they always went in with the goal of leaving the place 100 percent intact. Zero footprint.

This was not zero footprint. This was demolition. The place looked like it had been put through a wood chipper.

Another critical difference: they always went in with a team of at least four, ideally five or six. One on optics, one on comms, at least two on security, sitting with the family in rotation. One or two others, if possible, to rotate out the first two and give everyone a chance to sleep.

Boone didn't do sleep, not when he was on an all-time high. And he wouldn't bother with watching the family.

Even if the family was just one harmless old lady.

He went through Boone's stuff. Found a passport that read "Jack Lansdale" with Boone's unmistakable photo. No disguising those dead eyes.

On one section of wall there had sat a stereo system, but it was missing now. He learned why when he entered the bedroom and found the whole thing completely disassembled into its constituent parts. Hundreds of components, all neatly laid out on the bed. If Finn took the time to examine them, he'd probably find they were arranged alphabetically. Or by weight. Or some other system known only to the fevered brain who did the arranging.

Boone's drug spin cycle was out of control.

Finished with living room and bedroom, he went through the kitchen. Empty bottles of Appelsín, Iceland's favorite soft drink, starting to smell rank. Traces of orange powder on the counter. Boone was crushing up and snorting the pills.

Not a trace of any other food preparation.

He looked in the fridge.

Then the freezer.

And stood, looking in through the open freezer door.

Helga Guðmundsdóttir's head stared back at him.

Where the rest of Helga was, Finn didn't know and wouldn't have time to find out. He switched on phone #4 to call the detective—and that's when it dawned on him.

Follow the detective, he'd told himself. *She'll lead you to Boone.*

It hadn't occurred to him until this moment that it could work just as well in reverse.

That following the detective could also lead Boone to Finn.

The sequence of logical pieces fell like dominos.

If Boone had been following the detective all morning, betting that she would lead him to Finn, then he knew she was sniffing along the Jack Lansdale trail. Which meant she would know both his alias and what he looked like, whether through surveillance footage, witness description, or both. Which meant she was a loose cable, and every damn squid in the navy knew what you did with a loose cable.

You made sure to tie it back.

Helga's frozen eyes stared at him reproachfully.

You fucked up.

Fokking fokk.

Scrotal disaster.

Finn had unwittingly put the detective in the crosshairs. The moment she'd fulfilled Boone's purpose, which was to locate Finn, he would kill her.

Finn pulled out phone #4, the tracking phone, and looked at the screen.

She was at that moment in Parliament Hill.

Standing in his place.

She'd *already* led Boone to him.

She was already dead.

60

Krista stood looking at the wall, too stunned to curse.
It was blanketed with sheets of paper, an orgy of pencil sketches depicting the streets of the city in detail—the harbor, Fosshótel, the Tower, Hlemmur Square . . . and there was the duck pond, a knot of police crowding around the dead girl.

Herself, standing there among the others, cursing.

And off to the left, a printout of the newspaper photo of the dead girl's face, the "LITLA HAFMEYJAN Á ÍS!" photo—and next to that a detailed pencil sketch of Kateryna's face in the dead of night, glancing back over her shoulder as she ran, every bit as realistic as the photograph.

More realistic than the photograph.

And next to it, another. And another. And another.

Drawing after drawing of the girl's face.

Had to be twenty of them.

No, thirty.

He was obsessed with her.

He'd been following her.

He was the person she was running from.

Krista looked again at the newspaper photo and noticed something hand-lettered in the margin. She leaned in. Small, neat lettering, in pencil:

Part of a word—OM. Something religious?

She scrabbled for her phone and stared down at it. Opened her memo software and began furiously scrolling back through the days. Thursday . . . Wednesday . . . Tuesday—

There it was. In one of her own notes, dictated just after that confrontation with Einar over the diver's report about the scar and lettering on the dead girl's abdomen.

Hluti úr orði—OM. Eitthvað trúarlegt?

She stared from her phone back to the wall, and back to the memo on her phone. *Hluti úr orði—OM. Eitthvað trúarlegt?* Meaning . . .

"Part of a word. OM. Something religious," she whispered in English. Fuck!

The little bastard planted some kind of spyware on her phone! How the hell . . . ?

And then she remembered the photo.

"The fucking Unknown Bureaucrat!" she fumed to the empty room.

She thought back to how her mind had gone in circles, trying to work out the significance of the thing, why he'd sent it to her. Turned out, it had no significance at all.

It was nothing but a Trojan Horse.

As she stood staring at her phone, it let out a loud *bzzzz!*

She nearly dropped it.

Somehow, she knew who it was without even looking. She stabbed at the screen with a forefinger and put the phone to her ear.

"I'm standing in Boone's hide," said Marlin's voice. "Looking in the freezer at what's left of Helga Guðmundsdóttir." He reeled off an address.

"Why were you following Kateryna Shevchenko?" she demanded.

The moment the words left her lips, her brain registered what Pike had just said.

She had no idea who Helga Guðmundsdóttir was, but obviously she should have.

And soon would.

She slumped against the wall and gripped the phone tight. *Another homicide?*

"You should get a team over here right away," the voice was saying.

"Tell them to use extreme caution. And you need to get out of there immediately."

Krista's brain was racing at 100 kilometers per hour in two opposite directions at once.

Marlin was helping them solve their murders.

Marlin *was* a murderer.

Or . . . both?

"You're alone, aren't you," said the voice. "Flying solo."

She felt like her head was going to explode.

"Did you put her in that duck pond?" she shouted.

"Detective," the voice said. "Krista. You're in danger. Get out. And don't come this way—go straight back to the station."

"Is this whole Lansdale thing just a goddam distraction?! Did you kill your American friend? Did you kill Ólafur?"

"You're wasting time. Get out of there."

"Don't touch anything!" she barked through the phone. "Don't you move! Marlin Pike, I'm placing you under arrest for—for passport fraud, breaking and entering, stalking and assault, suspicion of murder, and God knows what else. And—and—and if you leave those fucking premises before I get there, resisting arrest!"

Silence. He'd disconnected.

"Fuck!" she shouted at the empty room.

In the time it would take to hoof it back to the station, retrieve her Volvo, and drive across town to the address Marlin had given, she could already be there.

If she hustled.

She burst out of Ragnar's townhouse and took off on foot, heading west.

61

The weather had taken another sudden lurch, the strange warm spell breaking like an interrupted dream and sending the mercury plunging again. The street slush was rapidly hardening back into ice, and now a thick fog was descending on the city.

As Krista fast-walked west out of Parliament Hill her visible horizon contracted, shrinking to the point where she could barely see twenty feet in front of her.

Approaching the duck pond from the east, she cut over to the bridge that bordered its southern edge.

Halfway across, she heard a sound.

She stopped for a moment and listened. Nothing.

She resumed her stride—then stopped when she heard the sound again. A sort of soft thrashing, then quiet.

Then the sound again. Coming from behind, toward the eastern side of the lake.

An unseen duck, enjoying the end of the brief thaw.

She let out a breath she hadn't realized she'd been holding.

She exited the bridge's footpath, coming out near the city's great cemetery. Anxious to reach Helga Guðmundsdóttir's home before Pike vacated the scene, she made for the graveyard's southeast corner to take a shortcut.

As she stepped through the cemetery gate, she heard the sound again.

Not a duck.

It sounded like the scuff of a boot on the pavement.

Pike? Could he have possibly gotten here that fast? She didn't think so. The sound didn't repeat.

Silence.

Get a grip, Krista.

Picking up her pace, she slipped farther in.

The old cemetery was cloistered in dark, looming trees, some as ancient as the graveyard itself. A place of moss, history, and ghosts.

A thousand years earlier, Krista's Viking ancestors took their axes to the forests that covered the countryside, leaving Iceland as a modern case study in deforestation. For the past hundred years citizens had poured their energies into a major reforesting effort. So far, they'd managed a gain of half a percent. Outside its cities, Iceland was still a mostly treeless moonscape.

Not here, though. Here it was a different world.

Krista felt like a child in a Grimms' fairy tale traipsing through Germany's Black Forest.

She stopped.

The sound again.

Not her imagination.

Not a fairy tale.

She felt her heart rate accelerate.

Someone following her.

She had reached about the halfway point on the path. The graveyard's western gate was maybe two hundred feet to her left. Closer than the northwest corner gate she was aiming for. Should she alter her path?

Should she move at all?

In the faint light filtering through the trees she caught a brief glimpse of a figure, about thirty meters back, stalking up the path.

Too tall to be Pike.

Ponytail.

A glint of light off a pair of glasses.

Boone.

A few images flashed through her mind, unbidden. The two corpses at the clinic, garish and ugly under the fluorescent light. The broken body of the American lying in the bloody snow. Poor Ólafur lying ghost-white, exsanguinated, in a duck pond of his own blood.

Stop it, Krista.

She slipped off the path to an outsize tombstone a few meters away and crouched down behind it.

The fog felt like a toxic substance, seeping in through her clothes, through her skin, into her bones. She wished she had worn more, silently cursed that freakish warm snap. Though without it there would be no fog. Would her situation be worse? Or better?

A new sound cut through her thoughts, short, soft and hard at the same time. Like the puff of a pneumatic brake, but quieter.

Heard it again. Puff, puff. Two sounds, in quick succession. Like two breaths of air.

And again. Two short breaths in sequence. Then silence. Like someone inhaling sharply, through his nostrils.

Like someone sniffing.

A shiver ran through her, starting at the base of her spine and shimmying up across her shoulders and neck.

She knew exactly what he was doing.

It was too bizarre, couldn't possibly be true. But she knew it was.

He was tracking her by scent.

Sniff-sniff.

She couldn't see him now, from her position behind the gravestone.

Only hear him.

She inched farther down behind the headstone, making herself as small as possible. Ten feet away a stone mausoleum stood staring at her. She cursed herself for not having investigated that as a hiding spot. Agonized over whether to lower herself even closer to the ground, which would present a smaller profile, but would also make it more difficult to bolt out of there if she came to the point of having to make that terrifying decision. Afraid to make the smallest movement.

Sniff-sniff.

Closer this time.

On this job, you don't want to be wearing any scents.

Ah, Einar had added, mocking her. *So the bad guys can't sniff you out. Verrry smart.*

She felt a trickle of sweat slipping down her sternum, traversing the skin between her breasts.

Smelled her own sweat betraying her, screaming out her location. God, no!

Krista closed her eyes and clenched her teeth, willing her adrenals not to bear down, willing her autonomic nervous system to stay the scent of fear rising off of her. Compelled her own breathing to slow and go still.

If the moment for flight came, it would need to be calculated and precise.

She forced her mind to reassert control.

Within seconds the perspiration dried, the cloud of fear vanished.

Without moving, Krista folded into herself. She became a glacier.

She became Snæfellsjökull.

The seconds squeezed past.

Sniff-sniff.

Breathe.

Wait.

Sniff-sniff.

Closer—and this time followed by a second, different sound. A quiet clanking rattle, like a ghost's tambourine. What the hell was that? It sounded to Krista like a handful of small, brittle objects clanking against each other. A set of thin, stone wind chimes, or a loose necklace jostling as its owner moved.

A necklace.

She felt the tiny hairs on her forearms and the nape of her neck standing erect, quivering like a porcupine's quills. A fresh flood of adrenaline poured through her bloodstream, flipping every switch, throwing every circuit.

She knew what had happened to the victims' canine teeth.

She couldn't say how she knew, but she knew.

He had made a necklace out of them.

A fucking necklace.

Perspiration burst out again, on her face, on her neck, under her arms, running down her sides and her chest in rivulets.

The clanking stopped.

SNIFF-SNIFF!!

She could feel herself about to bolt, her control giving way to panicked flight.

Breathe! she shouted inside her head.

Wait!

With excruciating care, she shifted her weight to her right foot and tensed her thighs and abdomen into the taut drawn string of a hunting bow, preparing to launch herself into a sprint—

When she heard another sound, this time coming from outside the cemetery.

Someone running.

62

Finn's instincts told him to slow as he passed the big cemetery, told him to go into stealth mode. But some other sense, some deeper instinct, pushed him to keep running at full tilt, noise be damned. Told him another life depended on his speed, not his silence.

So he was still darting through the fog at top speed when he sensed the flash of movement at the left edge of his field of vision, felt that static charge in the air a split second before he saw it—a figure bursting out of the cemetery's western gate and coming at him from his left flank.

The big obsidian blade leaping at his throat.

"Exsanguination doesn't happen like in the movies, gents. You don't hit the floor a dead man seconds after your assailant slits your throat. But it happens fast enough, and it kills you just as dead."

Finn's peripheral nerves fired off thousands of directives at once, screaming orders through a billion neurons, a trillion synapses, signaling a shift in tactics, constricting some blood vessels and muscle fibers and shouting at others to ease up—

"Depending on severity of the wound you can lose twenty-five percent of total blood volume in anywhere from thirty seconds to three minutes. You'll feel weakness, disorientation, nausea . . ."

Twelve guys in a room, sitting in a circle, instructor in the middle, another lifetime: advanced SEAL training in close-quarters combat—

"At fifty percent your organs start shutting down. Which you want to avoid. So here are two simple rules of close-quarters combat. Don't get shot. And don't get cut. Welcome to CQB, gentlemen."

Training and instinct rotated Finn's body to the left as he side-stepped to the right, like a fighter jet banking into a sudden dive, then continued the rotation, bringing his left leg around in a full 360-degree spin, lashing out with his boot—

And met nothing but air.

Too late to react, he felt the impact of Boone's steel-toe boot crashing into his right leg. The impact knocked Finn into an awkward two-step stagger, enough time for Boone to deliver a second kick, this one straight to the chest.

The second kick drove Finn to the ground.

As he fell he pulled his ring knife and a fraction of a second later it was flying toward Boone's gut—

And in the next fraction of a second Boone swatted it away with his obsidian blade.

Jesus, he was fast.

"Best way to avoid being shot or cut is to be the guy who shoots or cuts first. When you leave this room at the end of the week, you will be that guy."

Except that Finn and Boone had both been in that room.

And Finn had no gun to shoot with, and now no knife to cut with.

He popped up out of his roll and into a crouch, at the same time yanking off his belt and flicking it around his left arm, holding it across his front in a defensive stance.

The first slash bit deep into the belt, but the thick leather held.

The counter-slash was more destructive. Boone's blade sliced clear through one strap of Finn's backpack, severing the pack from his shoulder, then continued on its trajectory across his upper chest, biting deeper, slicing through his clothing and into his flesh.

The long knife stroke left Boone open and Finn charged in, launching a palm strike to the nose, throwing all his weight into it.

The impact broke Boone's nose and sent him staggering back, blood pouring from the burst capillaries and small vessels, before quickly recovering and running again at Finn—

And Finn turned his back on him.

It was such a shock, such an insanely, incomprehensibly foolish move, that it caused Boone to hesitate for half an instant.

Which was all Finn needed.

Finn was not a big man, and not as strong as some, but he was blindingly fast. In any face-off, speed was his prime advantage. But Boone was jacked up on massive amounts of chemical rocket fuel. Finn could read that on him like a billboard. Boone could match him move for move, and then some.

And Finn was cut.

The slash across the chest was not the perfect kill strike—there were ribs and clavicles and hard muscles to get past and the arteries and veins in the chest were tough to reach. But vulnerable enough. Finn was bleeding badly. He wouldn't last too many rounds. If he wanted to walk away from this contest alive, he needed something to increase his velocity.

Not chemicals.

Physics.

Angular velocity.

As long as Finn himself was the weapon, he would be dead in seconds. Fast as he was, he was too slow.

So don't try to be fast.

Be still.

A point of stasis.

A pivot point.

In the traditional Filipino knife arts, they had a favorite tactic they called "defanging the snake," which involved severing muscles or tendons of the forearm, thereby crippling the attacker's ability to grip his weapon. Finn had no knife to sever with.

But there was more than one way to defang a snake.

As he turned away from Boone, he shifted his weight to the right while whipping the belt off his arm, then launched into a counterclockwise spin on the opposite foot, gripping onto the tongue end of the belt and flinging it like a bullwhip.

Angular velocity.

As he launched off his left foot he made a split-second decision: head? or hand? A solid shot to the head could put Boone down permanently. And Finn didn't want that.

He didn't want Boone dead.

He wanted to ask Boone a question—and he needed an answer.

He spun one-and-a-half rotations, the steel belt buckle whistling through the air until it came into violent contact with Boone's knife hand, crushing several fingers and causing the knife to go clattering off over the pavement.

Boone dove for the knife, retrieved it in an instant, and turned.

Finn had vanished into the fog.

63

Boone stood before the wall, motionless, as he had been for the past five minutes. He couldn't decide whether he found this the most impressive thing he'd ever seen, or the most pathetic.

Both, he finally decided.

Sketch after sketch after sketch.

The freak was obsessed.

He walked over to the dining room table, yanked out a chair, and sat on it backward.

After a frustrating ten minutes at the cemetery searching for both the freak and the cop, Boone had backtracked to the freak's hidey-hole, forced his way in, and come upon this bizarre display of Chief Finn's impressively pathetic inner thoughts.

Boone had underestimated the freak, which was more disturbing than he wanted to admit. He never underestimated anyone. But the freak had survived.

And in the process, Evilbitch Ladycop slunk away.

Dang, Boone. You're pretty pathetic yourself, you know?

He looked at his two broken fingers, angled like miniature hockey sticks. Fourth and fifth fingers of his right hand. Boone didn't consider this a handicap. Once he'd finished thinking things through, he'd reset them, then reset his broken nose. No big deal.

Boone didn't feel pain.

It was one of his superpowers, one of many.

The pain was there, he knew that, but he didn't feel it.

Boone understood this. Ketamine had a peculiar range of side effects. It could induce dissociative states, including hallucinations and dissociative analgesia.

"Dissociative analgesia" being the cessation of any sensation of pain.

Not that it was total. The pain did have a clarifying effect. In this case, the effect of clearing away the hallucinations. That horse-hockey idea about being stalked by some Papa Bear–sent goon.

Paranoid delusion.

He understood that now.

You didn't send someone to vacuum up Boone.

Boone was the guy you sent when someone needed vacuuming.

If the paranoia came back again, well hell, he might just break another finger. Clear up the fog. But he didn't think that would be necessary. It had taken some forty-eight hours, but he'd got the Adderall and ketamine pretty well balanced. He was in good shape, getting stronger and clearer with each passing hour.

The freak was not.

The freak was falling apart.

Not hard to see.

Talk about "the handwriting on the wall."

Boone slowly shook his head.

The Little Mermaid on Ice.

Gee-*zus*.

The freak wouldn't come back here now. This place was burned, and he would know it. And Boone held little expectation that he'd be able to sleuth out wherever the hell the freak had gone to ground. But that was okay.

Dandy, in fact.

He didn't need to know where the freak was, because he knew where he'd be, sooner or later.

All Boone had to do was stake out the duck pond.

64

The lighting in the hotel lobby was low. Probably to conceal the grime. A patron lay sprawled on a couch, asleep on his back, mouth open, a mostly empty bottle of Brennivín cradled in his armpit.

Didn't look like the Iceland Miracle had spent much time here.

The Casablanca was one of the few places in Reykjavík, maybe the only place, where no one would notice blood on the lobby floor. Notice, or care.

The man at the desk didn't look up as Finn moved through the stale space.

He found the small bank of metal lockers.

Fished the tiny key out from a zippered pocket, fitted it into the rusted door.

Reached in and brought out the bolt bag he'd stashed in there earlier that day, before joining his walking tour of downtown Reykjavík.

There was no restroom on the Casablanca's ground floor. The elevator was out of service. Finn walked up two flights. Almost passed out three times on his way up the stairs.

You can lose twenty-five percent of total blood volume in anywhere from thirty seconds to three minutes . . .

Found a vacant room and broke in.

Alone in his new sanctuary, he switched on a low-wattage floor lamp and hobbled to the bathroom, set his bolt bag down on the vanity, and took a mental inventory.

Cash: useful. Marlin Pike passport: useless. Two phones, change of clothes.

First aid kit.

All he'd really lost with the backpack were his parka and more clothes. His keycard scanner. His ring knife.

And a great deal of blood.

You'll feel weakness, disorientation, nausea. At fifty percent your organs start shutting down. Which you want to avoid . . .

Copy that.

He leaned on the tiny sink and looked in the mirror.

Ragnar's wool sweater hung on him like rags. Even in a place like the Casablanca, it was surprising that no one had stopped him in the lobby.

Boone's knife had slashed him open nearly to the bone, the blade stopping only at the knot of scar tissue below his left shoulder, his old shrapnel wound.

The one Boone treated years earlier, when he saved Finn's life.

He sat down on the toilet seat.

Stripped from the waist up, tossing the useless remnants of shirt and sweater into the bathroom's minuscule trash can, then reached into the bolt bag and withdrew his precious first aid kit.

Extracted a small vial of tincture of benzoin, which he applied liberally to the slice across his chest.

He pinched his eyes closed and clenched his teeth. It was like cauterizing a wound with a hot laundry iron. He was glad he'd managed to hold on to the stuff, though. Otherwise he would've had to resort to an actual laundry iron.

That would have hurt worse. Maybe.

He leaned back against the restroom wall, letting the surges of pain subside, and thought about what had just happened.

He'd been face-to-face with Boone for only a split second, but the image was seared into his brain. Looking into those eyes—and seeing nothing there. It was like looking through a doorway into an empty room.

Two portholes into an abyss.

He thought about the running girl's eyes, staring up through the ice, eyes that spoke volumes, even if in a language he didn't understand, or at least not yet. But it was all there, the spill of urgent words, the message and meaning behind the red "OM" scribbled onto her abdomen.

And she was already dead.

How could there be so much there in a dead person's eyes—and in a living person's eyes nothing at all?

Finn struggled back to his feet and looked again in the mirror over the sink.

What would someone see if they looked in *his* eyes?

YOUDIDyoudidyoudid . . .

He turned away from the mirror. Closed the first aid kit and stuffed everything back into his bolt bag.

He started downstairs to pay for one night so he would be guaranteed not to be rousted. Give himself a good twelve hours of uninterrupted recovery time. Let the wound on his chest start to heal, or at least not start bleeding again.

Halfway down the second flight he stopped, turned about-face, and climbed back up.

There were two people at the front desk talking with the clerk in low tones.

Black coats, black-and-white-checked hatbands.

Showing the clerk a photo.

Could be an enlarged passport photo of "Jack Lansdale."

Or could be an enlarged passport photo of himself.

He had saved her life barely two hours ago, nearly gotten himself killed in the process. But he remembered those ice-blue eyes that didn't miss much. He had no doubt that Krista Kristjánsdóttir meant what she said.

Marlin Pike, I'm placing you under arrest!

The Casablanca had no side exits.

Finn returned to his temporary hide, slung his bolt bag over one shoulder, and went out the window.

65

There was a soft tap on the door, then silence. After a minute had gone by, the *tap-tap-tap* came again.

She cracked open the door and peered out. When she saw who it was she opened the door.

"I just need somewhere to lie down," he said. "Just for an hour. Maybe two."

She was staying in a studio apartment, her tiny building sandwiched in between a small guesthouse and a stand-alone home in a quiet residential neighborhood northwest of Parliament Square.

She ushered him into the place, which was laid out in classic one-room efficiency style. Tiny all-purpose table, two chairs. Love seat. Kitchenette. Single-mattress bed, basically a cot.

He collapsed into one of the chairs. Unshouldered his bolt bag and slung it onto the little table. Pulled out his first aid kit.

Oksana watched Finn check and redress his wounds.

He swallowed some pills—full-spectrum antibiotics and a mild painkiller—then looked at her, questioning. She nodded toward the cot in the corner. He limped over, moving stiffly, and lay down, back against the mattress, Oksana watching him, still not saying a word.

Once he was prone, on his back, and still, one arm thrown over his eyes, she spoke up.

"So. What happened?"

"Long story." Three syllables, and it already felt like too much work.

She shook her head. "Not story. Not all this." She waved her hand at the city around them. "You. What happened to you."

She wasn't asking about the wound on his chest, about the fight he was in. She was talking about something bigger.

"Why do you follow these two men?" she added. "With the third one. The one who fell."

"Colleagues," said Finn. "Former colleagues."

She looked at him, a long, probing look. Then shook her head again.

"You are not crime writer. You are, I think, American Spec Ops." She lit a cigarette, taking her time about it. Took a long drag, then tilted her chin up and blew out a thin plume of smoke. Looked at him again. "Not army. Navy SEAL, maybe."

Christ on stilts, she was good. Pretty acute observation for a history professor. Even a resourceful one. If that's what she really was.

"And your colleagues?"

"From my team. Former team." Every word an effort.

"So why are you here? Why follow them?" When Finn didn't answer, she said again: "What happened to you?"

Finn lay silent, eyes closed, for so long she was probably wondering if he was still awake. Finally he said:

"We were in Yemen together. Last summer." He stopped. How to explain this? "You know the name Ibrahim Asiri?"

"Asiri." Oksana frowned. "Al Qaeda?"

Finn gave a slight nod. "Underwear bomber, Christmas Day, 2009 . . . Asiri's work." The words resisted at first, then started to flow. "One time, the man packed a bomb into his brother's rectum to assassinate a Saudi prince. The prince wasn't hurt. The brother was. They found part of his arm embedded in the ceiling."

"I remember this," she murmured. "My friend at military intelligence directorate, he called it, 'premature explosion.'"

Finn almost smiled at that one. "Asiri got more sophisticated, worked on ways to make his bombs smaller, recruited a skilled surgeon to implant them. Tried it on dogs. But there were technical challenges. Back in 2012, we took out his surgeon in a drone strike."

Oksana nodded, remembering. "My friend called this 'surgical strike.'" She thought for a moment. "Asiri is dead, too, yes?"

"Fled to some secret camp in Yemen where he kept working on his technique. Recruited a new surgeon, another Saudi expat, brilliant, highly educated guy. His own personal Mengele. Who knows how far they got. We hit Asiri with another drone strike in 2017."

"But his Mengele is alive still?"

"We don't know. But if he is, he's somewhere in central Yemen. Which is why my team was sent there. To track him down."

Finn stopped talking.

What was he doing?

This was all classified information. He shouldn't be telling her any of this. Plus it was completely irrelevant. So why was he still talking?

You're avoiding the real point.

Carol's voice in his head.

You're talking about Yemen and Asiri because you're avoiding her question. So you don't have to talk about what happened. About what you did, or think you may have done.

Carol, who knew Finn better than Finn knew himself.

He took a slow, deep breath. It made his chest feel like he was being branded by a few dozen pissed-off porcupines.

"While we were there," he said, "some of my men did some bad things."

Oksana waited for him to say more. After a long beat she said: "You are blamed?"

"Hard to know."

Yes. He was blamed.

Whether they were right to blame him or not, well, the jury was still out on that one.

There was another long pause. Finn had the sense that she was studying him. Then she spoke up again, gently, as if she were a doctor probing a wound.

"You had close friend. And someone kill."

Finn took his arm down off from over his face and turned to look at her. He hadn't mentioned Kennedy or said anything at all about anyone having killed someone who was close to him.

He hadn't said the word "friend" at all.

"Loss recognize loss," she said.

Finn looked at her for another moment, then turned his head back and closed his eyes again.

"You know who did this?"

"No," he said. "I don't know."

"You look for revenge."

Finn paused before answering.

"I just want to know what happened," he said. "I owe him that."

She stood, covered him with a thin blanket, switched off the light, then went and lay down across the love seat.

The silence stretched out for five minutes, then ten. Then he heard Oksana's voice once more in the darkness.

"Your brother, Ray. Do you know who killed your brother?"

Finn was silent for a moment, then said, "Yes." The words again coming with effort. "I know."

He couldn't have slept if he tried. Though he didn't try: he needed to be on alert. Boone had almost certainly followed the detective to Ragnar's place. If he'd been inside Finn's hide, he would have seen the sketches in Finn's own hand. Which he would recognize. He would know that Finn had a keen interest in the dead girl's story, though he would not know why, any more than Finn himself did.

It was unlikely that he would be able to follow the trail from there to where Oksana was staying, at least not that quickly. They were probably safe there that night. But only probably. Which meant Finn needed to stay awake.

Not that he had much choice in the matter.

After twenty or thirty minutes he heard the soft, steady thrum of Oksana's breathing. Sleep had slipped up from behind and stolen over her, though judging from the faint murmurs and restless movements, it was not a settled sleep.

Another hour went by, and he made a decision.

It wasn't often that Finn backed down. But like any well-trained warrior, he knew the value of a tactical retreat. He would have to confront Boone again, he knew that. But this was not the place or the hour. He was too battered. If they met again, now, here, Boone would annihilate him, broken fingers or not.

And then he would never know.

He would find his answers. But not yet. Not now.

He crept off his cot to the little table where Oksana's phone lay, used it to send a text to Magnús arranging for a ride to the airport in the morning. Which might or might not work. If the DIA were already here, they would doubtless be monitoring the airport like cats watching a goldfish bowl. And just getting through whatever dragnet the detective might have set up could be challenge enough.

But he'd figure it out. If security at the airport made flying from there impossible, he would work out some other way to get off this Arctic raft.

One thing he knew for sure, he thought as he crawled back onto his cot.

If he and Boone did run into each other again before Finn had the chance to evac, only one of them would walk away alive.

During the night Oksana appeared out of the dark and slipped under his blanket, curling up next to him without a word.

Finn didn't think she had sexual intentions. Though he could not be sure of this, he guessed that what she was after was the measure of comfort offered by simple human contact. A moment of warmth in this cold place.

Finn had no problem with that.

For himself there was no thought of sex. Not entirely true; the impulse was there. Impossible not to be. But he was a ruin, drained by his months of sleeplessness, shattered by Peyton's words still echoing in his ears, and now crippled by his encounter with Boone. It hurt to breathe, let alone to move.

It hurt to think.

Besides, every time the notion of sex crept in from around the edges it brought with it thoughts of Carol and her last email message.

Remember who you are.

He had no idea.

Saturday

Plunging to single digits and below; winds from the north, snow flurries; driving conditions hazardous.

66

The phone buzzed.

Finn opened his eyes.

Oksana sat at her little table, smoking a cigarette in her no-smoking room. It was her phone on the table that was buzzing. She made no move to pick it up.

Bzzz!

Finn sat up, looked at the phone, then at her.

Bzzz!

She blew out a plume of smoke. "Is cop."

She looked small and vulnerable. As far as Finn could figure, she wasn't answering because she was afraid of what she'd hear.

Bzzz!

He glanced at his watch. Ten thirty, and still dark out. Half an hour till Magnús would arrive to ferry him to the airport, where he'd take his chances with security. He figured his odds of slipping through were better than 50 percent.

He stood, shakily, every muscle screaming, crossed the tiny room, reached out a finger and pressed TALK, then put the phone on speaker.

There was a brief pause, then Krista's voice, tinny and distorted over the cellphone's speaker, said, *"Halló, Oksana?"*

Finn leaned in and spoke softly. "This is Oksana Shevchenko's room."

There was another pause, then:

"Ah."

"I am Oksana," said Oksana. "You have some report?"

Finn lay down on the floor by the table, staring up at the low-slung ceiling. Felt like he'd never move again.

"In fact, I do. I'm wondering if you'd be able to come in to the station this morning? I'd like to bring you up to date on where we are with your sister's case."

Oksana inhaled on her cigarette, then blew out another plume of smoke. "Tell now."

A pause. *"If you don't mind, it might be easier if we could sit down together for a few minutes?"*

"Now is okay."

Finn heard Krista take a breath on the other end.

"All right. We heard from Tryggvi Pétursson, early this morning. He's had his people asking around, and this morning they brought a man in to us. The man has confessed."

Oksana and Finn exchanged a glance.

"Confessed what, exactly?"

Another pause. *"Oksana, are you sure you wouldn't prefer to come in and meet in person?"*

Without Marlin Pike sitting there listening, in other words.

"Confessed what," Oksana repeated. "Please."

"He says he assaulted your sister, but she managed to get away from him and ran, and he was too drunk to follow more than a block or two, at which point he passed out. Exactly where isn't clear."

Oksana sat still, looking at the end of her cigarette. Then turned her head toward the phone. "You think it possible he is lying?"

"You mean, that he didn't do this at all?"

"I mean, maybe this man chased Kateryna all the way to duck lake, then drown her."

The detective's voice softened slightly. *"The CCTV evidence doesn't support that, no. We expect he's basically telling the truth."*

"Who is this man?"

"A homeless gentleman, lives on the streets around Hlemmur Square. People call him 'Blámi.' Or in English, 'Blue.'"

Blue.

Electric blue silk sash.

Finn thought about the man he'd seen and his vaguely dogged shuffle.

"*We are considering the case as closed. I wanted you to know.*"

"You release body now?"

There was a long pause.

"*Unfortunately, it appears your sister was cremated.*"

Silence.

"*I'm so sorry. This was done in error. The ministry of justice is prepared to pay a substantial settlement.*"

From his vantage point lying on the floor, Finn could see the anguish on Oksana's face.

"*Oksana?*"

After a moment, Oksana whispered, "*Da?*"

"*I'm . . . so very sorry.*"

There was a moment's long silence, and in the stillness Finn thought he could hear both women's hearts collapsing.

"*Tryggvi asked if I would relay an invitation. If you're up to it, he would like to meet with you in person, out at his lake house. He'll send a driver whenever you're ready.*"

The detective gave the location's address and Tryggvi's phone number, then asked if she could speak for a moment with Pike.

Oksana reached over, took the phone off speaker, and handed it down to Finn.

"Detective," said Finn.

"Where is Lansdale?" Krista spoke in a voice barely above a whisper. Finn had the sense she didn't want anyone in her office to hear this part of the conversation. Probably didn't want anyone to know who she was talking to.

Flying solo.

"I find out, you'll be the first to know."

"Pike . . . what exactly is going on? What's your interest here?"

Wasn't that the $64,000 question.

"I find out," he said again, "you'll be the first to know."

"When I find you, I'm taking you in."

When I find you, she said. Not *if*. He almost smiled at that.

He'd changed his mind since the night before. The detective was bluffing. She didn't want to haul him in for questioning. What she wanted was the same thing he wanted.

To understand exactly why Oksana's sister ended up in the duck pond.

As she was about to disconnect the call, he said, "Krista."

"What, Pike." She sounded tired.

"I was sorry to hear about your partner."

He clicked off and lay back against the wooden floor, wondering why he'd said what he did.

He glanced up at Oksana, staring out the window, her face a tapestry of pain. "Substantial settlement," she said, spitting the words.

Like money would settle anything.

"Sister is smoke," she said.

Finn had no idea how to respond to that, so he waited to see if she would say anything else. When she didn't, he said, "You going out to meet with him?"

"*Da.*"

Finn considered for a moment. As soon as he could peel himself off this floor, he was out the door to meet up with his ride. He couldn't afford to delay his evac any longer. *Spoke with Diane about the boys' jungle gym, should be delivered no later than Friday.* And now it was Saturday.

He looked up at Oksana again.

"I have a driver who'll take you. Be here any minute."

The moment he made the offer he wondered why he'd done it. Now he'd have to find alternate transportation to the airport, which would only delay him further. And he needed to get out right then, as soon as possible, before DIA found him. Or Boone found him. Or Tryggvi tapped his network and learned who he really was. Or the detective with the ice-blue eyes changed her mind and the police hauled him in.

She nodded. "Good. Then I fly home to Kyiv, before all flights stop for New Year." She stubbed out her cigarette and gathered her cigarette pack, lighter, and phone into her purse. Looked down at him on the floor. "You rest. When I go, you keep room."

She slung her purse over her shoulder and walked to the door.

And Finn realized what he'd known since the moment he'd heard the detective say, *We are considering the case as closed.*

And the conflicted tone in which she said it.

He got up to a sitting position, then stood. Retrieved his bolt bag from where he'd dumped it on the table.

"I'm coming with you," he said.

67

As they drove east out of the city and merged onto
Ring Road, the sun rose to stare at them from the horizon, a hard, cold
sun that shimmered off the roadway's icy surface and did nothing to
mediate the sinking temperatures.

"In normal times," said Magnús in his tour-guide voice, "this is one
hour's drive at most, maybe fifty minutes. Today we go a little more slow,
in respect of the blackened ice."

It was the first time Finn had seen him since the day he arrived in
Iceland. The man looked bigger than he remembered. Or maybe the car
had gotten smaller.

Magnús had brought him something to replace his lost parka and ruined sweater. "America made," he'd announced proudly when he gave it
to Finn. A wool peacoat. US Navy spec.

Not exactly the best disguise for a US naval chief on the run, but Finn
was in no position to be picky.

Magnús had insisted Oksana sit up front, next to him, so he could
show her the sights. Finn did his best to stretch out in back, using the
peacoat as a pillow.

Every bump in the road was torture.

In movies, after the big fight scene the hero would recover more or
less instantly: a swig of bourbon, a few kisses from the leading lady, a
wince or two while someone put in stitches, and he'd be ready to fight
another day.

The reality was different. The beatings never went away. Finn had witnessed simple bar fights that ended in paraplegia or incapacitating brain damage.

And Finn had been through a lot worse than bar fights.

Even SEALs who never saw combat had some of the highest rates of TBI—traumatic brain injury—of any population group. Out on the water in fast boats crashing into waves, endless series of parachute jumps slamming them into the ground, rattling their brains in their skulls. Proximity to explosives. Shooting off thousands and thousands of high-velocity rounds. SEAL training was possibly the most percussive activity known to man.

And that was just the training.

They said a SEAL aged five years for every year he deployed. By that math, Finn was an old man, and right then he was feeling every tree-ring.

"Thingvallavatn is the largest natural lake in Iceland," Magnús was saying. "The Mid-Atlantic Rift runs straight up through the lake. It is the only place on earth where you can literally touch two continents at the same time."

The big man knew something of the tragedy his front-seat passenger had been through, and Finn had the impression he was keeping up the encyclopedia patter in an effort to keep her mind off her thoughts. From his position prone in the backseat, he couldn't tell if it was working or not. He doubted it.

"At the lake's northern point you'll see Parliament Field, where we held our old assemblies, over a thousand years ago. Justice was harsh in those days. Fingers were chopped off, sometimes whole arms," he rattled on cheerfully. "And, of course, many executions. There was hanging for thieves and beheading for male adulterers. Burning for witches and war-locks. There was also a whirlpool in a bend in the river, just above the lake, Drekkyingarhylur, the Drowning Pool.

"The Drowning Pool, now, this was reserved for the execution of women convicted of 'loose morals.' Since the 1600s we had nearly eighty—"

He abruptly stopped talking.

After a moment he said, "I almost forgot: to the south, not far from here, we have one of our famous geothermal plants. As you may have heard, one hundred percent of Iceland's energy come from geothermal and other renewables . . ."

Apparently their tour guide had finally realized he'd blundered into a wildly ill-suited topic. Finn was no expert in social graces, but even he could tell that the big man's attempt to change conversational lanes was hopeless.

". . . although our biggest industries now are tourism and bitcoin." Magnús chuckled. "You probably noticed the rows of Quonset huts and hangars out by the airport when you arrived. These were US air base buildings many decades ago, long abandoned. Now some are big data centers. The world's biggest cryptocurrency operation is right here in Iceland! Cheap energy and plenty of cold!"

After another paragraph or two about Iceland's economic resurrection he stopped, and the car lapsed into a desultory silence.

Finn hauled himself upright to look around at the scenery.

The sun hung low on the treeless horizon, ice glittering on the low desert scrub that spread in every direction. A landscape encased in glass.

After a minute or two, he lay back down.

They drove on.

68

The driveway sloped down from the access road to a parking area outside a garage built onto the back of the lake house.

Magnús brought the Yaris to a stop and Finn sat up again.

From the back, the place looked like a modest affair, not what he had expected from one of the wealthiest citizens of an extremely wealthy country.

Tryggvi had come out to meet them. As he approached the car and saw Oksana for the first time, his face visibly sagged. Obviously he was struck by her resemblance to her sister, just as Finn had been the first time they met. For Tryggvi, the reminder was clearly a painful one.

Magnús made brief introductions, then announced that he would remain with the car, if that was all right with their host, and let them have their meeting in private. Oksana made no effort to explain Finn's presence, and Tryggvi didn't ask.

Nor did he give any indication that he and Finn had already met.

He led his two guests down a set of wide slate steps that wound around the building to a small dock built out onto the lake.

The view was stunning. Ringed by low-lying, snow-dusted mountains, the lake stretched out for miles of majestic desolation, like an Arctic Ansel Adams print. From where they stood a strange, jagged line ran straight out to the horizon, like a massive zipper.

"My whole life," Tryggvi murmured, "the surface of Thingvallavatn sealed itself up every winter with a sheet of ice so thick you could drive trucks across it. The past fifteen years, the season has grown steadily milder and shorter, the ice itself more unstable. I try not to see this as a metaphor."

"For Iceland?" said Finn.

Tryggvi shrugged, that same, awkward shrug Finn had seen at the Fosshótel. "For humanity."

He turned and led them back up the slate path to a side entrance, where he stopped. Before entering the building he turned and spoke to Oksana.

"I wanted to meet with you to apologize in person. I am so deeply sorry my staff didn't . . ." He sighed. "That *we* didn't keep a closer eye on your sister. She was a good soul, a true innocent. I cannot fathom anyone wishing her harm, though I know only too well that such incomprehensible monsters exist on this earth."

He turned back again and stepped inside. Oksana and Finn followed into a large tiled mudroom, where they doffed their parka and peacoat and hung them on hooks. Racks of skis and snowshoes lined the walls, along with regiments of parkas and scarves and goggles; two kayaks hung from ceiling-mounted racks.

"I am afraid our city is not as safe as it once was," Tryggvi continued. "Perhaps your friend is right. Perhaps, like the ice over Thingvallavatn, the moral foundation of our Icelandic society is weakening. In some ways Iceland is a child who has reached the age of majority and come suddenly into a trust fund. Yesterday she was playing with trolls and sheep-bone toys, today she is driving her friends in a Maserati at 150 kilometers per hour. But she is still a child, trying to grasp what it means to be an adult."

He bade them follow him through a short hallway and out into a spacious kitchen and eating area, where he briefly introduced a burly groundskeeper and two other strapping staff personnel whose functions were not given. The cook was busy at the stove feeding the others and not introduced. She looked to Finn like a wrestler.

"While it took a few days," Tryggvi said over his shoulder as they exited the kitchen, "it was not difficult for my people to identify and locate the man responsible. I am sorry we were not able to do so more swiftly."

Finn noticed he made no reference to the police. Perhaps he found them too incompetent to deserve mention.

Tryggvi now ushered them into the "great room." Finn wasn't sure what a great room was supposed to look like, but this thing was cavernous. It was like a trick of perspective, some magic spell out of *The Arabian Nights*, or maybe *Doctor Who*: larger on the inside than it was on the outside.

The walls were sparsely hung with landscapes, each piece isolated against an expanse of white wall and lit discreetly by its own ceiling-mounted accent light. Natural-wood shelves lined the walls, widely spaced, holding a minimalist display of exquisite sculpted pieces. Oddly, no books.

There was evidence of culture everywhere, yet it struck Finn as somehow lacking in humanity. Beautiful but cold.

A massive plate-glass window looked directly out onto the lake.

Their host ushered them to chairs, and the three sat, each uncomfortable for their own reasons: Finn's his aching body, Oksana's her aching soul, Tryggvi's his apparent remorse and guilt of his inadvertent role in the tragedy.

"I know it would have been more convenient for us to meet in the city," Tryggvi said. "But I hoped you would accept my invitation for another reason. I wanted you to see the beauty that surrounded your sister in what we now understand were her final days. I also thought you might want to see the room where she stayed."

He paused, perhaps to give Oksana the opportunity to speak.

She gave a pro forma nod, looking not at him but out over the lake.

"If these thoughts only cause you more pain, I apologize once again. But I have seen much bereavement in my years. And sometimes it is a comfort to know these things. To have these memories of the departed one, to hold them as your own."

At this, Oksana's stoic reserve seemed to falter, whether prompted by the sensitivity of Tryggvi's words or the grief they triggered, Finn didn't know.

Tryggvi waited in silence, giving Oksana time to process the offer.

Finally, she turned her head and looked at him.

"I like to see the room."

69

The little room where Kateryna Shevchenko had spent much of the last eight weeks of her young life was sparsely furnished, yet it felt warmer than the great room. A small bed, fully made with quilt and bolsters. A bureau and mirror. A few cozy chairs. Bookshelves. A small writing table by the window, which like the great room's looked out over the lake.

The bookshelves were bare, as was every other piece of furniture. The room was conspicuously empty of any signs of habitation.

"Her personal effects have all been packed and prepared for shipment back home," Tryggvi explained. "To whatever address you would like to provide."

Oksana did so, reciting a Kyiv street address in quiet monotones, which Tryggvi dutifully tapped into a note on his phone.

Oksana rose from her chair and walked over to the window, looking out again at the lake.

"So peaceful," she murmured. "Exactly as she describe."

Finn noted a twitch pass over Tryggvi's face, but both men remained silent.

After a moment Oksana turned and looked at Tryggvi.

"Is possible I can meet Zofia?"

To Finn, Tryggvi's response seemed beyond strange. His expression didn't change at all—but he blinked, a slow blink of both eyes at the same time. Like two motorized window shades closing and opening together.

"Of course," he said, with a dip of the head halfway between a nod and a bow. "If you will give me a moment."

He left the room.

Oksana looked out the window again.

Finn waited.

Tryggvi returned a few minutes later looking apologetic. He spoke softly.

"I'm sorry. Zofia has taken this rather hard. She has, in fact, barely come out of her room in the past week. We've been bringing her meals, and at night, we have someone staying with her."

Oksana nodded dully. "Understand."

Tryggvi gestured toward the door to the hallway, prepared to lead them back to the great room. "If you're ready?"

Oksana stepped to the door, then turned to him and said, "Kateryna, she was sick?"

"Sick?"

"She write to me, say she is not feeling well. Sick."

Finn saw that same twitch in Tryggvi's face as he hesitated. He had the conflicted look of someone wrestling with what, or how much, to say.

"I wonder," he said finally, "if I might speak with you for a moment. Privately."

Oksana looked at Finn, then back to their host.

"Whatever we talk, he can hear too."

Tryggvi cast a sideways glance at Finn, then nodded. He gestured for Oksana to come back into the little bedroom, then shut the door. "Please," he said, gesturing to the bed.

Oksana sat, gingerly, as if afraid to disturb the neatly made covers. She ran her hand softly over the quilt, and didn't look up.

Tryggvi looked at them each in turn, then spread his hands, as if in a gesture of apology.

"I have not been entirely truthful," he began.

70

"The police asked me if there were any way Kateryna could have been using drugs. I told them this was impossible." Tryggvi paused and once again looked at each of them in turn. "This was a lie. I lied to the police."

He put his palms together and touched his lips to the tips of his fingers, a gesture Finn took to mean something like, *I accept my transgression.*

"It was too late to save her life," he continued. "It was not too late to preserve her privacy. Her dignity."

His voice dropped to a confidential, almost reverential tone.

"Saturday evening, as we now know, Kateryna slipped out of the house and, one way or another, found a ride into the city. Once there, we do not know where she went nor what she did. We will likely never know. But it ended, of course, in trouble . . ."

He let the sentence drift off, as if not wanting to paint in too much detail the picture of Blámi's attempted assault and its fatal consequences. When he began speaking again, he hesitated at first, as if unsure of how to phrase what he had to say next.

"Some weeks ago, not long after she first arrived, one of our staff found some . . . drug paraphernalia. Right here, in her room. Hidden in a mostly empty jar of peanut butter."

Finn heard a sharp intake of breath from Oksana.

"Of course, we let her know such behavior was not acceptable here, and certainly would not be tolerated at her eventual place of employ. She immediately apologized and seemed to understand this, and there were no further occurrences. But . . ."

This time he brought his hands together with fingers interlaced, a gesture of supplication that seemed to say, *I hope she meant what she said and stuck by that commitment—but who knows?*

Finn stole a glance at Oksana. Her face had gone pale. She looked like someone had struck her with a two-by-four.

After a long silence, Oksana stood. "Thank you for make everything clear," she said. "I will go now."

Tryggvi nodded and opened the bedroom door, ushering them back out into the hallway again.

They walked single-file back through the house, Oksana appearing not to hear Tryggvi's murmured words of sympathy, or even be aware that anyone was speaking, and came to a back entrance that let out into the garage space, which held three impressive vehicles. One of them, a black Bentley Bentayga, was currently being worked on by the chauffeur Finn had seen standing by the Tower elevator Wednesday evening.

Finn walked over to the front of the vehicle, where the chauffeur was bent over his task and leaned in next to him to get a look under the hood. "Wow," he said.

The other man shot him a look as dark as the Bentley's finish.

After another moment Finn rejoined the others at the exit out to the paved parking area, where Oksana had just stopped and turned to Tryggvi. "Leave today, for home," she said. "Not come back."

Finn signaled Magnús, who came over, gently took Oksana by the arm, and walked her back to the Yaris, leaving Finn behind for a parting word with their host.

Once Oksana was out of range, Finn turned to Tryggvi. "Was she pregnant?"

Tryggvi responded with that same strange, slow blink, both eyes together. Window shades down, window shades up. He then took a slow breath. In, then out. Finn sensed he was struggling to rein in a seething fury, holding off on a reply until his voice regained its usual even tone.

"There is a reason, Mister Pike," he finally said, "that Americans have the reputation for being a rude people. No, Kateryna was not pregnant." He glanced toward the retreating figures of sister and driver, then back to Finn. "Though I thank you for having the decency to wait until Miss Shevchenko was out of earshot to ask your question."

As he walked back to the car, Finn remembered something his big brother, Ray, told him as a kid, back in the Snake River woods. After catching a fly, Ray said, a frog would close its eyes for a moment—but not because it was blinking.

Because it was using the backs of its eyeballs to push the still-wriggling fly down its throat.

There were no reptiles or amphibians in Iceland, so Finn had read.

He wasn't so sure it was true.

71

" 'Fear not death, for the hour of your doom is set, and none may escape it.' "

It was perhaps the most famous line from the *Völsunga Saga*, one of Iceland's greatest epic poems.

If the doomed man in question were sitting right there on the bench next to Krista at that particular hour, he would roll his eyes and look for a way to slip out and go hunt down a Danish.

Krista smiled.

Evidently this greatly offended the older couple sitting next to her. Fuck 'em. She was aching on the inside, probably more than anyone else in the whole goddam church. She'd smile if she goddam wanted to.

Decked with a gigantic wreath and all the trappings of police regalia, Einar's coffin sat at the foot of the broad steps leading up to the altar where the minister gave his endless prepared remarks.

" 'Who can say what sorrows a seemingly carefree man bears to his life's end?' "

The *Völsunga Saga* again.

As the man's voice droned on Krista switched it off and tried to think about something, anything, that had nothing to do with why they were sitting there.

Einar's service was being held at Hallgrímskirkja, just as Birna Brjánsdóttir's had been a few years earlier. Only this felt less like a national trauma, strangely, and more like a national celebration.

The police had come through! They'd caught the man responsible for the Little Mermaid's death! The incident at the clinic? That was troubling, of course it was, but it could be put on hold for the moment, couldn't it? The American tourist's death was tragic, but, well, Americans could be foolish, couldn't they? And poor Ólafur. That was so sad, but then again, it was a good object lesson for Icelandic children: people who go down that path are likely to come to a bad end! Apply yourself, work hard, live a decent Icelandic life! Stay away from drugs and alcohol!

Even Einar had somehow become a part of the message.

The great detective's passing was tragic—but heroic, too, in its own way. It marked the end of an honorable life, serving the people of Iceland, helping to keep the peace.

And in the blink of an eye, the police had been restored to the place of honor as Iceland's heroes. Hey! It's New Year's Eve! Let's put the dark past behind us and light the way to happier times ahead!

Krista felt disgusted and ashamed.

She had left work right after making that disturbing call to Oksana. Her presence was hardly needed at metro today. The fog of tension that had suffused the building throughout the past week had magically dissipated. *Things were looking up*, as Einar might put it in another of his irritating Americanisms.

Coming up roses.

In Einar's honor, she'd tried to put her thoughts away and rejoin the memorial service happening all around her.

Her thoughts wouldn't cooperate.

The problem was, Krista *knew* the homeless man sitting in their jail cell at that very moment. Knew Blámi—Blue—as well as she'd known poor Ólafur, as well as she knew all the marginalized population of her city.

He had admitted his guilt. Did that mean he was guilty?

Well, just look at the circumstances.

The pressure to confess must have been substantial. And consider what he had to gain by saying "Yes, I did it." An assault charge in Iceland's lenient penal system wouldn't amount to much. Even if they convicted him of murder (which seemed highly unlikely), there was no death penalty. And prison life in Iceland was a good deal easier than the life he'd been living up till now.

Her entire department had rushed to indict the man, like pigeon hawks on a snared sparrow. Yet they couldn't release Logan the Aussie wunderkind fast enough.

It was all wrong. She knew it.

She just didn't know exactly how.

72

The interior of the Yaris was quiet the whole ride back. Oksana looked out her passenger's side window. Magnús just drove.

In back, Finn scrolled his phone—flip phone #4, the one he'd been using to track the detective's memos and movements, which had fortunately been in an inside pocket when he lost his backpack in the ambush outside the cemetery. The tracking wasn't working anymore. Evidently the detective had twigged on to his trick and ditched the phone, probably switched her old number over to a brand-new phone, leaving Finn's spyware behind.

But he still had all her notes from the week.

A few minutes of scrolling and translating confirmed it.

From her interview with Tryggvi Tuesday morning, she had detailed the whereabouts of the entire lake house staff. There'd been a follow-up interview with the groundskeeper the next day, the only person present on premises over Christmas. And that was it.

Nowhere in Krista's notes was there any mention of Zofia.

Why not?

Where was Zofia on Christmas Eve when her friend went missing?

Tryggvi had covered his reaction skillfully when Oksana asked about Zofia, but he'd been startled by the question. Finn had seen it in his face.

And that wasn't the only time. A minute before that, when Oksana commented that the lake was just as her sister had described, Tryggvi had reacted then, too. It was only a fraction of an instant, a micro-expression, no more noticeable than the twitch of a single eyelash. But Finn saw it.

A look of surprise.

Tryggvi had not known that Kateryna was in communication with her sister.

Maybe Kateryna had sent her texts surreptitiously.

Maybe she had sensed something that made her cautious.

Oksana appeared to accept the man's story.

Finn didn't.

Not that he thought the sex ring scenario worked. Anyone broker-ing a serious trafficking trade would deal in volume, not one or two women.

Then what?

Were Kateryna and Zofia set up to act as couriers, as the detective had speculated? That could fit. A private jet would get a very light touch on reentry to the US, no more than a cursory customs check.

Tryggvi might not have had any military background, but Finn sup-posed savvy businessmen lived by the same rule that had been drilled into him in his own Spec Ops training: never move without a backup plan.

Finn's guess was, if Kateryna was to be a courier, Zofia would be their backup. Just in case something went wrong.

And something had gone as wrong as a thing could go.

If Tryggvi was using the two women as couriers to transport some-thing to New York, what would it be? Drugs? Unlikely. Again: a question of volume. Someone like Tryggvi wouldn't go to the trouble of setting up this whole operation, no matter how well connected the client, unless the cargo was enormously valuable.

What would be that valuable yet portable enough to be couriered un-detected by a single twenty-something woman?

Intel? Extreme classified secrets, concealed somehow on their per-son?

Finn had no doubt that Tryggvi had the long-standing connections that could make such a thing possible. It could even be done without the courier herself being aware of it.

So: a maybe.

But a maybe was not the same thing as a *click*.

He left that question for the time being and moved on to the next.

The staffing at the lake house. What was up with that?

Hostile chauffeur/bodyguard. Cook who resembled Stone Cold Steve Austin. Burly groundskeeper and two others who had no discernible function, yet all three with that same merciless, unmistakably paramilitary look to them.

A security staff of three. Three at minimum.

Which seemed excessive.

It struck Finn that this was the first time since arriving in Iceland a week earlier that he'd seen any kind of dedicated security detail. And for a lake house?

Was she pregnant?

When Tryggvi denied it, Finn believed him. He'd never thought so anyway, Krista's speculations notwithstanding. He'd just wanted to see how Tryggvi would react.

And he did.

That strange, slow blink.

What wriggling fly was the old Icelander pushing down with the backs of his eyeballs?

The Yaris swayed once, then again. A gust of Arctic wind blowing down off the bay.

The temperature was dropping again.

As they exited off the Ring Road onto Seaway, the road into the city, Finn thought about something else he'd just now read in the detective's notes. It was from her interrogation of the hapless young medical student who'd said he might have seen Kateryna but was too drunk to be sure.

"*Svartur jeppi*," she'd written.

The first time he'd read it, the software translated "*jeppi*" as *Jeep*. Only he'd just now dug a little deeper and learned that the Icelandic word had a second meaning, namely "SUV."

"Svartur" meant "black," like the German *"schwartz."*

Svartur jeppi.

A black SUV.

Maybe a Bentley Bentayga.

73

"'Bravery is half the victory,' so says the saga *Haralds Harðráða*," the man declaimed. "Einar loved these old lines, loved the land that gave them birth, the land he gave his life to over twenty-six years of service. But as those close to him know, he was fonder still of another old verse, this one from the saga of Saint Ólafur: 'Too much ale, and a man's heart is laid open for all to see.'"

A ripple of mirth passed through the congregation.

Krista checked the time on her phone, for no particular reason.

She couldn't stop thinking, yet her thoughts went in aimless half circles. A detail was bothering her, and she couldn't nail down what it was.

"Yes, Einar Grímsson was a man who enjoyed his ale. And his heart was always laid out for all of us to plainly see. A man who . . ."

They'd run Kateryna's discarded clothing for DNA, pulled plenty of samples from her cuffs and collar, undergarments, socks, compared it to the samples from the toothbrush and hairbrush they'd recovered from Tryggvi's lake house. It was all Kateryna. Not a trace of a second person.

Her clothing had not been in any disarray at the scene, nothing torn, no sign of struggle. Like it had been simply removed and dropped to the ground.

Footprints were inconclusive. They were able to pick out Kateryna's and those of Gunnar, the little boy who found her, but random observers crowding in before the police arrived had pretty much wrecked any chance of identifying additional tracks.

And no CCTV of anyone following her anywhere near the pond, not of Blámi nor anyone else.

And even if poor Blámi was guilty of doing what he claimed he did—or for that matter, even if it was Logan who made the assault, or the attempted assault—none of that explained the sequence of events that actually put the girl in the water.

Nor the week-old scar.

There were whole chunks of this story still missing, and it was driving her crazy.

"'Cattle die, kinsmen die; the self must also die,'" the minister was intoning now. "'Yet I know one thing that never dies—the reputation of each dead man.'"

It struck Krista how anachronistic it was, how weird, hearing snippets of old Viking poems quoted like Scripture in a Lutheran service. But weird in a way she loved.

Weird in a way that was Iceland.

Though it was a different Old Norse saying that kept running through Krista's head.

A tale is but half told when only one person tells it.

Krista Kristjánsdóttir had the unshakable sense that she was still missing half the story.

74

As the three pulled in by the little apartment building, Oksana turned to Magnús. "You can give a ride to airport? I'm needing just a few minutes."

"No kind of problem," Magnús growled.

Oksana got out of the Yaris and disappeared into the building.

Magnús and Finn waited for her in silence.

After a moment, Finn spoke up from his prone position in back. "Iceland's industry. You have any aluminum mines here?"

Magnús shook his head. "The aluminum business is enormous here, but it's all processing. The raw material is shipped in from other countries. We can process it here at big profits, because of our big cheap energy."

"Are there any other kind of mines?"

"Not unless you mean geothermal plants. But"—he shook his head—"I don't know if you can exactly call those mines."

Last night I dream I visit mines.

I write back, Mines? What mines?

Oksana reemerged, carry-on bag over her shoulder and a sealed envelope in her hand.

Once in her seat she turned to Magnús. "Make one stop in town first. This is okay?" She held up the envelope. Finn noticed the neat printing on the front: Tryggvi. "Never said proper thank you."

It occurred to Finn that she actually *had* thanked the man. *Thank you for make everything clear*. But he said nothing. Maybe it was important to her to put it in writing.

"Next stop, Höfðatorg Tower," said Magnús, looking over his shoulder into the back. "All set?"

"Hold up." Finn sat up, pushed open the door, and got out, then came around to Oksana's door. She rolled down her window. "You go ahead," he said to Magnús through the open window.

"You sure?" said Magnús.

Finn shouldered his bolt bag and gave a thumbs-up.

"Maybe we'll see each other at the airport," he said to Oksana, knowing they would not.

"Maybe," said Oksana. She took his hand from the window frame, turned it over, and kissed his palm, then curled his fingers into a fist and gave it a squeeze. "Good luck with friend."

"See you around the block, Ghost Writer," said Magnús. Finn heard his laugh rumble as the Yaris pulled away.

He watched it turn a corner and disappear.

The streets were filling with people dressed up in sparkling outfits and snow boots. Like partygoers on an Arctic expedition. Which, he supposed, was pretty much what it was.

New Year's Eve in Iceland.

He rolled his shoulders a few times to get some circulation going. Looked around him.

Change of plans. No ride.

He could walk to the shuttle, near the harbor. That would work fine. Get him to the airport just as fast as Magnús would have, give or take a few minutes.

But something was bugging him.

He started walking east.

75

Krista got to her feet and slipped out of her pew as surreptitiously as possible, ignoring at least a dozen glares, including an especially dark look from Ylfa the she-wolf.

The memorial had not wrapped yet, but she couldn't sit there another minute.

She threaded her way up an outside aisle to the church's northwest-facing front entrance, through the great wooden doors, and out into the slate-gray courtyard, where an idling hearse stood patiently waiting for Einar.

Looking north toward the harbor, she could see the sporadic eruption of a few early fireworks. By midnight, they would fill the sky.

She began to walk east.

76

Finn knew he shouldn't be out in the open walking
like this.

He'd been lucky at the cemetery. But luck was a drug. One good hit
and you were hooked, always looking for another bump to carry you
safely through the next time, and the next after that. He knew better.
Boone could be anywhere. And Finn was in no shape to face him, not
now.

Yet he walked.

When he reached the duck pond, he stopped.

Sat on a wood-and-iron bench by the Monument to the Unknown
Bureaucrat, looking out over the railing at the ice spread out before him.
Less than a hundred feet away, she had walked into the pond and ended
her life.

And still no one knew why.

What did she see?

The question still whispering at the back of his brain.

What did she know?

Streams of people passed, out for the beginning of New Year's Eve
festivities.

The thing that was bugging him, the thing that made him get out of
Magnús's Yaris so he could walk and think, was something Dixon had
said.

*We're sitting here jerking off, waiting for a Go! and getting nothing but
radio silence.*

Why were they sitting there, waiting for a Go?

Why weren't the SEALs getting the order to finish their op?

Some limp dick bigwig in his Georgetown penthouse got cold feet.

Okay. But why?

The answer was so obvious that up till then, Finn hadn't bothered to give it a moment's thought. Tom had died, suddenly and in a most public way. Putting a kill-or-capture team in play in a friendly nation without their knowledge was an insanely risky proposition in the first place. It couldn't possibly withstand that kind of attention. The remaining members of the team had to be yanked before someone started looking at them too closely.

Obvious answer.

But what if it wasn't the right answer?

What if the reason they were recalled had nothing to do with Tom? If, for example, there was someone who simply didn't want their mission completed? What if there was someone who put pressure on whatever limp dick bigwig it was who pulled the plug?

Someone, say, with a network with tendrils that reached everywhere?

Someone who had gone out of his way to single Finn out and warn him away. Or try to anyway.

Finn stood, made his way out to the streets, and started walking east again.

It had been at least thirty-six hours since Peyton and Dixon were recalled. The odds that their suite had already been re-rented to new guests had to be high. Better than 50 percent anyway. And even if it hadn't, it would have been thoroughly cleaned.

Still, it was worth a look.

Looking for what?

Only one way to know.

The sun was setting behind him, casting the windows on the buildings ahead in a blood-orange glow that was already fading.

Darkness was falling.

77

She had no plan or direction. She just had to move, to get away from the maudlin display of sentiment that would make her old partner roll over in his grave.

His grave.

Just thinking the words made her chest ache all over again.

God help her but she missed him. His lame jokes and irritating routines, his B.O. and his Danishes and messy handwriting. His sharp eyes and fierce sense of fair play.

This is Einar. I'm occupied right now, solving the crime of the century.

As she walked she passed people everywhere, the streets filling up with the tide of New Year's Eve celebration. The whole city had taken the day off, relieved to say goodbye to the old year and eager to greet the new.

Krista was not ready to say goodbye.

She couldn't stop replaying the scene.

In the kitchen, building his drink.

Through the little hallway, to the bathroom.

Setting the drink carefully on the side of the tub, shutting off the water, climbing in, fastidiously drying off his hands on a hand towel, then lighting the little candle that would illuminate his final moments.

Placing his paperback facedown on the side of the tub to hold his place, just for a moment.

Picking up his glass and taking a long, sweet pull on his drink.

Setting the glass down again.

Settling back against the tub's backrest.

She stopped for a moment and wiped her eyes with the backs of her freezing hands. Looking around, she realized she was on her way to metro.

Why had she come this way? No reason in particular.

Darkness was falling.

She continued walking.

Her friend Einar, reading in the tub. It was so unlike him, that picture of a man sitting, peacefully reading a book in the tub. When was the last time she saw Einar reading a book? Never. The last time was never. Which made it all that much more poignant. An older and wiser Einar, in his final moments, enriching himself with a good John D. MacDonald.

Einar, who loved his telly and lived on his phone—

She stopped walking.

New Year's Eve partygoers buzzed and bustled around her, but she didn't notice them.

Einar, who loved his telly and lived on his phone.

Einar was never without his phone.

She thought back to her circuit through his little house, the day they discovered his body. Walking through room after room, taking in every mundane detail, trying to make sense out of all. Remembering what she'd thought as she repeated her hopeless pilgrimage.

A column of numbers that added up to a sum that made no sense.

Candle, book, drink.

Where was his phone?

78

Boone had never felt so clear.

He had followed Finn from the duck pond at a prudent remove, staying at least two blocks back. And they'd progressed no more than four or five blocks when, whaddyaknow, here came Evilbitch Ladycop, walking out of the big church and heading east herself.

Boone had to shake his head and grin.

What was this, Christmas all over again?

Neither one of 'em saw the other. And neither one knew Boone was on their tail.

Unbefuckinlievable.

Boone did not believe in God, per se (although as far as he was concerned, the jury was still out on Satan). But he did most certainly believe in the existence of Providence. Not an embodied deity sort of Providence, not as a "spiritual" thing. More like a mathematical field, like gravity, a sort of natural force that responded to the execution of excellence.

Right then, Boone was feeling the touch of Providence shining on him, lighting his path.

Which to be frank was a hell of a relief.

Boone would not admit this to anyone, not even to himself, but he was not proud of his last few kills since arriving here in this little one-horse town.

The fall from the roof, that was good. Clean. But the two at the clinic?

Too theatrical. A smart cop would have reason to frown and scratch his head, think a little harder than Boone would prefer.

Or *her* head.

And the drug dealer? That was a flat-out fuckaroo. Disaster. Even the rubest of rube blue boys (or blue *girls*) would have to wonder about "suicide" when the man's place was busted all to shit, his staged little cocaine after-party notwithstanding.

Boone had been off his game.

No more.

Boone was now very much on his game.

As a result of which he was now moving with a splash more circumspection in his coffee.

He had to assume the police knew he was here, probably even knew what he looked like.

This changed things.

Boone was fairly close to invincible. But close didn't cut it in hang gliding and homicide. Supremely confident in his abilities, yes, but he was not an incautious man. He needed to neutralize Finn and get off the damn island. Not get caught up in a mess with the locals, where he might have to kill in greater numbers and end up just spreading the mess around, rather than cleaning it up nice and neat.

He needed to follow, wait, and do it right.

Ladycop was a good block behind the freak, and within another two blocks the freak took a left, veering northeast, while Evilbitch kept on going due east.

Boone had a choice, and it was an easy one. Much as he would love to put out Evilbitch Ladycop's lights, that was for personal reasons, and Boone was nothing if not a professional. He had a job to do.

He let the bitch go and followed the freak.

79

Finn came to a stop in the street outside the entrance to the Fosshótel, standing where the detective had stood two days earlier, looking up at the hotel's windows, scanning for signs of him. Not far from where Finn had stood himself, the night before that, and seen the Northern Lights hovering over the Höfði House like a ghost.

He stood still now, looking up at the black sky—and it exploded in a burst of dazzling light.

New Year's Eve in Reykjavík was legendary, the most over-the-top display of pyrotechnics on the planet. Astronauts had reported seeing the Reykjavík fireworks from orbit. The mayhem wouldn't hit full stride until midnight, after everyone shouted *"Gleðilegt nýtt ár!"* but this year there were plenty of trigger-happy celebrants only too happy to jump the gun.

The sky above Finn's head went brilliant, then dark, then briefly brilliant a second time.

Flash—darkness—flash.

Finn jerked.

A memory.

Now it came again—

Flash—darkness—flash.

He bent forward, eyes closed, trying to catch it.

Morse code? Dit-dit-dit, dah-dah-dah, dit-dit-dit? An S-O-S? Didn't ring a bell. A flash, then darkness, then a flash. It meant something. Something weighty, he could feel it.

But he had no idea what.

Suddenly Finn felt a static charge shimmer in the air around him.

His eyes jerked open and he spun around, all his senses tingling, his peripheral nerves firing chemical fusillades like a brigade of one-celled Marines.

Streams of partygoers passed in all directions.

No sign of Boone.

dit-dit-dit, dah-dah-dah, dit-dit-dit

flash—darkness—flash

S-O-S

He took three steadying breaths. Then turned and proceeded in through the revolving door of the Fosshótel.

He stopped at the front desk and asked the clerk about his friends.

"The two Americans, whose friend . . . you know." He let his grave expression fill in the rest of the sentence.

The clerk's face fell. "Yes. I'm so sorry."

Finn leaned forward and spoke in the earnest hoarseness of the grieving-but-trying-to-move-on. "I'm just wondering, has their suite already been let out to new occupants?"

The clerk's somber expression turned to puzzlement. "New occupants?"

"No? I thought it might still be empty."

"Empty?"

"Since they checked out."

"Checked out?"

Finn cocked his head. What was it about his question this guy wasn't getting?

The clerk frowned, then looked at his computer screen and tapped a few keys. "But they haven't checked out, sir."

They hadn't checked out?

It was Friday morning when he got Stan L's message about George and Lenny being recalled. And they still hadn't checked out?

"Would you like me to ring them, sir?"

Finn put a self-deprecating grimace on his face and said, "No, no, not necessary. My bad. Sorry—I must have totally misunderstood their message."

He turned and headed for the elevators.

flash—darkness—flash

dit-dit-dit, dah-dah-dah, dit-dit-dit

S-O-S

80

Outside on the streets, the city fairly shimmered with New Year's celebrations. Inside, metro was quiet as a catacomb, no one but a few custodial staff and a skeleton crew to answer the phones, which seemed unlikely to ring at all.

A custodian let Krista into the evidence room. It took her all of ten minutes to check and double-check the inventory at the locker for Einar's apartment, then go through the physical artifacts herself, just to be sure.

There was no phone recovered at the scene.

Einar lived on his phone.

Back to her office.

She looked through his desk, every drawer. No phone.

The last time she saw him, when they had that big fight, he was sitting right there at his desk, eating a Danish. *And you look like hell*, she'd said. Her last words to him.

She tried not to think about that.

Had his phone been on his desk? Did he pick it up when he stormed out the door? She had no memory of seeing it, and it wasn't there now. It must have been in his pocket when he left. But then why wasn't it at his home?

She tapped on her phone's screen to wake it up, tapped on the memo app to open it—then stopped.

Looked at the phone.

Shut it off again and set it down on her desk.

The night before, after dragging herself home from the cemetery and locking herself in for the night, she'd deleted that subversive photo of the Unknown Bureaucrat. But did that delete the surveillance software Pike had smuggled onto the phone? She had no idea. So first thing that morning, she'd switched to a new phone, porting over only her address book and her notes. But had that data transfer brought over the sneaky little bastard's electronic stowaway, too? She had no way of knowing.

Fuck it.

She was sick of the phone anyway.

She rummaged through the top drawer of her desk and finally found her notepad and pencil stub in the back of the drawer.

Halló, old friend.

She opened the notepad to a blank page and wrote at the top:

EINAR'S PHONE—

God, it felt good to move her hand with the flow of her thoughts, feel the wood of the pencil between her fingers.

EINAR'S PHONE—SUNDAY MORNING—

She'd seen him on his phone at least a dozen times since then, but something about that morning stuck out. She wasn't sure just what. But something.

EINAR'S PHONE—SUNDAY MORNING—
ON THE ICE

When they were at the scene of the drowned girl, Einar was texting on his phone. Texting as he walked over to where she stood.

She'd thought nothing of it at the time. Why would she? Einar was always on his phone.

He'd stopped texting and relayed a report from one of the officers on the scene, then they stood together in silence, waiting to see if the divers could extract the body safely for an on-site examination.

The lead diver emerged and shook his head. They'd have to cut her out and transport her directly to pathology. "Like a fly in amber," Einar had murmured.

And started texting again.

Einar wasn't married.

Not in a relationship, as far as she knew.

Who would he be texting on a Sunday morning?

She reviewed the sequence in her mind again, more carefully this time. They'd stood together, waiting for a status update on access to the body . . .

He sends a text.

They learn they'll be transporting body to pathology.

He sends a text.

The body goes missing.

And then? Later that day a diver came back with his reported observations of the body. And Einar sat on the report. Until Krista learned about it quite by chance when she bumped into that same diver two days later.

Less than twelve hours after that, Einar was dead.

And his phone was missing.

She didn't want to think this was a sequence of events with any causative meaning attached to it. She would much prefer to see it all as a coincidence.

That thing that she and ten million other cops on the planet did not believe in.

"Einar, Einar," she murmured. "What did you do?"

All at once, out of the silence, Krista heard a sound.

The soft scuff of a footfall in the hallway outside her office.

She'd thought she was alone in this wing of the building.

There shouldn't be anyone there but her.

She slowed her breathing to steady herself.

Quietly, she rose from her desk and crossed the short distance to the closed office door.

Just as she reached for the knob, the door abruptly swung open.

81

Finn stepped out of the elevator onto the sixteenth floor, looked up and down the hallway. He was alone.

He walked to the end of the hall, where their suite was located.

The privacy sign was still on the door, exactly as he had left it two days earlier.

He let himself in with the passkey he'd lifted on his first visit to the Foss.

Always have a backup.

The suite was hot, the air stale and soundless.

Room by room, Finn began clearing the place.

All Peyton's and Dixon's stuff was still there.

As he slipped through the darkened suite, occasional bursts of fireworks outside lit up the living room behind him at random intervals.

flash—darkness—flash

S-O-S

He focused on his breath, slowed his heart rate. Continued on through the suite, listening, groping with his senses through the dark rooms.

Last bedroom.

Closet.

He approached the door, hand outstretched, then stopped.

The smell of wet straw . . . insistent buzzing of flies . . .

He was back at Snake River, he was back in Mukalla, there was death in the room, there was blood pooled on the floor—

He gave his head a hard shake, pinched his nose with his left hand and blew to pop his ears. He needed to stay present.

He grasped the knob and pulled open the closet door.

And stood looking at Dixon.

And Peyton.

Crammed together into the tiny space like forced puzzle pieces, limbs bent at impossible angles.

Eyes open, staring out at an eternity of nothing.

82

Krista was about to clock the figure standing in the doorway when she recognized him.

"Jesus, Jón! You scared the shit out of me!"

The young officer held up both his hands in front of him. "Sorry! Sorry!"

"The fuck you doing here?" She felt her heart pounding hard enough to burst open her chest.

Jón blanched at her language, then leaned his head in and looked cautiously around the office. "Okay if I come in? You won't tackle me?"

She let her shoulders drop. "Sorry, little jumpy." She stood back and to the side. "Of course. Come in. Sit."

Her heart was still thumping away like a jazz drummer on a solo. She stood at her desk while Jón pulled over a chair—Einar's chair—and sat a cautious few feet away.

"Why *are* you here?" she repeated.

"Right. So, there was something that kept nagging at the back of my mind. I came in to read over your notes from Tuesday, from your interview with Tryggvi?"

Wouldn't have done him much good. She hadn't yet put her notes from the week into the system. Another egregious breach in protocol. But Jón didn't need to know that. She took a deep breath to help her heart slow and lowered herself into her chair.

"Because?"

"I thought I remembered you saying something about Tryggvi being away over Christmas? In Europe?"

Krista nodded. "Left on his private plane, Christmas Eve."

"Yeah. So . . . I was curious about where in Europe." He shrugged. "Dunno why. I couldn't find your notes in the system, so I put a call in to the private hangar at Keflavík, asked about Tryggvi Pétursson's private jet, where it flew in from on Monday afternoon."

"And?"

The young officer leaned in toward her, elbows on his knees, and lowered his voice.

"They told me his plane hadn't been flown at all over the past two weeks. Not once. On Christmas Eve it was crewed and fueled up, ready to go, but after an hour it powered back down and never took off."

Krista sat back, stunned at the audacity of it.

It made no sense. Why would the man lie about something that could be so easily disproven? Unless he had assumed they were so incompetent that they wouldn't check. The thought pissed her off royally—at herself even more than at Tryggvi. Because, in fact, she hadn't.

She took another slow, focusing breath.

Who she was pissed off at and why wasn't really the point here. The question was: What was his plane doing all fueled up and ready to go on Christmas Eve. To where? Why? And why didn't it go?

Why did he lie about being here in town on Christmas Eve?

"What do you think?" Jón whispered.

She looked at him.

"Can you get me Einar's phone records for the past week?"

83

Finn spun around, hurling himself to the floor, rolling to the far wall, and leapt up to a crouched position facing the interior of the room.

Nothing.

He reached out with his senses and felt stillness radiating from every corner of the suite. Felt for that shimmer of static charge in the air.

Nothing.

There was nobody there.

He was alone.

Peyton and Dixon's bodies had obviously been there for quite a while. Hours. Possibly an entire day. No reason to think their killer was still there.

But no reason to think he wasn't.

He slid out through the doorway leading from the bedroom back into the living room space. Still being lit up by intermittent flashes. Still empty.

He stood still in the strobing darkness, ten seconds.

Twenty.

Thirty.

A flash of fireworks sent a sharp glint off an object at the window. After a moment, Finn approached. A spotting scope, mounted on a slim tripod, facing out. Facing northeast, directed toward Höfðatorg Tower.

Toward Peyton and Dixon's target, no doubt.

He bent down and looked through the scope. It was trained on a large floor-to-ceiling plate-glass window, looking in on a suite on the Tower's top floor, a hundred yards away.

As he watched, he caught a glimpse of a figure walking past the big window, then a moment later, pacing back the other way. On the phone? He couldn't see the man's face. The flashes of fireworks reflecting off the window made it impossible to get a clear view inside.

The three SEALs had spent hours there in that spot, watching. Like Jimmy Stewart and Grace Kelly watching Raymond Burr in *Rear Window*.

Finn wondered what crime this particular Raymond Burr had committed.

Taking his eye from the scope, he began searching the immediate area of the living room where he stood. Coffee table, end tables, sideboard. On the desk he found a laptop and a small inkjet printer, and next to that a stack of photos, apparently taken from that same spotting-scope vantage point with telephoto and printed out on the inkjet.

He found similar shots of the figure in the window, but taken during the dusky morning. The faint backlighting of the half-risen sun, combined with the lights still on inside the room, had provided a perfect view in.

Finn leafed through the photos.

Then stopped at one that framed two men talking together. He could clearly make out both faces.

And he recognized both.

One was Tryggvi.

The other was a Saudi.

No, not *a* Saudi.

The Saudi.

The man talking with Tryggvi was the reason his platoon was dispatched to Yemen six months earlier.

Asiri's Mengele. Top surgeon. Oxford-trained.

Oxford.

The Englishman.

Pandora.

Finn turned and ran out of the suite.

84

Krista scanned through the phone records Jón had retrieved using Einar's desktop computer, not knowing why or what she was looking for. Between last Saturday and Tuesday there were a meager handful of calls, but a considerable number of texts. Einar lived on text.

Everything stopped on Tuesday.

She walked back through the list, then stopped at a familiar number. She'd called that number, and recently, but when? To whom? She couldn't quite place it.

She scrolled back through her own notes, which she'd printed out before dumping her old phone. There. She'd written it down Tuesday morning, during her interview with Tryggvi, and called it later that afternoon.

Tryggvi Pétursson's private cellphone number.

Tryggvi.

And that's when it hit her. Like an earthquake. If Tryggvi lied about his plane, he could just as easily have lied about his staff's whereabouts that night.

The SUV.

The fucking black SUV.

Why do you say, "cruising"? Maybe . . . it was going slow. Like the driver was looking around as he drove.

Logan the arrogant prick was telling them the truth. He was nothing but a witness. A witness who had to be shielded from overly intrusive questioning and then quietly shuffled out of the country.

Because he saw the fucking black SUV that all their CCTV had missed.

And could possibly ID the driver.

"Krista?"

She looked at Jón, then back at her notes.

Why would Einar have been texting Tryggvi Pétursson's private cell-phone number on Christmas morning?

She checked the time stamp.

It was right about the time they arrived at the duck pond.

Under her nose the whole time.

Einar, Einar. What did you do?

She looked up at Jón again. "Who was this second number he texted, just a few minutes later?"

He bent over his phone, fingers flying, and had an answer in less than thirty seconds. "Works for the ambulance service."

She recognized the name: he was the driver from that morning. Who swore he delivered the body to pathology.

The body they said never arrived.

She put a call in to the driver and it went directly to voicemail.

She called the ambulance service and asked if this particular driver was available to come to the phone. When she was put on hold, she asked Jón if he could pull up Tryggvi's cellphone activity for the same time period.

The ambulance service came back on the line. "He's on vacation," the man said. "Been gone since the twenty-fifth."

And never coming back, thought Krista.

She scanned the list of calls Jón had just retrieved for her.

Immediately after receiving Einar's text message, Tryggvi placed a call to a number in the Reykjanes district, near the airport. Jón quickly looked it up.

A data center on the outskirts of Keflavík.

While Krista scribbled the address onto the back of an envelope, Jón sat looking at all the phone numbers he'd just written down. "I'm sorry," he said, "I don't quite get it. What does all this mean?"

She looked up at him.

"It means Einar didn't just climb into his tub and die."

He stared at her.

"Potassium chloride," she said, miming the action of a hypodermic plunger with her thumb and first two fingers. "Impossible to trace. Takes maybe a minute for the heart to seize up. While you wait, you just push him under. That's one possibility. There are others. I doubt we'll ever know the details."

He looked at the sheet of paper again, then back at her, disbelief and horror on his face. "Who would . . . ?"

Krista was already on her feet, picking up the envelope with the data center's address on it and shoving it in a blouse pocket.

"You should go home, Jón. And forget everything I just said."

85

Finn cut through the green behind the hotel building and in less than a minute he was stepping into the private elevator that exclusively served the Tower's penthouse. Once inside, he saw that the elevator car wouldn't budge, the door wouldn't even close, without someone swiping a key card to the suite over an electronic sensor.

Finn withdrew the key card he had lifted from the chauffeur at the lake house that afternoon as he'd stood admiring the Bentley and waved it over the sensor.

The door closed.

The elevator began its ascent.

He hadn't known he would need the key. Hadn't actually expected to use it. Just took it on principle.

They'd clearly had something to hide.

You were always better off knowing hidden things than not knowing them.

A minute later he stood just inside the penthouse entrance, perfectly still.

The big living room, which had been lit by low lights when he viewed it from the vantage point of the Fosshótel window a football field away, was now dark.

In the few minutes that had elapsed between dashing out of Peyton and Dixon's suite and entering this penthouse, the lights had been switched off.

The room was silent.

But Finn didn't think it was empty.

It didn't feel empty. Didn't smell empty. Sweat, cortisol, fear. Something.

The air was wrong.

A brief burst of distant fireworks splashed over the walls, painting them with hues of red, green, blue, a kinetic, high-combustion Aurora Borealis.

Then darkness again.

He focused his breath. Slowed his heart rate.

Searched through the faint afterimage left by the fireworks' flash, but couldn't find any sign of the surgeon.

He began inching through the foyer space, keeping to the wall on his right. Feeling his way with his feet. Reaching out with the antennae at the back of his neck.

flash

darkness

movement—

He froze. Held in place, suspended on the balls of his feet, eyes scanning everywhere, ears craning. Nothing.

But he had distinctly sensed movement.

It took another three seconds before he realized what it was.

The movement wasn't there. Wasn't with him in the Tower penthouse.

It was with him in Mukalla.

He was sitting, back to the wall, feeling the cool packed earth of the floor. It was dark, too dark to see detail, but he could make out the shape of two children lying still a few feet away.

FLASH

Heat lightning ripped open the room with a brief burst of light, and in the ozone glare the children's eyes stared up at the ceiling, sightless, black blood oozing from jagged gashes where their ears had been

DARKNESS

and then the lightning vanished, leaving him blinded by afterimages, his eyes straining to see but still flooded with residual neural impulses, and then just as the afterimages began to fade

FLASH

another shiver of heat lightning flared across the room, revealing the same silent tableau of horror, nothing more—

Yet he'd sensed something.

Flash, darkness, flash—and in that gap between the two flashes there'd been movement. A figure passing across the open doorway, right to left, as if timing the move so that it would happen between stabs of light and not be seen.

And it had worked. He couldn't see.

But he could smell.

Chicken manure.

Wet straw, soaked in blood.

The sweet astringent scent of burning khat.

Burning khat.

The Yemeni farmers all chewed khat. Women too. Even the kids. Sometimes they brewed it as tea.

But no Yemeni farmers smoked the stuff. Not the women. Not the kids. Nobody.

In that world, it was a singularly American habit.

And Finn knew only one American who smoked khat.

Thirteen-point-eight billion years ago, according to the scientists who studied such things, the universe consisted of an indistinct mass of infinite density and infinite temperature, a surreality that defied all known laws of existence. One trillionth of a trillionth of a quadrillionth of a second later, gravity separated itself out, and the world began to make sense.

For Finn, this was that moment.

In an instant—one trillionth of a trillionth of a quadrillionth of a second—he knew who was behind the massacre at Mukalla.

Who set them up.

Who silenced their lieutenant.

Not himself.

He didn't kill Kennedy.

And he knew who did.

Finn stopped breathing, struggling not to stagger forward from the impact of the revelation slamming into the back of his head.

Because the fine hairs on the backs of his arms were suddenly standing at attention.

Focus.

He'd sensed something—an infinitesimal change in pressure, a shift in the flow of air currents against his skin, something he couldn't identify but sufficient to trigger his instinct.

Flash—another explosion of fireworks painted the walls—

He jerked back a few inches.

There was the sharp *Crack!* of a gunshot by Finn's ear and the artwork on the wall directly behind where he'd just stood shattered, sending blasted shards of glass crashing to the floor.

86

Finn hit the floor.

The fucker had a gun.

A surgeon with a gun.

Now, there was an image for you.

Twenty-four hours earlier he'd fought off a former SEAL wielding an obsidian scalpel. Now he had a surgeon with a gun.

Finn listened for the sounds of alarm in the hallway outside, the shouts, the running feet, then realized there wouldn't be any.

Nobody would come running down the hallway.

There would be no knocks on the door.

No hotel staff wanting to know what was going on.

Because this was Iceland. On a bad year they had one gunshot death. In the entire country. Most years, none at all. No one even knew what a gunshot in their hotel would sound like. The *pop* of a handgun muffled by the penthouse's soundproofing would be just one more New Year's Eve hoorah.

The surgeon could empty his magazine at Finn, and nobody in the hotel would think twice about it.

Finn examined the afterimage left by the combustion of gasses from the gunshot.

Two afterimages, actually, a second apart. One from the flash of the fireworks outside, the second from the muzzle blast.

Plus his impression of the darkened room beforehand, before all the flashes started. Which wasn't much. The penthouse's floor-to-ceiling window let in just enough ambient light to make out basic shapes, nothing more. But that was still something.

There was a lot of information to process.

And just fractions of a second to do it.

The room was a large rectangle, close to a square. The big picture window faced roughly northwest, out over the harbor. The door through which Finn had entered was cut out of the suite's southeastern wall, so he stood opposite the big window. At noon he'd probably be able to see Snæfellsjökull, the volcano with the melting glacier. But not now.

The northeast wall was mostly taken up by a bar, with an access door set on the right, probably to a bathroom or bedroom.

The southwestern wall featured a couch, a tall narrow bookshelf containing a few vague art objects, and another access door, probably to a hallway and one or more bedrooms.

His own wall, the southeastern wall, sported a large overstuffed chair with ottoman, a few end tables with lamps, and nothing else. A few pieces of framed art on the walls. One now in pieces on the floor.

The room's center had held a small squat glass-top coffee table and a few curved hardwood chairs, but these had all been pushed away toward the bar, apparently to make room for something else. Finn thought he'd seen a small rectangular carpet placed on the floor, its near end pointing directly southeast.

Toward the suite's entrance, in other words.

Also toward Mecca.

A prayer rug.

Why not.

He'd known killers who did the rosary before murdering their victims. There were probably people who petted crystals and threw the I Ching while getting ready to kill. The world was a big place. Finn didn't judge.

That was pretty much the blueprint. Four walls. Four directions of the compass. Straightforward.

Finn placed the muzzle flash as coming from about eleven o'clock, which put the surgeon in the room's southwest corner. Not visible from the window, because the last foot or two of the window's span was blotted out by the retracted folds of floor-to-ceiling curtain.

Which was no doubt exactly why the surgeon had chosen that particular spot to hide in.

Also why Finn hadn't seen him in his initial scan of the room. He blended in with the bunched curtain.

The man was not dumb.

The fireworks flash hadn't provide the visual field of depth it would take to calculate distances. The second afterimage, from the muzzle flash, was no more helpful. But if he had to guess—and he did—he'd say the man was about eight yards away. Twenty-four feet.

Aiming a handgun at any range much over point-blank was harder than it looked. Most amateur handgun shots were misses. So were most police-held handgun shots. It wasn't like on TV. And in the half second the surgeon had after the fireworks' flash to register Finn's location, aim the pistol, and squeeze the trigger, he'd missed by only inches.

At twenty-four feet.

That was pretty damn good.

In the dark, Finn kept silently moving.

FLASH.

Crack!

A hole the size of a cigarette burn punched itself into the wallboard inches behind Finn's head.

Another shot, more data.

Pistol shots at close range did not go *BANG,* or *BLAM,* or *POW.* A typical muzzle blast from a handgun generated a shock wave with a sound pressure level of 140dB or more. Louder than a fighter jet taking off at 15 meters. The sonic boom produced by the projectile shoving air aside at supersonic speeds caused a loud whip-like *snap* or *crack.*

Different calibers and types of explosive round had different sonic signatures.

Finn judged this one to be a compact .38.

From the distinctive soft rack of the slide, he guessed a Walther PPK. A small semiautomatic that would fit nicely in the delicate hands of a surgeon.

Finn had by this point crept about five feet to his right and slipped into a low crouch, so the surgeon had had to make some quick adjustments before his second shot. Still, his miss was closer than his first.

Very damn good.

Finn silently plucked a picture off the wall. Holding it by its edge, he drew it back across his chest and flung it like a Frisbee in the general direction of the room's southwest corner.

Scuffle.

Dull crash.

Crack!

The surgeon's third shot went wild.

Finn hadn't expected to hit the guy with the hotel art, or even come close. Just close enough to provoke a reaction.

And he got exactly the reaction he was looking for.

Scuffle—the surgeon dodging and diving.

Dull crash—the picture making contact with the far wall and breaking apart.

Crack!—another gunshot, this one nowhere near in the same league as the first two, which was good, because that might rattle the shooter's confidence, might even induce a flicker of desperation, and desperate people made lousy shots and bad decisions.

Still, none of those three sounds—*scuffle, crash, crack!*—yielded any useful information. Finn didn't need them to.

It was the fourth sound he was after.

The sound that came on the heels of the first three.

The surgeon knew the suite's exact layout. Finn did not.

The surgeon had a handgun. Finn did not.

But Finn knew how to project total silence.

The surgeon did not.

The surgeon was quiet as a cat.

But even cats made noise.

Thus the fourth sound. The *hh, hh, hh* of rapid, shallow breathing, the kind of breathing you'd hear from a cornered animal. Or a person winded from exertion and trying not to make a sound.

Which gave away his location with a high degree of accuracy.

Finn wouldn't have a second opportunity to pry open doubt or desperation, or to gain a few seconds of leeway. The man was a surgeon: he knew how to focus under stress. He wouldn't react the same way twice.

The situation would only get worse from here.

If Finn was going to move, it had to be now.

He reached down in the dark with both arms, grabbed the coffee table by both edges, hoisted it in the air, and took off at a sprint, directly toward the surgeon—

Crack!

holding the table in front of him like a police officer's riot shield, not perpendicular to his line of movement but at a sharp angle to increase the chances of the .38 round deflecting to the side rather than penetrating the glass—

Crack!

because pistol shots fired at thick break-resistant glass, such as that used in expensive Danish glass-covered coffee tables, seldom penetrated with straight-line accuracy, which was the main reason cops carried twelve-gauge shotguns, so they could blast out car windows or apartment windows or any other obstructive glass that stood in the way of making an effective arrest—

Crack!

The surgeon's last shot finally shattered the tabletop, but too late—

Because in the next instant Finn hammered his left knee into the surgeon's gut and as the man's head went down it met Finn's right knee with an impact that caught him on the chin and took him out cold.

Five minutes later Finn walked outside into the building's underground valet area, a rolled-up rug slung over his shoulder.

A Tesla stood idling, key fob on the seat, trunk lid ajar. Neatly readied and waiting for its owner, who was probably on his way down at that very moment. No one else near the car. Which Finn took as a good sign.

Not luck. Finn avoided the concept of luck.

Call it a fortuitous circumstance. The trusting nature of Icelanders.

Finn tossed the rug into the trunk and slammed the lid shut.

Hopped into the driver's seat.

Floored it, roared up the ramp and onto the ice-covered streets.

In eight minutes he was on Route 1, Ring Road, on his way back to the lake house.

87

The data center was barely three kilometers south of the airport campus, housed in a huge, nondescript metal building that itself resembled a small airplane hangar. Decades ago it had been part of the US naval base there, back in the day when this part of Iceland was home to thousands of American military personnel. For years after the US military left, it had lain abandoned. No more.

The only clues to its current function were a long row of gigantic, whirring turbines running the length of the roof, and the armed security guard sitting on a folding chair, tucked into the recessed front entrance with a portable gas heater, iPad, and thermos bottle keeping him company.

Krista parked her car and switched off the ignition. Got out and walked over to the guard, who automatically set his iPad down and stood. She showed her badge, cuffed him, and left him locked into the backseat of her police car.

The iPad and thermos stayed where they were.

As Jón watched, she went around to the trunk and beeped it open with her key fob, reached inside and brought out a few tools.

A large pair of bolt cutters.

A Glock 17 handgun.

And an American Mossberg 500 shotgun, which she held out toward Jón. He blanched, but she ignored the look. He'd made his choice. When this night was over, he'd either be promoted or arrested. No way to know which.

Jón took the Mossberg.

Tonight, she thought. *Tonight our boy grows up.*

Neither of them had ever fired a weapon in the line of duty. Neither had ever *carried* a weapon while on duty. But they were trained to use them in a pinch.

Was this about to become a pinch?

She hoped not.

The two approached the front entrance.

It sounded like a small airplane engine running in there. Or maybe several small airplane engines.

She opened the door and they stepped inside.

88

A chaos of images and snippets of conversations crashed through Finn's brain as he veered off Ring Road and onto the exit for Route 36, the highway out to Thingvallavatn.

His every nerve fiber was still thrumming with the revelation that had crashed into him in the instant before the surgeon fired his first shot. The truth of what happened in Mukalla. But he couldn't afford the luxury of thinking about that now. He had to focus on what was happening right at that moment.

On the fact of the surgeon's presence there in Reykjavík, and what that meant.

So he let the images wash over him, nearly blinding him as he drove.

Kateryna, lying under her quilt, doped up and hazy, texting on her secret phone—

Last night I dream I visit mines—

Tryggvi's eyes in their slow-motion blink, pushing down the wriggling fly—

I write back, Mines? What mines?—

The lava fields and lunar landscapes, gouts of steam geysering up out of the treeless landscape on his ride in from the airport that first night—

The world's biggest cryptocurrency operation is right here in Iceland!

Bitcoin mines.

He forced his eyes to focus on the road.

Finn was bleeding. The chest wound had opened up during his struggle with the surgeon. He was fighting against the adrenaline ebb tide and plummeting blood sugar. Hadn't eaten a thing since the day before. Hadn't really slept in weeks.

His body was giving out.

Part of a word—OM. Something religious?—

They lost the body—

A black SUV—

A car flashed its high beams in his rearview, then accelerated and winged past him. Then another did the same.

He realized he'd let his foot off the accelerator and the Tesla was slowing.

Another car flashed its brights and zoomed past.

He straightened in his seat. Stepped on the accelerator and pulled his speed back up to 90 km/h.

Snowflurries swirled over the highway, turning everything to shades of white.

It was a struggle to keep his eyes open.

He began paying attention to the yellow poles placed at intervals along the highway's edge so drivers wouldn't go soaring off into the ice-covered moonscape. The poles were topped with thick silver stripes. He'd read about this.

One silver stripe = right side of road.

Two silver stripes = left side of road.

Good to remember.

Useful detail.

The snow picked up its pace, the yellow poles barely visible now as they flashed past.

Gusts of wind buffeted the car.

That week Finn had read a news piece about a motorist who stopped on this same highway and made the mistake of opening his door. The wind tore the door off its hinges.

He saw two great yellow eyes looming ahead, a tiger lunging at his face—headlights of an oncoming car visible just seconds before passing, their combined speed of 100-plus mph split by nothing more than a painted line on the road.

Another gust.

Bright beams in the rearview blinding him, another car winging around him and disappearing into the snow ahead.

Finn fought with the wheel for a moment, brought the Tesla back to center and powered on.

He let the fragments of images flood him again as the yellow poles strobed past.

Saddam, Assad, they are amateur . . . No one knows chemical and bio-weapon like the Russians—

Tryggvi has Russian client, very high up in Russian government, name is Petrov—

Pandora—

His mind working, assembling the pieces.

Kateryna sent her text about visiting Tryggvi's bitcoin mine one week before Christmas. Immediately afterward she started feeling ill, needing rest. Then stopped communicating.

She wasn't supposed to know about any of it. But she did.

She knew.

He thought through the timing of it.

Whatever they did, they'd planned it so she had a week to recover before moving her. If something went wrong on Christmas Eve and they had to start over with Zofia, simple arithmetic said they could be moving her tonight.

Christmas Eve.

New Year's Eve.

Maybe they favored making their move on a holiday, when the airport was mostly shut down.

Or maybe he was totally wrong about all of it.

Only one way to know.

A road sign went whipping past.

Thingvellir 2 km

Another car passed him, a big fucking Hummer, the pull of its backwash nearly sending him off the road.

Some stone drunk reveler hell-bent on making this New Year the fastest yet. Also the shortest.

The Hummer disappeared into the snow ahead.

Finn regained control of the Tesla.

A minute later he saw signs for the turnoff and eased off the accelerator. He slowed the Tesla off the highway and onto the unlit back road, relieved to finally be off the highway, out of the craziness.

As he neared the lake house, he pulled the surgeon's Walther PPK from an outer pocket and placed it on the passenger's seat, where he'd have instant access.

Buzzed down his window.

He might need to shoot before he even got out of the car.

Almost there.

He took a deep breath of the icy air to clear his head—

Too late to react, he heard the throbbing roar of a Powertrain V8 engine exploding out of nowhere and plowing into him.

A Hummer engine.

An eruption of ripping steel and aluminum tore at his ears, and his world tipped over.

89

It wasn't airplanes inside the hangar. It wasn't engines. It was computers. Tens of thousands of GPUs, stacked in endless rows like chicken crates in a gigantic poultry operation.

The noise was deafening. Any attempt to communicate with words would be useless.

Krista pointed at Jón, then at the opposite side of the passageway, then nodded toward the far end of the complex.

We'll go in parallel, me ten steps ahead.

You cover me.

They began walking, she with her Glock held out in front of her, he with the Mossberg at port arms.

She proceeded up the right side of the interminable aisle, the incessant clicking and beeping of computers flooding her ears, her eyes glued to the silent, dimly lit far end of the hangar. She didn't look back, knew Jón would be ten paces behind, creeping along at the same rate.

They passed nothing but computers and more computers, chewing away at their billions of cryptographic calculations, laying down infinitesimal layers of freshly minted transaction value to the global blockchain.

At the end of the aisle they came to a locked door.

Krista set the Glock down on the floor, hefted the great bolt cutter, swung it once over her head, and brought its full weight down against the lock, which gave way without protest. Or at least none that they could hear over the din behind them.

She retrieved the Glock and pushed open the door.

Lounge area. Fridge. Microwave. Small couch, television.

Two doors.

First door opened on to a tiny toilet.

The other was locked and secured by a heavy chain.

Krista hefted the bolt cutter again and placed the jaws of the thing around the chain, gave one hard squeeze, and the chain snapped apart.

The two looked at each other.

Jón readied the Mossberg.

Resisting the temptation to yell "Freeze!" Krista kicked open the door and burst into the room.

90

The Tesla fishtailed, careened across and off the road and down an embankment, the momentum flipping it over onto its roof, then tipping over another 90 degrees and coming to a stop on its passenger-seat side.

Finn unbuckled his seatbelt and fell to the passenger's side. He groped for the surgeon's pistol. Gone.

He pulled himself up to the hole where the windshield had been and crawled out of the wreck. Something had twisted or sprained in his left foot. Or maybe broken.

Worry about it later.

He took off in the direction of the house at a staggering lope.

He was dimly aware of the Hummer, which had gone skidding off the road on the other side before crashing into a boulder. Finn had no idea whether Boone himself survived the crash—who else could it be but Boone—and at the moment he didn't care.

He needed to get to the lake house before they left, if they hadn't already.

He limped another sixty yards before he spotted them.

In the glare of the spotlights that lit up the parking area, he saw the chauffeur bundling a nearly comatose young woman into the big Bentley SUV. Zofia, no doubt.

He broke into a shambling run.

The chauffeur heard him and turned.

The girl began slipping to the ground.

A bullet snapped past Finn's right ear.

A .45 round. Unmistakable. Nearly twice the stopping power of the surgeon's .38.

Although either one would kill you just as dead.

That's two guns in one night.

Not very Icelandic of them.

He pushed himself to run faster.

He heard someone shout something. Didn't understand a word. Finn guessed it was probably *Get her the fuck out of here!* or some Norse equivalent.

His head swiveled and he located the shooter, standing in the shadows just inside the garage entrance, taking aim. The burly groundskeeper. Even at that distance, Finn had no trouble making a visual ID of the man's weapon, a Heckler & Koch .45 semiauto. German reliability and accuracy. Damn thing just never broke. Finn had one just like it back in the States. So did every SEAL.

The chauffeur shoved Zofia onto the floor of the big car's backseat.

Finn was twenty feet away.

He needed to stop them from getting out and onto the highway.

Lives depended on it.

If Finn was right, a lot of lives.

He dove at the chauffeur's legs, too late.

Another .45 round cracked past him and lodged in the ice a few feet behind the spot where Finn's feet had just left the ground—

The Bentley spun its wheels, projecting a wake of ice and gravel flying behind it as it pulled out—

BOOM!

A shotgun blast—

The back window of the Bentley shattered—

Finn got to his feet and the shotgun fired again and again—*BOOM! BOOM! BOOM!*—tracking him as he dove and rolled and dove and rolled, a Cirque du Soleil acrobat in a war zone—

The Bentley was gone—

Finn heard more shouts and recognized Tryggvi's two unnamed security staff emerging from the garage and raising identical sidearms of their own, Finn noting without surprise that it was the cook behind the shotgun, and he braced for the fusillade as he dove and rolled a third time—

And saw Boone emerge from the darkness at the side of the building, plowing toward the cluster of shooters at a dead run, his killing lust out of control.

None of Tryggvi's staff were wearing parkas or wool coats. They'd all been inside when they heard the crash and run out. If they had stopped to don protective outerwear they might have had a chance of living through the night.

Too late.

Boone stabbed the first man in the kidney, twisting the blade as he yanked it back out, then plunged it hilt-deep under the second man's rib cage, burying it in his liver. A second later he punched the knife's tip straight into the side of the third man's neck, inserting the blade sideways, behind the critical veins and arteries, sharp edge forward, then slashed outward, the way a wolf would first bury his teeth deep and then rip the throat open.

The cook had just completed a half turn and brought the shotgun around to point at Boone but lost her chance at living by a fraction of a second as Boone slammed his foot into her chest and knocked her backward off her feet and then lunged, jamming his dagger into her exposed groin and slashing open the right femoral artery.

As the shotgun flew from her grip, Finn caught it.

Spun it around to point at Boone.

Unlike most of his Spec Ops brothers, Finn had never been a true lover of guns, possibly because the first time in his life he'd actually held one, he'd shot and killed his only brother. Still, guns had one undeniable virtue.

They worked.

In Finn's experience, the prime tactical goal in any fight was to finish it—fast. The longer a fight went, the more easily it spun out of control. Fatigue and battery bred missteps. Adrenaline took you only so far.

A single gunshot could end all that, violently and immediately.

One of the very few movie fights Finn truly appreciated was the Cairo scene in *Raiders* when the crowd parted, revealing an enormous fighter going through a dazzling sequence of scimitar moves designed to impress and intimidate. Indy just looked at the guy and shot him. Crude but effective.

Finn raised the shotgun and fired.

BOOM!

The swarm of buckshot tore into Boone's right shoulder, spinning him around and opening flesh and muscle like a blow from a butcher's meat hammer.

And rendering his right hand useless.

The obsidian knife went spinning out of sight.

Snake defanged.

Boone reeled and dropped to one knee, not from shock or impact but to make himself a smaller target—and to reach out and pull one of the fallen H&Ks from its former owner's lifeless grip.

With his left hand.

Because Boone was ambidextrous.

Which opened a question in Finn's mind.

Shotguns of this civilian, standard-barrel type were normally built to hold anywhere from two to ten shells. Five or eight were common configurations. In the US, shotguns sold for hunting were restricted by federal law to a three-shell capacity. The cook had already fired four rounds. Finn had shot a fifth. So the three-round rule obviously didn't apply.

Did this thing hold five rounds, or eight? No idea. He wasn't sure how things worked in Iceland. He'd had no reason to research this point.

Only one way to know.

He aimed at Boone's crouching figure and squeezed the trigger.

Click.

As Boone began to stand and turn, Finn charged him and punched the shotgun into his solar plexus like a jousting lance, sending him two steps back and then falling over backward, but not before taking a wild shot at Finn with the H&K as he fell—

Finn dodged and slipped on the ice, nearly went down himself—

The .45 slug flew over his body by inches—

Finn recovered his balance and did the only sensible thing—

He ran.

His only hope of making it to adequate cover before Boone got back on his feet was to reach the far edge of the garage and get around the corner of the building. The corner was about thirty feet away. With his damaged foot, the best he could do was maybe 10 miles per hour, which meant it would take about two seconds to cover the distance.

Crack!

Just as Finn began turning his head to glance back over his left shoulder, another .45 round snapped past, the slug tearing open Finn's left cheek as he ran.

Inch and a half to the right and it would have been his brain stem.

Lucky shot.

Or not.

Depending on your perspective.

Boone was on his feet now.

Finn was still a full second from the corner.

Boone gave himself the luxury of time to assume a stable two-hand stance and take careful aim.

All the time in the world.

Center mass a foregone conclusion.

Boone aimed.

Squeezed the trigger.

Click.

With a scream of rage, Boone hurled the empty gun away and broke into a sprint. His legs were inches longer than Finn's, his energy level at peak. He rounded the corner barely five feet behind Finn and launched himself in a flying tackle that caught Finn in the waist and slammed them both to the ground, the momentum carrying them across the slick of ice, down the sloping landscape—

And another twenty yards out onto the lake's frozen surface.

91

For the next ninety seconds the two men fought on, hurling punches and kicks, executing lunges and parries, spin-kicks and blocks, both men trying to end it, Boone by killing and Finn by incapacitating.

Finn now knew who killed Kennedy, but he didn't know who the rotten officer was who ordered the killing. For that he still needed Boone—alive.

Boone had only one fully functional hand. Finn's chest wound was bleeding and his tank was on empty.

But they both fought like wounded crocodiles.

Boone managed to grab Finn around the head with his bloodied right arm, pushing his left thumb and middle finger into Finn's face in an effort to gouge out his eyes. Finn punched him hard in the solar plexus, three times in rapid succession, weakening him just enough to escape the grip. Boone clawed and bit, Finn elbowed and grappled and kneed, the chill air's hush punctuated by grunts and panting and the smack of flesh slapping on flesh.

The pale starlight reflected off the lake's snow-covered surface, painting their struggle in a soft silvery glow.

The ninety seconds stretched out like one endless night.

As they parried and struck, feinted and lunged, Boone pushed Finn farther out, away from the shore and out toward the end of the property's long dock, where a strange, jagged line in the ice stretched out to the horizon.

Like a massive zipper.

The two men pushed closer.

The jagged line creaked and groaned.

Boone feinted left, then leapt at Finn, feet forward, locking his legs around Finn's trunk and pinning both his arms and driving him backward, and they fell and crashed together to the ice—

Which broke under their combined weight and momentum, plunging them into the lake's icy depths.

92

The battle continued underwater in an eerie silence, no more grunting, no more panting, their struggle reduced to one prolonged grappling match as the freezing water slowed every movement and rendered lightning strikes and knockout punches impossible, the cold a drag on their reflexes, the seconds ticking down to zero in glacial waters no human being could survive longer than a few minutes.

Welcome to Dante's ninth circle of hell, my friend.

And then it happened.

Boone got Finn in a rear choke hold—exactly the sleeper hold Finn had hoped to use on Boone to subdue him.

As the bigger man's arm slid around his neck, Finn automatically hunched his shoulders and tucked in his chin, but he couldn't stop the hold from taking.

He punched his right elbow with as much force as possible into Boone's solar plexus, the same spot he'd hit with the shotgun barrel, buying himself a fleeting instant of leeway, which he used to pivot to the side and thrust one arm up his chest and out, breaking Boone's grip. But just as he managed to extricate that arm and reach around the front of Boone's neck, Boone flung his own arms around Finn's new position, imprisoning him once more and choking off all further mobility.

More seconds drifted by as the two men strained in silence—strained against each other, against the cold, against the insistent drumbeat of oxygen deprivation.

Suddenly Finn felt a sharp pain.

Boone's necklace.

Two canine teeth, biting into his arm.

He tried to break free by giving his arm a quick upward jerk but couldn't move it more than an inch, which only served to jam the necklace in a half turn, twisting it so that the teeth were now pointed in the opposite direction.

Now they were biting into Boone's neck.

Finn tried to release the pressure of his arm, but Boone's iron grip held him in place, struggling for dominance, still pushing at maximum force to overpower Finn, not realizing he was causing the sharp cuspid points to dig deeper and deeper into his own neck.

Not feeling the pain.

Only the killing lust.

Finn struggled to break free.

Boone held, tightening his grip.

Dragging them down toward Death's encampment.

Both men had undergone brutal underwater training—"drown-proofing," they called it. But no one, not even a SEAL, was drown-proof. Under normal circumstances, the maximum underwater breath-hold was two to three minutes. Four, possibly. But the severe cold cut that time drastically. The exertion of hand-to-hand combat, even more so.

Now they were through Death's front door.

For another ten seconds, they struggled, locked together, both trembling with exertion.

Immovable object, unstoppable force.

Fifteen seconds.

Finn felt a sudden pulse of heat against his chest.

Arterial blood.

One of the necklace's teeth had punctured Boone's left carotid.

Finn couldn't budge.

A moment later Boone's grip relaxed by the faintest margin.

Finn yanked his arm free and jammed his right thumb and forefinger into the puncture wound, found the artery, and pinched it shut. He'd seen it done before. Knew it could work.

They stayed like that for an eternity of seconds, Boone still struggling, Finn holding on, his hand starting to cramp.

Recovery from blood loss was possible, even extreme blood loss. Finn had seen it done in the field. Boone had done it for him.

It was a question of time and intervention.

They had no time.

There would be no intervention.

Finn's hand began to scream.

He bore down harder, pushing the pain inside, burying it deep where it wouldn't distract him, and held on.

He couldn't keep holding forever.

Boone's struggles slowed.

Then stopped altogether.

Finn felt his reserves ebbing.

The oxygen supply in his lungs had thinned to a gasp, yet that wasn't what was sapping the life from him.

It was the cold.

The ninth circle of hell.

Hypothermia.

Finn's vision going black around the edges.

The darkness closing in.

Finn was treading water in the freezing cold October surf, struggling to save Sebastian's life.

Finn was locked onto the former teammate who came to kill him, trying to keep him alive.

Finn was stepping into the freezing cold duck pond and lying down and sliding himself under the ice . . .

His eyes rolled skyward, searching for air, and saw nothing but an expanse of midnight blue at the far end of a long, dark, blue-green tunnel, the water's surface a phantom of ghostly light twenty feet away, a mile away, a universe away . . .

93

Krista and Jón stood still, silent, gazing around the cramped chamber, lit only by dim illumination spilling in through the door. Jón found a light switch, and a soft incandescent light filled the space.

The center of the small room was occupied by a long steel table, surfaced with a thin mat and white linen covering. Large LED lights hung suspended around it on movable arms. There were several metal rolling trays arrayed by one end.

A bank of instruments and digital readouts lined that wall. An adjacent wall held several steel cabinets, each sporting multiple shallow drawers.

Krista pulled out the top drawer.

Scissors, forceps, clamps. Scalpels.

They were standing in an operating theater.

Another door, unlocked, opened onto a short passageway that gave way into an adjoining chamber, this one an equally small but much colder room with large steel drawers lining one wall.

Krista slid out one drawer, revealing a long shelf, extending some six or seven feet into the wall, also surfaced with a thin pad and white linen cover. It was empty.

She slid out another deep drawer.

Also empty.

A third.

And looked down at the body resting peacefully on its back.

Long incision across the abdomen.

Red lipstick letters.

"*Halló*, Kateryna," she said.

94

It was like gazing up through a semi-opaque surface at a dim diffuse light. What medium was he looking through—ice? Water?

Death?

Death. Had to be.

Out of the gloom an image resolved: two eyes peering through the darkness. Then a face, pale and terrified. A young boy, staring at him through the dimensional veil. A hole opened in the boy's face: a mouth, about to scream.

The image faded . . .

And now he saw a new image, a black Bentley Bentayga idling at the foot of a great glass Tower, the chauffeur getting out and walking into the building . . . There was a girl sprawled across the backseat of the car, drugged, asleep, but as he watched, her eyes slit open and something shifted and he wasn't him anymore, he was her, and she knew she

isn't supposed to be awake, isn't supposed to know what they did to her, what they have planned for her, isn't supposed to know about the Englishman or the mines or what goes on there, or where they are taking her now, or why.

She isn't supposed to know any of these things.

But she does.

A week's worth of drugs still weighs down her eyelids, still weighs down her brain, but she has heard enough to know.

She knows.

She waits until she is alone, then pushes open the heavy car door and staggers out into the cold.

There is almost no traffic at all.

Christmas Eve in Reykjavík.

She lopes across the pavement and falls around a corner, disappears behind the building.

Weaves her way across the green to the big hotel, around that building and out onto the street, and keeps going, block after block, doing her best to keep to back streets, to stay out of sight of the big SUV that must by now be crawling through the streets looking for her.

Six blocks

Seven

Deserted city streets.

Distant ruckus of drunken revelers, laughter, Christmas carol fragments.

Under the faint glow of streetlights a flurry of snowflakes drifts to the frigid cobblestone surface, then swirls aside as she sprints past.

She darts through an intersection. Then another.

Ten blocks.

Up ahead she spots the great stone church tower. She heads that way, passes the church, lungs burning, but she has to keep going . . .

The sound of her feet slapping the slick street surface drums against her ears—

Wait—was that a glimpse of someone passing on the far side of the street? (That was me, Finn thinks.) *She slows long enough to peer back through the murk. No one there.* (But I was. I could have saved her.)

She keeps going . . . feet slapping the cobblestones . . . reaches the next corner—

And there it is. Spread out before her like a banquet.

A patch of open water.

The duck pond.

She knows she is dead already.

There is nothing she or anyone else can do about that.

But she can still act.

She can still stop it.

From her pocket she pulls a stick of lipstick, bloodred.

Stares at it, her heart pounding.

Hands trembling from the cold, she twists the lipstick open, pulls up her shirt with one hand and with the other scrawls a single word upside-down across her abdomen.

Then lets the lipstick fall from her fingers.

And this is the Ukrainian word she scrawls in red lipstick on her own belly before stripping off her clothes and slipping under the ice and into the freezing cold water:

БОМБА

Not a mantra. Not OM.

Not WOMB.

BOMB.

95

Finn felt a strong hand grip him by the shoulder.

her back to the pond floor, she slides under the ice and pushes—

Then another hand on the other shoulder.

The vision of Kateryna's final moments faded as the two hands slipped under his armpits and dragged him up out of the water and onto the ice.

The hands pressing down on his chest, over and over.

Fingers pinching his nose. Mouth on his, pushing air into him.

Hands on his chest again.

Painful.

Fingers. Mouth.

Air.

A geyser of ice cold water belched up out of him. And another.

The hands slapped at his face. Wrapped him in a blanket. Dragged him across the ice, then up a rough incline.

The sound of crunching ice and snow.

Finn felt himself hoisted up and onto a car seat. Something thrown over him. A fresh parka. Heard the faint sounds of a door slamming, another opening. Felt the car rock on its chassis as someone else entered the front and sat. Felt the car door slam shut. Engine turn over and catch. Heat start filling the space around him.

The car began moving. Did a K-turn and pulled out of the parking flat, onto the access road.

"Wait," Finn croaked.

The car slowed to a stop.

Finn opened his eyes.

Magnús, looking back over his shoulder.

"Wait," Finn said again. He pushed himself half-upright and fumbled with the car door.

Magnús got out and opened the door for him, then helped him make his way off the driveway to the sloping berm where his wreck of a Tesla sat on its side, trunk sprung, lid half-open.

Finn reached in and started to pull at the rolled-up rug.

Magnús elbowed him aside, hauled out the rug, shouldered it, walked it back to the Yaris and tossed it in his trunk. It emitted a soft grunt. Then he came back for Finn, who'd meanwhile managed to extract his bolt bag from the passenger's side floor. Magnús walked Finn up the embankment and helped him into the rear seat, climbed back in the driver's seat, and pulled out onto the road to the highway.

They drove in silence for a minute or two before Magnús spoke.

"Saw you walking in town," he said over his shoulder. "After your friend dropped off her envelope. Thought you might be in the jam your-self."

After another minute he added, "On our drive today, your brain was going, tock-tock-tock." He tapped his temple with a huge forefinger. "Brain of a man with an unfinished story."

Finn felt the car slow into a turn, then accelerate. Getting on the high-way.

After another mile, Finn said, "Magnús?"

"Ghost Writer?"

"You never cease to impress me."

The big driver chuckled and drove on.

It occurred to Finn that his prolonged plunge in the icy water had probably constricted the blood vessels in his chest and torn cheek, slow-ing the bleeding, allowing clots to start to form. Maybe saved his life.

Finn dug in his pockets for his tracking phone. Gone. Probably at the bottom of Thingvallavatn. He rummaged in his bolt bag and pulled out a fresh phone. Burner #5.

He called the detective.

"There's a second au pair in a black Bentley SUV," he said the moment she picked up. "On her way to board Tryggvi's jet. Have the Airport Police stop the flight. Have your best surgical team meet them there. Also people who know ordnance disposal. Bring hazmat suits. And confiscate all the phones; they could be triggers."

"Triggers?"

"There's a bomb inside the girl. They removed it from Kateryna's body and implanted it in the new girl. Not a normal bomb. A bioweapon. Maybe an engineered super-virus, maybe something else. But contagious as hell. Probably enough to infect a city."

Magnús shot him a look in the rearview, and he half heard the detective say something under her breath that sounded like "fuck."

"If you raid Tryggvi's data center out by the airport, I'm pretty sure you'll find a full medical facility somewhere in there."

"I'm standing in it."

Impressed yet again. Good for her.

"Your team can use that facility to work on the girl. At least isolate the bomb. Maybe even save the girl. If that's even possible. She's heavily drugged, probably diazepam or some other benzo. Her name is Zofia."

"Zofia," she repeated. "Jesus."

"I'll drop off the surgeon who did it outside metro in about an hour. He's alive. Sort of. But your body count has gone up. Just outside Tryggvi's lake house. Boone's work."

"Fuck," she said again. "And Boone?"

"Have to wait till spring. Drag the lake."

There was silence for a moment on the other end, then he heard the detective exhale through pursed lips. "Is that it?" she said.

"That's it."

"Pike?"

"Here."

"I'm still going to arrest you."

"I know."

He clicked off. Lowered his window and tossed out the phone, then raised the window again and closed his eyes, letting the bump and roll of the road ease some of the aches.

Was that vision under the ice real? Had there been some kind of connection with the girl that night in the street, by the big church, something that allowed him to have a glimpse into her mind? Or was it just a narrative he'd constructed out of fragments of clues and logic and intuition. He didn't know. It didn't matter.

Either way, he knew it was the truth.

A courier, the detective had guessed.

What cargo would be that valuable? he'd wondered on his first ride back from the lake house. Now he had his answer. Asiri and his new Mengele had made strides, all right. A miniaturized bomb, probably not bearing much explosive force, just enough to rupture the seal and release its lethal contents. Sufficiently virulent to cripple New York, Finn's best guess, and torpedo the nation's economy.

The bioagent supplied, he supposed, by Petrov, Tryggvi's shadowy client. Or whatever higher-up he represented.

Though Tryggvi no doubt had his own interests at play somewhere in there.

Crippling the American dollar would also make cryptocurrency skyrocket. Anyone with a major stake in bitcoin would be in a very good position.

Last night I dream I visit mines.

Greyið, he thought, as he felt the Yaris change lanes. *Crying.*

Yes and no.

The girl's drowning was a terrible tragedy. No question there. But not a meaningless one.

No.

It was an act of heroism.

Kateryna willingly froze her own body, doing what she could to ensure she would be found by the police with her scar fully visible. Doing what she could to make sure they took extreme care in handling her.

She even left written instructions.

БОМБА

Her killers stole the evidence so their secret wouldn't be discovered. Covered their tracks as best they could. But not well enough to erase the trail of bread crumbs she left behind.

With her death, Kateryna saved tens of thousands of lives, maybe millions, in a place she would never see. She wasn't a victim. She wasn't a suicide.

She was a rescue swimmer.

Finn tasted salt on his lips. Touched his cheek with one finger.

Do you weep for him?

A rush of emotion swept through him, a strange and foreign feeling. And it came to him then, what it was about the girl that drew him so strongly. The girl frozen in time, staring out through the icy membrane that now separated her from the world.

Like a bug under glass.

Like looking at his own face.

He heard a sound, a thump, coming from behind. *Thump!* From the trunk of the car. *Thu-THUMP. Thump-thump. THUMP!*

Magnús glanced at Finn in the rearview.

"Bad man?"

"Very bad."

Magnús nodded and drove on.

After a few miles the thumping quieted down.

A quiet chuckling drifted back from the front seat.

From his position in back, lying curled on his side, Finn turned his head and squinted. Magnús was silent, watching the road ahead. The sound was coming from the front passenger's seat. The "death seat." A figure looking straight ahead, smoking a joint rolled of a shredded weed that looked a lot like marijuana but had a more astringent smell.

Smoking and chuckling.

And now another memory clicked into place.

That was how he ended up at the farmhouse in Mukalla.

That was how he knew where to go.

Middle of the night, hours after the failed raid. Base camp, everyone asleep. Except one, who rose and slipped out, silent as moonlight. And Finn silently followed, having no idea where they were going or why. Or what he'd find when they got there.

"It was you," he said, "running the whole operation. Not Keyes, not Dugan, not Meyerhoff. Not someone up the chain. You."

The figure in the front seat didn't turn, just sat smoking his hand-rolled khat spliff.

Another vision. Or another reconstructed narrative. Finn was too tired to guess which. Didn't matter.

Either way, he knew it was the truth.

"So how did it work, Paulie?" he whispered. "Did you tap one of the other guys, give the job to one of your gang? Some weak-minded drone like Peyton?"

There was no answer from the front seat.

"No, you wouldn't trust something that critical to a subordinate. You didn't even trust them to do their work at the farmhouse, had to go check up on them to make sure they got it right. Make sure they were so thorough it'd send the whole town a message. But hitting Kennedy? That you'd have to do yourself."

Silence from the front.

"How does that work, Paulie? How do you whack your best friend?"

The shadow in the front seat took a drag on his khat doobie, blew out the smoke, and chuckled.

"*Best friend?*" The voice oozed and buzzed into the backseat like motor oil covered in flies. "*You should know, Finny Boy, better than anyone. The whole friend thing is a grift. A game. You do what you do.*"

"You do what you do? That's it? Christ, Paulie. How do you ever sleep again?"

Once more, that ghostly chuckle and the oozing buzz.

"*You don't.*"

"You okay back there, Ghost Writer?"

Magnús glanced at Finn in the rearview mirror again.

The death seat was empty.

Of course it was.

Finn lifted a hand. "Still here," he croaked.

Just talking to ghosts.

The whole friend thing is a grift. You do what you do.

Was that true?

Finn closed his eyes.

He hoped not.

They pulled up in front of the entrance to the metro police station. Finn opened the back door and climbed out. "I'll walk from here."

"There are no more flights out till Monday," said Magnús as he climbed out and came around to the trunk to retrieve his rug-wrapped steerage passenger.

"I know," said Finn.

"You'll be okay?"

Finn zipped up his new parka. "Only one way to know," he said.

And he started walking.

Monday, January 2

Cold.

96

"Thank you, Mister Peyton. We hope you'll come back and visit our beautiful country again soon," said the agent at the ticket counter as she handed over the envelope bearing the passenger's cash receipt and boarding pass.

"I'm sure I will," lied the man with the wide-set eyes and scarred left cheek. He took back his passport and tucked it into an inside pocket as he limped back toward the main terminal area.

Photographic paper from Dixon's little inkjet, glue stick from the Fosshótel's business center. Hotel room iron, carefully applied through a hand towel. He hadn't been 100 percent sure it would fly.

But better than 50 percent.

And anyway, he had a high tolerance for risk.

Nobody bought tickets at airports anymore. He could have booked online and printed out his boarding pass ahead of time like a normal person. But Finn figured the closer to boarding time he booked, the briefer his exposure to any snooping eyes, human or digital—whether Reykjavík cops, Airport Police, DIA, or any one of however many other agencies might be sniffing at his trail by now.

High tolerance, but not foolhardy.

It wasn't quite time to board yet, so he headed to the lounge, where he sat at the same bar, in the same seat where he'd lifted Ragnar Björnsson's house key nine days earlier, and asked for a glass of water. No ice.

The place was humming with clientele, herds of travelers anxious to throw off the holiday doldrums and charge into the new year's business.

He was taking his first sip of water when he heard a voice directly behind him.

"Chief Finn."

He didn't turn.

No one had called him that in months. There was no one in Iceland who knew him by that name. No one alive, at least.

Yet Finn did not turn around. No point.

When you're made, you're made.

Besides, he recognized the voice.

The man took the seat next to Finn and placed his order. "Just tea, please. Hot. No, no milk. Just plain."

Finn waited till the tea arrived, then looked sideways at Ben, the Canadian photojournalist, and said, "How's the fox hunt going?"

The man pulled his steeping teabag up to just above water level, gave it a single squeeze against the side of the cup with a spoon, and set it to the side. Took a loud, slurpy sip.

"I found my Arctic fox the first day I was here. The moment it switched on its phone."

Elusive, highly intelligent little creature. Fascinating subject, really . . .

So Hot Tea and his unseen partner had been on him since the previous Monday. A full week. And had waited till now to move in.

Or maybe they'd lost track of him after he microwaved his phone.

"You had to show up here sooner or later," said Hot Tea, confirming that last thought.

Finn noticed there was no longer any trace of a Canadian accent.

He assessed the rest of the lounge's visible interior with his peripheral vision. Man by himself, few tables from the door, nursing a fizzy water. Hot Tea's partner.

Hot Tea and Fizzy Water.

Diane and Claudia.

Finn put up one finger, signaling their server, who came over and said, "Sir?"

"Icelandic rye, butter with lava salt?"

"You got it," said the server, trotting out his best American bartenderese. "Anything else?"

"Have you got a good single malt Scotch?"

"Lagavulin sixteen-year."

Finn touched his thumb and forefinger together, giving the kid the A-OK sign.

"Make it two," said Hot Tea. "And a second tea, if you would. Hot. Have you got Lapsang Souchong?"

"Of course," the kid said, in the vaguely patronizing tone Kennedy used to call "*Asshole* understood." The kid didn't seem to like Hot Tea much. "Comin' up."

Hot Tea raised one eyebrow at Finn. "Chief Finn, palling around with John Barleycorn?"

Finn shrugged. "I'm sure we'll think of something to toast."

Their server was back in moments with Finn's bread and lava-salt butter, then set down the twin shots of Scotch, and finally Hot Tea's Lapsang Souchong.

Hot Tea poured his shot directly into the tea. "The Lapsang's smoky flavor pairs well with the Scotch," he explained. Like Finn cared. He took a noisy sip, then another, nodding appreciatively. "Hot toddy, without all the fuss." He set the cup down. "I'll get right to it. We'd like you to come on board."

Finn broke off a piece of the bread, topped it with a thin pat of butter and generous dusting of lava salt, popped it in his mouth. Chewed. Swallowed.

"Doing what?" he said.

"Oh, this and that."

"Special assignment."

Slurp. "Something like that."

The Defense Intelligence Agency was nowhere near as high-profile as its cousins, the Central Intelligence Agency and National Security Agency. There were roughly a billion high-octane movies about the CIA. The DIA had *Spies Like Us* and *The Men Who Stare at Goats*. But low-profile had its benefits. Hot Tea was probably from some black-box "working group" buried deep within the DIA's massive classified budget. A spook wrapped in a cipher inside a black hole.

He was there to contract Finn off the books, under the radar, zero oversight.

NCIS have you now, like a monkey on a string? Maybe Dixon hadn't been so far off after all. Although a string held by DIA would be quite a different thing. All NCIS would have been recruiting was a snitch. Hot Tea was headhunting for a ghost with a long gun.

"And?" said Finn, already guessing what the enticement side of this devil's bargain would be.

"And, it's not out of the realm of possibility that the whole Mukalla thing could be made to go away."

A dozen Yemeni farmers and their entire families, toddlers to grandparents, ears sliced off, carved up like Halloween pumpkins, left lying in their own blood. Lieutenant Michael Joseph Kennedy, just as dead, the truth of his death just as mutilated, buried under a massive lie.

Made to go away.

Poof.

Hot Tea shrugged. "Could be a nice change. Stop running. Get back to doing something useful."

Finn broke off another chunk of bread, added butter and lava salt, and ate it, chewing slowly. "Do you guys know what actually happened that night?"

Hot Tea looked down and gave a deprecating sigh. Then looked at Finn.

"In the larger scheme of things, Chief Finn, it's not important what happened that night."

Not important.

Finn chewed another hunk of bread as he thought about that. "Do you know who killed Lieutenant Kennedy?"

"Chief Finn, I hope you won't take this the wrong way. But we don't really care who killed Lieutenant Kennedy. However, since you ask, I'll say there are some, and by 'some' I mean individuals whose opinions on such things carry some weight, who believe you did."

Finn said nothing, just took in the threat. Little bit of carrot, whole lot of stick. Although the way he said it, Finn got the sense there were cards he still hadn't laid out on the bar between them yet.

Hot Tea put both elbows on the bar and leaned forward.

"Do you know who my boss is, Chief Finn?"

Finn said nothing.

"The American people. Believe it or not, I answer to John, Jane, and

Jamal Q. Public, even though they have no idea I exist. And the American people don't want to know the details of what happened in Mukalla. It's not going to help them live their lives. It's our job to weigh priorities. And there are always, *always* priorities."

It occurred to Finn that Hot Tea's mission was not so different from Boone's.

Actually, no different at all.

Make it all go away.

"Nice work, by the way," Hot Tea added, "on the whole implanted bioweapon thing. To be honest, we did not see that coming. Tells us we're making this offer to the right man." He raised his teacup, toasting in Finn's direction. He put the cup to his lips—but stopped before taking a sip and lowered it again.

As if a new thought had just occurred to him.

"You haven't told your detective about Peyton and Dixon's disappearance yet, have you?"

Finn hadn't. He'd needed their suite for one more day. To recover, for one thing. Make sure his wounds didn't infect. He'd also had a little forgery to do. He'd figured he would call in the two dead bodies on 112, Iceland's version of 911, just before boarding his flight.

An announcement came over the airport's PA system, barely audible above the hubbub in the lounge. *"British Airways flight 251 to Heathrow will be boarding shortly at Gate 6 in the main gate area."*

Finn made no indication that he'd heard. Broke off another piece of bread.

"You know, Chief Finn, it's not unreasonable to think that *you* might be blamed for the disappearance of three Navy SEALs in Reykjavík. After all, we don't really know who killed them, do we?"

Ah. And there it was.

Trap fully sprung.

The way they'd spin the narrative—or one possible way, at least—it was Finn who was responsible for the massacre in Yemen, killing Kennedy when he got too close to the truth, and then silencing the three SEALs. It was a fox hunt, all right. And the hounds had closed in.

"Offer stands," said Hot Tea.

And it all goes away.

"Hard to refuse."

"Pretty much impossible, is how we see it."

"I have a question."

"Fire away. I imagine you've got a handful."

"Have you made the same deal with Paulie?"

Hot Tea's eyes narrowed; a slight smile played on his lips. "The third leg of the troika." He took another sip of his tea and said nothing.

"Do you know where he is?" Finn pressed. "Is he even alive?"

Hot Tea took a sip of his hot toddy without all the fuss.

Finn waited until their server was all the way at the far end of the bar before heaving a big sigh and saying, "All right, then."

He picked up his untouched shot of Lagavulin between thumb and forefinger and eyed it with wary resignation.

"Does this mean you're picking up my tab?" he said.

Hot Tea smiled and let out a satisfied sigh. "Good decision, Chief Finn. Welcome aboard." He drained his cup, smacked his lips, and turned away to get their server's attention. It took a good ten seconds before the kid finally noted his raised finger and headed their way.

With a look of mild irritation, Hot Tea turned back in his seat.

The stool next to him was empty.

97

The two DIA agents tried not to look harried as they hustled up to the podium at Gate 6. The gate attendant was in the middle of making an announcement.

"British Airways flight 251 to Heathrow, now boarding at Gate 6."

Her announcement completed, she turned to them. "Ben" quietly showed his identification, then the ticket purchase printout and passport photocopy they'd grabbed at the ticket counter.

"Doug Peyton," he said, finger on the passport photo. "Do you know if this man has boarded already?"

She glanced at the papers, then checked her roster. "No, sir. But he just checked in on standby. He would be somewhere in the immediate area. We're already boarding."

There weren't many passengers left to go. He had to be lurking nearby.

They needed to fade.

Ben nodded to his partner. "Better go cover the airport exits. I'll wait for him here."

The other man made tracks.

Ben walked away from the gate a short distance and slipped around a nearby news-and-magazine kiosk, where he could keep an eye on the boarding area without being seen himself.

One or two stragglers had just showed up and joined the tail of the line.

Only fifteen people left to board.

The line moved like a single organism, trundling its way through the gate and disappearing into the mouth of the jetway.

Fourteen people left.

So far no more stragglers. But there would be. At least one more.

Thirteen people.

Ben waited.

One floor down and through a second, separate customs checkpoint, a man with wide-set eyes behind wire-rim glasses stood at the far side of the gate, watching the exits.

He keyed a number into the phone he carried, hit SEND.

After two rings, a connection.

"Krista," said the voice on the other end.

"How is the girl?"

"Well, well," she said. "Blast from the past."

Finn said nothing.

"The surgery took six hours, right there inside the data center. Four to extract and stabilize the bomb, two to stabilize the patient." She didn't sound even vaguely surprised to be hearing from Finn. Or at least her voice didn't show it. "There's a team of British scientists working on the bomb itself right now, working out just what's inside there."

"The girl?" he repeated.

"They think she'll live. Once the sedation wore off, she told us what she could remember. Which was a shitload of nothing. Christmas morning she fell asleep right after eating breakfast. Everything after that is a blank."

There was a brief silence.

"So is that why you're calling?"

It was one reason. He had several.

"Tryggvi?" he said.

He heard her sigh.

"They won't rush to arrest him. Maybe they'll avoid it altogether. They'll investigate, but you'll never read about it in the press. Bad for tourism. And anyway, this isn't like the banking crisis. The Icelandic people weren't harmed."

Finn was struck by how much that sounded like Hot Tea. *The American people don't want to know the details.*

"You don't sound too happy about it," he said.

"You know how it is, Rescue Swimmer. 'Being an adult means accepting those situations where no action is possible.'"

Finn almost smiled at that one. "The wisdom of Travis McGee."

"The great John D.," she agreed. "Best thing to come out of America in the past hundred years." She paused, then said, "So, why *did* you call?"

"The two SEALs you questioned at the Fosshótel? They never made it out."

He heard her mutter something under her breath. It sounded like "fuck." "Boone?" she said, then answered her own question. "Of course. Jesus."

"I turned off the heat and cracked the windows. Should be cold in there."

She laughed, a sound he hadn't heard before. "Well, that was mighty fucking thoughtful." She took a big breath, then said, "Okay. I'll pass that on to the proper authorities."

Finn was silent. Thinking, *Proper authorities? Wasn't that her?*

"As my last official act," she added, "I arranged for Kateryna's body to be shipped back to Kyiv."

Last official act. Ah. So that was why she'd said "they," as in, *They'll* investigate him, but *they* won't rush to arrest him.

"I'm leaving the force. Left, actually. An hour ago."

"What will you do?"

"I like to write," she said. "Thought I might try my hand at crime fiction."

Finn had to smile at that. An actual smile. First time in a while.

First time in as long as he could remember.

"Hey, Pike?"

He put the phone back to his ear.

"Watch your six." She broke connection.

Finn removed the SIM card from burner phone #6 and crushed it under his boot heel, then broke the phone in half and dropped the pieces into separate trash cans. He walked to the podium and handed his boarding pass to the agent there.

"Standby?"

The agent looked at his boarding pass and passport and nodded. "Thank you, Mister Lansdale. Come back and visit us again soon."

98

Once in his seat, Finn withdrew an envelope from an inside pocket. It had been waiting for him at the ticket counter, nothing but the name "Jack Lansdale" written on the outside. Now he opened it. A handwritten note.

From Oksana.

He paused before reading to think it through.

She'd somehow known, or guessed, that he would be traveling as Lansdale. She must have seen the passport among Finn's bolt bag possessions early Saturday morning, in the few moments when he dozed off. And guessed he'd be on the first flight to the US after the New Year holiday.

Or maybe she left copies with "Jack Lansdale" written on them at *every* ticket counter with flights to the US that day.

How did she know he hadn't already left on New Year's Eve, before flights stopped? Maybe she asked Magnús. Or maybe, like Magnús, she just intuited that his business there wasn't finished when they parted ways.

He unfolded the note.

> I decide to stay through weekend and wait. Leaving now.
>
> Cop tells me they find Kateryna. So not smoke, after all. She is coming home.
>
> Thank you. You are good friend.—O

There was more writing on the back side of the sheet. He turned it over. A single line:

Kateryna is deadly allergic to peanuts. Never go near.

Finn thought about that as he refolded the letter and slipped it back into his pocket.

Deadly allergic to peanuts. Never go near.

Which meant there was no way she would have been keeping a peanut butter jar in her room. Which meant Tryggvi's story about her sneaking drugs was pure fiction.

Which Oksana would have known the instant he said it.

He remembered her face going pale in that moment. Like she'd been struck by a two-by-four. And the last thing she said to their host, as they left. *Thank you for make everything clear.*

Finn's eye was drawn to the screen next to him. The passenger in the seat beside him was glued to a breaking news bulletin on her iPad, and he could hear the anchor's urgent voice leaking from his seatmate's earphones.

"One of the great heroes of Icelandic culture and philanthropy has died," the voice was saying.

"Tryggvi Pétursson, icon of industry and to many the father of modern Iceland, passed peacefully in his sleep last night, of natural causes. Rumors of his having been poisoned by a Soviet-era nerve agent are being categorically denied by both the Icelandic government and the Kremlin . . ."

Finn tuned it out, strapped into his seatbelt, and closed his eyes.

Thought about the last time he'd seen her, holding that envelope with the neat printing on the front, on her way to Höfðatorg Tower. *Never said proper thank you.*

Remembering her voice, low and coarse with emotion:

I was teenager. Old enough to read autopsies. Old enough to not buy official bullshit story. I know all about Novichok.

Yes she did.

That was one seriously resourceful history professor.

Her seminars must be something.

The captain's voice came over the plane's PA system.

"Flight attendants, prepare for takeoff. This is Icelandair flight FI614, bound for JFK and continuing on to San Juan. Our flight time to the Big Apple is five hours and fifty-five minutes. Kick the tires and light the fires, ladies and gentlemen. Have a good sleep."

He looked out the window and thought about the note folded in his pocket.

Thank you.

You are good friend.

The plane accelerated now, pushing Finn gently against the seat back. It felt good.

He felt the plane lift and bank, climbing into the sky above the North Atlantic, passing over Bakkatjörn, "the pond out back," and the western coast of Reykjavík.

Looking down at the water, he felt the little neural *click* of yet another memory falling into place. What happened to Sebastian, that cold fall day off the deserted California beach.

On the edge of passing out, feeling Sebastian finally start to weaken, he gets his hands under Sebastian's legs and pushes with all his might, forcing the boy up and driving himself down deeper into the water, until he is at last able to wrench free from the boy's legs, then surging upward, his face breaking the surface and taking one great gulp of air before spinning the boy around and getting him into a solid cross-hold again, this time with his arm locked around the younger boy's chest, side-stroking for what seems like hours but is probably no more than a few minutes . . .

When he finally got Sebastian to shore and let go of him, the kid took off running, leaving Finn alone on the beach.

Never even said thank you, the little prick.

Finn remembered watching him run, thinking, *That's one.*

After a moment he leaned back against the airplane seat. Closed his eyes.

And slept.

Epilogue

Vieques

The figure stood on the rock cliff, still as the tropical sun, feeling the direction and velocity of the breeze against his closed eyes. Inhaled the smell of the coral and hot pink-white sand under an azure sky.

He stepped to the edge, accelerating as he covered the distance, and leapt out into space.

Two seconds later he pierced the clear turquoise water and plunged twenty feet down, then let himself slowly surface.

Opened his eyes, and swam.

Note from the Authors

The characters and events in this story are fictional; the surrounding circumstances are not. Ibrahim Asiri and his surgeon did indeed exist (though we have invented a second surgeon who survived beyond Asiri's demise). The Arctic is, of course, melting away, and the disparity of inventory between American and Russian ice-breakers is, at least as of this writing, as stark as Krista describes. The bits of Icelandic history are real, too—the Höfði House and its ghostly legend, the financial crash and Iceland Miracle, the murder of Birna Brjánsdóttir—as is Iceland's uniquely strategic geopolitical position. (The "unsinkable aircraft carrier in the middle of the Atlantic" observation, often repeated in foreign policy circles, goes back to Winston Churchill.) Tom Clancy's placement of Iceland as central to any future US-Soviet (or US-Russian) clash seems more prescient all the time.

The story of *Cold Fear* was born, as most stories are, from the collision of two unrelated ideas.

It started when Brandon took a brief trip to Iceland for New Year's Eve a few years ago, and reported back about his dive into the Silfra Fissure, a crack in the earth at the head of Thingvallavatn, Iceland's largest natural lake. "The water was near freezing, about 2° Celsius," he said, "and here we are, flowing along with this underground current, slipping through this tiny gap between the Eurasian and North American tectonic plates."

It is, as Magnús tells Finn and Oksana, the only place on earth where you can touch two continents at once.

We became intrigued with the idea that Iceland sits directly on a crack between two worlds, and everything that implies.

The second seminal idea came from a story Brandon's company, SOFREP Media, did years ago on Ibrahim Asiri, the bomber behind a handful of attacks including the failed Christmas 2009 "underwear bomber" plot. Asiri is long dead, and so is his surgeon-accomplice, but we wondered, if he'd gotten himself another surgeon who survived, what would he be doing today?

Asiri + Iceland gave us a stage set. But who were the players? What was the story about? We had a sense it started in the water, and ended in the water. A drowning, and a struggle not to drown.

John dove into research on Reykjavík, looking for water, and learned about Tjörnin, the pond at the city's center—where he bumped into a curious little tidbit: in the winter, when the pond freezes over, they keep the northeast corner heated for the ducks.

Click.

There was our story.

Navy SEALs are trained in every aspect of warfare and survival, giving them the capacity to function, if circumstances call for it, as an entire military operation rolled into a single individual: an army of one. Still, there is a reason they call it "the Teams," with a capital T. One of the overarching values instilled throughout SEAL training is the power of the team. "None of us is as smart as all of us."

As much as the mythology of storytelling loves the iconoclastic loner, no true hero slays his dragons in total isolation. Where would Finn be without Carol and Stan L., or Magnús and Oksana? (Or, in *Steel Fear*, Jackson and Monica?)

And the same holds true for authors. *Cold Fear* wouldn't exist, and you wouldn't be reading it, without the creative collaboration of our Team. Our thanks goes out especially:

To Silja Björk Björnsdóttir, author, native Icelander, and resident expert on all things Icelandic. Brandon spent just a brief winter's week in Iceland; John never set foot there at all. For the two of us to re-create the fascinating, baffling world of Reykjavík with anything remotely close to authenticity, we needed an exceptional guide to take our hand and walk us through it. That was Silja. Any errors or lapses in Icelandic accuracy are purely ours. (Example: Silja pointed out that in late 2020, the American embassy moved from the location where we had it, near the duck pond, to a spot east of the Fosshótel, but for the sake of our story, we left it where it was.)

To Alda Karen and Runar Thor, both native Icelanders and friends of Brandon's, who helped us navigate our way and connected us to Silja.

To Alyssa Reuben at William Morris Endeavor for helping us steer our course into the unfamiliar waters of fiction and crime writing; it's safe to say that without Alyssa there would be no Finn books.

To Anne Speyer, our intrepid editor, for helping us navigate our way from the first rough draft through the course-corrections it took to reach shore safe and undrowned. We used to wonder why novelists would heap such lavish praise on their editors in the backs of their books; we get it now.

To Jennifer Hershey, Kim Hovey, Kara Welsh, Kathleen Quinlan, Sarah C. Breivogel, Nithya Rajendran, and the rest of the crew at Bantam Books for giving us a solid home.

To Carlos Beltrán for his haunting cover design and Virginia Norey for her lean, clean book design.

To the insanely multitalented Johnathan McClain, for bringing the Finn stories to life on audio.

To Michael Bhaskar at Canelo and Ivan Mulcahy at Mulcahy Associates Literary Agency for bringing the Finn stories to the UK.

To Hilary Zaitz Michael and Jack Beloff at William Morris Endeavor, Ben Smith and Adam Docksey at Captivate Entertainment, and writer Aaron Rabin for their dedication to bringing Finn's story to the screen.

To David Krueger, M.D.; George Pratt, Ph.D.; and J. T. Swick II, M.D.; for once again lending their psychiatric, psychological, and medical expertise.

To Laura Mallonee for her vivid description of bitcoin mines in Keflavík, in her *Wired* magazine article "Inside the Icelandic Facility Where Bitcoin Is Mined" (Nov. 3, 2019).

To Jóhann Karl Þórisson, Reykjavík's Assistant Chief of Police, for filling in some details on the layout and function of his city's Metro Police Station.

To Arnaldur Indriðason for his extraordinary Inspector Erlendur novels; we picked up the Erlendur books purely as background reading on Iceland—and they ended up deeply informing not only our sense of Iceland but our sense of Finn himself (there is more than a bit of Erlendur in Finn).

To Lee Child for the breathtaking roofline quote that graced the cover of *Steel Fear*, our first Finn novel, and to Robert Crais, Brad Thor, Steve Berry, Daniel Pyne, Michael Ledwidge, Philippa East, Kim Howe at International Thriller Writers (ITW), Elena Taylor Hartwell at ITW Debut Authors, Ryan Steck at *RealBookSpy*, Jenny Milchman and Lisa Black and their cohorts at *Rogue Women Writers*, Sara DiVello (*Mystery and Thriller Mavens*), Steve Netter (*The Best Thriller Books*), George Easter (*Deadly Pleasures*), Michael J. McCann (*The New York Journal of Books*), and the folks at *Booklist*, *CrimeReads*, *Library Journal*, and *Publishers Weekly*, for the extraordinarily generous welcome they've given us to the world of crime writing.

To our close circle of beta readers, Ana Gabriel Mann, Dan Clements, Deb and Charlie Austin, Abbie McClung, and George Easter, the first human beings (outside ourselves) to read *Cold Fear* in its earliest forms, for their notes, critiques, and words of encouragement, all of which helped to make this a vastly better book.

And finally to you, faithful reader, for joining us in rooting for Finn and seeing where his story leads. We hope he'll eventually find his way *all* the way out of that Snake River cabin closet, and that you'll be there with us when he does.

A Guide to Pronunciation

Icelandic is an ancient language (arguably the oldest surviving Nordic tongue) and exquisitely beautiful to listen to. It is also—to American eyes and ears, at least—more than a little baffling. This brief guide won't have you speaking like a native Icelander, but it will put you close enough to each of the words below that you can throw a rock and hit it between the shoulder blades.

What we cannot fully convey on the page is how it *sounds*. Here's how Finn describes it: "It conjured up the sense of a magical kingdom. How elves or naiads would speak if they had human voices . . . each word spoken like a fresh mint being placed on a pillow" (chapter 10). We recommend hopping onto Forvo.com and listening to how native Icelanders pronounce each word. (And maybe listen to a Björk interview or two.)

Here are two broad guidelines, as Finn observes in chapter 3:

1) The stress nearly always falls on the first syllable. Thus, Laugavegur, the main drag in downtown Reykjavík, is LAU-guh'vay-gur, and Reykjavík itself is RAY-kya'veek. (We indicate secondary stress with an apostrophe.)

2) You put a hard roll in every R with the tip of your tongue, like you're imitating suppressed machine-gun fire, or a woodpecker: R-r-r-r-rekjavík. (And even at the ends of words: Laugavegur-r-r-r.) It takes a little practice, but it goes a long way toward Icelandic authenticity.

a	hat	á	cow
e	eh	é	yeh
i	hit	í	heat
y	hit	ý	heat
o	hot	ó	oh
u	put	ú	poot
ö	u as in fur		
æ	high		

ð   th as in feather, only with a hint of D in it ("feadther," if there were such a word). When it comes at the end of a word it's soft, as in thin.

j   y (just as in Spanish)

r   the R is always rolled, hard, like machine-gun fire. Try it, it's fun. (Good word to practice: Krista. Kr-r-r-r-rista!)

ng   nk

ll   tl

Krista Kristjánsdóttir	KRIS-ta KRIS-chans'doh-teer
Litla Hafmeyjan Á Ís	LIT-la HAF-meh-yan ow ees
Já	YOW
greyið	GRAY-idth
hangikjöt	HANG-key'kyoht
Reykjavík	RAY-kya'veek
Jóna Jónsdóttir	YOAN-a YOANS-doh-teer
Jón	YOAN
Magnús	MACK-noose
Öryggismiðstöð	UR-ig-gis'midth-stuth
Heil og sæl	HAIL og sighl
Lögreglan	LOR-ek-lan
Hverfisgata	KVAIR-fis-ga-ta
Tryggvi Pétursson	TRIG-vee PEH-tər-son
Höfðatorg	HUV-thah-tork
fyrirgefðu	FEAR-ear'gev-dthu
Thingvallavatn	THINK-vaht-lə'vaht
	(the final N is nearly silent)
hnífsár	HNEAF-sour

Björn	BYURN
Birna Brjánsdóttir	BEER-na Browns-'doh-teer
Eyjafjallajökull	EH-ya'fyaht-lah'yoh-kukh
Höfði	HUV-thee
Hallgrímskirkja	HAHK-kreems'keerk-yah
Snæfellsjökull	SNIGH-fəls'yokəl
Drekkyingarhylur	DREK-ink-ar'hey-lur
Völsunga	VUL-shunk-a
Blámi	BLAU-mee

Note: We use the ə symbol, technically called a "schwa," to indicate a neutral, unstressed vowel. (English is full of them; e.g., "little bauble" = littəl bawbəl.)

About the Authors

BRANDON WEBB and JOHN DAVID MANN have been writing together for a decade, starting with their 2012 *New York Times* bestselling memoir *The Red Circle*. Their debut novel, *Steel Fear,* was nominated for a Barry Award and named "one of the best books of 2021" by *Publishers Weekly*. To stay informed on the next Finn X thriller, join their website:

WebbandMann.com

After leaving home at sixteen, BRANDON WEBB joined the US Navy to become a Navy SEAL. His first assignment was as a helicopter search-and-rescue (SAR) swimmer and Aviation Warfare Systems Operator with HS-6. In 1997 his SEAL training package was approved; he joined more than two hundred students in BUD/S class 215 and went on to complete the training as one of twenty-three originals.

He served with SEAL Team 3, Naval Special Warfare Group One Training Detachment (sniper cell), and the Naval Special Warfare Center (sniper course) as the Naval Special Warfare West Coast sniper course manager. Over his navy career he completed four deployments to the Middle East and one to Afghanistan, and redeployed to Iraq in 2006–2007 as a contractor in support of the US Intelligence Community. His proudest accomplishment in the military was working as the SEAL sniper course manager, a schoolhouse that has produced some of the best snipers in military history.

An accomplished and proven leader, Brandon was meritoriously promoted to Petty Officer First Class, ranked first in the command, while assigned to Training Detachment sniper cell. Shortly thereafter he was promoted again, to the rank of Chief Petty Officer (E-7). He has received numerous distinguished service awards, including Top Frog at Team 3 (best combat diver), the Presidential Unit Citation (awarded by President George W. Bush), and the Navy and Marine Corps Commendation Medal with "V" device for valor in combat. Webb ended his navy career early to spend more time with his children and focus on business.

As an entrepreneur and creator, Webb founded two brands, SOFREP. com and CrateClub.com, and bootstrapped them to an eight-figure revenue before successfully exiting the Crate Club in 2020. He continues to run SOFREP Media, his military-themed digital media company, and as its CEO has created several hit online TV shows, books, and podcasts, including the series *Inside the Team Room* and the award-winning documentary *Big Mountain Heroes*.

Webb is a multiple *New York Times* bestselling author of nonfiction and is now focused on his new thriller series with his creative writing partner, John David Mann. The first in the series, *Steel Fear,* is a high seas thriller that follows the US Navy's first serial killer. Brandon pursued his undergrad studies at Embry Riddle Aeronautical University and Harvard Business School's two-year OPM program. He is a member of the Young Presidents' Organization and has served as an appointed member on the veterans advisory committee to the US Small Business Administration.

He enjoys spending time with his tight circle of amazing family and friends. When he's not traveling the world, being in the wild outdoors, or flying his planes upside-down or on floats, you can find him at home in San Juan, Puerto Rico.

brandontylerwebb.com
Facebook: /brandonwebbseal
Twitter: @brandontwebb
Instagram: /brandontwebb

JOHN DAVID MANN has been creating careers since he was a teenager. At age seventeen, he and a few friends started their own high school in New Jersey, called "Changes, Inc." Before turning to business and writing, he forged a successful career as a concert cellist and prize-winning composer. At fifteen he was recipient of the 1969 BMI Awards to Student Composers and several New Jersey state grants for composition; his musical compositions were performed throughout the US and his musical score for Aeschylus's *Prometheus Bound* (written at age thirteen) was performed at the amphitheater in Epidaurus, Greece, where the play was originally premiered.

John's diverse career has made him a thought leader in several different industries. In 1986 he founded *Solstice,* a journal on health and environmental issues; his series on the climate crisis (yes, he was writing about this back in the eighties) was selected for national reprint in *Utne Reader.* In 1992 John helped write and produce the underground bestseller *The Greatest Networker in the World,* by John Milton Fogg, which became the defining book in its field. During the 1990s, John built a multimillion-dollar sales/distribution organization of over a hundred thousand people. He was co-founder and senior editor of the legendary *Upline* journal and editor in chief of *Networking Times.*

John is the co-author of more than thirty books, including four *New York Times* bestsellers and five national bestsellers. His books are published in thirty-eight languages, have sold over 3 million copies, and have earned the Axiom Business Book Award (Gold Medal), the Nautilus Award, Bookpal's "Outstanding Works of Literature (OWL)" award, and Taiwan's Golden Book Award for Innovation. His bestselling classic *The Go-Giver* (with Bob Burg) received the Living Now Book Awards "Evergreen Medal" for its "contributions to positive global change." His books have been cited on *Inc.*'s "Most Motivational Books Ever Written," HubSpot's "20 Most Highly Rated Sales Books of All Time," *Entrepreneur*'s "10 Books Every Leader Should Read," *Forbes*'s "8 Books Every Young Leader Should Read," CNBC's "10 Books That Boost Money IQ," NPR's "Great Reads," and the *New York Post*'s "Best Books of the Week." His 2012 *Take the Lead* (with Betsy Myers) was named Best Leadership Book of the Year by Tom Peters and *The Washington Post.*

Over his decade of writing with Brandon, John has logged hundreds of hours of interviews with US military service members, along with their spouses, parents, children, and friends, to gain an intimate understanding of the military life and Special Operations community. In preparation for writing *Steel Fear* he spent time on the aircraft carrier USS *Abraham Lincoln,* where the novel is set.

John is married to Ana Gabriel Mann and considers himself the luckiest mann in the world.

johndavidmann.com

Facebook: /johndavidmann

Twitter: @johndavidmann

Instagram: /johndavidmann

About the Type

This book was set in Minion, a 1990 Adobe Originals typeface by Robert Slimbach. Minion is inspired by classical, old-style typefaces of the late Renaissance, a period of elegant and beautiful type designs. Created primarily for text setting, Minion combines the aesthetic and functional qualities that make text type highly readable with the versatility of digital technology.